ANTIGODDESS

TOR BOOKS BY KENDARE BLAKE

Anna Dressed in Blood

Girl of Nightmares

ANTIGODDESS

The Goddess War: Book One

KENDARE BLAKE

TOR
TEEN

A TOM DOHERTY ASSOCIATES BOOK

NEW YORK

ANTIGODDESS

Book design by Mary A. Wirth

A Tor Teen Book
Published by Tom Doherty Associates, LLC
175 Fifth Avenue
New York, NY 10010

www.tor-forge.com

Tor® is a registered trademark of Tom Doherty Associates, LLC.

Library of Congress Cataloging-in-Publication Data

Blake, Kendare.
    Antigoddess / Kendare Blake.—First edition.
        p. cm.—(The goddess war)
    "A Tom Doherty Associates Book."
    ISBN 978-0-7653-3443-5 (hardcover)
    ISBN 978-1-4668-1221-5 (e-book)
    [1. Adventure and adventurers—Fiction.   2. Sick—Fiction.
3. Athena (Greek deity)—Fiction.   4. Hermes (Greek deity)—
Fiction.   5. Cassandra (Legendary character)—Fiction.   6. Hera
(Greek deity)—Fiction.   7. Goddesses—Fiction.   8. Gods—
Fiction.   9. Mythology, Greek,—Fiction.]   I. Title.
    PZ7.B5566Ant 2013
    [Fic]—dc23

                                                        2013018467

Tor Teen books may be purchased for educational, business, or promotional use. For information on bulk purchases, please contact Macmillan Corporate and Premium Sales Department at 1-800-221-7945, extension 5442, or write specialmarkets@macmillan.com.

First Edition: September 2013

Printed in the United States of America

0 9 8 7 6 5 4 3 2 1

ANTIGODDESS

OWL FEATHERS

The feathers were starting to be a nuisance. There was one in her mouth, tickling the back of her throat. She chewed at it as she walked, grabbing it with her molars and pulling it loose. Warm, copper-penny blood flooded over her tongue. There were others too, sprouting up inside of her like a strange cancer, worming their way through her innards and muscle. Before long she would be essentially a girl-shaped, walking chicken, constantly plucking at herself.

She reached between her lips discreetly to take the feather out and twist it between her fingers. The movement wasn't subtle enough; she caught the tilt of his head at the edge of her vision.

"Feathers," she snapped.

"You should stop making out with your owls."

"Shut up." Neither of them wanted to talk about the feathers, any more than they wanted to talk about the way he was starting to look thin and gaunt in places. It was easier to ignore the afflictions than to talk about what they meant.

So they just walked, in the same direction that they had been walking for three days already, under the damned sun, in the middle of a damned desert, looking for the last of she who used to be called the Mother of the Earth.

"We should stop," he said. The distance of his voice told her he already had.

Her legs kept moving, dark denim hot against her knees, for another five paces just to make a point before she kicked at the dry sand, flinging up dust and small stones and probably pissing off a lizard somewhere.

"She's here."

"How do you know?" he asked. "I want water."

She tossed him the leather cask without looking and listened to the slow slosh as he drank. He threw it back and she took a swallow, felt another owl feather making its way into her windpipe, a sore, fluttering spot when the water passed over it. The water was unpleasant too. Lukewarm and dust flavored. She stretched her arms and stared up into the sun.

"It's a good thing we don't sunburn." When they left the desert they'd be the same shade they were when they started, despite yards of exposed skin. She glanced at his jeans, his tight t-shirt, and at her own tattooed wrists and thin black tank top. A shadow passed overhead: a buzzard. She snorted. "Look. He probably thinks we're a couple of lost rave kids. A quick meal. Won't he be disappointed."

He turned shielded eyes to the sky and chuckled. "Will he? I wish we had come from a rave. Next time you drag me to the middle of a desert, it had better be for music and glow sticks. Not some goddess who's probably not even here. Give me that disgusting water back."

"She *is* here. Can't you feel her? She doesn't have the energy to hide." She tossed the water to him and he crouched down to rest, the leather of water hanging loosely down to the dirt. When he shook his head, a cloud of dust fell out of his close-cropped brown hair.

"I can't feel anything," he said. "Except the blasted sun and weariness that shouldn't be there."

She watched him. Hermes, the god of thieves, an eternal seventeen year old bitching like an old man. It was almost funny. It would have been, if they weren't both dying, and he hadn't been so thin. The muscles in his arms were becoming sinewy, and his cheeks had hollows they hadn't had before. He must've lost five pounds just since they reached the desert.

"You should eat something." She knelt in the dirt beside him and took off her pack. There was dried beef inside and fruit.

"This is humiliating," he muttered as she handed him the food.

"Death without glory always is. Of course, I never thought it would happen to us." She swallowed again, and the pin of the feather poked her. She took another drink of water. In the old days, she would have been able to wish the feather right out of existence, to burn it up with a thought, into nothing but a hiss and a curl of smoke. It was still hard to believe that this would be her end, that it would be so quiet and slow, her lungs filling up with feathers. It would be like breathing through a pillow. She wouldn't even be able to scream.

"We should have seen it coming. It's not as though it hasn't been foretold and written about. The twilight of the gods." He scraped up a handful of dust and tossed it into the air. He arched his brow.

"Dust in the wind. Funny."

"Everything born must die, Athena."

"So says convention." She pushed herself back up and squinted into the harsh light. For as far as she could see everything looked the same. Cactuses cropped up in strange little families. Tumbleweeds rolled along on their way to nowhere. It was flat, and barren, and the last place she wanted to be: dying in the middle of a desert.

She held out her hand and pulled him up.

"Everything born must die," she repeated. "But I sprang fully formed from our father's head. So that doesn't exactly count, now does it?"

1

COIN TOSS

It was an odd little scene, a pocket of stillness in the middle of the cafeteria shuffle and noise: two boys at a corner table, watching a silver coin flip end over end. The girl across from them called it in the air, "Heads" or "Tails," her voice indicating it was far less interesting than their bug eyes suggested. She'd called it correctly thirteen times in a row. She could've called it a hundred more.

"How are you doing this?"

"Magic," Cassandra Weaver replied. The coin spun. "Tails."

Aidan Baxter caught it and slapped it down against the back of his hand. He showed it, tails side up; the silver eagle shone under the glare of the fluorescent lights.

One of the boys held his hand out.

"Let me see it. Is it weighted?"

They studied it curiously, turning it in their fingers, scratching the edge, tapping it on the table. They flipped it themselves a couple of times. But it was just a quarter.

"There's got to be something," the taller boy muttered. He looked at Cassandra like it might be her. Something that she was doing.

Warmer.

But there was nothing special about her. No mystical tell, no ethereal eyes. Just normal, brown, blinking ones. He looked at her brown hair, hanging down around her shoulders. Too average. Not even a streak, no punk-rock pink or gypsy ribbons. He turned toward Aidan.

Colder.

No one ever bought the magic. They always thought it was a trick, or an angle. Some boring explanation so their world could keep its dimensions and still be explained by the ABCs. By laws and math. That was the way they wanted it. If they learned the truth, they wouldn't look at her with wonder. They'd be disappointed. Maybe even have her stoned to death.

"Seriously. What's the trick?"

"Seriously?" She watched the coin spin and called it again. She could tell them she was counting the spins. That it wasn't much different than scamming a game of poker. They'd believe that. "Seriously, I'm a genuine, bona fide psychic. Always have been."

He smirked. "Right."

She glanced at Aidan, and he smiled.

"It's true," he said as Cassandra called "Heads" almost before the quarter left his fingertips. "Pretty annoying, actually. I could never cheat on her and get away with it. And don't get me started on the things she sees before they happen."

Cassandra stifled a laugh. Mentioning her visions was farther than they usually went. But it wouldn't matter. The skeptical muscles in the freshman's face just clenched harder. They were muscles she knew well.

Aidan snatched the coin back. "So. Think you can beat her?"

For a second the boys' mouths opened and closed like fish and Cassandra thought they might try. Sometimes they did. Once, a girl managed to call it right five times before she missed. Maggie Wegman. Just a petite blond girl who sang in the choir and played volleyball. Cassandra watched her sometimes in the halls, wondering if the five times had been a fluke, or if Maggie might be a little bit psychic too.

Might be nice if she was. We could start a club for freaks. I could be like Professor X.

She smiled to herself, and shook her head when Aidan gave her a weird look.

"Don't waste your time." Sam Burress winked at her from across the table, his brow arched beneath his black stocking cap. She hadn't thought he'd been paying attention. "Nobody beats Cassandra. Half the school's lost money to these two." He gestured between her and Aidan with a carrot stick before biting through it. "Better just pay up. Get your friends to play and she'll give you a cut."

The boys opened their wallets and forked over ten dollars apiece.

"This isn't hard-earned allowance money or anything, right?" Cassandra asked as she took it.

"Nah," said one of the boys with a shrug. He had a sweet face and a mop of brown hair. "It's a really cool trick."

"Thanks. I stayed up for three days watching Criss Angel to figure out how to do it."

His face lit up, relieved by the explanation. "I knew I saw this somewhere." He picked up his plastic lunch tray and nudged his friend to leave, back to their own table. Before he left, he winked at her. No hard feelings, and now when they passed each other in the hall, they'd nod.

"Why'd you say that?" Aidan asked after they'd gone.

Cassandra shrugged. To make them feel better maybe. Or maybe just to get the wink. Some goodwill instead of wary glances later on.

Aidan shook his head.

"Your showmanship is slipping. Do I need to get you a crystal ball and a bunch of gold jewelry?" He slid closer to her on the bench, blue eyes dark and devilish, then picked up her hand and kissed it. "They're going to start thinking it's me. That I've got a trick to tossing it. Maybe you should breathe heavy, or roll your eyes back in your head."

Cassandra snorted. "What am I? Some guy at a carnival?" She shoved him with her shoulder. "You really love this about me, don't you?"

"I really do." He kissed her temple, like that was where it came from. "Amongst other things." He turned away to take a bite of bland lunchroom burrito and to scoop the cherries out of his fruit cup into Cassandra's. The hood of his gray sweatshirt was over his head, covering his golden hair just like it always was at school unless a teacher made him take it down for class. He looked like a street urchin, sitting there with his knee tucked up, scarfing his food.

But a good-looking street urchin.

Cassandra reached to touch his cheek.

"No PDAs while I'm eating." Andie Legendre swung her leg over the bench opposite, disrupting Sam and the rest of the table. They clucked and rustled like birds disturbed on the roost as they moved down. "You'll appreciate that rule when I have a disgusting boyfriend of my own."

"Yeah, we will," Aidan said, too enthusiastically for Andie's taste if her expression was anything to go by. "Besides, when are you ever going to get a boyfriend?"

"Whenever I find one who's more manly than I am." She threw a carrot at him.

"So never, then."

Cassandra punched Aidan lightly in the shoulder, but he and Andie both laughed. It wasn't exactly untrue. Andie had been named cocaptain of the varsity girls' hockey team that fall, even though she was still a sophomore. And she was taller than most boys. And stronger.

"Trade you?" Andie scooped Cassandra's burrito off her tray and deftly swapped it for a tri-cut potato. Half the burrito disappeared in one bite.

"Tuck your hair back." Cassandra reached forward and slid Andie's black hair behind her ears. "You're going to eat it otherwise."

Andie snorted. "So what? It's clean. You guys been scamming freshmen again?"

"How'd you know? Are you psychic now too?"

"Yeah. I used my magical ability to see you from the lunch line."

Cassandra's eyes drifted through the cafeteria. It was always so loud. Pervasively loud. A constant, multitone buzzing interspersed with the clack and clang of trays and silverware and chair legs dragged against the floor. At least fifty conversations going on at once, and everyone had at least one ear or one eye on someone sitting at a different table.

Cassandra crunched through her tri-cut potato and tuned out the noise. There were worse things to be than psychic. A mind reader, for example.

"Hide me." Andie ducked low.

"From what?"

"Christy Foster."

Cassandra turned. An auburn-haired girl with a sprinkling

of freckles across her nose and cheekbones was headed their way with an imperious look on her face.

"If she tells me one more time how captains need to set an example I'm going to fling rice in her hair."

"Andie!" Christy called. "What are you wearing tomorrow?"

"My jersey," Andie replied with a curled lip as Christy breezed past.

"Good. Because captains set an example."

Andie's spork hovered dangerously above the rice, but in the end she just threw the spork. It bounced off Christy's shoulder harmlessly. She didn't even acknowledge it. Captains set an example.

"You guys coming to the game tomorrow?" Andie asked.

Cassandra cocked her head regretfully. "History test Friday. I have to study."

"Aidan?"

"I have to help her."

"You guys are lame." The roll of Andie's eyes confirmed the point. Andie never studied. And not because she was a natural scholar, but because she couldn't be bothered to give a shit.

Cassandra nudged Aidan. "Friday night's open," she said. "Bonfire party at Abbott Park?"

"That's better." Andie grinned. "I'll spread the word."

Studying might've been a mistake. Two hours in, it was clear that Cassandra already knew everything, and Aidan was bored. He reclined on pillows stacked against her headboard and slid farther down them by the minute. He was never really any more interested in studying than Andie was.

"You wish we were at the game?" he asked.

"A little." Or a lot. Watching Andie's game with a hot

chocolate and a long piece of red rope licorice sounded ten times better than what they were doing. Notebooks and textbooks and loose-leaf handouts lay strewn around them in carefully organized circles and piles, the pages exposed so the words could whisper "U.S. History" into the air like a cloud. She glanced at the clock; it was too late to turn back.

"Are they going to win?" Aidan asked.

"Yes," Cassandra replied sulkily.

Aidan took a drink of his soda and set it on the night-stand. Then he started discarding books and papers, casually dropping her carefully ordered stacks onto the floor. Each moved pile opened up space between them on the bed. He shrugged out of his zip-up hoodie and crawled toward her.

"What are you doing?"

"Don't worry. You'll like it."

"Are you sure?"

He paused. "Fifty, sixty percent sure."

Laughing, she let him take the last notebook out of her hand and heard it hit the carpet as he laid her on her back. The room was quiet as they kissed, the bedspread and walls grown used to their antics. They'd been making out in her bedroom for almost a year. Sometimes, when he wasn't there, the air seemed full of him still, imprinted with a thousand memories of things they'd done. Everything inside the walls was tied to him somehow, right down to the walls themselves. He'd helped her paint them white six months ago, when she'd finally had enough of the lavender of her girlhood. But they'd been lazy, and distracted, and they'd left roller marks. In a certain light, the lavender still showed through at the corners.

"My parents will be home any minute," she said.

"Yeah?"

"Yeah. So disentangle your hands from my bra."

[19]

Aidan smiled and rolled onto his back with a groan. "Ow." He pulled a textbook out from under his shoulder and tossed it onto the floor. "We study too much."

"You know why I study so much."

He looked at her and held out his arm; she rolled closer and rested her head on his shoulder.

"The future, the future, I know. You don't know where we're headed. A little weird for a psychic."

"Shut up." She nudged him in the ribs.

"I'm kidding. But I'm telling you. It'll fill in. It's the only thing it can do."

Cassandra said nothing. They'd talked about it before. The dark spot waiting up ahead, somewhere around her eighteenth year. The day when she'd no longer be able to foresee things. It was a strange thing to foretell, her own lack of foretelling. But she knew it, just as surely as she knew on which side a coin would fall. She wouldn't be psychic forever. One day it would be gone, like a light going out.

It'll fill in, he always said. And she supposed he was right. But since they wouldn't be able to scam freshmen for cash forever, they'd better have a backup plan. Like college.

Cassandra listened to Aidan's heartbeat, the hot rushing of blood so strong beneath her cheek. When she'd first told him she knew her gift would disappear, she'd asked if it would make her less. If it would make her boring, or ordinary. He said no, but sometimes when she made a prediction the look in his eyes was so intense. Almost proud.

"Do you think I'll feel stupid?" Cassandra asked.

"Stupid?"

"After I can't see anymore. Will it be like a blank? Like words on the tip of my tongue that I can't quite remember?"

"No." He kissed the top of her head. "I don't think it'll be like that."

"What do you think it'll be like?"

"I think it'll be like . . . life," he said after a few seconds. "Like other people lead. I think you'll go to college, and I'll go to college, and we'll get a place together. That's what you want, isn't it?"

It was. Despite a few misgivings, most of her couldn't wait. It might be nice to not know for a change. More of an adventure. Aidan said that some people would kill to have her ability, but she didn't know why. It never came in any particular use.

"Yes, that's what I want. That's why I study."

"Not a good enough excuse. I'm the richest orphan in the tri-state area. We don't need scholarships."

"*You* don't need scholarships," she corrected. "Not all of us get to live out a reversal of the musical *Annie*." She remembered how curious she'd been three years ago, when she'd heard that Ernie and Gloria Baxter, neighbors for as long as she could remember, had adopted a teenage son. A trust-fund-rich teenage son.

Aidan grinned. "I guess it was a pretty hard-knock life. Living in all those group homes."

Cassandra lay quiet. He joked, but it was probably more true than not. Part of her still didn't understand why he'd chosen to live in state-run facilities and group homes instead of with whatever remained of his family. A family as wealthy as his had to have surviving members. A drunk uncle, at least. But she knew better than to ask. He shut down whenever she brought it up. "You worry too much." He sounded drowsy. She'd have to rouse him soon, or they'd wake to a vision of her dad's extremely annoyed face. "You and I will be together, Cassandra. You don't have to be psychic to see that."

2

THE MOTHER OF THE EARTH

They walked for two more hours before he stepped on it. Or rather, before he stepped on *her*. Demeter. The one who used to be called the Mother of the Earth. It was much like stepping on the edge of a long-collapsed tent. Pebbles skittered across the leathery surface, making soft, echoless thumps. When they knelt to inspect the edge, they couldn't find one. She simply disappeared into the dirt.

Athena ran her hand gently across the skin, because that's what it was. Skin. Stretched as taut as a drum, dried out and tanned.

"Hermes," she whispered. "I didn't expect her to be like this." She didn't know what she had expected. Part of her had hoped that Demeter had escaped the fate of the rest of them, that her link to the fertile earth had kept her well. Instead she seemed to be suffering worse.

"Maybe you shouldn't touch her," Hermes whispered. When she looked at him quizzically, he shrugged. "It seems indecent, doesn't it? We don't know what part of her this is, and—well, honestly, what if she's already dead?"

"She's not." Athena bit her lip on the question of why he couldn't tell. Every god had different talents. Maybe Hermes couldn't detect any of them. But the slight vibration that had been in Athena's bones since they made it to the desert had grown to a dull yet soothing hum. Using her fingers, she traced the line of the skin a few steps to her right. Reluctantly, Hermes did the same to their left. When they were twenty paces away from each other, she stood and put her hands on her hips. Then she lifted her boot-clad foot and stepped down, pressing her weight onto the layer of skin. It didn't move, but Hermes was at her side in an instant, dragging her back.

"What are you doing?"

"What we came here to do," she hissed, and jerked away. "We have to speak to her, if she can even still speak. And the only way to do that is to find her mouth, which is obviously nowhere near here." She looked around bleakly. The skin could stretch for miles. And even street- and century-hardened as she was, she didn't relish the idea of tramping around on it for what could be hours or days.

"Demeter!" Hermes shouted. They waited in the stillness. It was difficult to believe that the stretched skin at their feet was actually her, the summer goddess, lush and full of bounty. People had once made offerings of grain and grapes. They had danced in her honor.

"You don't have to come," Athena said finally. "I'll understand if you don't."

"This is stupid." He put a hand on her arm. "You should call an owl."

"We're in the middle of the desert."

"Don't play dumb." When she continued to, he gestured to a patch of tall saguaros, their arms raised. To Athena, the cactuses seemed to be waving stupidly, traitorously. "There are owls here."

Of course there were. She could see them. And hear them. There were close to a dozen tiny elf owls within calling distance, and every one would do her bidding. She rubbed her tongue against the roof of her mouth and felt the hardness of a new quill growing beneath the surface.

It isn't their fault. We all go our own way. Hermes eats his own flesh, Demeter gets stretched to the point of tearing, and I choke to death on the inside of a bird cage.

Athena looked at her companion. They were both haggard and dirty. Hermes' vibrant skin was caked with dust, and rings of armpit sweat grew larger on his gray t-shirt. She glanced down and brushed at dirt marks on the belly of her black tank top. Her hair hung down her back in dark, rough tangles.

"What are you doing?" he asked.

"I don't know. I just got the idea that when we saw her, we shouldn't look like . . . such punks."

He laughed and flicked a lock of her hair over her shoulder. "Then you should've dyed over those purple streaks before we got here. It's too late now. We look how we look." Despite his words, he brushed at his jeans. "We're really going to see her. Aunt Demeter. After so long." He smiled. "And much sooner if you'd just call a damned owl." His breathing was slightly labored, but hope lit up his eyes for the first time since they'd started their search for answers.

God of thieves, she thought fondly. *Always looking for the easy way out. But this is only the beginning.*

Still, he had a point about the owls.

"You win." She lifted her hand toward the nearest group of saguaros.

It was like pulling a string. A tiny, yellow-eyed bird dove out of the cactus and made a beeline for them. Athena lowered her hand and it flew around and around her in a tight circle, clicking its small beak. It would have liked to land on her. She could feel that. The owls were still her servants, and the fact that it was their feathers that were killing her would probably have saddened them more than it did her, if they had been able to know.

It isn't the feathers that are killing me. The feathers are being used to kill me by something else. Some force. This damned Twilight.

In a flash of eyes, she told the elf owl what she wanted, and it zipped off across the expanse of skin. It would search for days until it found Demeter's mouth. It would search until it died of exhaustion.

"Was that so hard?" Hermes asked, and plunked himself down in the dirt to wait. He squinted up at the sky, blazing so brightly it appeared white. "About five more hours of daylight, you think?"

Athena snorted. "I could do with less. The sun is making my nose ring so hot I might accidentally brand my face." She lowered down to the sand and propped her elbows on her knees.

Hermes, always one step ahead when it came to relaxation, stretched out, arms crossed behind his head. "If Apollo was here, we could ask him to turn it down." He turned to her. "Where do you think he is, anyway? Off in the jungle with Artemis, maybe. Twins of the sun and moon, hanging out in some Mayan temple."

Athena smiled and said nothing. It was nice to imagine. But the truth was probably far uglier.

Hermes reached into his pack for some beef jerky. He wanted to ask a million questions; Athena could see that. But they'd been over most of them before, and she didn't have new answers.

But Demeter might. She's always given me wise counsel. She has to have heard something that we haven't.

"Have you thought about what comes next?" he asked.

"One thing at a time, brother." It was a stupid question anyway. She thought about it every minute. Where they were going, and what must be done. The thousand what-ifs and maybes, and finally what might be at the end. The ultimate end. Dying was a strange, almost invigorating feeling. She couldn't remember ever feeling quite so desperate before.

The owl returned in the dark. Its yellow reflector eyes floated toward them, sinking slowly, and disappearing when it blinked. Hours had passed while the sun sank below the sand, and she and Hermes talked of idle things that had nothing to do with the task that literally lay before them.

As the bird dipped lower, she could feel the whisper of its exhausted wings. She gave it permission with a tilt of her head, and it landed on her shoulder in a soft, grateful clump. Hermes jerked. Cold came on quickly in the night-time desert, and the two had taken to resting back to back, staving off the chill. He turned and regarded the drowsy owl.

There was no moon. The scene in the sand, two gods speaking to a bird at the edge of an expanse of stretched skin, was invisible to anyone else. But Athena could see into the owl's eyes clearly.

"Where is she?" Hermes asked. "Er, where is her . . .

mouth?" He didn't ask whether the owl had found it or not. It wouldn't have returned if it hadn't.

"A few hours' walk," Athena replied. "That way." She stretched her arm out and pointed southeast.

Hermes sighed. "A few hours. Everything used to be so much easier. Do you remember when I could fly?"

She laughed. "Of course I remember. It isn't easy to forget someone running all over the place like the damned Flash. It was pretty geeky, frankly."

He snorted. "Even when you're dying, you're still a bitch."

"What are you complaining about anyway? You can still catch a bullet."

Athena heaved to her feet; the owl on her shoulder gave a shudder. She glanced sidelong at it and whispered, "Rest now, little one. And be well." It blinked and ruffled itself, then flew off into the black to disappear into its cactus. She held her hand out. Hermes took it, and she pulled him up.

We should be at the mouth by morning. The strangeness of the idea made her pause, but after a few seconds, her boot found its way back onto the skin. It sank down like the surface of a trampoline. She couldn't feel the dirt or gravel beneath it, but couldn't help imagining the grinding that had to be going on beneath her heel. Maybe Hermes' idea of flying wasn't so ridiculous after all.

She looked back. He lingered on the edge, looking guilty or anxious, she couldn't tell which. Then he shrugged and carefully put his feet down until he was by her side.

"At least she'll know we're coming," he said.

"We should be getting there soon. The sun's coming up. What do you think she'll say? Do you think she can hear us? Where are her ears?"

Athena walked on in silence. After six hours of traveling on the skin, it didn't feel any less unnatural beneath her boot heels. She wished Hermes would shut up. But he was nervous, and when he was nervous, his tongue moved as quickly as his wings used to.

"You're lucky I'm stretched flat." Demeter's voice was a rasp, thin as the wind that raced across her leathered body. "If I had any decent lung left, I would've sucked in your bird and you'd never have found me."

Athena scanned the skin beneath them. Hermes had zipped to her side and was doing the same.

"We'd have found you eventually, Mother of the Earth," she said. "We would have just had to put more boot prints into your hide first."

Demeter laughed, and when she did there was more air to it, more force. Athena wondered briefly if the goddess wasn't sandbagging, and the pun almost made her snort. But the idea that Demeter was stronger than she seemed, that the skin could snap over the top of them at any moment, trapping them like a great bat's wing, kept her quiet. She and Hermes both carried small pocketknives, but she didn't want to think about what it would take to slice their way out should Demeter decide to try and keep them.

"Sit, children," Demeter said.

Hermes did so immediately. The walk had been long, and his gray t-shirt was black with sweat. But after only a few seconds, he stood back up and looked at Athena with an odd expression.

She paid him no mind. She was still looking for the mouth, an eye, anything. Had all of Demeter's features been spread out as she was stretched?

"How did you come to be this way?" Athena asked, stepping slowly toward the sound of shallow breathing.

"I am used as the earth is used," Demeter replied. "Pulled thin across the land and consumed. Sucked dry, bleached white. And so I have been laid thin for decades. For centuries."

"Why didn't you seek us out for help?" Athena asked. She saw what looked like a ragged wrinkle in the skin, like an elephant's kneecap. And then it opened, revealing a glassy, dark eye, which swiveled sickly toward her and fixed her with a sharpened pupil.

"We are not all like you, Gray Eyes," Demeter whispered. "Goddess of battle, fighting through the millennium. Unable even now to lie down and accept your fate."

Hermes walked to the eye and peered down at it. "We're *immortals*," he said loudly. "Why should we have to accept this?"

"Immortal doesn't mean forever, Messenger."

Hermes scoffed. "We shouldn't have even come here. She's as useless as that old turtle from *The Neverending Story*. Nothing but riddles and double-talk."

Beneath their feet the skin quickened, tightening like the muscles of a snake before a strike. They were lifted three inches, and Athena cast him a sharp look. He was always impatient, always twitchy. Someday it would get them into trouble they couldn't get out of.

"You say I am the goddess of battle, and so I am," Athena said, careful, unlike Hermes, to keep the modernity out of her voice. "But wisdom was also my charge. And I can't understand this. That is why I come to you. To learn what you know."

"I know many things with my ears pinned to the dirt. They walk across me and spill their secrets into the sand. But you cannot escape this. You shouldn't." Demeter's voice was low, spoken through tense lips and teeth. Her eye swiveled up and down the length of Athena's body. "Look at you. Ink marks your skin. You bear a whore's jewelry in your nose. Why should you escape when my daughter is already gone?"

"Persephone," Athena whispered. The queen of the underworld and Demeter's daughter, stolen from the summer lands and dragged below to be the bride of Hades. It made sense that she had died faster than the rest. She was half-dead already, one side of her an ageless, golden-haired maiden, and the other a rotted, sagging corpse. When Athena closed her eyes, she could see Persephone's demise: the black skin slowly consuming the peach, the blue eye becoming cloudy, then milky, and finally falling into her skull. She swallowed and frowned, unsure whether the vision was true or just the product of her imagination.

"I'm sorry," Athena whispered. "I was sorry the first time she was taken from you. You know that. I wanted to get her back."

Demeter sighed, and the skin moved them with an uneven rattle. "What do you want, Athena? Why have you come, dressed like a harlot, asking stupid questions?"

"It's high noon in the desert," Hermes snapped, blowing sweat off of his upper lip. "Was she supposed to come wearing a high-collared robe?"

Athena placed a hand on his arm. Demeter's words didn't bother her. They didn't feel insulting so much as grandmotherly, and she regretted not covering her tattoos and taking out her nose ring. It was lucky that the purple streaks in her mahogany hair had mostly grown out.

"If you seek to stop this, then leave me out of it," Demeter said. "I want to lie here until I tear. I want to rip into leathery ribbons and be carried away by birds." She laughed another low, papery laugh. "If you want answers, go to the Oracle. She will guide you."

"The oracle? The oracle at Delphi?" Hermes scoffed. He looked at Athena. "There's nothing there but a half-ruined temple and mushroom-induced hallucinations. There never has been."

"She didn't say anything about Delphi," Athena muttered. Of course she'd never considered going to the oracle. There was nothing mystical about that temple in Greece. The only thing that had once made it wise was the fact that Apollo had deigned to imbue it with knowledge. But he hadn't hung around there for centuries. He hadn't hung around anywhere that she knew of. They had all scattered across the globe, becoming hermits and nomads, and maybe it was that as much as anything that had spelled their doom. They had lost one another. She hadn't seen any of them, save Hermes, for over a hundred years, unless you counted the dreams and flashes. And now she was looking for them all, scrambling around to save them, when she hadn't really cared for most of a millennium.

"Please," she said. "Just tell me what you know."

"You can't stop it, Athena," Demeter said. "I see the feathers blooming under your skin. You'll be weak. You'll be too late."

"But there is a way to stop it."

"I don't know. Not without great cost. There are tools that might help."

"What kind of tools?" Hermes interjected, impatient as usual.

"Those that you have known before," Demeter said. "Some of them walking are nearly as old as you are. They are threads that were cut, and then rewoven."

Hermes turned to Athena. "What is she blathering on about?"

"Reincarnation," Athena said thoughtfully.

"Oh," Hermes snorted. "So we're Buddhists now, are we?"

"What would they be good for?" Athena asked, ignoring him.

"What they were always good for," Demeter answered. "They still are, fundamentally, what they *were*."

Hermes stepped closer to the eye. He seemed to hesitate to speak to it, but in the absence of a mouth, there were few other options. "I still don't understand," he said awkwardly. "How will humans, even reincarnated ones, help us to stop . . . whatever this is?"

"You still don't know *what* this is," Demeter said.

"This is the twilight of the gods."

The skin shook as the goddess laughed. Pebbles bounced on her surface at the vibrations. Athena and Hermes shifted their weight uncomfortably. It was like standing on a drum.

"The twilight of the gods," Demeter said when the rumbling had stopped. "But not all of the gods. Some of us are the bitches of fate and will persevere."

"What do you mean?"

"I mean you're not fighting our deaths. You're fighting a war. A war against your own. And you will lose."

"A war against our own?" Hermes asked. "Why would we fight each other? We're dying."

Athena swallowed. Some of them would fight for exactly that reason. Dying wasn't something gods understood. It certainly wasn't something many would do well.

"You'll kill each other now, because you can. What was impossible is now possible. And if that wasn't reason enough to try, you are the Titan's children. You'll kill each other. Consume each other, to survive."

The skin shifted softly from side to side. It took Athena a moment to realize that it was Demeter settling into the dirt, ruffling her skin like she was pleased with herself and ready to drift back to whatever sleep she had, stretched across the desert.

"Go and find the Oracle," the tired voice of Demeter said, drifting off. "If you can, and if she'll help you, after what you did to her. You three. But maybe you'll be lucky, and she'll hate the others more than she still hates you."

"Enough riddles. Who is the Oracle? What can she do?" Hermes stomped his foot and Demeter gave an "Oof!" Athena gave Hermes a stern look. It was rude to stomp your aunt, no matter how dire the situation.

"The Oracle is a prophetess. Find her. Make her remember, and she'll be much more than that." The eye fluttered shut.

"You won't help," Athena whispered.

"Do I look like I'm in any position to help?" Demeter snapped, and the skin coiled back to attention. "And you, with your whore's jewelry and pathetic knife. Are you in any position to fight?"

Athena walked to the eye and knelt. Gently, she placed her palm above the lid, and the tired eye drifted shut. "Perhaps not yet. But I will be soon."

3

THE CALM BREAKS

Abbott Park sat in the middle of the Spirit River Nature Preserve, an oblong strip of green land slowly yellowing its way to autumn brown. It was mid-October, and Kincade, New York, had already had a few hard freezes, just enough to make everything feel brittle and solid. Cassandra, Aidan, and Andie huddled on the outer edge of the fire circle, atop the remains of the low stone wall that seemed to begin and end at random, dotting the border of the park like an uneven stitch.

"You spread the word well," Cassandra said, watching forty to fifty of their classmates mill around the three fire pits in the park. "Almost as well as if the word was 'legs'." She blinked and laughed, breath leaving her throat in a thin cloud. After a surprised pause, Andie and Aidan laughed back.

"Are you drunk?" Andie asked.

"No." She looked down into her half-empty red plastic cup. The beer inside had gone sad and flat a half hour ago.

"Sorry. I'm just tired." Tired, and working on a headache. Some people had managed to get a few cars down the Jeep trail the DNR used and were blaring music out the windows. Not everyone agreed on the choice, and Muse competed with Florence + the Machine. The result was just a whole lot of shrill.

"It's probably all the studying." Andie bent her knee up and dug her boot into the edge of the wall, her arms folded over it. There was more than a little disdain in her voice. "I don't know what your effing hurry is. College is two years away, and all it means is the end of us."

"Are *you* drunk?"

"Shut up." Andie pulled down on her tan corduroy jockey cap like it could obscure her reluctant grin. "I'm not even drinking. The greenhouse is closing up for winter. They want me to go in early tomorrow to help out."

"Cheers to your last day of work." Aidan raised his cup.

"Cheers to the end of paychecks, trust-fund boy." Andie smiled. Cassandra smiled too. She'd always thought it was strange that a girl who never noticed pretty flowers would want to spend all summer potting and pruning in a greenhouse. Until Andie explained that she got to move saplings and haul around dirt.

"You know, you could always go to college near us," Aidan said. "Or with us."

Andie huffed, and tugged her red wool coat tighter around herself.

"With my grades, the only way I'm going to college is with a hockey scholarship. So I'll probably wind up in one of the Dakotas."

Cassandra and Aidan looked at each other and suppressed smiles. The night was getting colder. Around them the party was tightening up. Groups increased in number and clustered closer together. Cassandra watched moving lips, flashes of white teeth, and cheeks made gaunt by the firelight. She caught the eye of one of the freshmen from lunch, the one with the mop of brown hair. He smiled and nodded; she nodded back. Even in the orange glow she could see that the tips of his nose and cheeks were rosy. She leaned back into Aidan. With his arms wrapped around her, she was nowhere near cold.

"The Dakotas would be cool," said Cassandra.

"Cool? Check a map," Andie snapped. "They're square states. Square states are boring."

Aidan laughed. "People go on vacation to the Dakotas all the time. My parents went there for one of their anniversaries or something."

Cassandra prodded him in the ribs. "You're not helping."

The fire in the pit nearest them started to flicker and Cassandra checked her watch. Eleven. Not that late, but late enough. They probably wouldn't put any more logs on and just let the flames weaken down to embers. After that, someone would haul a bucket down to the creek and wash out the pits, leaving a sizzling charcoal soup to soak into the ground by morning.

"You asshole!"

Twenty heads lifted and twisted toward the sudden shout. Someone yelled back. It took less than a minute for whatever it was to escalate from words into roars and squeals. Cassandra, Aidan, and Andie rose to their feet to try to rubberneck. As the scene came into view the music seemed suddenly quieter, the acoustic equivalent of tunnel vision, or maybe someone had actually turned it down to hear the fight better. Only the tops of heads were visible, and the view worsened as a crowd gathered. Andie bobbed and weaved; at one point she jumped.

"It's Casey," she announced. "And Matt." Casey was a friend of theirs, a forward on Andie's hockey team. Matt was a junior, the backup goalie for varsity. They'd been dating about a month. A few choice swear words hit the air, and a flurry of mingled, screeched accusations. There was more than one girl involved, by the sound of it.

"You don't seem surprised," Cassandra said. Andie shrugged.

"Misty Walker has been sniffing around Matt since that weirdo from Buffalo dumped her. Someone's trying to break it up." She craned her neck. "I think it's your brother."

"Henry?" Cassandra peered toward the fight. There he was, in the middle of it, about a head taller than everyone else. "I didn't even know he was here."

"Well, there he is. Playing team manager, as usual." Andie squared her shoulders. "I suppose I should help. Captains have to set an example, and all that crap." She twisted her way through the people and joined the fray, her hands on Casey's shoulders to push her back. A few friends of Misty Walker's snarled at their heels, but a raised index finger from Andie put their tails well between their legs.

"You about ready to go?" Aidan asked.

"As soon as Andie's done playing captain."

The fight looked to be over as quickly as it began. No one was shouting anymore and Matt was clearly trying to explain the situation to Henry; he looked embarrassed and ashamed, head low, feet scuffing the dirt. Casey's face was red with fury and firelight, and Cassandra frowned. When the anger faded, all Casey's toughness would fade with it. She'd spend the rest of the weekend thinking about Misty and Matt and what she would have to say at school on Monday.

"Is it weird that this never happens to us?" Cassandra asked, still leaning back on Aidan's chest.

"That we never pull each other's hair out at campfires?"

"No." She smiled. He knew what she meant. No girl had ever "come sniffing" around Aidan. No one had ever tried to entice him away. Even though he was far better-looking than Matt Bauer. "You know what I mean. No one even flirts with you."

"Yes, they do."

"Well, they don't flirt *with feeling.*" She turned and saw his face, amused and blinking, feigning innocence. It was probably the one expression his features couldn't hold.

"They must know it'd be a waste," he said. "We've got some very smart girls in Kincade." He smiled and she pushed her fingers into his hair. "Hang on, is this your way of hinting that some guy is flirting with *you?*" He slid his hands underneath her jacket, warm fingers pressed around her waist to the curve of her back. "Because I guess that would mean . . . I'd have to flay him. It'd be pretty grisly. I'd probably go to prison."

"Probably?"

He grinned. Blood coated his teeth.

"Aidan? I think you bit your lip."

"What?"

"I—" Cassandra stopped. It wasn't just his lip. Blood seeped up into his eyes. Glimpses of his tongue as he spoke words she couldn't hear looked cracked, split open, wet and red. Pinpricks stood out on his cheeks and forehead, tearing the skin as she watched. Something pressed through as she looked closer, frozen in horror as his face degraded right in front of her. Feathers. White, and speckled brown. After they wriggled free they fluttered to the ground, leaving bleeding gashes behind, all over his body. He was a monster, holding her shoulders, his sliced-open lips mouthing her name.

4

BEWARE OF BARS BEARING JACKALOPES

The first building they saw as they left the desert was a bar. A bar aptly named the Watering Hole. It stood alone, a dusty clapboard one-story structure ten miles from the middle of nowhere. Long rectangular shafts of yellow light cut across the dirt from the windows. Athena and Hermes hadn't seen the bar on their way in, because they hadn't passed it. After their encounter with Demeter, they hadn't turned around the way they had come, but kept on walking and crossed over the top of her. It had taken four hours to get off the skin, and another six before they came across anything but cactus and sagebrush. Dusk had come and gone, and Hermes had wrung their water skin dry five miles ago. As they approached the building, Athena stopped short, and Hermes drew up alongside her. A light breeze kicked up from the west and chilled them, making the hairs on the back of their necks stiffen.

"Tell me you have money," he said.

"Of course I do," she replied. "But if I didn't, I'd drink that place dry and burn it down."

Hermes laughed. "Now you sound like me."

Inside the bar, they were surprised to find a handful of patrons and much less dust. The floorboards still squeaked under their feet, and on one wall there was a mounted head of some rabbit/deer monstrosity labeled a "jackalope," but the bar was polished hardwood, and a stone chimney held a small fire. To Athena it felt like coming home. It was primitive and firelit, and even the ridiculous jackalope felt familiar, a lame contemporary of the old creatures: the Chimera, the Minotaur, the Sphinx.

When they sat upon the swiveling stools, exhausted and confused, only the last remnants of their gods' pride kept them from resting their foreheads on the bar. Not that anyone would have noticed. The patrons, all men, ignored them completely, immersed in their beers and in the baseball game playing on the surprisingly nice flat-screen TV. Behind the bar, the bartender absently dried glasses with a white terry towel, his eyes trained on the game while he rolled a toothpick in the corner of his mouth.

"Yo," Hermes called out irritably. "Can we get two waters?"

"There's a two-drink minimum," the bartender replied without looking over.

"That wasn't posted anywhere," Hermes grumbled, but Athena set her pack up on the bar.

"Two waters and two Bud Lights then," she said.

Hermes' eyes widened. "Bud Light? I'd rather dehydrate. How about a Rolling Rock?"

"Bottle okay?"

"Fine."

"I'm going to need to see some IDs."

They flipped their wallets open and tapped sand out onto the floor. The bartender checked them, but it was just for show; he didn't seem to care if they were fake as long as they were IDs.

"Let me see that." Hermes snatched Athena's license out of her hand. "Twenty-one. Mine too. You should change yours so people don't think we're twins."

"Why should I change mine? I don't look twenty-two. You change yours."

"You barely look nineteen. That's not what I meant. But with the way you *are* . . ."

"What's that supposed to mean?"

There was a sharp hiss and a pop as the cap was taken off of a beer. A few seconds later, the bartender set the Rolling Rock and a frosty mug of Bud down in front of them. Athena tossed a ten onto the counter and he spared her a wink. She didn't think he'd bring back change, and she didn't have the energy to argue. In days gone by she might have smote him, turned him into a tree or a statue or something. Glory days.

She took a long drink of her beer. He'd forgotten to bring the waters, but it didn't matter. The Bud was ice cold, the carbonation a satisfying burn in her throat. Behind them, a meager cheer went up from two or three patrons as apparently something good happened to whatever baseball team was being rooted for.

"Do you want to talk about it?" Hermes asked after half of his Rolling Rock was sitting comfortably in his stomach.

She nudged the roof of her mouth with her tongue. The quill of the owl feather was more defined, but still several days from poking through the skin. When it did, she wouldn't be able to help herself from yanking it free, drawing blood and leaving a ragged, stringy wound. Then it would probably turn into a canker sore because she wouldn't be able to stop sucking at it.

She shook her head, but said, "I guess we have to." Their voices were low, cloaked in that way that they still knew how to do, so that people could hear that they were talking but if pressed would never be able to remember just what it was they had been saying.

"It wasn't exactly what you wanted her to say, was it." Hermes sighed.

"I never expected it to be easy." She shot him a look. "I just thought maybe we'd band together this time instead of tearing each other apart. How stupid of me."

"Some of us will band together. Only . . . to eat the other band. Still a team effort, depending on how you look at it."

Athena snorted. "And these reincarnated tools? I never figured on dealing with humans again." Even though she had lived among them, blended into their population almost since the day they tossed her and her brethren off of Olympus and sent it crashing into the sea.

"So much bitterness. I thought the humans were your friends. That they came even before us."

"They did. Once." *Before they forgot me. When I was a true god.*

Hermes took a long drink of Rolling Rock. "So what happened? Some hideous mortal break your heart?"

She laughed, genuinely and ruefully. "Shut up, Hermes."

He shrugged. "Guess not. Still the virgin goddess then, eh? I don't know why. You have no idea what you're missing out on."

"It's a choice," she said. *And more than that. It's what I am. What I've always been.* "But you're getting off point. You heard Demeter. We need to find the tools. The oracle. Whom she seemed to think is a 'she.'"

He sighed. "An oracle. In this century you can find one on every block. Neon palm with a blinking eye in the center. You can call them on the phone. How are we supposed to find the one she's talking about? And why would this human even help us?"

Athena clenched her jaw. Find her. Make her remember, and she'll be more than a prophetess. It sounded like another of Demeter's riddles. But Demeter wanted them to survive, no matter what she said. She'd been a curmudgeon as long as Athena had known her. The kind of aunt who slapped your hand off the table but gave you a dozen cookies if you just asked properly.

"The prophet will help us. We'll convince her. We'll make her remember."

"Right. Somehow."

"Will you shut up? We have to find her first."

Hermes shrugged. "Maybe if we tell her we can prevent the war. A war between the gods means a dirty, bloody mess, and not just for us."

"So we should lie."

He shrugged again. "Maybe not. If we have to go down, I wouldn't mind if the mortals went down with us. It sort of eases the blow. Is that wrong?" He took another long swallow of beer. "To tell the truth, I sort of thought that it was the humans who were doing this to us, somehow."

"We still don't know what *is* doing this to us. This whole thing feels strange. I'm dying, and I feel like something's *starting*. Like something is on its way. But maybe that's just how it always feels. Not like we would know."

Hermes took a swallow of Rolling Rock.

"A war against our own. Killing each other to survive. I wonder who we'll go against?" He started to say more, and then summed it up with a shake of his head. The truth was,

the gods had never really cared that much about one another. Bonds were fickle and morality generally nonexistent. They changed sides constantly. "Those bastards." He
looked at her incredulously. "How could any of them think
of killing me? Me! All these millennia, all I've done is be
helpful. Deliver a message here, fetch a hero there."

"Necessity is a strong motivator." Athena rubbed her
tongue across the bump of feather on the roof of her mouth.
The others were dying too, in various ways and shapes. She
knew that much. And killing each other wasn't really such
a strange way to survive. Their grandparents, the Titans, had
eaten their own children toward the same end.

"Another round?" The bartender stood directly in front
of her, an impatient stare on his face like he'd been there
for days waiting for her to notice.

"Yeah," she said, and reached into her wallet for a twenty.
He took the money and their empties. They waited to speak
again until he'd brought the fresh drinks. He still forgot the
waters.

"Are you sure the oracle isn't in Delphi?" Hermes asked.

"She called it a 'she.' Which I guess rules out Tiresias."

"Not necessarily. There's no rule that says you have to be
reincarnated as the same gender."

"How would you know? You should hope there is. Or
our task becomes harder. So rattle off some female prophets." She took a long drink and set her mug down hard with
a heavy clink. "All I can think of is the Sybil, but she was
never one person. She was a line passed down over time."
She took another drink. The temptation to let this business
rest rose up, strong and cloying. Her back hurt, and her eyes
hurt. There were feathers seeding her internal organs. Beside her, Hermes' labored breathing hadn't abated. Maybe

it never would. They could just drink here, in this small, comfortable bar, and forget about things. They could stretch out across the land like Demeter and sink into the dirt.

Haven't I lived long enough? Shouldn't a goddess have the grace to accept this?

"She also said you screwed the girl over." Hermes squinted while he thought. "The three of you, she said. That mean anything?"

"I've screwed a lot of people over."

"Yes, you have."

"So have you," Athena snapped.

"But we're talking about *you*. So think."

Think. What prophetess did I screw over with the help of two other gods? A prophetess strong enough to help us now, somehow . . .

"Oh, shit." Athena turned to him. "It's Cassandra."

Hermes' eyes glowed brilliant blue and stood out like methane torches against his dirt-streaked face. "Of course it's Cassandra," he said. "She's talking about Cassandra. God, we're idiots." He clapped a hand to his chest.

Cassandra of Troy. A princess and prophetess during the Trojan War. She'd warned her city that they would fall to Achilles and the Greeks, but no one had listened.

Because she was cursed. Someone cursed her to never be believed.

Not just someone. A god. Their brother, Apollo.

"It's so simple," Hermes said. "Cassandra of Troy."

Athena blinked. Hermes was getting ahead of himself, as usual.

"Don't get too excited. We might be wrong. And you should hope we are." She took a drink.

"Why?"

"Because I fought against her, last time. I sided with the Greeks to burn down her city and murder her family. I started the war."

Hermes waved his hand dismissively.

"Sides change all the time." He tightened his thinning fist, spread his fingers, and watched them tremble. "But I guess . . . Even if we find her, she won't be the same person we knew once. She's probably happy and not a part of this anymore."

The sympathy in his voice edged just nearer to sorry for himself. Death was softening him up. Athena didn't remember him having an excess of compassion for mortals in the past. It was sort of touching. And they didn't have time for it.

"You're not even half right. She probably is happy, but she's also the same prophet we knew once, and that means she always has been, and always will be, a part of this."

She took a long pull of her beer, but it tasted bad. Cold water was what she'd craved since they'd come in. She looked at the bartender to order, and found him staring straight at her. When she opened her mouth, he opened his in a broad, strange smile. A smile that quickly stretched until it split into bleeding cracks across his cheeks.

Beside her, Hermes took a drink and crinkled his nose. "Yuck. Did someone salt this while I wasn't looking?"

"Hermes." Athena put her hand on her brother's arm and together they looked around the bar. The baseball game was forgotten. Every pair of eyes was on them.

As the seconds ticked by, the flannel shirts and thick, tanned flesh of the bar patrons hung looser. Blue and silver scales began to show through at their temples and cheeks like harlequin-painted sequins. One moment she was looking at a middle-aged man dressed in a John Deere ball cap and tan shirt, and a blink later seeing a clawed, finned thing in a melting human costume.

Athena's eyes did a full sweep and came back to rest on the bartender.

Who wasn't the bartender anymore. Only the slightest resemblance to his previous form remained. The bone structure around the eyes and cheeks was still intact, and there was something about the curl of aquatic lip, peeled back against piranha-jagged teeth, that was reminiscent of the way he had smirked when he dropped off their beers. Beyond that, everything had changed. Black, speckled scales peppered his skin. His irises were gone. Slight webbing fluttered between his fingers, and his legs had molded into one long, muscled appendage. He stood balanced on it like a snake's tail curled beneath him. At the end a broad fin waved lazily.

All of this she saw in an instant, and in her silence, Hermes looked as well. He reacted with more force, spinning off of his stool and sending it swiveling unevenly to the floor with a sharp thud.

"Nereid," she said lowly. They had of course seen the oceanic creatures before, swirling about their master, Poseidon, the god of the sea.

"Make that plural," Hermes added. The other bar patrons had almost finished shedding their human makeup: shirts and jeans slid down scaled and rubber-skinned legs. When the Nereids stood, they made a wet squelching sound like they'd been sitting in a mud puddle, and a look at the seat of their chairs revealed a flesh-colored pool of water. Their disguises ran off of them in rivulets.

"Neat trick," Athena said to the bartender. "Who taught it to you?"

She glanced around. It was hard to believe that these

monstrosities had once been jewels of the sea. That they swam in swirling patterns and entranced fishermen from their boats. The silver hair and shining body was gone, evolved into cracked scales and oily eyes. They reeked of salt and old blood.

The bartender didn't answer her question. But it didn't take a genius to figure out the Nereids had been planted there. They'd been waiting, and they'd listened to everything she and Hermes said. Once the two of them got to the interesting part, it was time to lose the masks and get down to business.

"Six of them, two of us," Athena said.

"I think Uncle Poseidon's trying to send us a message." Hermes kept his eyes on the group of Nereids clustered around the television, still droning out a baseball game in the seventh inning.

Athena flexed her muscles. *I'm tired, I'm tired, I just crossed the fucking desert*, they protested, but beneath the protest was springy strength.

"I guess it'd be rude if we didn't reply."

The attack came all at once. The group darted forward, knocking over whatever tables and chairs got in their way. Their movement reminded her of a pod of fish, fast and synchronized, as if they shared one brain. Athena was up instantly, moving almost as fast as Hermes, who had grabbed the first of the pod by the throat and didn't waste any time tearing its gills out and throwing them to the floorboards where they bounced like bloody, rubber filters. Athena drew her legs up to perch on the seat of her stool. With a grimace, she flung herself headlong into the bunch, and felt a sharp fin slice through the skin of her underarm. The wound barely registered. Claws gripped her legs, her shoulders, and the strength in them was almost enough to pop her joints.

The air filled with the smell of salt and a watery, raspy sound that the Nereids made from their lampreylike mouths.

Athena reached for the nearest body, and her fingers slid against the slick mucous coating the skin. She almost didn't get a grip, but with a deep breath she twisted her arms and tore the head free. The body fell to the floor and flopped, webbed hooks still grasping. Then she used the head like a bludgeon, swinging it wide and knocking three of the others back. The head flew out of her hand and knocked into the TV. It crashed to the ground and sparked.

"Don't kill them all," she hissed, and Hermes shot her a disbelieving look.

"I'm killing until they stop," he shouted, but he pulled his fingers out of the gills of the creature atop him and punched it in the face instead.

Athena feinted backward as the hooked finger-claws of the last Nereid in front of her passed dangerously close to her face. There had been a time when no god or mortal would have dared try to disfigure her cheeks. The attempt now struck her as incredibly rude. She reached out and smashed Hermes' bottle of Rolling Rock against the bar, feeling cold beer fizz over her knuckles. The jagged edge went right into the Nereid's belly, and she sawed her way up to its chest. The thing fell, jerking, at her feet. Her breath came fast and light, angry but not labored, and unfettered by feathers, which was a relief.

With most of its patrons now dead and the TV broken, the interior of the bar was quiet. The sound of Hermes struggling with the last one, on his back against the rough wooden floor, was oddly magnified. So were Athena's steps as she walked calmly over to him. She scooped a chair up in one hand, the legs scraping along the wood as she used her other hand to flip the Nereid off of Hermes, planting it on its back. She drove the legs of the chair through its shoulders, through the floorboards, all the way into the tightly packed dirt beneath.

Hermes got to his feet and brushed himself off.

"That was fun," he muttered, staring down at the Nereid as it hissed and thrashed and tried to pry the chair loose. Black blood oozed from the punctures in its shoulders and pooled on the floor. Hermes reached for Athena's arm. "You're hurt."

She jerked away. She was looking down at the carnage, counting bodies. And the count was off.

"Where's the bartender?" she asked.

"God," Hermes said.

The door to the bar hung open, literally. It had been opened with enough force to rip the top hinge off, and swayed back and forth at them like a shaming finger. Without sparing each other a glance, they ran to the door and through it, into the black. Cold wind prickled their skin as their eyes searched the dark for movement. The bartender could be miles away. He could be anywhere.

Stupid, stupid. She was becoming careless, sloppy. It was a mistake she never would have made two thousand years ago.

"Wait," Hermes said. He sniffed the air. Athena sniffed too, once, tentatively. The breeze carried the scent of salt back to them.

"Go," she said, and he ran, faster than she could, though she ran too. His footfalls grew fainter as he raced ahead of her, god of thieves, faster than a Nereid, faster than an antelope. Soon she could only hear her own breath and the wind in her ears. The scent of salt grew fainter. As her eyes adjusted to the dark she made out the landscape, shadowy buttes and clusters of cacti. Stars sparkled brightly overhead, witness to their embarrassing chase. When she heard a faint whisper, her legs pushed harder. It was the whisper of water. They were too late.

When she caught up to Hermes he had already stopped by the edge of the creek. It was black and tiny, barely more than a four-foot stream, but it moved fast over the sandy bottom and swirled in rippled eddies against rocks. The Nereid had slid into it like a sharpened blade and disappeared. It would find its way to an ocean in less than a day, and then it would spill its secrets to its master.

"Don't go in," he hissed when she stepped into the water. He yanked her backward, and her feet splashed angrily, but he was right. They would never catch it now. And who knew what might come after them, who knew what was waiting in some darkened underwater cave.

"Poseidon," Athena said darkly, and then she screamed his name, her battle cry ringing out into the empty air, vibrating into the sand and water, and she hoped he heard it before his little guppy got home to whisper.

"What do we do now?" Hermes asked, walking briskly by her side. "Athena! It knows everything. We don't know anything!"

She didn't reply, just kept walking, stiff-legged, back to the bar. Hermes' questions bounced annoyingly around her ears and echoed in her head. Telling him to shut the hell up was tempting. But instead she silenced her own mind. Somehow, she had been elected captain and commander of this damned little enterprise, and as such she didn't have time to indulge in panicked, useless questions, or snapping at her sibling. Her focus was on one thing: the Nereid trapped back at the bar. She hoped beyond hope that it wasn't dead. An image popped up behind her eyes: the creature straining, twisting the chair loose and scrambling out into the night. The idea made her break into a sprint.

It was their only link, their only chance to find out what Poseidon knew, to find out why he had obviously allied against them. They needed the Nereid to talk.

When they burst into the busted bar, she thought they were sunk. The Nereid lay motionless, tacked to the floor like some bizarre crucifixion. A blood puddle surrounded it at least three feet wide. But then the mouth moved. It looked like it might be swallowing.

They went to it and knelt. Hermes gripped the chair, but Athena stopped him and shook her head. If they removed the chair, the wounds would only bleed faster.

"Hey," she said, not terribly gently, but at least in an even tone. When the Nereid didn't respond, she patted its cheek softly. Then with a little more force.

"Can it even talk?" Hermes asked, grimacing.

"The bartender could talk. And the rest could whoop it up over that damned baseball game," she replied.

"What if that was part of the enchantment?"

"If it was, then it's an even better trick than I thought."

The Nereid was coming to, swiveling its eyes slowly to the left and right. It was disoriented and weak. Whether it would be able to impart anything useful before it cacked off, Athena wasn't sure. But neither she nor Hermes had any powers of healing, aside from basic first aid, so there was nothing to be done about it now.

"What were you doing here?" Hermes asked loudly and slowly, like he was talking to a simpleton, but Athena gave him a shove. Why waste time on the obvious? The thing was bleeding out all over their feet. In another five minutes, there'd be nothing left to do but wrap it in yesterday's newspaper.

"What does Poseidon want?" Athena asked instead. "How did he know we would come?" Although she figured she knew the answer to the last one already. Demeter was wise, and easy to find. Demeter had also been Athena's ally before, and not terribly fond of her sea-ruling brother, Poseidon. There were probably similar surprises planted around every god she might have approached: Artemis, Apollo, Hephaestus. Heaviness squeezed her heart. They were so far behind. A war that she had no idea about was already being fought. For all she knew, those who would have been her allies had already been found and killed, or turned to the other side. And now Poseidon would find Cassandra and use her prophecy for himself, or worse.

"Who does your master work for?" She shook the Nereid by the shoulders. Its lips pulled back in a hiss as the rods of wood pressed back and forth inside its wounds, but it didn't answer. It even appeared to be smiling. "I can make this last forever," Athena lied.

"Time to talk, Swamp Thing," Hermes growled. "Or we'll do things to you that will make those piercings in your torso seem like Shiatsu massage."

The Nereid looked at him fearlessly, and Athena ground her teeth. It was humiliating to be so weakened. It was humiliating to be chasing Poseidon's tail. He was an overgrown puffed-up mermaid. He had never bested her in anything. And now her pompous, fish-eyed uncle was six moves ahead. He had to be working for someone else. He'd never been strategic before. He would never have had the foresight to plant spies.

"You think I fear that?"

Athena blinked down at the Nereid. Its voice was a thin, rasping croak. Air squeaked from its mouth as it tried to laugh.

"You can't stop what's coming, battle goddess," it said, and peered at her with black eyes. "You'll die, and he'll die, we'll all die! We're all dead!" It grinned. Purple-black blood coated its teeth in a thin slime. Then it quieted and grew somber. "But my god will live. He will live a slave, but he will live."

"A slave?" Hermes snorted. "Who could turn that trident-bearing prick into a slave?"

Athena looked down at the Nereid. It stared at them with almost delirious satisfaction, breath coming in shuddering gasps. It would be dead in seconds.

"Who are we fighting against?" she asked. "If you believe what you say, if we're all dead anyway, then it won't matter if you tell me or not."

For a second the creature stared at her stubbornly. And then it blinked. Motion caught the corner of her eye and she watched its webbed fingers flicker in a hesitant, reluctant way, down toward its own thigh. Athena looked, but wasn't sure what she was looking at. It appeared to be a series of scars, poorly healed and tightly puckered in fist-sized crescents.

"What are those?" Hermes asked, cocking his head and peering closer.

"They're teeth marks," Athena replied in a dull voice. She ran her hand over them gently, and the Nereid tensed. Athena shook her head to soothe it. The anger had leaked out of her as her fingers had traced those scars. She thought she could see wetness clouding the Nereid's eyes and understood. They were tears of humiliation and powerlessness.

"Do you want me to see?" she whispered, and the Nereid strained toward her. She stretched out her hand and pressed her palm to the creature's forehead.

The world was water. Clear greens and blues and diamond sand. Cold surrounded their bodies, but didn't chill them; it was a constant breeze upon their cheeks. They might have been in any shallow cove anywhere in the world. Beams of white light cut through the water and illuminated the sea floor in rippling patches. And someone was screaming.

Many of them were screaming. It had been so still a moment before, glittering and calm. Now the water churned, it turned dark, it stank of blood. Sand was kicked up to mingle with the red cloud, a cloud that would attract no sharks, and continued to grow along with the sound of screaming. In the center, a bearded figure seemed to be nothing more than arms and teeth, reaching fingers and clenching jaws. He was eating them, wrenching their flesh loose, tearing their limbs free, cracking their bones. He called them and they came, because they always had, because they had to, and he swallowed them in chunks. Some died gratefully. Others, like this one, survived to swim away and heal, until the next time he called.

Athena jerked her hand away, and the Nereid's head dropped to the floor and bounced. It was dead, and she was glad that it had died here, at the hands of those it called enemies, rather than be murdered by him that it called master, that it called father.

"Take a breath," Hermes said. He had her by the shoulders and she put her hand over his. "What did you see?"

I saw Poseidon gone mad, Poseidon surviving in the way of the Titans, only worse than the Titans, more savage, disgusting.

She gestured to the bite scar. "Poseidon did that. He ate most of his Nereid's leg." Bile rose up into her throat and cold ran over her in waves. The Nereids were Poseidon's most loyal servants. They had loved him, and he them, since the moment of their creation. They were his children. And he was eating them.

"That is . . . disgusting," Hermes said. "It's like sampling the family dog."

"Anyway, it's nothing useful," she said, and spat onto the floor. A taste of bad fish coated her mouth. She had to get out of the bar, away from oily blood and salt. Hermes helped her up, and she bolted jerkily for the door. She didn't breathe deeply until she was fifteen feet into the night air.

"Are you all right?"

"Yeah," she said, and spat again. Then she started walking. If she didn't get away, she might throw up all of her beer, and that was beer she had paid plenty for.

"What are we going to do?" Hermes asked for what felt like the millionth time.

"You're going to burn down that bar, and then catch up to me," Athena said without turning. "And then we're going to find Cassandra. Before they do."

5

INTO THE DARK

The backseat of Henry's Mustang was way too hot. They'd cranked the heat up, not wanting Cassandra to get a chill, but it was stifling, and when she came back to herself she jerked upright, trying to get air. Her foot knocked against the side armrest and made everything worse; it felt cramped, too hot and too small. The camel-tan interior bled through her vision and as the car lurched to the left her stomach heaved.

"Open a window," she mumbled.

"Roll the window down," Aidan said, and a moment later the cold hit her face. She sucked it in hard through her nose, feeling it saturate down to her toes.

"Is that better?"

"Yeah." She blinked at him. She was half on his lap, her legs twisted down behind the passenger seat. The dome light was on and Henry was driving, a little too fast maybe for the way he kept glancing into the back.

"Is she okay?" he asked. "Are you okay, Cassie?"

"I'm okay."

"Do I need to drive to the hospital?"

"No," Aidan answered for her. "I think she's okay. Just head to your house."

Henry's eyes met hers in the mirror; she nodded.

"Where's Andie?"

"Right behind us."

Cassandra lifted onto her elbows and looked back. The familiar headlights of Andie's silver Saturn followed close behind. She took one more deep breath. She must've blacked out. When she remembered why, her eyes snapped to Aidan, but he was just Aidan, no feathers or blood. He reached up to touch her face and she jerked away. There had been feathers coming through his fingers as well, red-tinged quills breaking through the joints and twisting out from beneath his fingernails. It made her fingers sore just thinking about it, like a nail had been torn off.

"Hey, it's okay." Aidan held his palm up and didn't touch her until she'd relaxed. He looked from one eye to the other, checking her pupils.

"She's never done that before," Henry said from the front. "Has she eaten today?"

"Probably not enough. And then she had a beer on top of it." But not a lot of beer. Not so much that she'd hallucinate. They turned onto Ticonderoga Drive, which led to Somerset Street and their house. Henry kept watching her in the rearview mirror, ready to jerk the Mustang around and drive to the hospital at the first sign of distress. When they pulled into their driveway, he came around to get her door.

"Hold still," he said when she got out. He put his hand on her chin and turned her face into the beam of their garage door light. "Do you hurt anywhere?" Cassandra moved her shoulders and shifted her weight from foot to foot. She shook her head. "Do you remember what happened?"

"I think she's fine," said Aidan.

Henry ignored him.

Andie's Saturn turned into the driveway, bathing them in its headlights. Her shoes squeaked on the pavement a few seconds later.

"You screamed and fell down." Andie's brows knit. "That's weird even for you."

"Nice going," Henry snapped. "I wanted to find out if she remembered what happened."

"Shut up, Henry." Andie shoved him, but did look sort of regretful.

"Let's just get her in out of the cold," Aidan suggested. They walked with her to the front door in a tight formation, ready to catch her if she fell. It was nice of them, but the tone of the conversation had started to change, taking a turn toward talking about her like she wasn't there.

When they got through the door, Cassandra squirmed free and took off her coat and shoes, grateful that her hands weren't shaking. "I probably just didn't have enough to eat today," she said. "Andie keeps stealing my lunches."

"You never fight me for them."

Inside the house she felt better. There was space to move, even in the entryway, and it was familiar. Home. The TV was on in the den, and canned audience laughter from the sitcom rerun their parents were watching carried down the hall. A hint of garlic laced the air, along with roasted chicken.

"I think I'm fine now," she said, right before a black-and-silver German shepherd barreled past her legs on his way to Henry.

"You kids have fun?" Their dad came into the hall holding an empty snack bowl. Cassandra looked at Henry. When he looked away first, she knew he wouldn't say anything.

"Nobody better smell like beer." Her father stopped short in front of them and scrutinized their faces. He adjusted his glasses and leaned closer to give her face a sniff.

"Dad."

"Cassandra smells like beer."

"A glass and a half. Over like three hours. I swear."

He gave her the eye and grilled everyone else. They came up clean.

"Sixteen-year-old girls don't need beer," her dad said, but it was a tired lecture. He'd been talking to them about drinking responsibly since they were thirteen. "You might be grounded. I'm going to talk to your mother." He reached a long arm into the kitchen and set the empty bowl on the counter. "Honey," he called. "The kids are hammered!"

"What?!"

"Kidding, dear." He smiled, but when he raised a finger his voice was stern. "I am going to talk to your mother." He turned away back down the hall. "You kids just be careful."

Aidan insisted she get into bed, so she sat, still dressed in jeans and her blue cardigan, her blankets pulled up to her waist and the big black-and-silver dog stretched along one side. Andie sat on the edge of the bed and scratched his ears.

"Can't believe Henry let you borrow Lux," she said. "He must think you're dying."

Cassandra stroked the dog's furred shoulder, and Lux tilted his head toward her and whined. He'd stay with her until she fell asleep, then sneak out of her room to go crawl in with Henry. Despite being adopted as a family dog, he'd been Henry's from the start.

Andie stood up. "Listen, I'll call you after I'm done at the nursery tomorrow. You need a ride home, Aidan?"

"I can walk."

Andie waved, and they listened to her footsteps tramp down the stairs. There was a short, muffled exchange with Cassandra's parents, and a few seconds later, the front door opened and closed. Lux's ears pricked when she started her car. For a few deep breaths it was silent, and Cassandra sat in her bed, cuddled into her blue comforter. Whatever it was she'd thought she'd seen, it wasn't real. Feathers didn't sprout from people like leaves. They didn't slice through a body and tear them up from the inside out. And Aidan was fine.

"So," Cassandra said hesitantly. "Did I make a scene?"

Aidan shrugged from the foot of the bed, where he lay reclined on one elbow.

"A little. Sam said it was a nice diversionary tactic from Casey and Matt."

Cassandra smiled. It was what she expected. Kincade was full of nice, nonbigoted people. She'd been a little strange all her life, but no one ever made her feel it. When she went back to school on Monday, a few would ask how she was doing, whether she was okay, and when she said she was fine, they'd talk about something else. It seemed strange sometimes, like something was in the water.

It feels like a shield, she thought, but didn't know why she thought that.

"You going to tell me what happened?"

"Mmm-hmm." In a minute or so. She wished they were somewhere else, at the kitchen table, maybe, or in the den had her parents not been in it. Her room seemed suddenly childish, with its white dresser and vanity and gauzy blue curtains. There was a jewelry box on the vanity that played music; her mother had gotten it for her when she was six. She wanted to throw it out the window.

None of this is mine.

"Cassandra?"

"You're not going to believe me," she said, and he gave her a look. Of course he would believe her. He always did.

"I saw you, standing in front of me. Except you weren't right. There were cuts—wounds—and there were feathers coming out of them."

"Feathers?"

"Everywhere. Brown and white. Like they were slicing through you somehow. Even through your tongue and"— she made a face—"under your fingernails."

Seconds ticked by with Aidan staring at the blanket. It wasn't exactly the quick comfort she'd expected.

"It was really real. I think I could smell the blood, the disease, even through the cold." She swallowed, careful not to inhale too deeply. That smell might stay with her the rest of her life: sweet, cloying, and sick. It reminded her of counting pennies from her piggy bank.

Beside them, something struck the window, and Lux nearly punctured Cassandra's lung scrambling off the bed to attack. It was gone before he'd managed to bark twice, gone in a thump and a flash of silent feathers, but they'd both seen what it was: an owl. An owl had landed on the windowsill. It had balanced for an instant, all tufted ears and yellow eyes.

"Lux, quiet," said Cassandra, and the dog gave one final bark before returning to jump back onto her lap. Aidan went to the window and rubbed his sleeve through the fog of dog breath.

"It's gone."

"That's a weird coincidence," Cassandra said.

"Yeah." Aidan returned to the bed but didn't sit. He reached for his jacket. "Listen, I'd better let you get some sleep. You and your dad."

"My dad?" she asked as he walked to her door.

"You think he actually goes to bed before he hears me go out the door?" He smiled, then paused with his hand on the knob. "You know I won't let anything happen to you, don't you?"

"I know. Are you weirded out?"

"No. And if I am, I like it."

The sensation of cold hit her first. It shocked her insteps and made her toes clench. The dead, half-frozen grass spread ice all the way up her legs, and slow, chilly wind took care of the rest of her.

It's cold and it's dark. And I'm flipping barefoot. Where am I?

Moonlight showed the bony trunks of pines, green needles silver in the night. Up ahead was the orange glow of a dying fire, and the wind rattled through dry, brittle things.

Abbott Park?

No, not Abbott Park. There was no crumbling, patchy stone fence, and the trees were different. No sound of moving water from the stream either. Wherever she was, it wasn't in the hills of Kincade. It was wide open, and flat.

This is a dream.

But every physical sensation was there, from the cold on her goose-bumped skin to the irritating wet of thawing grass between her toes. Even the weight of her body. It felt completely real, to move and blink, to feel her hair shift across her back.

But I've had these dreams before. This must be someplace I'm going. Soon.

Cassandra stood silent, waiting for whatever mundane tidbit the dream wanted to impart. She crossed her arms. Stupid. The last thing she remembered was lying in her bed with a warm dog beside her. Now she was in the middle of a frigid, overgrown field, edged by pine trees.

I'm dreaming of an overgrown field. I'm not really in one. Just show me what you're going to show me already.

Nothing happened. She waited, and then walked toward the place where the small fire ebbed in a hand-dug pit. She wondered who dug it; maybe her dad, or Henry. Maybe this was a preview of a really miserable future camping trip. When she stepped into the small clearing, off the grass, her wet feet turned the dirt to mud that stuck to her soles.

"Damn it."

Her voice rang out too loud and made her jump, which made her feel stupid. Cold air crept down the neck of her sleep shirt and the embers of the fire inhaled and glowed brighter. She put her foot over them to get dry, but couldn't feel heat. Her foot dropped lower and lower, until she stood on the embers.

This is different.

"This is different." Her voice was too loud again, though she'd spoken softly. But she didn't care. Something was off here; something was unfamiliar. What was off was hard to say. It felt . . . altered.

I don't know this place. I'll never know this place.

The urge to leave rose up in her neck and shoulders and rushed down to her feet. The instinct to back up, to return the same way she'd come and disturb nothing.

Maybe then they'll never know I was here.

But who did she mean? Her heel shuffled backward, out of the coals she couldn't feel, and in her hurry she sent pebbles and sand skittering across the ground, loud as her voice. She jumped back, and gave a short yelp when her feet ran up against a rough wool blanket.

It hadn't been there before; she was sure of it.

There's something under that blanket.

She knew it as surely as she knew it hadn't been there a moment before. She wouldn't touch it in a million years, but she bent, and her fingers found the edge.

Don't.

Her heart hammered. The adrenaline would wake her up as soon as she lifted the blanket. Too soon for whatever was underneath to move. But not too soon to see it.

Don't, idiot.

Her fingertips tightened on the edge of the wool and pulled until his face came into the light.

His face. Just a boy. Not much older than she was, relaxed and asleep. Shaggy, dark hair hung across his forehead. He was handsome, with angular cheekbones. The sight of him filled her with cold dread.

I know him. Or I did. I would if he'd open his eyes. If he opened his eyes, they'd be dark, dark brown. And they'd be so clever.

But she couldn't know him from anywhere. Not from school, even though he seemed about Henry's age, maybe seventeen or eighteen. The gentleness of sleep wasn't at home on his face. This boy was a flashed grin, narrowed eyes, a quick tongue. An image of him flickered: fierce and confident. She wanted to hit him in the head with a rock.

It wouldn't do any good. It's done. It's started.

"What's done? What's started?" Words flew into her mind. Her own thoughts, but she didn't understand them.

The wind shifted, and drew her gaze up and away from the boy, into the trees. She couldn't see anything but black shadows between trunks. Maybe that was where she was supposed to go. Her way out.

"No." No. She stared at the darkness. *That's not the way out.* "There are wolves in the woods." *Not wolves.*

Not anything. She glanced down at the boy, then back to the trees. The shadows had shifted. Something had changed. A tree that was there before wasn't where it was supposed to be.

Not a tree.

She stood still and stared for so long her eyes started to go dry. Cold wind whipped across them and made them water, but she didn't blink. She wouldn't blink and let it fool her in that moment. Eyes wide open, she stared into the dark. Until the darkness lost its patience.

It moved, picking its way from shadow to shadow. Slowly at first, and then faster.

Cassandra's stomach fell through her feet and her mouth tasted bad suddenly, like she'd gargled with cemetery dirt.

"Get up."

The boy didn't move. Even as whatever waited in the trees came closer, close enough to hear the sounds it made, insect clicking, like jointed legs and jaws. An image flashed in the dark part of her mind: one red, faceted eye above a disturbingly human nose. A human mouth that opened to reveal a second set of mandibles.

"Get up!" Whatever it was in the woods, it was almost out. And when it came from the trees it would spring. She didn't want to see its face. She looked down at the sleeping boy. Maybe it was better this way. Better that he sleep through his throat being torn out. If he woke he'd be afraid, and he could never outrun it.

Cassandra backed up, the wrong way, back into the dying coals. *This is not the way out.*

The smell of caves and mold scented the air. She couldn't remember where she'd come from, or how long she'd been there.

A face broke through the trees, pale as the moon, with a

ruined mouth and one red eye. It saw the boy and scrambled forward, on him before she could stagger back, before she could think of finding a weapon or what she would do if she had one.

The boy's eyes flew open. He pushed against the chest of the creature as its fingers sought his eyes and mouth. A flash of silver showed through the blanket, and he dragged a knife across the thing's eye cluster.

Dark blood sprayed across his face and arm, and the creature rolled and curled in on itself, hissing and clicking its mandibles. When it came back to all fours, its head twitched and one of its forearms kept flicking at its mangled, dripping eye, or what was left of it.

The boy drew himself up from underneath his blanket. His eyes never left the creature, and his knife never left his hand. He slipped quietly to the left, and Cassandra moved out of the way.

You weren't sleeping. You were never sleeping.

He smiled. "You know I don't have all night."

Cassandra turned toward the boy in surprise just as the creature sprang, and it knocked her down as it passed. Rolling onto her elbows, she watched the two struggle. The creature's back pressed down into the smoking embers and it screeched. The boy kept his face away from the clacking jaws, and his arm jerked hard, once, then twice. The creature twitched and gurgled.

"I suppose it wasn't exactly fair," he said as he continued to stab. Dark blood coated him up to the wrist. "Robbing you of your one"—stab—"stupid"—stab—"eye." The creature lay limp, and the boy pushed it away and sat back on his haunches, breathing heavily. "But fair is overrated."

"Who are you?" Cassandra shouted, looking from the boy to the dead monster and back again. He'd killed it.

Feigned sleep and killed it, with no fear. His voice was accented, London-street, but not strained. He might've sounded more upset if he'd just come out of a scuffle in his local pub. Cassandra pushed off the ground and stood beside him. They watched silently as the body of the creature stiffened. Its pale, blood-streaked face stared up at the sky accusingly, and its arms and legs drew in and curled like an arachnid's carapace. He'd left the knife in its chest. When he reached forward to pull it out, it made a sick sucking sound that made Cassandra want to retch. She swallowed hard.

The boy studied the blood on the knife and wiped it on his sleeve.

No surprise in your eyes. You knew it was hunting you. You knew what it was.

She studied his profile.

I know you. I knew you. I liked you, and I hated you.

"Glory of Athena," the boy whispered, and made a reverent gesture before bowing his head.

The next attack came too fast. The second Cyclops leapt onto his shoulder and drove him forward, facedown into the stiffening body of the first. Cassandra screamed as it dug its jaws into his shoulder and neck, tearing skin, but it was his screams that finally drove her away, out of the dream.

Aidan's footsteps fell heavy on the bridge. Frost crunched beneath his feet as he walked down the center of the road, listening to the whisper of the river water thirty feet below, barely perceptible as it flowed lazily past downed trees and rushed against a steadily spreading sheet of ice. He didn't bother to listen for cars. It was late and the road was quiet.

His ears were on the sky, on the branches creaking above his head. He was listening for feathers. For wing beats.

An owl's feathers made no sound. That was how they hunted. They watched silently, heads spinning round, eyes wide as dinner plates. They watched, and they swooped without warning, talons breaking the backs of an unsuspecting rabbit, or mouse, or unlucky house cat. It seemed cowardly. It seemed like a cheat. And he expected better, especially from her.

He stopped in the middle of the bridge and stared up at the blank spot in the sky that the road left, cutting through the vast forest that surrounded Abbott Park. It was there somewhere, the owl that had flown up against Cassandra's window. He had to find it.

That's a weird coincidence, Cassandra had said. But it wasn't. No matter how much he wanted it to be. Their time of calm would end. Unless he stopped it.

The moment Cassandra spoke of feathers breaking through skin, he knew. He knew that somewhere his sister was dying, with feathers cutting through her body. His self-righteous, battle-ready sister. And now she wanted something. Something that had to do with Cassandra.

"You can't have her," he said, and his breath left his throat in a cloud of steam. He had to find the owl. It wouldn't be hard. It was Athena's servant, but it was still just an owl. It wouldn't race to her side to whisper in her ear. It would fly, and hunt, and sleep, and reach her in its own time.

The wind came up hard and sudden; the sound it made moving across the bridge and over the river was like a scream. The river would be covered over soon, locked down under ice and snow, only breaking through in the spaces where it sped up, past rocks and through spinning eddies. Aidan breathed the cold in deep but couldn't feel it. Cold had never been able to touch him. Not in all his long, immortal life. He was a golden glow. He was light, and heat. He was Apollo, the sun, and he'd burn down anyone who tried to hurt her.

Movement high up in the pines caught his attention and he moved, darting off the bridge, running low and quiet. He reached the owl in moments, watching from beneath as it swooped from branch to branch. He watched its brown speckled belly, its flight feathers stretched out on the wind like fingers. It didn't pay any attention to him, so far below on the ground. Not even when he leapt up to catch it when it dove.

The sensation of being pulled down out of the air had no time to register in the bird's brain. Neither did the feeling of its wings being crushed, or its neck being broken. There were no final thoughts. Only vague surprise and no regrets.

Aidan looked down at the feathery mess in his hands. The owl was dead. Silenced. He stroked the feathers.

"You didn't feel it. And it wasn't your fault." The bird was so light in his hands. Maybe he shouldn't have killed it. Maybe they could have caged it and kept it as a pet. Cassandra might have liked that.

But how many more would she send? He couldn't cage them all. His hands tightened. Questions filled his ears like they'd been shouted. What did she want? And how many others would she bring with her?

"I've waited too long for Cassandra." The fear he felt ran down to his fingers; he could feel feathers trembling. "I've waited so long, and now I finally have her. And I'll kill every one of you if you try to ruin it." He looked down at the poor dead owl. "Even you, Athena."

6

FAR JOURNEYS

Athena jerked awake, back tensed taut as a bowstring. There had been a dream, a flash of vision, something breaking. Something awful. She couldn't remember what it was. All that remained was the adrenaline, sparking through her veins and driving sleep far, far away.

"What is it?"

She glanced over at Hermes, ever the insomniac, even in his weakened condition.

"Are you all right?" He came and knelt beside her. His bony hands on her shoulders were warm to the point of being feverish. "Is it the feathers? Can you breathe?"

"I'm fine." Her voice was clipped and terse. He took his hands off and rolled his eyes; she muttered an apology. She was never a bitch on purpose, but accidents were happening more and more frequently where Hermes was concerned. Taking out her frustrations on him wasn't fair.

"I don't know what it was." She sighed. Talking was starting to be uncomfortable. The feather in the roof of her mouth pressed down insistently, and the flesh that covered it was tender and inflamed. Soon a bit of it would break through the skin, and she would wriggle it loose and tear it out. They say the mouth is the quickest-healing part of the body. She wondered who "they" were. Mouth wounds seemed to take forever to go away. And a torn strip the length of an owl's wing feather would be one hell of a canker sore, if it turned to that.

"Maybe just a bad dream," Hermes said softly.

"We don't have 'just dreams,'" she replied. "At least, I don't."

"I don't either. It was just something to say. Anyway, if you don't remember it, then it isn't much use." He gave her a piercing look, making sure nothing was flooding back. "Might as well call it 'just a dream.'"

"I guess."

Hermes stood up and stretched his thinning back. He was starting to look like a PSA against anorexia. She held in the soft snort of bitter laughter that accompanied the thought. It wasn't funny. Nothing was all that funny anymore.

They had traveled hard over the last two days and made it out of the bleak extremes of the desert. Their camp was set on a quiet curve of the Green River in eastern Utah. A soft patch of grass made for a decent bed, and the water was drinkable enough. A scraggly coniferous tree provided shelter. They were living like vagabonds or fugitives, with as little human interaction as possible. Such a lifestyle had always suited Athena, but Hermes was a house cat, and she could tell sleeping on the ground was getting on his nerves. He didn't hide it well. He constantly tossed and *hmph*ed and stretched his back.

"Are you hungry?" Athena asked.

"Usually," he replied sulkily, and she tossed him a can of peaches from her pack. He cracked the tin cover off and ate them with his fingers. Dawn was about to break over the river, beautiful and pastel. At least she'd managed to sleep through the night. It hadn't been an easy task since the encounter with the Nereid.

Her mind constantly returned to the vision that the poor creature had shown her. She saw it again and again, the blood-cloud whipped up in the saltwater, heard the gurgling and panicked currents of fins in death throes.

And the glimpse of him. Of Poseidon. Twisted beyond imagining. She could've sworn she'd seen a piece of coral cutting through his shoulder, like it was growing into his skin. Or out of it. Perhaps their deaths were eerily similar.

Regret, stronger than she'd imagined, clenched down on her stomach. They'd never been close, but seeing him that way still felt wrong.

Would he feel the same way? Seeing me pull feathers from my throat?

Probably not. He was weaker than she was and always resented that. He resented that Zeus had made her so strong. He resented that Zeus had that much strength to give her.

But it still felt unfair.

He should be on the sand somewhere, tanned and golden. He should be in the ocean, on a fucking surfboard with a nymph on each arm.

That was what might have been, if fate were kinder. Instead he was a monster, on the opposite side of a war.

Trying to humble me, as usual. She allowed herself a rueful smile. It lasted only a second before dropping off her face. Poseidon was ahead of them, after all, and setting traps too clever to come from his mind alone. He had help, and she suspected she knew who it was. Who *they* were.

"When can we go to a *city?*" Hermes thumped the dirt with his fist. She supposed it did make for a shitty mattress.

Athena laughed. "I knew it. Missing your pillow top and manicured nails?"

Hermes threw a peach at her; she dipped low, birdlike, and caught it in her mouth. He curled his lip. "Excuse me if I'd like to have some comfort during my final days."

"These aren't your final days," she said, but he seemed not to hear. He was looking off to the west with his back to the breaking dawn, his fingers suspended over the jar of peaches.

"Maybe we should just live it out," he said quietly. "Just enjoy what time we have left. Haven't we had enough?" She turned away from his glance and watched the water of the river pass. It moved without pausing, without taking notice. It was indifferent to them. That was how she had been for a long time. The world forgot her, and she forgot it, passing through cities and existing on the fringe, an ob-server rather than a participant. But now it was different. She couldn't explain it to Hermes, who had lived among the humans and, she suspected, lived right up to the hilt, but dying to her felt strangely similar to waking up.

"No." He sighed and ate another slice of peach. "Not for you. I can see that. I can see it turning in your brain. You've got your old cape of Justice on again. You're getting it in your head that you could be a hero. Athena and Hermes, last of the sane gods, saving the humans and righting the wrongs." In the soft-hued light of morning, with the sun coming up over his back, she couldn't tell how serious he was.

"Don't sound so high and mighty. You've played the hero before."

Hermes snorted. "Rarely. And never front and center. Face it, sis, I was always the Green Lantern to your Iron Man."

"Don't be such a nerd. Besides, you're mixing Marvel and DC."

"Who's the nerd?" Hermes arched his brow. Then he softened. "My point is, there is no point. We're dying, so we panic and band together. So what? What the hell are we trying to save, anyway? We have no purpose. We're obsolete gods in a destructive world. The earth wouldn't shed a tear, not even for withered old Demeter."

"There was a time when we mattered," said Athena, but Hermes shook his head.

"No. There was a time when we *lived*. Rather than just existed. But that hasn't been for centuries. I walked with mortals, played with them, ate with them. I've used up more of them than I can count or remember. But I stopped living. Look at us, Athena. No family, no friends—"

"You're my family. You're my friend."

He squinted at her and smiled sarcastically. "You need a helping hand and I'm afraid of dying. You can't fight alone and I don't want to *be* alone. We call each other 'sister' and 'brother,' but I don't know if it means anything. Maybe it never did. Gods are cold. War, killing, and stabbing each other in the back is really what we do best."

What he said was true enough. What they were probably wasn't worth saving. But it didn't mean she would let herself go. She sat peacefully a few moments, watching the water pass, swirling and dark in the early dawn. Then she sighed.

"I want you to stop it." They locked eyes. "It's the talk of the dying, and I won't hear it. I know you, Hermes, whatever you might say. You'll sing a different tune when this is over, if we come out on top. You'll fly again, you'll laugh again." She tore her eyes away and looked back toward the river. "You'll call me 'sister' and mean it."

"Athena," he said, but she stood up and started to gather

her things, rolling her thin blanket into her pack and walking toward the water to fill her leather cask.

"Never mind," she said. "Let's just get moving."

"Moving where? Why do we even need to find this girl? Prophets. What good is foresight? We know we're dying. We know that Uncle Poseidon will try to kill us so he can live."

Athena crouched by the river, filling the water cask and letting the cold river slide over her fingers, over her wrists with their bracelets of tattoos. The reflection that looked back at her was a girl's face.

Not a warrior's face. Not a general's face. But it will be again. Soon.

"Demeter said she's more than a prophet." She stood and shook her hands dry. "And Poseidon wants her; that has to mean something. That trap of Nereids—"

"Might've been just laid for us. Maybe he doesn't want her at all."

"But he'll kill her to thwart our plans. It's the only lead we've got," she said. "At the very least, we'll be headed in the same direction Poseidon is going."

"We might want to run the other way."

"So they can kill the girl, take all our advantages, and hunt us down later?" Athena shook her head. How could he talk of running, of retreating? The fight had barely begun. "Besides, do you really want to let our uncle tear some poor reincarnated prophetess to bits? You're not that cold, and I've got my cape of Justice on, like you said. So let's go save her."

Hermes shoved onto his feet and stuffed his unrolled blanket into his own pack.

"How are we supposed to find her?"

"We go to those in the know," Athena replied. "Those who can track her. Circe's witches. Chicago."

"That's halfway across the country." Hermes groaned and

stared east, like he was trying to catch a view of the Sears Tower. "Do you remember when the world was smaller? When we could get anywhere at the snap of our fingers? God, I miss Olympus."

"Yeah, well, it's gone." She shouldered her bag and started walking.

"Can't you send another owl? What if Cassandra's in Arizona and we have to come all the way back here?"

Athena shook her head. She could feel the owls, like she always could. And they knew what she sought. But they weren't trained spies. They were birds. The chance that one would happen to see Cassandra as they hunted their nightly mice was slim. And even if they did, who knew how long it would take to get back. She looked up at the sun, rising hot over their shoulders.

"We don't have that kind of time."

If this guy looks at my chest even once more, I'm going to crack his rearview mirror into a thousand pieces. She stared at the reflection of the driver, a middle-aged man with a tan, fading widow's peak of hair, hair that looked as fragile as strands of sugar. The backseat of his '90s model Caprice Classic smelled like stale aftershave and dirty socks, but it was comfortable. Soft, cinnamon-colored velour, with their packs sitting on either side of her, serving as armrests.

Hitchhiking had been Hermes' idea. A fast, comfortable way to travel, but as soon as the maroon sedan had stopped for them on the shoulder of Highway 40, she'd gotten an uneasy feeling. Not a feeling of danger, but rather of sliminess. The driver welcomed them in with a coffee-stained smile, yellow to match the old stain spots around his collar and armpits. His name was George, and he was in sales for a company that manufactured air filters. Athena had jerked her head for Hermes to sit up front, and when she made herself reasonably at home in the backseat, George had adjusted his mirror to roughly the level of her breasts and his eyes had lit there like flies ever since.

In times past, a mortal caught ogling would have been treated to a fairly nasty fate. The loss of all his teeth, perhaps. Or his eyes turned to stone inside his head. But times weren't what they once were. Her power over mortals had dwindled to the point of near nonexistence. She couldn't even give him a migraine.

Hermes chatted away in the passenger seat, asking lots of questions about George's travels and the air filter business. It took a few minutes, but gradually, George's attention shifted from Athena's rack to Hermes' curiosity. As he tried to explain the complexities of the perfect air filter sales pitch, Hermes snuck Athena a wink. She smiled and leaned back, trying to cool, trying to relax, trying to think of what exactly they were going to do once they found this girl, Cassandra.

To be honest, Athena barely remembered her. It had been so long ago, and she'd been sort of preoccupied managing the *entire* Greek Army. Back then she had fought for the other side, hadn't cared whether Cassandra lived or died. An image of the princesses of Troy rose through the mists of memory: two girls, one tall, one shorter, both graceful in fine woven robes. Trojan gold sparkled around their necks and on their wrists. One had dark hair, the other a rich honey color. One had to be Cassandra, and the other the eldest, Polyxena. She had no idea which was which.

Doesn't matter, she thought. *When we find her, I'll know.*

"You kids got parents waiting?" George asked with his eyes again in the rearview mirror, this time finding Athena's face. "I've got a daughter not much younger than you, and I think I'd have a heart attack if I knew she was out hitching."

"We've just got our dad now," Hermes said. "And he's pretty liberal."

"Besides." Athena smiled. "We're older than we look."

"Can't be that much older." George took a moment to scrutinize each of them. "I'd say you're barely out of high school. Am I right?"

Athena and Hermes exchanged a look. "According to our fake IDs, we're twenty-one."

George laughed. "I don't want to know about any of that. Though I can't believe—" He looked from Hermes to Athena in the mirror. "They must be some pretty good fake IDs."

Athena smiled. If he'd look into their eyes for more than a moment, he'd see their true age. The forever behind them. But he didn't.

George would take them as far as Kansas City. From there they might catch a bus. A bus to the witches, and from there on to a prophetess. Unless of course they were too late and arrived to find her already taken. Or worse, arrived to find ragged pieces of her strewn across the floor of her house.

Would she have been my friend, Athena wondered, *if we had fought on the same side all those centuries ago?*

It was a strange question, one she had never thought she would ask. In any case she couldn't imagine it. She couldn't imagine them having been on the same side. Back then her anger had been so fresh. Her disgust had been for all of the Trojans, all of the royal house of Priam and every god who opposed her will to stomp Troy into the bloody sand.

It seemed stupid now. Such a battle, such alliances, and

for what? For pride. For pride and for vanity. She should have been above it. But then, none of them had been. Only her father had remained neutral, and as the war progressed, original wrongs and causes were overshadowed by the play of gods. Gods wanting to see who was strongest, using humans like chess pieces, like avatars in a video game.

I actually allied with her. It was hard to believe, even so many centuries later. It had been one of the few times that they had been able to stand in the same space and not spit daggers. Hera. Her stepmother. She had fought at her side against the Trojans, against Aphrodite, Ares, Poseidon, and Apollo.

It all started on a quiet hill on the slopes of ancient Mount Ida. She remembered how she had seethed and how ridiculous she had felt, done up in her best gown, her hair, usually hidden beneath her warrior's helmet, flowing in dark plaits and curls down her back. Hera had been there too, wearing a crown of peacock's feathers, her cheeks creamy white, breasts thrust out proudly, angrily. Together they watched Aphrodite study her prize: one golden apple, marked, "To the Fairest."

"I suppose you'll both be sour now," Aphrodite had said in her high, girlish voice. "But you can't dispute the judgment."

Paris, the younger prince of Troy, had been the judge. His task was to award the apple to the fairest of the three goddesses. Of course they had all offered bribes. Aphrodite, golden goddess of love and passion, had offered him access to the most beautiful woman in the world. Hera, Zeus' queen and goddess of marriage, offered a fine kingdom and a world of power and riches. Athena had tried to ply him with promises of glory on the battlefield. And then, as Paris sought to deliberate fairly, Aphrodite had let her robe slip.

What was a boy to do? At the time, Athena had thought him the stupidest of men. But the passing centuries gave her more perspective. He'd been a seventeen-year-old boy, staring at the most beautiful naked woman in creation. Thinking with the brain below his belt was only natural.

But back then, she hadn't taken the rejection kindly. She couldn't remember ever having felt more jilted, more insulted, or, frankly, more stupid. There she was, done up like a debutante in her finery, when she'd never cared about finery. She'd put on their costume and danced to their tunes, and she'd paid for it. And then all of Troy had paid for it.

"Enjoy your little piece of fruit," Hera had said acidly, glaring at Aphrodite. "A pretty trinket to add to all your other pretty trinkets. Let it comfort you, that you have nothing else."

The sweetness left Aphrodite's face. "Nothing else? I have everything that this apple represents. And you are angry, because you are second to me."

If Hera is second, that makes me third, Athena remembered thinking. It had been difficult to hold her head up. She'd never wanted to be more beautiful than them. But she had always known herself to be smarter, and standing in her gown, staring at the golden apple and still ridiculously *wanting* it—she had failed herself.

"Leave her be," she said to Hera, and turned her shoulder to Aphrodite dismissively. "What can she know of our worries? What can she know of kingdoms and battles and glory? She's a silly, braided harlot. Good for men's dalliances, then tossed aside. Is that apple anything to compare to our legacies? Of course not."

Hera's eyes flashed electric blue. Then they calmed and adopted a mighty, motherly quality.

"You are right, stepdaughter," she said, her voice throaty

and deep. "We should have tossed that bit of gold to her the moment it rolled into the hall." She had reached out then and lifted Athena's hair gently off of her shoulder. Such an actress. The gesture had seemed so genuine; it had almost fooled Athena herself.

"You hateful witches," Aphrodite had spat. Angry tears had welled in her eyes. "You're jealous, that's what you are."

"Jealous?" Hera asked innocently. "Jealous of what? Your ability to sleep with men?" She made a soft scoffing sound. "I sleep with Zeus, the greatest of all. Athena—" She laid a hand on Athena's shoulder. "Athena sleeps with no one, and has no wish to. So go. Go on, Aphrodite. Let your prince dip his little wick into some beautiful woman. What can it matter to us?"

Aphrodite had no response other than to burst into tears and flee. Athena and Hera had watched with catlike smiles. With acid and malice, they had planted the seed of the Trojan War. Aphrodite had cried to her lover, Ares, and he had pledged his allegiance. So she had stolen the Spartan Queen Helen, rather than merely allowing Paris to sleep with her, and Greece went to war with Troy, battering it to the ground, and Cassandra and all of her family with it.

It had been easy. Hera's cleverness and natural wickedness lent itself to the plan. No one in the world could pull a double-cross or lay a trap like Hera could. A trap like the one she'd set for Athena and Hermes in that bar in the desert.

Athena had known almost immediately. The whole setup reeked of her so-called stepmother. Though she hesitated to impart this hunch to Hermes, who feared Hera above all other goddesses, and with good reason.

Athena leaned her forehead against the cool window glass, and watched the scenery flow by. In the front seat, the conversation stopped in favor of a low and off-key sing-along with Bob Dylan. George had his shirt sleeves rolled up to the elbow and tapped his stiff fingers against the steering wheel in time to the music. It made her smile, watching him and Hermes sing with their heads thrown back. When he didn't have his eyeballs plastered to her chest, he seemed like a nice guy.

Hera orchestrated the trap and Poseidon sent his Nereids to do the dirty work. The glamour, though, she thought lazily, *the spell to make those ugly Nereids look like people. That's what gave you away, Aphrodite. That part of the trick was yours.* The tables had turned. Allies had shifted. Two thousand years ago, the three of them had made the world burn. Now it seemed they would do it again.

"Tell me more about these witches."

Hermes shouted at her from the shower. He was *still* in the shower, and had been for the last thirty-five minutes. Steam was beginning to curl out in ghostly fingers from beneath the door.

"What more do you want to know?" Athena asked, raising her voice over the noise of the jets of water. She stood at the mirror that stretched over the large basin sink, combing her hair.

"What do you mean 'more'? You barely told me anything, yet."

Which was true. They'd slept most of the bus ride up from Kansas City, causing curious titters from the other passengers as they eventually began to wonder if the two ever needed to pee. A couple of fourth graders traveling with an aunt had briefly entered into a very serious double-dog-dare situation regarding which of them would hold a mirror under Hermes' nose. Then Hermes had started to snore.

"They're Circe's witches," Athena called. "You remember Circe, don't you? She led a coven on the island of Aiaia."

"What?" Hermes barked, and she rolled her eyes.

"Come out of there already! Do you know how much water you're running through?" She tugged at a tangle in her water-blackened hair. "And the inside of that room must look like a sauna."

Moments later the shower shut off and he emerged, letting out a massive cloud of steam. He ruffled his hair with a towel and smiled, looking pampered in a white Holiday Inn bathrobe. They had rented a standard room after Hermes flashed his puppy-dog eyes. He'd had enough of hoboing.

"Check out the fog," he said. "It's like a Van Halen video." He air guitared, and she smiled in spite of herself. "Nobody uses fog machines anymore. Except I saw the Foo Fighters do it last year. Mostly as a joke."

Athena tossed her combed hair back over her shoulder. A large, wet stain had soaked into the front of her gray t-shirt. She tapped at the antique silver buckle that adorned her brown leather belt.

"Nice," Hermes commented. "Where'd you pick it up?"

"Thrift shop in Albuquerque," she replied. "Now try to focus."

"Fine," he said, and left the room. "I remember Circe. Of course I do. She was a sorceress, had a habit of enchanting men and turning them into beasts. But unlike you, I haven't stayed in touch with the descendants of times gone by." Sounds came of him rifling through his pack, pulling out clothes and putting them on.

"I haven't stayed in touch with them either," she said.

"But it doesn't hurt to stay in the know. Circe herself is dead, obviously, but her island remains, in an altered state. Witches of her tradition have lived in covens through the centuries, in Greece, then later France, and now here in Middle America."

"Chicago's an underrated town," he observed. "Or maybe I just like the wind." He popped his head back into the bathroom, dressed now in a brown hooded sweatshirt. "They're not still turning men into animals, are they?"

"Guess we'll find out," Athena said, and smiled.

The witches had gone corporate. They occupied two floors of a warehouse on the lower east side. The sign on the building read THE THREE SISTERS, but in truth, over twenty women lived and worked within. Athena and Hermes entered the lobby, which was done up chicly in marble and brushed chrome. The receptionist, one of those bookish, sexy types with carefully pinned hair, glasses, and a low-cut blouse, gestured to the elevator at once. She watched them calmly. Athena barely saw her pick up the phone as her view was reduced to a slit by the closing doors.

Good, she thought. *They know who we are.* It would make things easier; eliminate annoying explanations and demands for proof. It also lent faith to the fact that the witches still had power, a question that had plagued Athena since her decision to come to them. A millennium was a long time to foster a mystical thing. The reduction in her own strength was evidence of that.

The elevator reached the upper level, and the doors opened on a wooden crate-gate, the type often found in warehouses. The rest of the interior had been completely redone: impressionist art hung on the plastered and painted walls, and marble columns stretched to the ceiling, but apparently the wooden gate had been left for ambience. Athena bent down and lifted it with a soft whirr, and they stepped into the center of a very large reception area. A circular brushed-chrome desk sat ahead, and behind it a receptionist so similar to the girl downstairs that one might have been just a hologram of the other. On the wall, a row of plush, cushioned sofas in shades of cream and gray rested. In them sat not customers but girls, beautiful girls in tight, attractive clothing, who looked at them with expressions of curiosity and obvious welcome.

"Holy shit, it's an escort service," said Hermes.

"And not only that."

They turned to find a girl nearly as tall as Athena standing beside them in a finely cut black suit. Hermes jumped, and she smiled at him warmly.

"I am Celine," she said, and Athena recognized a name passed down through generations. She offered her hand, and both shook it. Athena was surprised to see Hermes blushing. Celine was strikingly beautiful, with shining red hair, peach skin, and legs that seemed to stretch for miles beneath the elegantly tailored skirt, but Hermes' tastes rarely ran toward women.

"Do you know who we are?" Athena asked.

"I know only that you are of the old ones," Celine replied. There was a trace of a French accent in her voice, as soft as an echo. "Mareden, the girl in the lobby, is one of the strongest telepaths in the world. She phoned a moment ago to say that two visitors were here whom she could not see into. Only those among the old ones could be so strong. We know only that."

Athena scanned the room again. Celine had come from a doorway to their left. The girls on the sofas had ceased to stare and had gone back to posing with lithe, languorous grace. Beauty was everywhere. The very air was perfumed with some soft, floral scent. The room was meant to seduce, to comfort, and to quicken the pulse. When Hermes went to introduce himself, she stopped him with a hand on his forearm.

"Have you seen many old ones?" Athena asked casually.

"Never in my life," Celine replied. That gentle smile, the graceful squaring of her shoulders. "Until two days ago. When one showed up on our doorstep, beaten nearly to death. Is it he whom you are looking for?"

Athena and Hermes exchanged a look. "Can you take us to him?" they asked together.

Celine laughed softly. "But of course. However, you may find him . . . indisposed."

They were led down a long hallway, through a conference room with a high-tech projector and glass walls, and into the back area of the warehouse, which was a system of cubicles, what looked like an office kitchen with a sink and refrigerator, and several closed doors. While they walked, Celine talked to them of The Three Sisters.

"We are, as you so quickly observed, an escort company," she said. "But not only that. Twenty-three girls live and work in this space, performing a variety of tasks, including high-end mystic consultation for many businesses you would know by name. Others manage our worldwide distribution department of occult supplies and books, most of which are written here, in house."

"High-end mystic consultation?" Hermes asked skeptically.

"*Oui*." Celine smiled. "Those who have the most power

are the most inclined to believe in more power, in *endless power*. They are also the most desperate, the most fearful of losing everything. And so they pay us—for spells, for charming girls, for feng shui, in some cases."

"And you have twenty-some girls, all living and working here?"

"*Oui. Vingt-trois*. Twenty-three. Our apartments and quarters are downstairs, and in the basement. We are all coven members, all descendants of Circe and her clan. Everything you see here"—she gestured around her, to the walls, the floors, the art and sculpture that adorned it—"comes from the coven, and everything we make goes back into it."

Athena listened with half an ear. Her mind raced ahead, scrutinizing every closed door. This old one, who was he? Who would they walk in and find? Every muscle in her body was tensed and ready for the possibility of a trap. Her eyes and ears tuned to every movement, every sound. Beside her, Hermes chatted with Celine, but she knew he was ready as well.

This reeks of Aphrodite. He feels it too.

Celine moved slightly farther ahead of them and pivoted. They had come to the end of the warehouse, to another elevator. She crossed her arms over her chest as they waited for it.

"Will you not tell me your names?" she asked, eyebrows raised. "We are your hosts, you our guests. It is my right to ask this question, is it not?"

The elevator arrived with a soft ding. They stepped inside.

"Who do you think we are?" Athena asked. She was genuinely curious. No mortal should recognize her, or Hermes either. They looked nothing like any of their paintings and statues. No vacant eyes or marble butt cheeks.

The question, when Celine posed it, had an innocent ring, but her face darkened, becoming almost trancelike. Her pupils dilated and for a moment her hair swayed back and forth like a dancing mass of red snakes. She looked at neither Athena nor Hermes for several seconds. When the elevator doors opened on the basement level, her eyelids closed. When they opened, her eyes were back to normal.

"Please," she said, and motioned for them to leave the elevator. "This is our personal level. We do not conduct business here."

"But this is where you've taken the old one?"

For a moment Celine hesitated and seemed almost fearful. "You must understand," she said carefully. "He was very badly injured when he came to us. He had been traveling for such a long time. He was weary; he needed comfort and care."

"Comfort?" Hermes asked with a cockeyed expression. He looked around at the hardwood floor and leather furniture, the long oak bar along the west wall. In one corner a fireplace sat dormant, with what looked like a rug made from an entire polar bear laid before it. "I can imagine what kind of comfort you can provide here."

"We can provide such comfort for you as well, *cher.*"

Hermes swallowed.

"In the elevator," said Athena. She'd have shoved an elbow into him had Celine not been looking. "You never answered my question."

Celine inhaled deeply and smiled. "I do not know who you are. They do not tell me."

"Who are 'they'?" Hermes asked.

Celine shrugged, confident and charming. "They," she said and laughed. "I do not know. They who spoke to the Sibyl, I suppose. They who whisper in dreams." Her head cocked at him for a moment. "You seem so thin to me, *monsieur*. You look so very frail, so very human. It is a good disguise. Had it not been for Mareden, we might never have known."

Hermes looked away uncomfortably. It's no disguise, that look said. No disguise and not of my power. Athena's jaw clenched. He should be more careful. If they didn't know, then they didn't need to.

"And what about me?" Athena asked.

"You are flawless, *mademoiselle*. But then, so many women are, in these times."

It was true. Thanks to creams and collagens and nips and tucks, goddesses walked the earth in abundance. Celine herself was, to many eyes, much more appealing than Athena. Celine, who wore beautiful clothes and cared for her body well.

Athena glanced at Hermes. He was dying for an introduction. Revealing who he was to mortals was probably one of his favorite pastimes. And there was no more point to putting it off.

Athena held out her hand, and Celine grasped it.

"I am Athena," she said, and felt the pulse jump beneath the other woman's skin. "And this is Hermes."

"Athena," Celine said carefully. Her eyes darted down the hallway; the flicker of movement was almost too fast to notice. It had probably been unconscious. "And Hermes. We are honored to have you." She turned and resumed walking.

"She took that well," Hermes muttered, probably disappointed there hadn't been more of a starry-eyed reaction. But Celine was so collected and precise. Her response was exactly what Athena had expected.

They were being led to a room at the back, toward a dark mahogany door at the end of a long hallway lined with doors of a lighter chestnut color. The sound of Celine's high heels clicking on the floor was distracting and loud, but Athena could still hear soft strains of music coming from behind the wood. There were also other, more animal noises: laughter and soft moans.

My eyes must be bulging from their sockets, my ears grown elf tips. Her heart too was in overdrive, and she shoved the tip of her tongue up hard against the sore feather in the roof of her mouth to bring herself back down into her shoes. They were there. Celine's hand rested on the silver doorknob. Then she withdrew it.

"Perhaps you would wish to wait at the bar," she offered. "I could bring him to you very quickly."

Athena said nothing. All of her attention was focused on the door and what lay behind it. Her heart hammered for an ally, for hope, for any help at all. *Let it be Hephaestus*, she thought wildly, *reasonable, sturdy Hephaestus. Let it be Apollo, strong and brave.* But maybe she shouldn't hope for either. Both of them had fought with her, but they'd also fought against her on various occasions. And Hephaestus was Hera's son, and Aphrodite's husband.

It doesn't matter. He's always had a mind for reason. He's always been my friend despite them.

The door opened in her imagination on a dozen different scenarios. In her mind's eye it opened to reveal Hephaestus, twisted and mangled almost beyond recognition, suffering and useless. It opened on Poseidon, flashing jagged coral teeth behind his mossy beard. Water ran in rivulets down his bare legs; in his hand he held a black trident with razor-sharp points. She saw Ares of the smoldering eyes, saw him leap like a wolf for her throat. All of these possibilities flashed through her in an instant, but she said nothing.

"As you wish," said Celine, and turned the knob.

There were four of them on the bed. Three beautiful girls, one blond-headed, one black, and one red. The fourth was a young man with wild brown hair. They were half-dressed at best. The boy in the center leaned into the arms of the softly laughing blonde, while the others knelt by his knees, kissing his chest and fingertips. His eyes were closed. There was a glimpse of gauze on his neck, and more could be seen peeking around the sides of his ribcage. Athena knew him immediately. His angular face, the infuriating, exhilarating confidence that came off of him in waves. Flashes of memory rose across centuries and pasted seamlessly onto the moment, flickering in her eyes like tiny electric sparks. She smiled wryly.

"Odysseus."

7

DYING GODS

Cassandra's mother hummed as she moved between the stove and the table to place a platter of bacon down next to a steaming stack of pancakes. The smell made Cassandra's stomach turn, but she tried to smile. There are times when your parents' best intentions feel almost ironic in their complete and utter wrongness, but it doesn't do to hurt their feelings. Really it was Henry's fault; he'd mentioned that Cassandra looked sort of pale. Their mother had grabbed the skillet without another word.

Two days had passed since the dream. She kept expecting it to fade, to be chased away by waking life. But her head was still full of blood, of monsters that smelled like clay and moved like bugs. If she didn't eat for a week, that'd be just fine.

Henry and her mother buzzed about the kitchen, talking about the day, trying not to trip over each other as they coordinated eggs and toast. A crack preceded a sizzle as an egg hit the pan. Henry inhaled hungrily.

"Mmm. They're so much better when you fry them in the bacon grease."

Cassandra's stomach rolled.

"Cassie, why aren't you eating?" Her mother motioned to the food, so she took a piece of bacon off the platter and forced her teeth to bite through it, then fed the rest to Lux when nobody was watching. The spread of food grew by the minute: Henry plunked down a pitcher of orange juice to join the platters of bacon, toast, pancakes, and cubed cantaloupe. Just one piece of bacon wasn't going to satisfy the breakfast police. Cassandra wondered if pancakes were good for dogs. Lux certainly seemed to think so.

She was still in her pajamas, and her bare feet rested on the cold kitchen floor. The sensation felt flat, less cold than the frosty grass of the field she'd stood in two nights ago. Except she hadn't really stood in that field. But the kitchen she sat in now felt no more or less real.

She'd seen someone die. Someone she'd known, only she wasn't sure how. She remembered his eyes, the steady way they'd faced down the attack. He'd been confident, right up to the end. Cassandra wasn't so brave. If she closed her eyes the creature's face jumped up behind her lids. She heard the clicking of malformed jaws, louder than Henry and her mother's voices. And the screams. Of the boy being killed. She swallowed hard. The dream wasn't receding. Instead it folded over, stretching into the world where she was awake, where things like Cyclops didn't exist.

Cyclops. Even though they weren't anything like what she would have described if someone had asked what a Cyclops was, she knew their name. Why didn't she know his? Was she supposed to do something? Had she been meant to save him? Could she still?

I don't want to save him. I want him to stay away.

But she didn't want him to die.

"Cassie. Do you want a ride to school, I said." Henry sat beside her at the table, halfway done with his plate of food. He looked frustrated. He must've asked twice already.

"It's nice out," she replied. "I think I'm going to walk."

It wasn't, truly, that nice out. But the chill on the tips of her nose and fingers felt better than the claustrophobia of Henry's front seat. And she hadn't been in the mood to deflect his worried questions. He would have known that something was off. Anyway, in that way she had of knowing things, she knew Henry was going to hit a chunk of concrete on Meyer Road and stop to check his car for ten minutes. Annoying.

Cassandra was showered and dressed, with her hair brushed and lip gloss on, but she felt vacant, distracted, like she might walk into traffic at any moment. When she'd gotten ready, first in front of the bathroom mirror and then at her antique white vanity, it had all been on autopilot, a lucky thing that she'd done it so many times and that she never varied her makeup and rarely her hair.

Her feet stepped along the sidewalk, quick and indecisive, the walk of someone running from something without knowing where they were headed. Kincade High School was only another ten minutes away. Maybe she wouldn't go. If she took a right on Birch she would head farther into town. Left and she'd eventually find herself on the highway, and if she followed that as it wound northwest, she'd hit the state park. There didn't seem to be enough ground in either direction. Her feet slowed, then stopped.

This was supposed to happen. The visions changing. All the little things led up to this.

What part of her thought that? What part of her felt it? But part of her did. And if she was honest, part of her thought it made sense. Something was starting. Something was happening.

Maybe this is the point. The reason I've been a little bit different all this time. Maybe this is the start of whyever I was given this—

"Curse," she whispered. Curse. She didn't know why that word passed through her head. She'd never thought of it that way before.

When she finally walked into the school, she was fifteen minutes late. The building was always kept at what felt like several dozen degrees too hot, and it melted the frozen tips of her fingers and ears too fast, so by the time she got to her locker on the second floor her face and hands tingled and stung. Aidan was there waiting and had the locker open before she reached it.

"Hey."

"Hey." She skinned out of her jacket and stuffed it inside.

"I was getting worried. Didn't you get my texts?"

"Huh?" She pulled her phone out of her pocket but didn't really look at it. "Yeah." She flexed her fingers. "Cold hands. Figured I'd just see you when I got here." Textbooks with frayed edges and laminated folders slid through her clumsy grip. The blood inside her hands hurt and felt slushy, like if you tore them open it'd look like a red ICEE.

"I shouldn't have come." She pressed the books back into the locker and let them drop; they boomed against the thin metal and fell in a heap of open covers and bent pages.

Aidan looked at the pile and cocked his brow. "Not up for English this morning?"

Cassandra shook her head.

"Music to my ears." He took her jacket out and helped her back into it.

"You look better already."

She smiled. "I don't feel better already." But she did, a little. With her hands curled around a mug of hot chocolate and a half-moon cookie in her stomach, she felt close to okay.

Aidan sipped his coffee. "Well, maybe if we got you something besides sugar. Do you want a sandwich?"

"Not yet. Maybe in a while." Her phone buzzed but she ignored it. A few seconds later, Aidan's buzzed as well. Angry texts from Andie, demanding to know why they'd ditched without telling her. Cassandra sipped her cocoa and looked out onto the quiet street. The sky was gray and overcast. Everyone passing by had their necks tucked into the collars of their jackets, eyes solidly on the sidewalk or straight ahead. No stopping to admire the scenery. Cold wind reminded them that winter was coming, and they were bitter about it.

"I dreamed the other night." She looked down into her cocoa. "Except it wasn't a dream."

"Tell me."

She told him about the Cyclops, about the boy with clever eyes and shaggy brown hair. Her voice sounded like someone else's voice, monotone, and so even it might have been prerecorded. When she was done, her lips pressed together wearily. It had only taken a few minutes to tell.

"He died?" Aidan asked.

"He was screaming."

"But did he die?"

"I don't know." She swallowed. "I think so." Thinking about it again brought a whiff of caves and old decay. She covered her cocoa with her hand. Only the warmth of Aidan's arm around her back kept her in the booth. It still felt like she should do something. Like she should stop it; as if that were possible. Aidan sighed: a sound of relief. He kissed her temple, her ear, her neck and told her everything would be fine, the way you'd calm a child, or a crazy person.

"It won't be all right. This isn't normal. Not even for me. It isn't just calling coins, or knowing when it's going to rain. I saw you cut to ribbons by feathers. I saw a Cyclops *eat* someone, and I don't even know how I know what a Cyclops is." She kept her voice low, even though they were in the back of the café, in a corner booth. The confession felt strange. The words clung to her teeth.

"You have to trust me," he said. "Everything will be fine."

"You should be the one trusting me. I know things. And what I know right now is that everything is not going to be fine."

"But it is. I'll make sure it is. I know things too."

"Yeah?" she asked. "Like what things?" He was looking at her so intently. His mouth opened and closed on words. Aidan never hesitated, or sputtered.

It must be really horrible to be around me sometimes. I must've really freaked him out.

She sighed and he squeezed her tighter.

"I know I love you," he said. "We'll figure this out. I promise."

The hockey arena stood on the outskirts of town, an enormous structure painted a bleak, pale blue with what seemed to be a mustard yellow racing stripe along the roof. It sat beside four outdoor rinks and across from the lot where the bus garage was. The town used it for all manner of events: birthday parties, senior skate nights, and figure skating lessons, but the presence of so many yellow buses stamped it forever as being part of the school, and the specter of tests and teachers hung over it in a perpetual cloud.

Cassandra and Aidan leaned against the hood of Henry's Mustang while Andie and Henry stood on the sidewalk and talked about pucks and passing and goalies who couldn't get their legs closed. They'd been lucky to get a close space. Even though it was a mid-week game, the lot was jammed. Andie was in all her gear except for her skates and helmet. Her black hair was back in a ponytail, her bangs kept off her forehead with a purple bandanna. Her shoulders and ass looked enormous in the padding. It was strange that something so awkward and full of bulges could be so graceful once you strapped blades to its feet.

"I'd better go play captain," Andie said, and motioned to Cassandra. "Want to walk me back to the locker room?"

"So you're not mad anymore about us ditching Monday, right?" Cassandra asked as they walked down the cement steps. Andie had given her the cold shoulder for the better part of Tuesday, but by Wednesday seemed to have forgotten all about it. "It wasn't planned or anything. I got there late. You were already in class."

"It was for the best anyway. If I'd have ditched, they'd have benched me tonight, and I bet your brother twenty bucks I'd get a hat trick."

Cassandra smiled. Going to the café with Aidan had helped, and she was glad Andie wasn't pissed. Afterward, they'd gone back to his house and spent the day curled up together, watching movies. Or not watching movies. It had been too long since they'd done that, kissed until their lips hurt, the heat of his hands making her dizzy. After that there'd been no more visions and no more dreams. Maybe it had been a fluke, an anomaly, or a temporary bad spell, sort of like psychic food poisoning.

"And you didn't mean what you said Friday night at the party, did you? About us not being friends after high school?"

Andie made a face and flipped her blue Gatorade into the air. "Please. Since when am I serious?" She pulled open the door of the locker room. The sounds of Velcro being stretched and adjusted, sticks rattling, and the excited voices of a dozen girls spilled out to mingle with the cold hum of the arena lights. Andie ducked inside and said, "See you after." Then she paused. "Hey, are we going to win tonight?"

No.

Cassandra smiled. "I'll never tell."

She and Aidan got seats in the bleachers low along the home-side blue line. It was the best spot to watch from, and they didn't have any trouble getting it; girls' games weren't as well attended as the boys'. Most of the people there were parents and older alumni with a few pockets of students in twos and threes peppered throughout.

The opening puck dropped and everyone cheered. Christy passed to Andie and she took control, weaving through defenders and getting off a shot that barely missed, ringing off the post.

"I'm going to get a hot dog." Aidan stood. "Do you want anything? Red rope licorice?"

"And maybe a hot chocolate?"

He smiled. "Yeah. Maybe." He edged past her and she watched Andie try to dig the puck out of the corner, apparently by elbowing a girl on the opposing team repeatedly in the face. There were shouts from the crowd, and a bark. Someone must've brought a dog to the game.

The ref blew the whistle for a new face-off after another missed shot let the goalie freeze the puck. The crowd quieted, except for the dog. It got louder. The bark was rough and raw.

That's no dog.

Another bark joined it, and another, until the arena could have been filled with them. The sounds of snarling and growling came from every direction. Cassandra turned her head, hoping ridiculously to see a Labrador retriever or a husky. Maybe a team of them. But there were only people. When they opened their mouths to shout, snarls came instead.

Sweat broke out across Cassandra's forehead and panic coursed down to her feet.

I should run.

Don't be stupid. It's only a vision. Nothing worse than any other.

Only it was. It was like the dream. She sat still as stone, trying to ignore the urge to fly, to jump up and run screaming through the arena, through leaves and steaming jungle.

Leaves and steaming jungle. Something was out there.

They're already chasing me.

The mad barking took over her ears, changing to something else, losing the dog quality that made a bark familiar. This sound was feral and wild. It came from wet, hungry throats. Across razor teeth. It was a sound you ran from until blood broke into your lungs and your legs failed.

They'll be on me as soon as I fall. So fast. They could take me any time they want, but they like it better that way. With me broken and degraded. Without the breath to scream. They'll tear me into ribbons and gulp me down. I'll see their necks and shoulders jerk while they do it. I'll hear the shredding of my own skin.

Except it wasn't her they were chasing. She knew that even as she was terrified, even as the temperature inside the arena spiked, the humidity so stifling and heavy it felt like breathing water. Leaves took over her vision, hanging heavily from branches, enormous and dark green. Strange ferns peppered the ground, curled in like alien fingers. The light was hazy, indirect. Tree trunks stood choked with vines.

It smells like dirt. Rich, black dirt. And something else. Something nauseating and sweet. Rotten.

"Cassandra?" Aidan set the food on the bleacher and knelt by her knees.

"It's not me."

"What? Cassandra?"

Had she said it out loud? Sweat beaded on her forehead. The jungle was incredibly animal, alive and sinister. But the sound was the worst. Rustling leaves and roots being crushed underfoot. Branches being pulled and snapped back. The sound of something giving chase.

"It's not me they're chasing."

"Tell me what you see." Aidan's hands slid over her knees.

"Be still," she whispered. "Don't run."

"Run where?"

No. Not you. Not us.

She fixed her eyes on the sheet of ice that was no longer ice but humid forest. She fixed her eyes on the girl, who was Andie but no longer Andie.

Silvery hair flew out behind her like a flag as she ran, ducking vines. It was stringy with sweat and dirt, but still had a glow, like a pale moon. She wore brown clothes, torn and streaked with dirt. Her feet were bare.

"She's so fast," she whispered. "She's run for miles. She's almost laughing. But there's blood. So much blood on the leaves."

Aidan squeezed her tighter. She saw it, dripping down from the shining green, a trail for the slathering tongues behind her. The dogs that weren't dogs could smell it. They would taste it as they passed.

"Blood on the leaves," Cassandra whispered. "And in her silver hair. They're going to tear her apart."

"No," Aidan whispered back. "No." He pressed against her and buried his face in her hair.

Cassandra spat on the asphalt of the arena parking lot, where she sat in the seat of Henry's car, her legs out the open door so she could get air.

"My mouth tastes disgusting." Like bitter leaves and something organic she couldn't quite identify but that re-minded her of snails.

Leaves. Leaves from a forest I've never been. Where a girl is running to her death.

"Here." Andie rifled through her backpack and handed her a half-eaten Nestle Crunch. Cassandra peeled the foil and took a bite, tasting chocolate, crisp rice, and snails. It coated her mouth, like the scent of carrion and humid rot coated the inside of her nose. After a few chews she twisted and spat it out.

"Thanks anyway."

Andie nodded. She leaned against the car, back in her street clothes except for the purple bandanna in her hair. Henry and Aidan stood farther off. They looked lost. Aidan looked worse than that. When he'd helped her out of the arena, Cassandra had felt him shaking.

She exhaled a cloud, spat again. The parking lot was shad-owed and empty, lit only by three sets of large fluorescent lights. The game was still going inside, but there were a bunch of little kids skating on the outdoor rinks beside the arena. The sound of the ice shearing beneath skates and the kids' exuberant shouts made their corner of the dark lot all the more somber.

"This is getting old," said Cassandra.

"What is 'this' exactly?" Andie asked. "Tell me you're not pregnant."

Cassandra snorted, but Aidan didn't seem to be listening.

"I'm not. I don't know what 'this' is. I miss the days of coin tosses and weather prediction."

"Is that gone?"

"No. You're going to lose in there, by the way."

"Maybe we should take you to the hospital," Henry suggested.

"I'd rather you didn't."

"But maybe we should." He stuffed his hands into his pockets and his shoulders slumped. She felt bad, pulling him away from his friends for the second night in less than a week. But he didn't look irritated. He looked worried and no more enthusiastic about the hospital than she was.

"Are you dizzy?" Andie asked. She held her phone in her hand, trying to WebMD it before jumping to any conclusions.

"No," said Aidan. "No doctors. No hospitals. No Internet searches." He was still apart from them, staring into the pavement. Something was wrong.

"Well, what are we supposed to do then?" Henry asked. "It could be a tumor, you know."

"It's not."

"How do you know? She's been seeing all this weird shit—that's what it was again, wasn't it?" Henry looked at Cassandra. "It was like in the park."

"Sort of. It wasn't the same. It was a girl this time, running, in a jungle. She was cut, or hurt, or something. She was being chased." Cassandra paused. "And she didn't seem human."

"What?" Andie asked.

Cassandra blinked. It hadn't occurred to her until then. The way that the girl ran was so effortless and so blindingly fast. No one bleeding the way she was should be able to run like that.

She shrugged. "What are you listening to me for? It was a hallucination. Maybe I really should see a doctor."

"It couldn't hurt," said Andie. "I saw an old John Travolta movie once, where he got all these special powers and it turned out it was just this weird brain tumor, activating dormant brain parts."

"So what'd they do? Did he live?"

Andie blanched. "I'm sure that's not what it is."

"Aidan?" Cassandra asked. He had sunk down against the cement wall with his hands between his knees. She got out of the car and walked to him.

"It's not a tumor," he said quietly. "And it wasn't a hallucination." He took Cassandra by the hand. "The girl you saw in that jungle. I think she was my twin sister."

Twin sister. Aidan didn't have any sisters. Or at least he'd never mentioned one.

After the initial confusion and flurry of questions, he'd refused to say any more in the ice arena parking lot, so they drove to Andie's house, which was empty on Wednesday nights when her mom worked the night shift at the county hospital.

"What do you mean it was your twin sister?" Cassandra asked. "You have a sister?" Aidan closed his eyes and shook his head. But it didn't mean no. He was stalling. Whatever it was he needed to say, he couldn't figure out how to say it.

"Maybe you should sit down."

Cassandra looked at Andie and Henry. Who was he talking to? They were all standing: Henry by the sink, and Cassandra across from Aidan. Andie lingered near the refrigerator like she was trying to decide whether she should offer them something to drink.

"Cassandra. Maybe you should sit."

"Don't worry about me." She felt fine. The vision of the jungle had shattered and been shaken off. Aidan looked like hell. Like he might be sick, and it scared her. She wished she knew what he was going to say; she tried to will the knowledge into the dark space in her mind. But it never worked like that. It never worked the way she wanted it to.

"I don't know how to tell you this." He looked at them from under his brows. Gold hair obscured his eyes almost completely. "It's going to sound crazy."

Cassandra nodded. What right did she have to not believe? Whatever he said, she would take it. She would take him at his word, like he'd always taken her. Blood pounded in her ears alongside the ticking of the wall clock. Her eyes strained in the shoddy light cast from the fixture above the sink, the only one they'd turned on when they got to the house.

"I never wanted to tell you," he said, and stopped. "That's not true. I always wanted to tell you. I just never wanted to have to." He looked at her. "I'm not who— I'm not what you think I am."

Not what?

"The girl. You said she didn't seem human. And she isn't. And neither am I, exactly."

Three seconds ticked off the clock before Andie and Henry started to laugh.

"God, you really scared us," said Andie. The laughter stopped slowly, awkwardly, when neither Cassandra nor Aidan joined them.

"You're serious. Cassandra, he can't be serious."

Except he was. She'd never seen him look the way he did now, so somber and scared, and—

And regretful.

He took a deep breath and pushed away from the chair.

"I didn't expect you to believe it at first. I figured on having to prove it." He looked at Cassandra's hands like he wanted to touch them, but he didn't. "Follow me."

He led them to the second level and up to the sparsely furnished loft space where Andie and Cassandra used to have slumber parties, hanging out on beanbag chairs, reading magazines and eating popcorn.

"What're we doing up here?" Andie asked. Aidan didn't answer. He walked to the window. It overlooked the walkway of paving stones and the small front yard. It took him a moment to get it open; the locks were sticky, and when he jiggled them the glass rattled in protest. Winter air rushed into the loft as he pushed the pane wide. It bit at their necks and made them blink against the cold.

Away we go, into the dark.

He didn't look back before he stepped into the window and dove out headfirst.

"Aidan!"

Andie screamed and Henry did too; they almost knocked Cassandra over rushing to look down, expecting to see their friend's head burst like a pumpkin on the walkway. The front door opened and closed. Footsteps came up the stairs, and there he was, unhurt.

"I'm sorry," he said quietly.

He was a god, he said, and always had been. Or at least, that was what they used to be called. What they were now, he didn't know. It seemed like the wrong word when he was so limited, so much less than he'd been before. But there were still things he could do, the extent of which he wasn't quite sure. It had been too long since he'd pushed himself, or since he'd been pushed. He'd lived as Aidan for a long time. He was Aidan. But he used to be called Apollo.

Apollo. God of the sun, and of prophecy.

Cassandra lifted her eyes.

"And the girl? Your twin?" Andie asked. They were downstairs again, sitting at the kitchen table. Talking about it like it was normal. Andie and Henry looked like they expected to wake up at any minute.

"Artemis. Goddess of the moon and of the hunt." Aidan squeezed Cassandra's hand, folded in his. She hadn't run or slapped him. She hadn't even shouted. But her fingers were as cold as a corpse.

The way he talks, when he says those words. His voice isn't even his voice.

"What was happening to her?" Cassandra asked.

"She's dying," he replied. "She'll run until she can't run anymore, or until whatever you heard behind her catches up." He ran his hand across his face, over his eyes. "You said she's almost laughing. Did she seem insane? Crazy?"

"I don't know."

But you hope so. You hope she's so mad that she won't un-

derstand it when the teeth tear into her skin. That she won't feel it.

She wanted to reach out, hold him closer. It was strange to hurt so much for someone she wasn't even sure she knew.

"I haven't seen her in eight hundred years. My sister. She went deeper and deeper into the wild. Away from men and machines. And I never followed. She belonged there, I thought. Where no one could touch her."

"I don't understand." Cassandra's hand in his felt like stone. "What's happening to her?"

"She's dying. I think they're all dying. In different ways."

"I thought gods didn't die," Henry muttered. "That they were . . . immortal."

"We are. I don't know what's happening to them. Something's changing."

"What about you? Is that what I saw? Those feathers?"

Aidan squeezed her hand. "No. I'm all right. I think those feathers belong to another sister."

Another sister.

"Do we need to find her? Artemis?" Cassandra swallowed. The name felt clumsy coming out of her mouth. "Can we help her?"

"No." Aidan shook his head. "No. If we go, they'll find you. I think they're looking for you already. And I don't think she can be saved."

"What do you mean, they'll find her?" Andie asked. "Who's looking?"

"I don't know. Others who are dying. I think that's what the dreams mean, and the visions. I think it means they're coming for you."

"Why?" Cassandra asked. But she knew. It was something about the visions, and the way she knew things. It was changing, and they could feel it, like a beacon. They'd use her however they could. They'd squeeze the contents of her head out into a glass.

"What are we going to do?" Henry asked. He hung back in the shadows, his broad shoulders slumped, arms crossed. The question sat awkwardly on him. Cassandra was surprised he hadn't left. Henry was always so logical.

"Your hands are cold," said Aidan, and Cassandra felt them start to warm, heat radiating from him into her fingers. It was sweet comfort. And it was an invasion.

"What are we going to do?" she asked.

"We're going to do nothing," said Aidan. "We're going to hide, for as long as we can."

"You've put too much phenolphthalein in it."

"Huh?" asked Andie. Sam nudged her out of the way to examine the titration vials. Pink liquid danced inside the delicate clear tube. Dark pink liquid. He pushed his stocking cap farther back on his head like he could get a better view.

"You put in *way* too much," said Sam.

Andie and Cassandra looked at each other vacantly. Poor Sam. Andie wasn't much use as a lab partner on a good day. On a distracted day, she was a walking booby trap. Cassandra's partner was luckier: Jeff Larson, a brainy kid who preferred she not do anything anyway. The pink in their liquid was barely visible, just a scant tint, like the rose coating on a pair of sunglasses Cassandra had owned as a child.

They were doing acid-base titration, ten lab teams of students neutralizing the pH of an unknown acid while Miss Mackay looked on, walking behind the stations in her rather unnecessary white lab coat. Cassandra sighed. She and Andie weren't partners so much as assistants. They handed things to Sam and Jeff when asked, but mostly stayed out of the way. Cassandra kept her eyes on her station, trying to avoid eye contact with Andie. Whenever their eyes met it was there on the tips of their tongues; they had to clench their teeth to keep from screaming it. Aidan was a god.

The words were underneath everything else as Cassandra walked through the day, a day that felt stiflingly normal. At Andie's locker that morning, her team had gathered around to talk about the game and Cassandra's head had almost exploded. And when Casey seethed about Misty and Matt, Andie's eyes bulged dangerously from their sockets.

Talking about anything else felt ridiculous, like talking about what to have for lunch back and forth across a black hole.

"Can you get me the handout?" Jeff asked.

"Sure." Cassandra reached for it and her arm almost knocked the flask of base off the table. He looked at her irritably.

Aidan watched from across the room, standing with his own lab partner. He smiled. They'd seen him go headfirst out a window. She'd felt the inhuman heat of his hands and wondered why she'd never noticed it before. But she still loved him. He was still Aidan.

(Aidan but not Aidan.)

And he hadn't changed.

"He's still our friend," Andie had said to her and Henry when Aidan left them alone. "We can't treat him any different just because of his past. Right? If we say anything, he'd probably get locked up in a government lab or something."

"He's a god," Henry said. "They'd never be able to hold him." And then he'd shaken his head like he couldn't believe the words out of his own mouth.

Cassandra wasn't sure. He didn't seem like much of a god. Who knew what he was or wasn't capable of? She looked away, back at the glass tube, the liquid inside still slightly pink. The past was the past. But it stretched out so far, farther than even her imagination could go. How could she catch up? It seemed impossible that she could matter to a being like that. Her whole life would pass and to him it'd be no longer than a moment. Aidan would remain, and eventually their time together would diminish to a dot.

"Maybe we should give up." Sam leaned against the table staring at their titration, which seemed an even darker pink than before. He raised his hand, the white flag for Miss Mackay. Beside Cassandra, Jeff kept working, adjusting drips and reading and rereading the handout. The flask of base on the table rattled with his efforts.

"Easy, Jeff. You're going to lose something." Cassandra reached out to steady it. Then she felt the vibration through her feet. She glanced at Andie, who had finally gotten into a real argument with Sam over how the mistakes had been made and whose fault it was. Neither of them noticed the shaking.

But there was shaking. Reverberating through the entire room. The glass of the titration stations blurred at the edges. Metal desk legs clanged against the linoleum floor; the back row of desks started to slide. Somewhere, a piece of wood split with a loud crack.

Around her, clear glass tubes bounced, and several Erlenmeyer flasks hit the floor and shattered. But everyone kept working. Even Jeff beside her, though she had no idea how he was able to.

"Stay still."

"Cassandra?" Aidan asked. She heard him from across the room. The floor shifted violently and her legs buckled.

She had to grab on to the table to keep from falling. Jagged cracks raced through the linoleum and up the walls, splitting it like an earthquake, and Aidan walked across the room. Dust from the ceiling fell into his hair. An intense heat grew somewhere below them, and the floor rippled like water.

Get out. We've got to get out.

The light fixture fell from the ceiling and sliced into Miss Mackay's head, right through her pixie cut and into her brain, cleaving her skull open. Cassandra's stomach lurched. Miss Mackay walked calmly toward Andie and Sam, talking while reddish fluid ran down her cheek and dripped from her chin onto her white lab coat.

Aidan grasped her shoulders. "What's happening?"

Pressure. It built below them, sucking the air out of the room, and it built in her brain until she thought she might scream. Then it exploded, hurling her backward, boiling her insides. Only the strength in Aidan's arms kept her on her feet, but she pulled him down, crouching against shattering and flying glass. Women screamed. They were screaming, and then they *weren't screaming*, which was worse. In the aftermath she smelled dust. It filled her lungs and choked her. She couldn't hear anything over the ringing in her ears.

Miss Mackay knelt by her side and Aidan said something; they each took an arm and dragged her to the eye-flushing station. She found herself bent over into two soft jets of water. The cool of it brought her back, out of the dust and broken things. Away from the blood.

"Hold your eyes open as much as you can," Miss Mackay said. "How much got into them? Cassandra?"

"None," she said shakily. "I mean, I'm okay. I thought it got into my eye, but it didn't. It doesn't hurt."

"Are you sure?"

"Yes."

Miss Mackay sighed. "Okay. You scared me. We haven't lost an eye in here in years." She clapped Aidan on the back. "I'm kidding. Just to be safe though, keep your eyes in the water for a little longer. And rinse all over your face." She stayed until Cassandra did it, then ordered the class back to work. Cassandra wondered if she'd ever be able to look at her again without seeing her head split open.

"Hey," said Aidan, his hand on her lower back. "What just happened? What did you see?"

She took a deep breath and looked up helplessly.

"A building just blew up somewhere."

8

THE ISLAND OF CIRCE, REDUX

"Ay caramba."

The scene in the room hadn't paused when the door opened. It was a jumble of caressing, and giggling, and soft sighs. The scent of amber incense wafted up, cloying and strong.

"Shut up, Hermes." At the sound of Athena's voice, Odysseus' eyes fluttered open; his brow creased as he tried to focus.

This is just like it was before.

The scene from thousands of years ago and the room she looked into now. Odysseus had been marooned on Circe's island after the Trojan War. His men had been transformed into pigs and beasts, and he'd been taken as Circe's plaything. He'd lingered there for a year in Circe's bed, while Athena labored to send him home.

And here you are again. Tangled up in a ball of witches.

Athena and Hermes stood in the doorway as Celine snapped her fingers at the girls, telling them to grab their things, quickly, quickly. This evoked whines of protest, but the look in Celine's eyes silenced the noise. All three left in a flurry of bare legs and perfumes that made Athena's nose crinkle as they passed. Before she left, the blonde ran a lingering hand across Odysseus' chest while he lay dazed in the center of the bed. Celine looked at Athena, for a moment seeming like she was going to explain. Then she ducked her head solemnly and quit the room, closing the door behind her.

Hermes walked quickly to the bed and peered down into Odysseus' face. He narrowed his eyes and scrutinized him, his mouth dropped open comically. Athena stayed where she was, near the door. She hadn't known what to expect, but it certainly hadn't been this. To have the reincarnated body of her favorite hero lying before her had jolted her brain to a catatonic stillness. She felt almost peaceful. Shocked but peaceful.

"It's really him," Hermes said. "Younger. Better haircut. But it's him. Wily Odysseus." He bent and pushed the boy's head with a stiff forefinger. "Something sure as hell took a good bite off him."

Athena took a deep breath and walked to the bed and looked down on his face. Two thousand years had passed since she'd seen him last.

Odysseus. I thought your story was told. That you'd live and die on Ithaca, quietly, with your loyal Penelope.

Odysseus lifted his hand to his forehead and grimaced like a man fighting a cheap whiskey hangover.

"Hey," Hermes said sharply. He snapped his fingers before Odysseus' face, then looked at Athena. "They were like freaking Dracula's wives. I think they put the whammy on him. What should we do? Cold shower?"

"That won't be necessary," Odysseus replied. "But if you could hand me my shirt, that'd be nice."

"He's British," Hermes observed while he bent to retrieve the rumpled cloth from the floor. "That's interesting."

"Not as interesting as what he's doing here." Athena glanced around at the silk pillows. "Didn't you get enough of this two thousand years ago?"

Odysseus sat up wearily and caught the shirt Hermes threw. When he slid into it, Athena could see the halting protests of his torn back muscles, but he didn't wince or moan. His fingers stayed steady as he buttoned it up and stared at her. There was nothing in his expression, but she expected that. He never gave away anything that he didn't want to.

"Enough for a lifetime. But this isn't the same lifetime, now is it?"

The same lifetime. Not by a long shot. In the old days, he'd been a king. A leader of the Greeks during the Trojan War. He'd fought alongside Agamemnon and Achilles. He'd helped them break down Troy's walls. Cassandra's walls.

And now we find you here. At the same time we seek her.

Odysseus rolled the sleeves of his black shirt up to the elbows. When he stood, he was as tall as he had been then, tall enough to look into her eyes. "In any case, I was looking for *you*." He stepped closer; the movement was intimate and challenging. "Athena."

"You know who I am."

His brows knit and he smirked. "You knew who I was."

"Hello?" Hermes waved his hand. "Anybody know who I am?"

Odysseus looked over his shoulder. "Messenger. Nice to see you again. You're looking a bit thin. You given up meat or something?" He looked at Athena and jerked his head back toward Hermes. "Why couldn't you send him for me like you did before? Would have been nice to have a winged escort. Might've kept the fucking Cyclops off my neck."

"He can't fly anymore," she replied, and ignored Hermes' offended glare. "And I think I've seen you home safely often enough."

"Right, right, right. You fought Poseidon so I could make it back to Ithaca after the war, and I'm supposed to be eternally grateful. Never mind that it took ten bloody years to get the job done, and that everyone I was traveling with died—"

Athena laughed. The sound cut through the air, surprising everyone.

"You can't blame me if you keep pissing off Poseidon. Though you might just come in handy. Perhaps I could feed you to him as a distraction."

You're still so much the same. Clever. Balanced on a razor's edge. They gave Achilles all the credit for the war in Troy. Manslayer, they called him. Sacker of cities. But it was you who thought of the Trojan Horse. Hollowing out that wooden steed to sneak Greeks inside the city. Without you, Achilles was nothing.

"Enough of this." Hermes' voice was deep and impatient, and uncharacteristically godlike. "There are questions to be answered and work to be done, and since when do I have to remind you of that?" He arched his brow at Athena. "Banter with your favorite hero later, when we're not knee-deep in throw pillows and body glitter in the middle of a brothel bedroom. When we're not fighting for our lives."

Odysseus smiled. "I see he's still dramatic."

"Shut up." Hermes crossed his arms. "Why were you looking for us?"

Odysseus' eyes flickered from him to Athena. "For protection," he replied. "Why else would you seek out a goddess?"

"We've got our own problems," said Hermes. "Sister's suggestion wasn't half bad. Maybe we should use you as a distraction. Throw Poseidon off our scent for a while."

"Counterproductive, mate." Odysseus turned and walked to a Louis XV–style chair in the corner of the room. It was covered in garish red velvet to match the walls. Everything in the room was a shade of red. It was supposed to be seductive. Instead it evoked claustrophobic thoughts of blood and being swallowed whole. He picked up a green-and-black canvas pack from the seat and slung it over his good shoulder, then looked back at Hermes with a grin. "If Poseidon and his little harem get hold of me, you all"—he gestured to them with a tilt of his chin—"are dead."

"What are you talking about?" Athena asked.

"Listen. I know that Hermes isn't on some wonky diet. His body's eating his flesh away. He's dying. All the gods are dying. I also know that Poseidon and his lady friends have a plan to keep that from happening, and it involves gathering weapons and eating the two of you. And then maybe sinking the whole world under the fucking waves or some bollocks."

"How do you know that?" Hermes asked.

"Never mind how I know that. The important thing is, I know what they're after, and they know that I know. Figured that out when that insectian Cyclops popped out of the dark like a frakking jack-in-the-box." He flexed his injured shoulder and grimaced.

Athena looked at her brother. When the door had opened, she'd prayed for an ally. Instead she found an informant. Still, a gain was a gain.

"Let's get out of this nauseating room," she said. "And then you're going to tell us everything."

They found Celine waiting near the bar. Three glasses of red wine sat on the polished wood beside her. When they approached she stood, her expression apprehensive but pleasant.

"I have sent the girls away," she said, and gestured to the wine. "Please. Join me. Take some refreshment."

"That seems about right." Odysseus set his pack down on the floor and moved toward a glass, but Celine took it gracefully away from his seeking fingers.

"You are not of age," she said.

"I'm eighteen," he said. "In the UK, that's age plenty."

"Ah, but you are in America now." Celine smiled. Athena grinned and tipped up her own glass. Odysseus gestured toward her.

"Come on. I'm almost as old as they are."

Celine lifted her chin and pursed her lips. Her head shook demurely, once, right to left. "No, no, *monsieur. They* are ageless. You, though an old one, have a new body. And that body is not yet of age."

Athena drank while Odysseus grumbled, trying to look like she was enjoying it. But swallowing took some effort, both because of the feathers in her throat and the liberal amount of honey Celine had added to the wine. It was meant as tribute, but it hadn't been watered, and tasted too heavy and sweet. Hermes guzzled his like water. Athena grabbed a few blackberries from a silver tray to cut the sugar.

"Are you pleased to find him?" Celine asked. "We healed him as best we could, in the tradition which has always been our way." There was nervous unease in her eyes, like she thought Athena was about to wrench her head off of her shoulders.

"You've done well. And you have nothing to fear from me. I'm sure that Odysseus had no objections."

Celine smiled. "And now you will take him and leave us in peace." She sipped her wine, and Athena watched her shoulders relax.

"Don't you want to know what's happening?" Hermes asked incredulously. "Two gods and an old one turn up at your door, and you don't think that something might be, I don't know—afoot?"

Celine sipped again and stood. "I have no doubt. And no care. We keep to ourselves. We keep our own, and let the rest of the world do as it will. We do not interfere with it, and it does not interfere with us."

"And if it did interfere with you?" Odysseus asked.

"It has not for over a thousand years," Celine replied, and shrugged. There was a disaffected air in her demeanor that Athena didn't like. It was passive and haughty. "It would be best, I think, if you went as soon as possible."

"We need your help," Hermes pressed. "That's why we came. We didn't even come for him." He gestured toward Odysseus, who smiled and raised a grape in a "thanks and fuck you" salute.

Some of the serenity drained out of Celine's large brown eyes. Her warm smile faltered and became brittle.

She's afraid. She's known all along the danger we brought with us.

It must've killed her to put on a demure face and play the polite hostess. Everything inside her must've screamed to lock the door, to protect herself and her coven. But what was a locked door against a god? Even a door locked by witches. It wouldn't have done any good.

Athena saw the denial quickly chipping away from Celine,

taking her calm, capable exterior with it. These witches were not warriors; they were not Amazons. They had never been allies of anyone save themselves. But they had to help. They were needed.

"We have given you shelter and care." Celine stood and folded her arms in front of her, then pulled them, trembling, to her sides, palms up. "We are glad to offer you food and drink, rest and relaxation. And then we ask you to leave at once. As your host, it is our right to do so."

"Don't pull that 'code of Xenia' bullshit on them," Odysseus said. "They're your gods, not your guest-friends."

"They are no one's gods," Celine snapped. "Not anymore."

Odysseus looked at Athena with wide eyes. The look demanded action. It called for punishment for such disrespect. Athena smiled. He had always had so much pride, and it had always been so easily wounded. Only her hand on his forearm kept him in his seat. She stood and sighed.

"You've hit the nail on the head, Celine. We are no one's gods." Athena's tongue drifted over the feather nestled beneath the swollen skin on the roof of her mouth. It had begun to emerge. A quarter inch of smooth quill could be felt, and it tasted faintly of birds. "We are barely gods at all, anymore." She locked eyes with the other girl, drawing herself up, and in Celine's eyes she knew that she must seem huge, larger than life and shimmering, blotting out the world. Mortals were easily dazzled. Even witches. "You think by turning us away you will save The Three Sisters, that you will save your coven and your world. But you are wrong."

"No," Celine said softly. Her hands fluttered and shook as they clasped together and started to wring.

"The gods are dying. We're banding together, one side against the other, and those who seek to kill us would gladly

send you and twenty-two other witches with us. Circe's coven has to choose a side."

Athena could see the mantra repeating inside the frightened woman's head. *We are not fighters*, it said. *We are modernized, we are comfortable, we keep to ourselves and let others solve their own problems.*

"No. You are immortal! You do not need us!"

"Have Circe's witches become such cowards?" Odysseus spat. "I remember when they trapped my men to put them in stew!"

Celine ignored him and touched Athena's hand. "You are immortal," she said again, her voice growing high with fear. "You do not need us. We ask nothing from you. Please go!"

The entreating touch was the last straw. It had been many centuries since humanity had bowed to Athena, but these were Circe's witches. These were the descendants of her people, and they had no right to refuse. She looked at Celine's small, pale hand and felt pity. Felt guilt. She would have liked to be strong enough to do as she asked, to go and fight her own battles. Celine's repeated words, "You are immortal, you are immortal," stung her ears. Suddenly she reached into her mouth and grasped the short, exposed quill of the feather. When she yanked, it tore free with a long, meaty sound. Behind her, Hermes moaned.

Blood drenched her tongue and teeth. The feather hung limply from her fingertips, and she slammed it down onto the bar top. It was disgusting, coated with blood and bits of her skin. Celine put her hands to her mouth, her eyes wide and losing their reason.

"I am a walking wound," Athena hissed. She swallowed red salt and came close to retching. "And still I'm *asking*. The ones who come after me won't be so polite. So make

your choice. But don't fool yourself. You're going to have to get off your ass and help someone." She spun and struck the bar chair, sending it flying, and headed for the back of the warehouse. When she saw the exit door, she pushed through it and pounded her feet against the steel stairs. She didn't stop until she'd shoved her way out into the brick-walled alley.

Stupid.

She touched the ragged hole in the roof of her mouth with the tip of her tongue. It felt like setting her whole head on fire. She spat blood onto the pavement. With the adrenaline wearing off, it was starting to sting and throb. She bared her teeth. Tearing it out had been so easy.

"Athena."

She didn't turn. She didn't want to betray her surprise, but she'd been so preoccupied with the pain that she hadn't heard the door open behind her.

"Don't sound shocked," she said. "You already knew."

"I knew you were dying," Odysseus said. "I didn't know how." He placed hesitant fingers on her arm, like he was afraid to feel another quill breaking the surface. She jerked.

Yes, I'm hideous. Get the fuck away.

He cleared his throat.

"They'll heal you," he said. "They're right good at doing that."

"I don't doubt it. You're looking downright spry for just taking on a Cyclops." She turned and met his eyes. He looked so *concerned.* It shamed her. And it touched her. He'd always been her favorite hero. She'd never given much thought to whether she'd been his favorite goddess.

He grinned and held up his fingers.

"Two Cyclops."

"Whatever you say. But Circe's witches can't heal this."

She gestured to her mouth. "This I will have to bear. And if I can't stop tonguing it, it's going to turn into one mother of a canker sore."

He stared at her, and she watched his mouth open and close, words and phrases trying themselves out in his head. It was amusing to watch someone with so quick a tongue try to find the right thing to say. In the end, he didn't say anything. He just lifted his hand and gently wiped away a dot of blood from her lower lip.

"That was awful of me, in there." She gestured toward the door.

"Gave Miss Celine the fright of her life." Odysseus smiled. "I thought she was going to faint dead away. But desperate times call for desperate measures. You did what you had to."

"That's what these are, I suppose." She looked at him carefully. He could meet her gaze like so few were able. But just then he couldn't quite manage it. "How did you know?"

He paced away and shrugged. "I don't know. Up until I was six, I was a carefree lad growing up in Stoke Newington. Still had this ridiculous name, of course, but everyone around home just called me Ody, which I wish that you would do."

"That's Garfield's dog's name. But if you insist." She swallowed gingerly. It hurt when anything touched the roof of her mouth. Keeping her voice normal was difficult.

He grinned and went on. "Anyway, one summer I was on holiday with my family at Brighton Beach. My older sister and I got to messing around. I hit my head on something and went over the rail. I maintain that the something I hit my head on was actually a rock that she threw, but she denies it. The point is, I almost drowned. Stopped breathing, stopped pumping blood. I was dead. And then *I* wasn't dead, if you get my meaning."

"You were yourself again."

He raised his eyebrows and ran a hand through his brown hair. It was a tangled mess, and his fingers snagged in it. Probably on a sticky patch of some kind of massage oil from his time in the room of many bosoms, was Athena's guess.

"I was myself again. Remembered everything. Ithaca, Troy, everything. That fucking endless journey home." His face grew serious. "And you. I remembered you."

Athena dropped her eyes. How many times had she thought of him, over the centuries? Every clever human who wasn't as clever as he was, every pompous act of bravery that wasn't as brave or as pompous as his would have been. Now he was there, eighteen again, young and strong with the same quick, dark eyes and the same sideways smile. Asking her to protect him when it was the last thing she had time to be doing, and she couldn't even find it in herself to be angry about it.

"Thought I was plum crazy, for the longest time. But I kept my mouth shut and I watched, and I listened. I lived like a normal bloke, played some rugby, scammed on the Tube. And then three months ago, she came for me." Odysseus cleared his throat.

"She?"

"Everything all right out here?" The door behind them opened, and Hermes popped his head out. He looked from Odysseus to Athena and handed her a glass of water.

"Thank you," she said. "Everything's fine." She glanced at Odysseus. His hands were stuffed deep into his jeans pockets. The look was decidedly awkward, almost guilty.

What must Hermes be thinking, finding us like this? He'd better not be thinking anything, if he knows what's good for him.

She took a swish of water and spat onto the sidewalk. The water came out clear. The ragged channel on the roof of her mouth stretched from just behind her teeth to nearly down her throat. She didn't know what was going to hurt worse: talking, or having her tongue sit on it idly in a constant, hot pressure.

"Well you'd better get back in here," said Hermes. "Celine has finally grown a spine. The coven's going to help us. She's assembling them upstairs."

"Can we trust them?" Odysseus asked.

"They were frightened, but they're not idiots. I've convinced them that they can back us and live, or back Poseidon and live as slaves."

Athena smiled. "Well done, Hermes."

Celine met them when the elevator doors opened on the top floor. In one hand she held a clay bowl, filled with dark, steaming liquid that looked like unfiltered tea. When Athena stepped out, she gave it to her. It smelled of strong, bitter herbs.

"What's this?" Athena asked.

"Please, accept it," Celine said. Her mild smile was gone, replaced by a nervous, distracted intensity. "It is only a simple potion, to help with your pain." She motioned for Athena to drink. The taste was faintly lemony. It stung the roof of her mouth; she had to clench her jaw to keep from wincing. But as the initial acid sting wore off, a calm numbness spread within her mouth.

"Thank you," she said.

"You are welcome. And please forgive my cowardice." Celine's eyes met hers, unwavering. "It will not happen again."

Athena nodded. They walked quickly together down the hall. When they reached the conference room, Celine extended her arm to direct them inside. At a glance, at least fifteen girls of varying heights and features stood around the long, oval table. They had arranged themselves attractively, so that the different shades of blonde, brunette, black, and red moved through the room like a mellow rainbow. Each wore a well-cut suit and a silver necklace. It was a sharp contrast to Athena's well-worn t-shirt and cardigan and Hermes' brown hoodie. Still, none of the witches regarded them with disapproval. The mood was serious, fearful, and tense with power.

"I have assembled everyone I could." Celine motioned for them to join her at the head of the table. "Bethe, Jenna, and Harper are out of the office today, working on consultations." She nodded to the women, who moved forward and sat down in their chairs. Then she held her hand out to Athena. "Please," she said, and sat herself. "Tell us what we must do."

Athena could feel Hermes and Odysseus standing just behind, one at each of her shoulders. They expected her to talk, to make a speech, to rouse the troops as she had once done. Part of her resented it. She hadn't been a general for two thousand years. The blank row of faces that lined the table seemed miles away, viewed across mountaintops. These were modern women; mystical or not, how could she talk to them about the wars of gods? This wasn't anything like it had been in those days. This was no great hall where kings drank and feasted, where braziers burned late into the night. It was a damn boardroom.

She took a deep breath.

"I trust that Celine has told you who we are." She regarded them gravely. "And now I will tell you why we have come.

"There is a war being fought among the gods. It's not like other wars, wars that conquered cities or which were staged for our amusement. It's the Twilight, the death of us all, and you know that there are those who would not accept that without a struggle." Not a single eye moved while she spoke. No one made a sound. "*I* won't accept that without a struggle. The gods, my family, are set to consume each other. My aunt Demeter has favored us, and told us of tools, weapons that will help."

"Who are the enemies?" The voice came from the left side of the table. Athena recognized the blond girl from the room where they had found Odysseus, but just barely. She looked different fully clothed.

"Poseidon," Athena replied. Then, hesitating, she glanced sidelong at Hermes. "As well as Aphrodite . . . and Hera."

Hermes shifted his weight, but stayed quiet.

The witches exchanged glances.

"Hera has always been a friend to women," said a redhead with striking green eyes. "And Aphrodite has ever been a friend to the coven. Why should we help you over them? You've always chosen the causes of men over us."

Athena swallowed. She wasn't exactly wrong. But times had changed. "Not always," she whispered.

"Look." Hermes stepped forward. "You don't know Hera like we do. And don't forget what I told you about Poseidon."

Celine raised her chin. "What do you need from us?"

"We need to find a prophetess. The reincarnation of Cassandra of Troy. That's why we came to you. Poseidon and Hera are seeking her as well. We don't have much time."

"What can she do for us?"

Athena swallowed. "We don't know. Not for sure. But Demeter thinks she's a weapon, and I believe her."

The redhead shook her head and looked across at the blonde. "It seems reactionary. And blind. Not at all a winning battle plan."

Odysseus bumped Athena's shoulder as he moved to the front.

"Don't forget who you're talking to," he said darkly. "This is Athena. She knows strategy better than anyone. She'll tell you what she wants to tell you. Hell, she might even be lying. But what choice do you have?"

"How can you want us to do this?" asked the blonde, who Celine whispered was called Isabella. "You ask for our help and offer us no protection in return. After you go, your enemies will become our enemies. What's to stop them from burning us to the ground?"

"The chances that they'll even come to you are slim," Athena replied. "They don't know we're here."

"That's not good enough."

"Isabella," Celine cautioned, but the girl looked at her like she was mad.

"The gods will tear us apart. They will send things after us." She looked at Odysseus imploringly. "Can't you stay at least? Can't one of you protect us?"

"No," Athena said.

A number of protests rose from around the table, but Celine hushed them.

"This is not for us to question," she said mildly. "The gods would do more if they could." She looked each of the girls in the eye. Physically, she looked no older than any of them, but the fact that she was their matriarch was plain. "The coven of Circe will support Athena. We will help her locate this prophetess. And then we will worry about ourselves." The witches around the table lowered their eyes in silent compliance. Celine snapped her fingers.

"Mareden," she said, and the trim receptionist stood from where she sat at the end of the table. "A map on the projector, please. Lilith, we will need candles." A buxom redhead pushed her chair away and quickly left the room. It was less than a minute before she returned with a silver tray laden with white pillars. As she passed, each witch took one and set it before her.

"What're they doing?" Hermes whispered out of the corner of his mouth.

"They're doing what they do," Athena replied. She touched both Hermes and Odysseus on the arm and walked them back a few steps. She had only a vague understanding of magic, but whatever was happening, they weren't a part of it.

Behind them, on a large white screen, a stretched map of the world appeared from the projector. It always looked so odd to Athena, miles and miles of sand and saltwater, rocks and ice and green, represented in lines and labels. Mareden stepped away from the laptop and returned to her place at the table, taking a candle from the tray as she passed. Once she was seated, the witches linked hands, beginning with Celine and moving counterclockwise. It had an odd visual effect, almost serpentine. They closed their eyes.

"Light," Celine said softly.

An almost inaudible puff sounded as the candles produced flame all at once. Athena took a quiet breath. It was beautiful and strange. Each small tip of fire was identical to the one beside it.

"Now," Celine said. "Find me Cassandra of Troy."

For a long second, nothing happened. Then the whispering started, whispers of words long forgotten. The sounds came on together, as if the women shared one brain. Whispers quickly became quiet chants, twenty intermingled voices, and Athena thought she heard Circe be invoked; she thought she heard them call the Moirae, the Fates, but she couldn't be sure. The air in the room grew colder, even as the candle flames grew. They grew until they were spears of light flashing across the women's cheeks. Then the chanting stopped, all at once. Together, twenty heads turned to the image of the map. Their eyes were coal black, and blank.

Athena looked. On the map, one tiny sparkle of light shone, like a gem embedded in the screen. She walked closer. The sparkle was in the northeastern United States, in New York state. Her eyes narrowed.

"Kincade," she said, and looked triumphantly back at Hermes. "Someplace called Kincade."

Odysseus smiled his lopsided smile, his expression both relieved and disbelieving. Around them, a collective exhale rose as the women came back to themselves. The candle flames shrunk. Several of the witches blinked their eyes rapidly. Celine licked her thumb and forefinger and snuffed out her candle. She stood as the others extinguished theirs.

"You have your answer, goddess," she said.

Athena nodded. Kincade, New York. On the map it looked like a small town in the middle-upper part of the state. The population couldn't be that large. Maybe they were finally catching a break.

"Thank—"

She didn't get a chance to finish. Her words were cut off by the wooden, rickety sound of the elevator door being pulled up. Celine's brow creased curiously. Everyone in the warehouse was collected in the conference room, and the front doors to the building had been locked. "Mareden," she said.

"I'll see to it." Mareden rose quickly and left. Her footsteps clicked toward the reception area, and then they heard her voice, asking if she could be of service. There was no reply before she started to scream.

Athena and Hermes exchanged a glance, but Celine and

her sisters reacted without thinking. They shrieked Mareden's name, charging from the conference room in a struggling, panicked wave. Athena, Hermes, and Odysseus were left in their wake. Hermes' eyes moved toward the back of the warehouse, toward the emergency exit and fire escape.

"We can't just leave them," Athena said, and started moving, following the sounds of gasps and cries. Behind her, Odysseus asked Hermes what was happening, and Hermes replied that he didn't know. But she knew. A cold certainty wrapped itself around her heart. They'd been found.

As much as she wanted to run, she forced her legs to be slow, to creep up onto the scene. At first only the backs of the witches were visible, rigid with fear, as they stood in a semicircle around Mareden and her attacker. But even before she saw a face, she heard familiar laughter, throaty and full of malice, that made her pause. It sounded like an echo out of a deep well.

Hermes froze. Athena moved forward again, slinking like a cat. Between the frightened bodies, she glimpsed a tall, ivory shoulder and a head of shining dark blond hair, like ancient gold.

"I've been all up and down your floors, daughters of Circe," Hera said. "You've set yourself up quite nicely. What a pity that I've come too late for you to choose the correct side."

"We do only what the gods tell us," Celine said. She lowered her eyes in a gesture of piety.

Clever. But it won't make any difference.

"What do you want?" This came from one of the other girls. Hera's head snapped to the left sharply like a snake's, and the left side of the circle shuddered. But no one stepped back. Every set of eyes stayed carefully trained on Mareden, who stood motionless in Hera's grasp, the back of her head held in the goddess's hand.

Athena wondered if she could feel the power in those fingers, if she knew that in one crunch of Hera's knuckles, the back of her skull would cave in like it was made of sugar.

"I want you to tell me what you have told Athena," Hera replied.

Athena stepped into the circle.

"I'd be happy to tell you myself. If you'd only ask nicely."

In the quiet it was possible to hear Hera's smile stretch across her face before she turned. When she saw Athena, her eyes glittered. She cut an imposing figure, as usual. But the years had changed her as it had changed them all. Gone were the locks of hair falling to her waist. Now she kept her blond hair cut fashionably short. Her clothes too were modernized and expensive: she paired a cream-colored silk top with tailored gray slacks. A headband adorned with a peacock's feather, her sacred bird, was affixed to her head. Zeus' wife, Athena's stepmother, pivoted on sling-backs with kitten heels. She glanced at Athena's frayed jeans and smiled, then shoved Mareden away. Relief passed through the witches in a wave, and they came forward to catch her. Then they crept backward, toward Hermes and Odysseus.

"Didn't you used to be clever enough to run away?" Hera asked.

"Not a day in my life have I needed to run from you," Athena replied.

The two goddesses faced each other for the first time in over a thousand years. From a distance they would have seemed like two normal, mortal women with smooth cheeks and groomed hair. But to those in the room they were thunderstorms encased in skin; the current of the air between them crackled with the possibility of violence.

"That was a long time ago." Hera smiled. "Since then I've grown stronger. You've only grown dead." She casually brushed the fingertips of one hand along her bangs, tucking them back. The other hand she kept curled in a tight fist by her side. Unnaturally tight, it seemed to Athena. She looked closer. The skin of that fist was smooth and poreless, whiter than the rest of her skin. Something was wrong with it. She blinked and looked harder. Just above the bones of the wrist there was a small roll. It took her only a moment to realize that it was the line where the arm became flesh again.

"You're turning to stone," she whispered, and then she laughed. "That's fitting. Guess I'm not the only one growing dead, eh? Whatever that means."

For a moment, Hera's eyes darkened, and Athena tensed. She would engage her if she had to. And she would move fast, before that stone fist of hers could smash through any of these poor witches' faces. But Hera's expression cleared and became almost light.

"Athena, look at you. Scrambling around, seeking answers from sorceresses, playing by all the rules. Haven't you learned anything from this century?" Hera's hand strayed into her back pocket. "You have to break the rules to win. And humans have come up with such excellent toys." The thing she held in her palm was no larger than a tube of lipstick. It was trim and black. On the top was a small green light, and what appeared to be a button.

"Oh, fuck," said Hermes, as her thumb pressed it down.

The bomb had been planted somewhere on one of the lower floors. The blast was strong enough to cause the whole building to quake. The sound was deafening. Only Athena, Hermes, and Hera had ears enough to hear the shocked screams of the witches. It happened in an instant, one bright instant of fiery light and flying glass, wood, and concrete. The floor beneath them rippled like it was made of water before exploding into pieces.

Hermes moved too quickly to be seen. He raced around the circle and grasped Celine, Mareden, and one more of the witches, and vaulted through the window headfirst. It was impossible to tell whether the glass broke because of him or because of the explosion.

Athena acted almost as quickly, pivoting and running toward Odysseus. Her arm caught him by the waist and she went through the window after Hermes. They had dropped only half of the forty feet when the force of a second explosion catapulted them forward into the concrete of the building across the street. Athena was barely able to twist her body in front of Odysseus before they struck the wall. When she finally hit the ground her bones felt loose, like they'd been rattled inside her muscle.

"Go, go, go!" she shouted at Hermes. He had the witches in his arms. He nodded and ran, faster than any living thing, just a blur streaking through the panic as people from nearby buildings began to empty into the streets, screaming.

Another strong rumble surged through the ground, and Athena leaned forward to cover Odysseus as, behind them, the warehouse that held The Three Sisters collapsed in on itself in a cloud of dust and crashing brick. She stifled a frustrated scream. No one inside could have survived. She peered through the dust, moving her head to try to see through the people running in all directions.

Hera stood unharmed in the center of the rubble and twisted metal. Her shirt was torn and her pants were filthy and streaked with dirt, but there were no wounds. She stared directly at them. Athena heard her voice clearly above the chaos.

"When they said that someone would oppose us, I hoped it would be you, Athena." Her smile was malice and poison. "I sincerely hoped it would be you." She raised her fist, the fist of stone, and slammed it into the ground. The impact set off a shockwave, and the foundation of the building next to them began to crack.

"Come on," Athena said to Odysseus, and pulled him to his feet. She didn't let him run on his own for long before she lifted him by the shoulder and went faster.

9

PREMONITION

Andie grabbed Cassandra's arm. Something had apparently happened on the movie screen that Cassandra should take note of. Or something was about to happen. Andie had already seen the thing twice, so she couldn't be sure. Either way, it didn't matter. To Cassandra, the movie on the screen was images and noise. A distraction. Something meant to block out the memory of blasted dust and flying glass, and screaming.

It's not working.

Despite the sheer volume of the theater and the thick smell of buttered popcorn, despite the color and spectacle of everything happening in the made-up story playing out before her eyes, the only thing she could see or hear was that explosion. It was huge, on repeat inside her head. It spoke of the death of innocent people. Lots of them. And it hadn't happened yet.

Cassandra stood and made her way to the end of the aisle, ignoring Andie's startled questions about where she was going. She shoved through the theater doors and stalked through the lobby, past the concession and the restrooms. She didn't stop until she was outside. The cold and dark seemed as far as she could get from the explosion. From the heat and choking dust. But the minute she was clear of it, her mind started it up again from the beginning.

How many of them would die? Who were they? And what did it have to do with her? Because it had something to do with her, that much she was sure of.

Why can't I stop it? What's the point of seeing, if I can't stop it?

She walked quickly around the side of the building, down the shadowy alley that somehow still managed to smell faintly of buttered popcorn.

"Cassandra?"

She jumped at the sound of Andie's shout.

"Cassandra? Are you out here?"

Cassandra craned her neck and saw Andie walking through the parking lot, looking in every direction. She drew farther back into the shadows and walked behind the theater, then slipped across the alley, staying in back crossways until she couldn't tell what she was behind anymore.

Andie couldn't help. The distraction hadn't worked. And Cassandra hated to see that look on her face, when she knew it.

As she walked her brain went back over every option she could think of to stop the explosion, options she'd already crossed out as infeasible. She couldn't call in bomb threats to every building in every major city. But maybe she really could talk to the police. They employed psychics sometimes. They might believe her.

Even if they did, it wouldn't make a difference. They couldn't figure out where it's going to happen any better than I can.

She ground her teeth as she walked, and felt the passing

wind slowly freezing her ears and making them sting. Her arms and fingers were cold too. She'd left her jacket back at the theater.

"Cassandra?"

She gave a little yelp as Aidan appeared in front of her, and jerked so hard in the opposite direction that she almost fell on her butt. He held his hands out.

"It's just me! Andie called me. She said she couldn't find you."

Cassandra laughed bitterly, and pointed her finger at him.

"See, why couldn't I foresee that? You, jumping out of that alley. At least that would be something I could use!"

His shoulders slumped. He frowned. For a second she wished he wouldn't care so much, so she could complain about things he couldn't fix without feeling guilty.

"Why did you leave the theater?"

"Why do you think?" She put her fists to her temples. "I'm sorry. I don't mean to snap. It's just driving me crazy." She peered up at him. "How did you find me?"

"I wasn't far away. It just took some looking."

"You're not stalking me, are you?"

"A little. But it's warranted. Come here." He held his arms out and she went. He folded her into his chest and kissed the top of her head.

"Aidan, I've never wanted to stop anything so badly. I've never seen anything that felt so important. I mean, I felt horrible for your sister, but—"

"I know. It's different. But it's the same. You can't stick your neck out. You can't be found."

He was so warm. She twined her cold fingers under his shirt.

"You make me feel safe."

He sighed. "Don't say that."

"Why not?"

"Because it shames me, that I can't protect you from them. From this." He drew back and looked into her eyes. "But I'm trying."

"I don't blame you. This isn't your fault."

"You're so cold."

Waves of heat flowed from him into her, through her chest down to her toes and fingertips. Like sunlight. A safe spot she could curl up in. She pulled free.

"What's wrong?"

"Nothing. Just, don't do that right now. I want to be cold. I want to walk in the dark until I can't feel my toes."

"You want to suffer, because you can't save them."

"I deserve that. I don't even know who they are."

But I'm the reason they'll die.

She was sure of it as soon as the shock of the initial vision wore off. Those women, whoever they were, would die at the hands of gods who were looking for her.

Cassandra paced. She seethed. She wanted to pummel the cement of the building beside them until her knuckles bled and her hands were broken.

I don't want to hide. I want to save them.

She took a deep, slow breath, and clenched her teeth. More even than saving them, she wanted to stop the gods. Grind them into paste if she had to. Sudden heat tingled in the palms of her hands, and she shook them in the cold air.

"Can I tell you a secret?"

"Always."

"Part of me wants the explosion to happen. So it can be over. A small part. Because—"

"Because every hour that passes until then is like walking in a shadow." Aidan nodded. "Because at least once it's over, you won't be able to do anything about it anymore."

Cassandra nodded. Of course he understood. He always understood.

And he would. He's so wise. He's a god.

The sudden bitterness of the thought caught her by surprise. The knowledge of the explosion had kept her from thinking too much about Aidan and what he was. But she realized she hadn't kissed him since the night he'd told them the truth.

I will. Just not now.

He gestured with his head and shoulder down the alley. So harmless looking, with his hands stuffed into his pockets.

"Can I walk you home now?"

10

SCATTER

Weeping. Weeping, they were all weeping. Celine, Mareden, and the third witch, a petite brunette creature called Estelle. Athena stood to the side with Hermes and Odysseus, trying to not be annoyed. Trying to be patient and sympathetic, like she should be. God knew the witches had reason enough to cry. Reason enough to be downright hysterical. Their sisters were dead. Their home was destroyed. But Athena was angry and shaken, a combination she never wore well. After a few more seconds of watching the moaning huddle, caked with dust and dried blood from several cuts, she turned and stalked into the trees.

"Hey, wait up."

She glanced back and saw Hermes following. He looked tired, and streaked with sweat and grime. They had run so far, left Chicago behind, the skyline dwarfed by miles of distance. Athena looked back at it from the copse of trees where they'd stopped. A plume of smoke curled up from the east side. It looked to Athena like Hera's waving arm, bitchy and gloating.

"Fuck!"

"Sister—" Hermes held his hands up while Athena battered her fist into the bark of the nearest trunk. The tree trembled but didn't fall.

Athena looked at her torn and bleeding knuckles in disgust. Bits of bark were embedded into the skin.

Hermes didn't press her. She'd plant her set of bloody knuckles square in his jaw if he did. Hera had beaten them, and losing in battle was something Athena had never gotten used to. A million questions weaved through the air. How had Hera known where they were? How had she gotten so close without them knowing? Close enough to plant a bomb? But Athena didn't have any answers.

"I want you to take them," Athena said suddenly. "Take them and hide them. Do it well."

"Where?"

"I don't care where!" she screamed, then bit down on her tongue when she heard the cries of the witches sharply cut off. They had so many reasons to be afraid. They didn't need to be afraid of her too.

Celine's potion had started to wear off, and the wound in her mouth throbbed. The wounds on her knuckles throbbed. It seemed she could feel the point of every impact that the pattern of bricks had imprinted into the flesh of her back in a hot, sore bruise. Cuts from window glass and sharp-edged steel stung in a dozen places. Evidence of her defeat. It was in every one of her wounds and in the wounds of Hermes. It was in Odysseus' cuts and those of the witches. It was fifteen miles away, seventeen bodies broken and torn open, buried in rubble.

"I don't care where," she said again, this time more calmly.

"Think of anywhere. Take them far away if you have to. Or let them decide. Just do it well. Make them safe."

"There's nowhere safe." Hermes looked at her wildly. "Did you see that? Did you see her? She's still a god."

"So are we." *So are we. But not like that.*

"Her and Poseidon together. Aphrodite. How are we supposed to stand against that?"

"I don't know. But we will."

We'll stand. But we won't win.

She closed her eyes and thought of Hera. Of the impact of her fist into the ground. She'd felt it all the way up to her knees. With Poseidon, Hera could take whole cities of lives, and she would. Just to sharpen her teeth. All the better to bite through Athena's neck.

"What do we do?" Hermes looked up into the sky. "What *should* we do?"

"What are you talking about?"

He glanced at her. Guilty. "I'm talking about not winning. Bad choices." He shook his head. "I don't know what I'm talking about."

Athena stood still. Irritation mixed with anger and fear. "You think you made the wrong choice. Picked the wrong side."

"That's not what I said."

"It's what you meant." She kept her voice low. Tried to keep it calm, but it came out accusatory. "You're afraid."

"Of course I'm afraid," Hermes hissed. "And Hera might be a high-riding bitch, but she's afraid too. You can understand that, can't you?" He shook his head. "She's doing what she has to, like she's always done."

"Killing people to save herself?"

"To save her family."

"We're her family!" Why was he talking like an idiot?

"Will you give us up?"

Athena and Hermes turned. Celine stood a short distance from them, the jacket of her suit torn to reveal a long swath of pale arm. A deep cut ran down her leg, leaking blood into the grass. She had lost one of her shoes and discarded the other, so she stood evenly, if a little weakly.

Does she blame me? Athena looked at the girl, at her tear-streaked face and hitching chest. *Do I have any right to tell her not to?*

"No. We won't give you up." Athena glanced sideways at Hermes, who looked away.

Celine held her head high, dignified. Whether it was a show of strength or just the force of habit Athena didn't know. Her red hair hung limply, matted down with dust.

"Then we must find the others: Jenna, Bethe, and Harper. They may be in danger. Will you help us?"

For a moment Athena only blinked. It was Hermes who stepped forward and nodded. He looked at his sister.

Thank you, brother.

"We'll go now, and I'll come back for Mareden and Estelle."

"Yes," Athena replied. Exhaustion crept up in the wake of adrenaline. "Be careful, and quick. We don't know how much Hera knows, or what she intends to do."

"She had a hard-on for you, that's for sure," Hermes said. "You shouldn't stay here. Take Odysseus and go. I can meet you in Kincade."

Athena glanced back through the trees. Mareden and Estelle huddled on the ground, embracing each other. They weren't listening to anything that was being said. They didn't care. If Hera found them again, they wouldn't even run.

"I'm not going to leave them," Athena said. "So you'll have to hurry. It won't be easy for you to move so many witches at once." She paused. Recommending that the witches split up was out of the question, after what had happened. "Get them to the nearest safe place. Celine, you should keep on moving once he gets you there. Lay low. Do you have some friends?"

"We have many, all over the world," Celine replied. "And they are very discreet."

"Good," said Athena. "Then get going. I'll watch over Mareden and Estelle. Hermes—" She grasped his arm suddenly and stood for a second, looking down at it. She hadn't meant to do it.

He might never come back. The next time I see him he might try to kill me. Or he might run and keep on running.

But there was nothing she could say. No guarantee she could ask for.

"Don't give up," she said finally. "We haven't even started yet."

He patted her hand and she let go. "I'll be back." He offered an arm to Celine and she took it. "The god of thieves might be easily rattled. But that doesn't make him a coward." He turned to go, but before she walked with him, Celine looked at Athena.

"I'm glad that you came to us in time to learn the whereabouts of the girl."

Athena said nothing. It was the last thing she'd expected.

Celine shrugged. "Blaming you would be easy. But it is not so simple as that. We would have been forced to choose a side. It would have come to this, eventually. So I am glad that when you found us we were strong enough to help you. And I am glad that you were there to save us." She paused, and fresh tears rolled down her cheeks. The voice that issued from her throat was the same as ever, though her lips trembled. "The last of Circe's coven." She nodded to Hermes, who led her a few paces before picking her up and starting to run. It was only seconds before they were no longer visible.

Will they be all right? Athena stared into the trees where Hermes had gone. Would any of them? They'd stepped into it right and proper. The odds of survival slipped by the minute, and the odds of a victory were somewhere between winning the lottery and dying of spontaneous human combustion. She flexed her torn hand and rubbed her tongue against the roof of her mouth. The pain felt like weakness. Where would the next goddamn feather turn up? In her heart? Or maybe it would corkscrew right through her eye.

She thought of Hera, so strong, and as maliciously clever as ever. Her death was a slow turning to stone. It was a walking metaphor. And instead of making her weak it only made her more of a monster. They were up against too much. Poseidon would crash the sea into every continent and Hera would apparently bomb the shit out of the rest, all while brandishing her damn stone fist like a battle-axe.

What did it feel like, to have your flesh slowly harden into rock? Did it feel similar to the way the feathers felt? Stinging pains and dull, aching throbs?

"I hope it hurts like fucking nails in your eyes," Athena muttered. "And I wish that it had started with your face."

Behind her, Odysseus cleared his throat. She turned to see him standing beside the tree she had struck with her fist. There was a patch of bark missing eight inches across and three inches deep. Sap oozed from the wound like sticky, amber blood. Embarrassment clenched down in her chest; she didn't like him knowing she'd lost her temper. It wasn't in tune with the goddess she'd always been, the one he must remember.

Odysseus examined the splintered wood and flashed a cockeyed grin.

"Whatever the tree did, I'm sure that it's sorry."

Athena sucked on her tongue. "I miss the days when one glare from me was enough to turn you into a trembling puddle."

Odysseus laughed. "In all our long history, I don't remember any days like that." He gestured over his shoulder, back toward where Mareden and Estelle still sat. "They're all right," he said. "I just couldn't . . . stand there anymore. They don't want comfort, you know?"

"I know." What could have comforted them? They wanted their sisters back, their lives back. They wanted for none of what was happening to be happening. It was impossible. Not even Zeus at the height of his powers could perform those kinds of miracles. And even if he could, he wouldn't. She could practically hear his voice in her head, as clear as it had been when she'd sat near his knee on Olympus.

What has happened was ordained by Fate. It governs all things, and we cannot see into its mind, child, no matter how mighty we are.

Over and over she'd heard those words, or a similar variation. The Fates. The Moirae. Three beings of destiny, above the gods. Zeus always called them "It," but they were really three: three sisters. He was mostly right, though. They acted as one, spoke as one, sometimes moved as one as they worked their golden loom, weaving and unweaving peoples' lives. And shearing them off just as quickly. Fate was the only lesson a god needed to learn. It was their only hard limit.

Athena exhaled bitterly. Since then she'd learned a lot more about limits. Limits of strength and limits of life.

"How fast do you heal?"

Athena blinked. She'd been caught up in her own mind and hadn't noticed Odysseus drawing closer. He held her injured hand up to his face, surveying the tears in the skin and the drying patterns of blood crisscrossed over her fingers and wrist.

"Faster than you'd think for someone who's dying," she replied, and he smiled.

"You should put something on it anyway," he said. "I've got some ointment and bandages in my pack, from back at The Three Sisters."

Athena sighed. All the anger that had fueled her flight through Chicago had leaked out. What still lingered was weak and exhausted, just fumes. Odysseus brushed his fingers across the back of her hand, lightly and carefully. The touch was soothing and sweet. She could've closed her eyes and fallen asleep standing.

Instead she pulled away and clenched her fist, breaking the newly forming scabs on her knuckles.

"Don't baby me," she said. Odysseus raised his eyebrows.

"Wouldn't dream of it." He smiled his familiar smile and walked back through the trees. Athena counted to ten before following.

Hermes was back before nightfall. He came without Celine and would only say that he had found the others and that they were safe. Athena didn't ask where they had gone. The fewer people who knew, the safer the witches would be.

"Are you going to rest for the night?" Hermes asked, and Athena looked over her shoulder at Odysseus, who sat with his back against a broad tree trunk. His eyes were closed, but he was listening, she was sure.

"We've rested enough." She glanced into the darkening

sky. Hera was out there somewhere. She knew it, but she couldn't feel it like she had been able to sense Demeter's presence. The bitch had cloaked herself somehow. *Either that, or I'm just growing weaker.*

"Are you sure?" Hermes asked. His eyes stole down to her hand. Odysseus' bandaging stood out on her knuckles, bright white. "Did you do that yourself?"

"No. Odysseus had some salve from the witches."

"Oh," Hermes said.

Athena cocked her head. "Is something wrong?"

"No."

"Then get going. Why are you dawdling?"

Hermes did his best to appear intimidated and couldn't quite manage it. "You're not the warm and fuzzy sister I left here a few hours ago."

"You're not the confused and cowardly brother who ran off a few hours ago. Are you."

"No." He smiled with closed lips. He liked her better this way, no matter what he said. She could see it. This way was normal. It made him feel safe.

Hermes rolled his shoulders back. "Well, stay off the main roads when you go. They're calling this a terrorist attack, which is at least accurate. But Fox News is saying it leveled half a block, and that's a total exaggeration."

Athena looked around at the trees. When they'd fled Chicago, they'd done so in a state of panic. They hadn't even gone the right way, which would have been east, though it was probably a lucky mistake in case Hera had been watching in an attempt to follow. She and Hermes hadn't stopped running for miles, darting like rabbits into the first patch of forest they found. They'd changed directions then and run through trees for another four miles. She wasn't certain where they'd ended up. She thought it was part of Palos Park.

"Look, there are forest preserves all over down here, looping to the east. We'll stick to them as best we can. Drop the witches and then meet us at Wolf Lake. We'll start hitching from there."

"I don't know where Wolf Lake is," Hermes protested. "Some of us haven't committed every stretch of the globe to memory."

"So get a map."

"No money. It was inconveniently blown up back at The Three Sisters, remember?"

Athena looked at him carefully. He was being thick on purpose. Since when had the god of thieves needed money for anything? He was already wearing a fresh set of clothes, some new jeans and a Hollister t-shirt that had obviously been lifted from somewhere.

"Besides, it would be a good idea if I went ahead to Kincade and checked things out. We don't need any more surprises."

"Am I slowing you down, Hermes?"

He didn't answer, just smiled an odd little smile. He looked good, all things considered. With his muster up and his eyes bright, he hardly looked sick. It was the weariness that really made his bones show. Plain old fatigue, pulling his skin down toward the ground.

Athena sighed.

"Fine. Go on ahead. But be careful. And don't do anything until we get there. We won't be more than three days behind."

"Absolutely." He smirked and walked away toward where Mareden and Estelle waited. Their eyes were dry, finally, and their faces lit with tenuous hope. They had been certain that Bethe, Harper, and Jenna had somehow been killed too. When Hermes got to them, they each stood to one side and slung an arm around his neck. Only Mareden looked back at Athena, and when she did it was without expression.

"Aren't you worried we're getting lost?" Odysseus asked. They'd been walking for two hours and had left the Palos Park Woods. The going was easier for a stretch as they crossed over highways, but then they'd gone back into the trees. It was full dark and the sky overhead hung a dull, over-cast black. Light in the forest was basically nonexistent. Odysseus kept close to Athena. She did her best to pick the path with the least obstructions, but it was a miracle he hadn't gone face-first over a root.

"How do you know we're going the right direction?"

"I just know."

"But how? There's no moon, and no visible stars. And it feels like we're traveling in a curve." He adjusted his pack on his shoulders. "Don't you think we should pop out of these trees and check? How can you see in this? I'm going to end up arse over ears."

Athena groaned. "You're worse than Hermes."

"Well, I'm only saying."

"Don't question me. I'm a god. Dammit." She turned back and saw him smile in the dark.

"You could just piggyback me, you know."

"Is the great Odysseus getting tired?"

"Not in a thousand years. It'd be faster is all. During that uphill stretch I was halfway to jumping on without asking."

He reached forward and managed to slip his finger through one of her belt loops. She froze like he'd stabbed her with an ice pick and slapped his hand away. The grin fell off his face in the span of a second.

Athena blanched. "Sorry." Grabbing her belt loop had been a harmless gesture, meant to keep him on the right track and on his feet rather than facedown in dirt and ferns.

"Don't worry about it. Nothing like being smacked away like a three year old to remind you of your place."

"Don't be like that." She watched him. He didn't hide his facial expressions in the dark like he did in the light. The embarrassment and disappointment on his features were plain. He shook his head.

"I'm not. Like anything. It's just been a long time. I thought you might've loosened up."

"Don't count on it."

He smiled. "Look, I didn't mean anything by it. I feel like I know you, is all. Like I've known you for a long time. Ever since Brighton Beach, getting my memories back—I guess it never occurred to me that you wouldn't feel the same way."

He made her feel guiltier by the second. "I do feel the same way. I have known you. For a long time."

"Don't worry about it. You've been alive these few thousand years. What do my two lives matter to you?"

"Will you shut up? They matter plenty. When I saw you back at The Three Sisters I thought—" She paused as the smirk broke through his cheeks, then laughed. "You still can't touch me."

"But you're still my goddess?"

"*Because* I'm still your goddess. Now keep moving." As she turned, she caught a flash of disappointment cross his face. That was real. She'd seen him through so many things in the past. She'd seen him sad to the point of madness, seen him sulk when his pride was wounded. But she'd never seen that look before.

I've never seen that look from anyone.

"Wait."

"What?" He tensed, thinking she'd heard something. She lifted her hand toward his face curiously. Her fingers traced the air along his neck and shoulders. She could feel the heat of his skin.

An image of the red room at The Three Sisters rose in her head, adorned with satin and crystal beads. The sounds of his breathing as he lay on the bed, still dazed. None of his lovers in his previous life had ever wanted to let him go. Circe had kept him for a year. The sea goddess Calypso had kept him for seven and would have married him if Athena hadn't demanded his release.

She looked at him in the dark. Could he really be so much better than any other? What was it about him? What did his lips feel like, parted against your neck, or grazing along your shoulders? How did his arms feel when they crushed you against his chest?

She'd never felt any of those things. Not once.

Not even with you. And of all mortals, I loved you best.

Athena blinked and snapped her arm back to her side. She grimaced. The movement hadn't been quiet. She watched Odysseus carefully. His eyes wandered and stilled again.

"If you're having trouble keeping up, just say so," she said quickly.

"I'm having trouble keeping up," he said with a wry smile.

"All right. We have to keep moving, but—" She thought of ways to carry him along, using her arm to hold him up beside her. "I'll help you." She reached out and took his hand. The gentle pressure of his fingers sent a jolt down her spine. Then she tugged him forward, and they walked quickly before breaking into a run. As they went she pulled him up and along, and sensed his fear change to exhilaration as they streaked through night-black trees, their feet barely touching the dirt.

Athena stuck her thumb out as the tenth pair of headlights approached in the morning fog. Hitching was a pain in the ass, especially when there was fog so thick that the driver couldn't see that the thumb was attached to a good set of legs. Visibility was also a factor when it came to Odysseus, who consistently stepped too far out into the lane and was going to get his arm taken off at the very least.

They were on Route 6, walking the shoulder and hoping to get a ride that would take them onto the freeway and, if they were lucky, out of Illinois. Two more cars passed by in the pink-orange light of dawn; the second one honked loudly. Athena and Odysseus gave it matching middle fingers.

"Just some scared house lady," Odysseus mused. "Probably scared to death that we're going to steal her car, cut her up, and stick her in the trunk while we go joyriding."

"You can't really blame her," said Athena, gesturing to her clothes, which were still torn and caked with dirt. Blood had dried to brown spots and patches on her knees and the belly of her t-shirt. Odysseus looked even worse. Unlike Hermes, they hadn't taken a trip to the local mall.

Hermes was probably halfway to Kincade by now, Athena supposed. He was probably holed up in some swanky hotel and figured that "laying low" meant using a very convincing alias to book it under. Athena frowned.

Don't worry so much. He can take care of himself. He's done it since forever.

But things were different. They were all vulnerable, and she regretted letting him go ahead on his own.

"Why are we looking for Cassandra, anyway?" Odysseus asked.

"You remember her?"

"Of course I do. She was a right comely little princess. Maybe not so much as her sister, but . . ."

Athena rolled her eyes. "Do you remember her with something besides your penis?"

Odysseus laughed. "I remember that everyone said she was a prophet, but nobody believed what she prophesized. They said she was crazy. Even when everything happened the way she said it would. People were jerks, back then."

"It wasn't the people." Athena put her thumb out for another pair of headlights, but they went right by. "It was Apollo."

"Apollo? Patron god of Troy?"

"He was in love with her. He was the one who gave her the gift of prophecy to begin with. But then she pissed him off, somehow, so he cursed her. He made it so she'd always see, but no one would ever believe her."

"Sounds pretty crazy-making." Odysseus waved his arms at an approaching minivan.

"Don't flag the ones with children inside. They're never going to stop for two bloodied vagrants, and they might call the cops."

"I thought maybe they'd think we were in an accident and pull over like good Samaritans." He sighed. "So when we find Cassandra, what makes you think she'll help? She must hate gods, after what was done to her."

"She probably doesn't remember. And even if she does, not all gods are bad." She smiled over her shoulder. "Some of them work for years to save the skins of cocky, ungrateful heroes."

"Hey! You coming?"

She turned toward the voice, shouted from the rolled-down window of a silver, late-model Ford Taurus. A jacket-clad arm hooked out onto the door and gestured for them to come on.

Odysseus grinned and slung his bag over his shoulder. In the fog they hadn't even noticed the car pulling over. They walked up and Athena got into the front seat. Odysseus piled into the back and immediately tossed his bag down to use for a pillow. He'd probably be snoring in less than a mile, but he shook hands with the driver before flopping onto his side.

"Name's Derek," the driver said after they had introduced themselves. "Where you headed?"

"We're trying to get out to New York," Athena supplied. She held the front of her cardigan closed to keep the rips and blood hidden.

"Oh, yeah? Freak Show Central?" Derek checked his mirrors and pulled back onto the highway.

"No, just upstate," said Athena. "We have friends there." Derek made an affirmative sound with his nose and roof of his mouth, and said nothing. Behind her, Odysseus shifted clothes around in his bag, getting comfortable.

"I can take you quite a way," Derek said. He rubbed at his face quickly with the back of his hand. "I'm headed to Erie, Pennsylvania. Driving straight through."

"That's just fine." Athena yawned. Part of her didn't want to sleep. She knew the fresh, stiff hell she was going to be in for when she woke up. All of her muscles and tendons would have clenched down and shrunk three sizes. But it wasn't a matter of choice. It took a lot to weary a god, but it happened eventually.

"Thank you for picking us up," she said. "We might've stood out there all morning, with the fog as thick as it is.

I'm surprised you even saw us." Her lids slipped shut. She was asleep before the driver could answer, and when he did, her eyes were closed, so she couldn't see the look on his face.

Had Athena been more alert when she had gotten into the car, she would have noticed a few strange things about their driver. His clothes didn't fit right, for a start. His pants were too tight to even button, and they were too long. Inches of fabric collected around the tops of his Velcro tennis shoes. The clothes didn't match, either. He was wearing a combination of green and red that would have looked wrong even around Christmas. And then there was the smell, sour and medicinal, hiding just underneath a camouflage of Brut 57.

But Athena hadn't been more alert. She had fallen asleep, slumped against the passenger-side window. She and Odysseus slept together, oblivious to the car's increasing speed. The Taurus' engine was surprisingly quiet, even at a hundred miles an hour, and the freeway was wide open ahead, except for a large tanker semitruck, shining silver as it plodded along in the right lane. Neither one of them stirred as they passed it. The truck driver watched with annoyance and told another driver over the CB that some idiot in a silver Taurus was out to get them all killed. He didn't really take the thought seriously until the car moved over the center line, and the passenger door opened and a young woman flew toward the speeding pavement.

The move was quick and well done. He pushed Athena's door open and shoved her out toward the ground, with the intent of sending her rolling across the asphalt, directly under the sixteen tires of the semi just behind.

It wouldn't have been fatal. She was dying, that was true, but she still couldn't be *killed*, not by any conventional means, anyway. It would, however, have ruined her eye, and left bloody red scales of road rash across her cheek, shoulder, and arm. The impact of the semi would have cracked her bones like dry branches.

She thought all of this in the fraction of a second it took to catch hold of the swung-open car door in the reflexive instant she felt her neck tense just enough to keep her skull from bouncing off of the pavement passing by below.

She hung suspended between the open door and the front seat, her knee wedged underneath the dashboard, and flexed. Her hands wrapped around the interior door handle, trying to pull it shut while the driver swerved. Something struck her hip and she yelped. Looking back she saw the end of some kind of steel or lead pipe, just before it raised and came down again, this time closer to her rib cage. The impact had the opposite effect of what was hoped for; it made Athena's muscles contract sharply, and she managed to pull the door most of the way shut.

In the backseat, Odysseus woke. After a few startled seconds of coming to, he plunged forward and began to fight with the driver for control of the steel pipe. The Taurus careened sharply to the right. Athena winced. If they turned too far, or went off the shoulder, they would flip like a coin.

"The wheel!" she shouted at Odysseus, who stretched out and grabbed it. With the door mostly shut, she had just enough leverage to draw her leg up and piston her boot-clad foot into the driver's ribs, snapping at least two. The impact drove him into Odysseus, and the car swerved again.

"If you want me to drive, you have to give me some room." Odysseus tried to hang on to the wheel as the car accelerated in mad spurts. It revved and shot forward as the driver's foot pushed the gas pedal unintentionally down to the floor.

Athena reached up and grabbed the driver by the throat. She yanked hard and for a moment he was on top of her, before she heaved herself up and shoved him toward the still slightly open door. The front seat was cramped, and Odysseus' shoe heel scraped her cheek as he climbed over from the back and dropped down to drive.

"She'll have him if she wants him," the driver said, and Athena paused. She was holding him by the collar and the door had popped open again. He hung suspended over pavement passing by at ninety-five miles an hour.

"She can have anything she wants. Anything she wants," he babbled. His eyes fixed on Odysseus, bloodshot and stark raving nuts. "I wanted to give him to her. I wanted to. He's right there." His arm stretched out toward Odysseus, trembling. "And then we drive away, we drive away and you're gone. You're gone, awful bitch—"

"Throw him out the bleeding door!" Odysseus growled. "Or I'll put that pipe through his teeth."

Athena ignored him. She stared at the driver, fascinated. Tears welled in his eyes. He was manic and sad, a special kind of sad that was reserved for when you failed someone you loved.

Athena snorted.

"That silly brat."

"What?" Odysseus asked. "What are you talking about?"

"This is her attempt," Athena said incredulously, and shook the driver by the collar. "She sends a lovesick lunatic to try to take me out? Her assassin is a mooning mental case?" Her eyes narrowed in disgust. "She must be the laughing-stock of that little trio."

Odysseus let the car slow. Athena wrested the pipe away

from the driver and tossed it into the backseat. He cried, hard, with his eyes clenched shut.

What were they going to do with him? Aphrodite's little assassin. They could tie him up, she supposed, and gag him so they wouldn't have to listen to his ranting all the way to Kincade. Once they got there, she might be able to find a way to put him to use.

She cried out as pain pinched down on her hand. The bastard was biting her. Half of his teeth had disappeared into the skin between her thumb and forefinger. When she let go, he grinned an enormous blood-tinged grin and shoved himself backward out the open door before she could stop him. They heard the sharp crack of his bones striking the pavement and felt the car lurch as the back tires caught some part of him underneath.

Athena looked out the back window. He was a rumpled set of clothes tumbling and flapping down the middle of the road. The semitruck was only a mile or so behind. The body would be found, and they had better be nowhere near when it got called in. She yanked the door closed tightly and stared ahead. Odysseus breathed hard, and the car slowed. He'd been shocked into coasting, his foot off the gas.

"Don't slow too much," she said, and grasped his knee, guiding it down. "But don't speed. We need to—" Exhaustion hit her in a strong tide. It felt like someone had cut her adrenaline line and it was leaking out of her in a rush.

"We need to what?" Odysseus asked gently.

Athena put her fists to her forehead. "We need to get out of Dodge," she said, "and then we need to get out of Ford."

Odysseus' brows knit. "Is that a cutesy, Americanized way of saying we need to get out of here and then ditch the car?"

Athena smiled. "Sorry. I'm suddenly very, very tired."

Aphrodite, you sneaky little idiot, she thought. *Why do you always have such shitty timing?* She let her head fall back against the seat. Odysseus reached for her bitten hand. The semicircle of teeth marks oozed blood.

"I've got more salve and bandages."

She jerked her hand away. "Forget it. I'm not walking around with both hands gauzed up."

"Suit yourself. But that bloke's mouth was like a toilet."

A groan issued from her throat, made up of every frustration she'd had over the last day and a half. It filled the car almost to bursting. She wanted to slow down, to take stock, but her brain refused to obey. It raced ahead, thinking of good places to get off of the interstate, mapping out alternative routes and figuring where they might be able to score another car, because more hitchhiking sounded not appealing at all. All she really wanted to do was rest. To go back to sleep and wake up to the radio playing a good song and gold and red fall trees going by in the window. But there was no time for that.

"What I want," she said, "is to know why the hell she was after you. Why are they after you? Why did you come halfway around the world to seek my protection?"

Odysseus looked grimly ahead when he answered. "They want me because I know what they're after. They want me because without me, they won't be able to get it. And I came to you because you're the only god strong enough to stop them."

11

MESSAGES FROM THE MESSENGER

The explosion in Chicago was on every channel. It didn't matter whether she flipped from CNN to ABC, there was the same live image: smoke rising into the sky, and an enormous pile of wreckage on the corner of a block. It was a mess of crumbled rock and steel girders, dust and flashing red and yellow lights from fire trucks and rescue crews. Some of the neighboring buildings had been hit too, and wore dangerous-looking cracks snaking up their sides. Before the bomb it had been a small, restored warehouse, converted to house a consultancy of some kind. No one was sure yet how many had died. Estimates varied wildly from twenty to several dozen, depending on the network. There were other casualties too: people who had been walking on the sidewalk or driving past. There were surprisingly few injuries. It killed you, or it left you alone.

"It's terrible," Cassandra's father said. He and her mother had been watching the coverage since he'd come home from work. The smoke reflected in his eyeglasses and was made tiny. "It's going to cost the city a hell of a lot to re-build." He shook his head and sighed. *That's what the world is coming to,* the sigh said.

"Who would do that?" her mother asked. Reporters cried terrorism but were having a hard time pulling together a motive, and the only groups who had come forward to claim responsibility were the ones who came forward to claim responsibility for everything. One program suggested the consultancy was actually a high-end escort service. That at least would make it a more likely target.

Cassandra sat on the couch beside Henry and stared at the screen. She hated it. Hated everything about it, and whoever had done it. The feeling coursed through her like liquid metal; she felt it in her wrists. Hate. Frustration. Every time a reporter named groups who might be respon-sible, she wanted to scream. They'd done that. Dying gods. Aidan's malignant family. They'd done it on their way to her.

"If it turns out it was a brothel, this news coverage is going to get a whole lot uglier."

"Why?" Cassandra snapped. "Are the reporters going to start saying that they deserved it? That they deserved to get blown into a million pieces, because they were whores?"

"Cassandra!" Her parents looked at her, mouths open as she stalked out of the den and headed for the backyard. The smell of meatloaf in the oven made her want to break a window. It was so domestic and unaffected. Business as usual. When she burst into the backyard, she almost hit Henry in the face with the door as he followed with her jacket.

"Hey," he said.

"Hey, what?" He didn't try to touch her as she paced, just tossed her the jacket and let her walk it off, watching as the rage leaked out through her feet and through the steam of her breath in the cold air.

"There were no words. No names. No sense of place. Not even the weather. I didn't know where it was."

"There wasn't anything you could do."

She slowed. "Then why did I see it? What's the point?"

"Maybe there is no point. You just know things, and they just happen. That's how it's always been."

"Henry, that is so not good enough." And it wasn't right, either. Something was coming, just around the bend. She felt it, an odd sense of *increasing*, like the world starting to spin faster.

"You'd better get back in there and tell Mom you're okay," said Henry. "She's been asking if something's up with you."

"I know, I know. I should eat meatloaf and smile. Talk about school." Cassandra took a breath. The itchy feeling in her wrists was gone. Only vague tiredness remained.

"Well, yeah. That's what Aidan said, right? Act normal."

Act normal. Don't make waves or trip anyone's radar. He seemed so silly, suddenly, thinking that they could hide. Thinking there was any way around what was going to happen.

"Would you tell Mom and Dad I'm going over to eat at Aidan's?" she asked. "Tell them we had a fight or something, and that's why I flipped. Do you think they'll mind?"

"I think Dad'll be thrilled. He's been waiting for you two to fight for a year."

Aidan lived in a two-story house on Red Oak Lane. It was less than a half mile from Cassandra's. The wind cut through her jacket as she stood out front, urging her to walk up the driveway with cold fingers against her back. Inside, Aidan stood in the dining room, clearing the table and talking to his mom.

His adopted mom. His mom who is nothing close to his mom.

She watched the way they talked, easily and always smiling. Gloria Baxter was a petite woman with narrow hips. She wore corduroy pants in different colors and kept her hair dyed golden blond, the same shade as her adopted son. She worked as a bookkeeper for a lawyer's office in town, and Cassandra had known her longer than she'd known Aidan.

Gloria put her hand on Aidan's shoulder and kissed his cheek. He said something that made her laugh. It looked so natural. She'd seen them act that way countless times. She'd seen them argue too. All of those exchanges flickered through her mind as she watched this one. It was all playacting. None of it was real.

Aidan saw her through the window and waved. Gloria turned and waved too, and moments later, Aidan walked her up the driveway to the door. Inside smelled like marinara sauce and Parmesan cheese; the kitchen and dining room windows were still slightly fogged from the steam of boiling water.

"Hi, Cassandra." Gloria smiled. "You just missed Aidan's spaghetti. But there are plenty of leftovers. Are you hungry?"

"There really is a lot left," said Aidan. "Too much for my dad to eat."

"No, thanks." Cassandra smiled a little weakly. Aidan slipped his hand beneath her hair onto the back of her neck.

"You okay with dishes, Mom?" he asked.

"Sure. You cooked."

Aidan led Cassandra up the carpeted stairs to his bedroom and closed the door behind them.

"Hey," Aidan said. "I saw the way you were watching us."

"I don't know what you mean." She skinned out of her jacket and tossed it on the bed.

"Sure you do. And I get it. But she is my mom, Cassandra. She didn't raise me, but I love her just the same."

Cassandra nodded. Just the same. What did he know? But he had lived a hundred lives. He might have had a hundred parents. So maybe he did know. Maybe he knew even better than she did.

She looked around the room like she'd never been there before. The green quilt on Aidan's bed always smelled like Tide. His laptop sat closed on his desk, the top covered with stickers. Some of them were ones she'd given him. On the back of the door hung a vintage movie poster for *Vertigo*. Beside it on the wall was one of Radiohead and, next to that, a closet full of hooded sweatshirts. She gestured to the movie poster.

"You always did like vintage stuff."

He nodded.

"Were you there for the filming? Spend a lot of time with Hitchcock?"

"Cassandra."

"Or maybe you hung out with The Doors." She looked over her shoulder at a poster of Jim Morrison. "Any of their songs about you?"

"Don't do that. If you want to know anything about who I was, I'll tell you."

"Not about who you were. About who you are. I'm trying really hard not to feel like this room is one big prop. Even the messiness." She toed a pile of dirty clothes lying by the foot of the bed. "It all feels very . . . quintessential teenager."

"You still know me, Cassandra."

"I know. I know you, and I don't." This was shaky ground. Until very recently, she'd thought her life was only just a little strange. Aidan sat on the bed and touched her cheek. He pushed his fingers into her hair. The feel of his hands was so familiar. How many times had he laid her back on this bed? How many times had he told her he loved her? She didn't want anything to change. No matter how strange it was, he still made her feel so safe.

"I'm sorry I lied. But I think you can see why I would."

"Would you ever have told me, if this hadn't started happening?"

"Well, I would have had to, I guess. In about twenty years when I still wasn't ageing."

Cassandra smirked and pushed him. "Jerk."

"I'm sorry! I don't know when I would have told you. I was scared to." He looked away, shoulders slumped. "I didn't want you to look at me the way you're looking at me now."

Cassandra frowned. He was still Aidan. He'd never been anything different than what he was. She just hadn't known. And she did understand why he would lie. It wasn't the sort of thing you printed up on a t-shirt. There wasn't really anything to forgive. "I just . . . have to get used to it."

"Okay." He nodded. "What about Andie and Henry? Will they get used to it?"

Andie and Henry. They talked to him, but with strange looks on their faces. Sometimes there was so much sheer concentration on Henry's face, she thought he was going to pop something.

"I think so."

"What? What are you thinking?"

"I'm just wondering, about my—" She gestured toward her head.

"Your prophecy?"

"Yeah."

"What about it?"

She hesitated. "Do you . . . Do you know anything more about it? Why it's there?"

Aidan smiled. "No. I just like it, that's all. It makes you special. And don't ask if it's the only thing that makes you special. You know it's not."

"It's just—you've always been so proud of it—"

"I haven't been proud of it. I've been proud of you."

She blinked. He'd cut her off so fast, almost like he was offended. "It's just brought up a lot of questions. About everything." Her teeth clenched. "And I don't want you to be proud of it anymore. It's a curse. That's all it ever has been." She stared at him, hard. She shouldn't feel guilty for saying that. Even if his face looked like she'd just broken his favorite toy.

"Okay. I'm sorry."

"Don't be sorry. Just promise that this is the only secret you have. You're not also a secret agent, or married, or actually my great-great-grandfather."

He looked into her eyes. "I promise."

Blood coated the entire chest and collar of her shirt. It came from a gaping wound that wrapped around her neck in a grotesque second mouth. Blood spilled out from it, running in thick drops over her white button-up and down the front of the maroon waist-apron that had been part of her uniform at the Java Joint coffee house that summer.

Cassandra stared into the mirror at her dead reflection. Her face was powdered pale to the point of being tinged blue. She touched her hair and her fingers stuck to it and came away streaked with red.

"I told you I didn't want a head wound."

"Don't whine," Andie said from behind her. "It'll dry, and it'll all wash out." Andie fussed at the blood and squirted more of it into Cassandra's hair, then down the front of herself. The two-ounce squeeze bottle of FX blood was almost empty. About time too. They were already late to Sam's annual Halloween party.

"Do my guts look okay?"

Cassandra turned. Andie wore a dark blue corseted dress. A pile of intestines and other inner organs lay across her lower midsection. She'd squirted some of the fake blood over the top of it and smeared it around so it looked sickly real. She was dressed as Mary Kelly, the last prostitute dissected by Jack the Ripper.

"I think they still look like rubber." Andie sighed and tugged at the edges of her dress, trying to make it seem like the intestines were coming from inside, rather than lying on top.

"They look good." Cassandra wiped blood spatters from the sink with one of the dye-stained towels they used when they tried to put highlights in their hair. Mary Kelly was supposed to have been her costume, but she didn't have the stomach for so much intestine. It was gross, even on Andie. And all the makeup had a sour, faintly medicinal smell. It was weaker than the smell inside of a rubber mask, but worse, because you couldn't take it off to get away for a minute.

"I don't know why we couldn't have just gotten the Slutty Bo Peep and Slutty Cleopatra costumes like I wanted."

"Because Halloween is for guts. It's not a fricken Victoria's Secret audition."

"This from someone whose dress is pushing her cleavage up into her chin. You're not historically accurate, you know. I'm pretty sure when they found Mary Kelly, Jack had sliced both of her boobs off."

Andie looked horrified. "Sick."

"Well, yeah. He was Jack the Ripper."

Aidan was going to the party as Jack. He and Cassandra were supposed to be a matched set, but the costume fit Andie just as well. Cassandra glanced at her friend's corset. Truthfully, Andie had a little bit more up front to fill it out. A knock on the door preceded Henry's head, clad in a pirate hat.

"What's taking so long? Aidan's downstairs already, and if we don't leave soon we'll have to walk for blocks."

"What are you supposed to be?" Andie asked. Henry gave her a look, and so did the stuffed parrot on his shoulder.

"I don't know what's going to scare people more," he said lightly. "Those guts, or the sight of you in a dress." He ducked out the door just in time to avoid a spray of blood. Cassandra wiped it from the wood.

"Cheer up," Andie said. "Sam's Halloween parties are legendary." Cassandra didn't know what was so legendary about fog from dry ice and punch with spiders floating in it, but there was always a DJ and an impressive array of food that might or might not be a prank in disguise. And Andie's expression was so hopeful. Cassandra smiled.

"You are going to surprise a few people in that dress."

Andie tried to squirt her, but the bottle of blood was empty.

Aidan and Henry waited in the entryway, talking to Cassandra's mother, who was dressed as an enormous yellow canary. She was Tweety Bird, complete with orange tights and huge orange feet. Her parents were going to a Halloween party of their own, something thrown by the higher-ups at her dad's marketing firm. Somewhere in the house, a man-sized Sylvester the Cat was lurking.

"Oh." Cassandra's mother smiled, her face coming out of the bird's mouth. "You girls look disgusting."

"Thanks, Maureen," said Andie.

"It's my handiwork," said Aidan. He wore a long black cape and top hat. A long-bladed fake knife was tucked into his vest.

"You kids are pretty sick," Maureen said. "Here. Have some Snickers and Milky Ways before you go." She reached for a Tupperware megabowl filled with fun-sized candy bars. The contents had already dwindled; most of the neighborhood kids had been through earlier that evening, ringing the doorbell in packs of witches and superheroes.

They grabbed their candy and headed for the door. On the way out, Cassandra's mother caught her arm and whispered, "I'm glad you and Aidan made up."

"Me too." Cassandra smiled.

"Have fun. And be careful." She watched them through the window until they pulled out of the driveway in Henry's Mustang, then let the curtain drop.

"For a scrub in a stocking cap, Sam has a really nice house." Andie whistled through her teeth. Sam's house was a gigantic stone monstrosity that was basically a mansion. It sat at the top of a pine-covered hill, near the end of a winding street lined with similar stone beast houses. The curve of the horseshoe driveway was already packed with cars and more were parked along the curb. Henry muttered "I told you so" and hunted for an empty space. When he tried to parallel park between two SUVs, he misjudged the distance and braked hard. Andie jerked forward in the passenger seat.

"Watch it. You're going to wrinkle my intestines."

"If you hadn't taken so long with those stupid things, we'd have been able to park in the driveway."

"And if you had your eyes on the road and not on my décolletage, you wouldn't be trying to park in a space that's too small."

Henry blushed. "Just don't get any of that stupid blood on the seat."

They found a space and walked. It was cold, and they weren't wearing coats. The temp had dropped down below freezing and it was threatening to snow. Andie shivered as she tugged at her rubber innards, but she had to be less cold than Kjirsten Miels and Leslie Denton, who ran past dressed as some kind of risqué fairies with yards of exposed skin. As they approached the house, the music pumped bass through the frozen lawn, and screams from cheap scares drifted through the brick. Andie tucked a curl of intestine behind a lobe of plastic liver and knocked on the door. Sam swung it wide, dressed as the Headless Horseman. He had a black stick horse under his arm, and the bloody stump of his neck glistened wetly above his head. He looked them over and his eyes widened.

"Boobs, Andie!"

"Shut up, Sam. You should've put your stocking cap on your stump. You look weird without it." He laughed and let them pass. Something was said to Henry about having a peg leg in his pocket or just being happy to see her, but Andie and Cassandra pretended to not hear.

Sam put an arm around each of them and pointed to the food, the drinks, the DJ. Cassandra looked over her shoulder at Aidan just as the door closed and thought she saw something move in the driveway, a flash of something between a maroon Explorer and a tan Malibu. Aidan caught her eye and smiled. She smiled back and let Sam lead them through the foyer.

The temperature change inside the house was extreme. The proliferation of bodies had heated the rooms far more than the thermostat intended. It felt oddly like walking into their overheated school.

"There's the punch," Sam said, preparing to leave them in the kitchen. "If you want anything spiked, let me know." He mounted his stick horse and spun away.

Andie went to the punch bowl and filled a plastic cup while Cassandra looked suspiciously at a bowl of some kind of pasta salad.

"Think it's a prank?"

"Yes, I think it's a prank. Who has pasta salad at a Halloween party? Stick to prepackaged foods."

Another pirate spotted Henry and yelled. There was a small group of them dressed that way, all eye patches, peg legs, and gold teeth. Beneath the makeup, Cassandra recognized some of the varsity players. Henry waved but didn't leave.

"You don't have to stay glued to me all night," Cassandra said.

Henry glanced at Aidan and smiled. "I'll be back in a bit."

Cassandra took a deep breath and chewed on a cracker. The kitchen smelled like pizza; three boxes sat on the table. Cassandra went to grab a slice of Canadian bacon and caught a whiff of alcohol. A puddle of something clear dripped onto the floor. She mopped it up with a napkin and sniffed. Vodka.

"Hey, Cassandra."

"Hey, Megan. Careful, something spilled." She grabbed

the girl's shoulder when she slid. Megan's costume was Slutty Bo Peep, her blond hair in pigtails and a cotton bonnet on her head. She used her sheepherding cane to prop herself up and took a slice of pizza.

"I really need to eat something, or I'm going to pass out. Can you hold my sheep?" She handed off the small inflated animal, blue eyes painted onto white plastic. Then she picked up a napkin and walked off, forgetting her livestock entirely. Cassandra set it on the table.

"How can she be that drunk already?" Aidan asked, watching her wobble back to the dance floor.

"How could I have suggested Andie buy that Bo Peep outfit?"

Aidan shrugged. "It would've looked nice on you." He wrapped his cape around her shoulders and stole a bite of pizza.

Getting to the party late was a good idea. They'd missed the awkward start-up, when only a few people were there and the music echoed through the space. Now it was packed, and people danced and crowded the furniture. Not a single chair or sofa arm was unoccupied and the noise stuffed itself into their ears: cackled laughter and constant conversations weaved through the beat of music. It seemed like everyone had come in costume; there were so many masks and layers of makeup it was hard to tell who was who. Girls were mostly flash and glitter, lipstick and sequins. At least five wore fishnet stockings.

Andie stood surrounded by girls from her hockey team. They pulled her toward the back of the house and up the stairs, where Sam had set up a haunted house.

"Aidan! Cassandra! You coming?" She gestured up the stairs.

Cassandra waved her off. Maybe later. Though the

haunted portion of the house probably wouldn't exist later. Whoever was doing the scaring upstairs would get bored, and people would start using the dark rooms to make out.

There was an odd synchronicity to her thoughts as a giant human condom passed by en route to the punch bowl. Cassandra laughed.

"What?"

"Nothing. Giant human condom made me laugh."

Aidan grinned and watched the condom walk away. It was basically a huge square of gold foil with legs.

"I'm glad we came. I missed the sound of you laughing." He put his hands around her waist and pulled her close.

Color rose into her cheeks, visible even beneath the smear of white makeup. She swallowed. Being touched by him was different now, even if she didn't want to admit it. The heat in his hands, and the strength, made her heart pound. He kissed her and she forgot where she was and wrapped her arms around him. He lifted her like she weighed nothing. When her feet hit the floor it took an extra second for her brain to catch up.

It's like he's never touched me before. Like he was holding back the whole time. And now everything's different.

"That was hot."

They looked across the table. Megan stared at them with wide eyes. "Sorry. Forgot my sheep."

Cassandra giggled into Aidan's shoulder. "Let's just . . . go find Andie."

Somehow they managed to snag a corner of sofa in the living room, far enough away from the DJ that they could carry on a conversation. Andie sat on the arm, careful to keep her bloody entrails off of the leather, in case it would stain. A few feet in front of them, the Quentin twins showed off their new matching tattoos. The pulled-down sleeves of their costumes revealed twisting black tribal marks. Amy's was on her right shoulder, and Angie's on her left. Standing face-to-face in identical clothing, they were like mirror images.

"They only dress the same on Halloween," Andie mused. "It's weird. I wonder if they have a secret twin language."

"Not every set of twins has weird secret twin languages," said Aidan. "Artemis and I didn't. Though I could read her mind sometimes." He paused and looked down. Andie blinked and basically ignored him. Cassandra squeezed his hand. One day it wouldn't hurt to talk about Artemis. Or maybe it always would.

Andie went back to studying the tattoos.

"Twin symmetry aside, it's sort of cool looking. Not something I'd get, though. I don't think I could get a tattoo. It'd be there forever unless I sprang for the laser treatments. And I hear those hurt like a bitch."

Cassandra nodded and watched a bunch of werewolves ogle Andie's chest from across the room. There was no shortage of skin for their eyes to feast on, but Andie's skin was a surprise. Even Sam had stopped by more than once to put an arm around her and tell her something or other.

"Hey," Cassandra said. "Boys are staring."

Andie scowled. "Hey! I'm a murder victim." She pointed to her exposed guts. The wolf howled and his friends laughed. "Perverts. What kind of sicko gets turned on by a dead girl? I'm going to find your brother."

Andie walked away, bobbing and dodging through groups of people and dancing bodies. The way some of them were gyrating, you'd think they were trying to turn the party into a bacchanal. Cassandra's mind slid back to Aidan and the kiss they'd had in the kitchen. She turned and whispered in his ear.

"I think it's time we checked out the haunted house."

He smiled, and the heat from his body jumped. "Follow me upstairs in a few minutes." When he got up, his fingers trailed along her leg.

Take a breath. This is bordering on unhealthy.

With Aidan gone, she looked around and tried to be inconspicuous. In the corner of her eye, someone sat in a porcelain mask, dark eyes watching her through the cutouts. But when she turned, there was no one there. Cassandra blinked.

Probably just my imagination.

Everyone seemed to be caught up in their own conversations, and no one had asked her to do the coin trick yet, which was nice. She wasn't in the mood.

How long had it been since Aidan had left? Long enough to go after him? There weren't any clocks on the walls and she hadn't checked her phone for the time. She stood and walked toward the hallway. More than likely she'd stumble into the wrong dark room and get yelled at by some couple. Or she'd open a door and have a skeleton jump up and rattle in her face.

The music changed to some song that sounded like a remix of My Morning Jacket. The closer she got to the music, the more people shouted to be heard, and through the crowd she saw Henry's face rise up over the other faces like the dorsal fin of a shark. She veered away toward the stairs, so he wouldn't see her sneaking off to meet Aidan. But then he also didn't see someone grab her from behind and pull her through an open door. Her yelp of surprise was drowned out by laughter and music, which itself was muted when the door closed in front of her.

"Shh," a male voice said into her ear. "And don't struggle or you'll fall down the stairs."

She looked down. Her feet balanced precariously on a stone staircase leading to the basement. The light where they were was dim and yellow, thrown from a single blurry bulb. It smelled like stone and was kept cool enough to make her arms prickle. After the heat upstairs, it felt almost good.

"What are you doing?" she asked. It was the first thing she thought to say. After the initial surprise of being grabbed, her heart began to thump its way back to normal. She was at Sam's house, at a party. Someone had grabbed her to play a prank or something. It was probably someone she knew.

Except it isn't. The strength in these fingers is like the strength in Aidan's fingers.

But it wasn't Aidan. If it was, she wouldn't still be tense, ready to grasp the railing should whoever it was decide to throw her down the steps like she was a pile of rags.

"I'm not doing anything. Just making introductions." His grip loosened, and she twisted to look behind her. She found herself staring into a white harlequin mask, the cheek painted with gold glitter tears. Green and purple feathers adorned the head. It was something you'd see at Mardi Gras, or Carnival in Rio.

"You were watching me," she said. The eyes behind the mask regarded her without blinking. She didn't recognize them. When they swept up and down her body, the movement was unnaturally quick, curious. "What? What are you looking at?"

"I'm not sure. To be honest, you aren't quite what I expected. I thought you'd be taller. Or that you'd be sparkling." He smiled, revealing beautiful white teeth. The movement highlighted the gauntness of his face. His clothes were slightly loose and the mask was the only costume piece he wore. The rest of him was clad in jeans and a navy-blue t-shirt.

"Who are you?"

He leaned close, gave her a sniff. "You wouldn't believe me if I told you. Or maybe you would. Odysseus did."

When the door opened behind them, his hands were on her faster than she could blink. He drew her down the stairs until he hit the wall at the bottom. Glass clinked and rattled. He'd run up against a rack of wine bottles. More bottles lined the walls of the small room to their left. They were in a wine cellar.

Aidan stood on the stairs above them; the cape of his costume swayed against his knees.

"Let go of her." The way he said it left no question that he knew who he was talking to. The grip on her shoulders tightened slightly, but a soft bark of laughter shot past her ear.

"Look at you. I don't believe it."

"Shut up. Let her go."

He did, and backed down the stairs, farther into the cellar. Cassandra found herself farther inside too when Aidan walked forward. The staircase was narrow and didn't allow room for her to pass. The boy who'd grabbed her still smiled, and he reached up to push the mask off his face.

Cassandra looked from one to the other. The stranger was thinner, and his hair was chestnut brown, but the bone structure of his face and the shape of his eyes were the same. Even the way they stood. They could have been brothers.

They are brothers. They're family. This is Aidan's real family.

Aidan held his hand out and drew her toward him, putting himself between her and the stranger. A ripple of fear coursed down her spine and she tugged on his hand. They should run. Whoever he was, he was dangerous, even if he did look like he hadn't eaten in weeks.

"Get out of here, Hermes," said Aidan.

"Hermes?" He smiled. "So she does know. That's excellent. Big sister will be very pleased."

"Who's 'big sister'?" Cassandra asked. She stepped out from behind Aidan. Their voices rang loud against the stone walls. The slightest shuffling of her feet was loud, even over the muffled music coming through the cellar door.

"Don't talk to him, Cassandra," Aidan whispered. "Please don't."

Hermes looked from one to the other, eyes narrowing. "You haven't just gotten here. You haven't been looking for her like we have. What are you doing?"

"Shut up, Hermes!"

"You've been living here. Like one of them." His eyes traveled over Aidan. "And you look so healthy."

"You don't. And I gather that she doesn't either."

"She looks good. Sturdy. Just like always."

Aidan smiled. "Jumping to her defense? She must be worse off than I thought."

"That smile. There's the Apollo I remember. Cocky and vain."

Cassandra held her breath as the two verbally circled. The wine cellar felt tighter by the minute. Beside her, Aidan seemed taller suddenly. Stronger.

"Cocky and vain. And stronger than you."

Hermes shrugged. "It was a mistake to grab her; I see that now. Athena told me not to. She warned me. Stay back." He jerked backward as Aidan leaned forward. "Tsk, tsk. If I get my limbs torn off now, I'll never hear the end of it." He took another hasty step backward and knocked against the bottles. Glass rattled like a nervous titter running through a crowd. "I was just saying hello." His eyes darted to the staircase.

"You should have stayed away."

"Do you know what's happening? You should be glad I got here first."

Cassandra grasped Aidan's arm. "Wait. He knows what's going on?" Aidan shook her off like he hadn't heard. "Aidan."

Hermes' brows knit. "Aidan?" He grinned. "It's nice. I like it. And I can see that you love the girl, so I'll be on my way."

"And you'll never come back?" Aidan's arm shot out and grasped a bottle by the neck, then dashed it against the wall. Red liquid and green glass exploded and splashed onto the floor; the sharp smell of alcohol flooded the air. He still held the neck of the bottle; the jagged edge dripped wine.

Adrenaline went through Cassandra like a gunshot. He was going to kill him, or at least try. "Aidan—"

"Go upstairs, okay? Find Andie and your brother. Take them home." He edged her out of the way.

She looked at the glass in his hand. "No."

Hermes had lost all traces of levity. He stared at Apollo with dread and more than a little exhaustion.

"Are you choosing sides?" he asked.

"There are no sides," Aidan replied. "Not for me. There's only her." The shard of glass twisted in his grip.

"What're you going to do with that?"

"I'm going to slice you open. Bleed you out onto the cement. That ought to slow you down for awhile."

Hermes' mouth opened and closed. "I can see that nothing I say is going to matter. Whoever you are, you're not the brother I hoped for. No ally. Nothing but a traitor." He looked at Aidan with disgust. "And from the look of it, you're not even dying."

Light flashed on the glass in Aidan's hand. "Maybe I am. Come closer and find out."

Hermes glanced toward the door and Cassandra nodded slightly.

Go. Get out of here before you ruin everything.

He smiled. "Uh-uh. It's been a few thousand years, but if I remember correctly, I'm no match for you on my own." He looked at the sharp glass. "If I come any closer, most of my spleen is going to end up skewered on the end of that bottle. I can almost feel it already, sliding into my guts. No thank you." He looked at Cassandra. "Sorry, sweetheart. You're sort of a pretty girl, very nice I'm sure. You'll forgive me for this later."

Hermes pulled a wine bottle from the wall and threw it at her head. Cassandra screamed, but Aidan jumped in front of her and caught it. It gave Hermes just enough time to rush past them and leap over the railing onto the stairs.

"Big sister's on her way," he said. "I'm going to love watching you explain this to her."

Aidan growled and leapt for him. The tip of the broken bottle sliced through the back of Hermes' shirt and into the skin but went no farther. He was out of the cellar and fleeing before Aidan even regained his balance.

Aidan ran up the stairs and out into the party.

"Aidan!" Cassandra shouted. She vaulted up the stairs and caught him at the open front door, staring into the night. "Don't!"

He looked at her frightened face and dropped the bloody shard of bottle, then pulled her close.

"Are you all right? Did he hurt you?"

"No." She shook her head, and he felt her arms and down her back. "But he was one of them, wasn't he? One of you. Where is he?"

"The fast-footed prick is probably a half mile away by now."

She glanced over his shoulder. Andie and Henry had heard her yell; they were coming through the crowd, their faces concerned.

"I have to go after him," he said.

"No."

"I'm stronger than he is. I promise."

"What about your sister? The big one he talked about."

"I'm stronger than her too."

She narrowed her eyes.

"Come on. It might not be a lie. She's dying, after all." He kissed her quickly and ran out the door, black cape flying ridiculously behind him.

"Hey." Sam poked his head out beside her. "What's up? Where's he going to so fast?"

"Family emergency," said Cassandra, and walked down the front steps with Andie and Henry not far behind.

Andie snored. It was loud on a regular night, worse after having her lungs shoved into a corset for three hours. She slept in Cassandra's bed while Cassandra lay on the floor in a sleeping bag, watching the pale light from the bulb over the driveway basketball court float up through her window. The dull thud of a rubber ball hitting pavement assured her that Henry couldn't sleep either. She stared at the glowing red numbers of her alarm clock. They hadn't advanced much since the last time she'd looked. Aidan hadn't called, but she thought he was okay. She hoped he was. No certainty of his death had leaked into the dark space between her ears, anyway.

Cassandra sat up and threw the covers back, then grabbed

her bathrobe and went downstairs to join Henry by the basketball hoop.

"Can I play?" Cassandra asked, closing the front door softly.

"Sure." He tossed her the ball and she almost dropped it.

Basketball wasn't their game. They were both surprisingly bad at it. But chasing down missed shots seemed like just the thing to tire them out and hopefully drive them to sleep. Cassandra made it all the way to *S* in a game of HORSE before either one of them brought it up.

"I still don't think he is what he says he is." Henry took a shot and made it off the rim. "I mean, I know he jumped out that window, and he's definitely strong. Superhuman, even. But a god? Come on."

"You didn't see them tonight," said Cassandra. "You didn't see the way Hermes moved. Or hear the things they said."

Henry scoffed and threw a shot up into the backboard. It bounced off and Cassandra chased it down the driveway. She took her own shot, missed, and blew into her frozen hands. Touching the cold ball was starting to hurt.

"So what do you think he is, if not a god?"

Henry shrugged and dribbled absently. "A government experiment maybe. And now he's got amnesia about it, or paranoid fantasies or whatever. It happens all the time."

"Where?"

"TV." Henry smirked. "To be honest, Cassie, I'm trying not to think about this too much."

That was well and good for him. But she had to think about it. Because big sister was coming, whoever that was, and she was coming for her. "Henry?"

"Yeah?"

"You know how I won't be psychic for much longer?"

Henry bounced the basketball, nodded. "Sure. Eighteen

or whereabouts you always said. It'd just go up like a puff of smoke." He drew up and took a shot; the ball dropped through the net and bounced off the driveway into the dead grass. "What about it?"

"Well, what if I was wrong? What if that dark spot in the future isn't me not being psychic anymore? What if it's me not being around anymore? What if I just—" She held her hands up and let them fall. "Die?"

Henry took a breath and let his shoulders slump. He still had traces of pirate eyeliner under his eyes and it gave him the look of a cartoon villain.

No. A dark, reluctant hero, maybe. But never a villain. Henry doesn't have a villainous bone in his body.

It didn't surprise her that he was the one having the hardest time accepting Aidan being what he was. He was always so grounded, solid, and practical. A six-foot-tall rock people leaned on. Sometimes Cassandra wondered if he believed in her psychic stuff at all, or if he just said he did because he loved her.

After a second, Henry retrieved the ball from the grass. He shook his head.

"Nope."

She smiled. "Nope, what?"

"Nope, that's not going to happen." He dribbled and passed her the ball. The impact stung her fingers.

"How do you know?"

"I just know," he said, and took a defensive position, trying to get her to drive past him. "Maybe I'm psychic too."

Aidan stood in the backyard of his parents' house, leaned against one of their pine trees and listening for movement. The only thing he heard was a gentle wind and the soft squeak of his mother's porch swing swaying slightly back and forth.

His adopted mother. The mother who was thousands of years too late to be his real mother. He'd never thought of her that way before. She'd always been Gloria, the woman who loved him enough to call him her son. And Ernie was always just his dad. But everything was coming unraveled. The way that Cassandra had looked at them through the window that day; he couldn't get it out of his mind.

There wasn't much time left. He'd fought against believing it ever since Cassandra's visions had started. But denial didn't do anyone any good. Not even a god. Especially not a god, when Athena was on her way. A fight was coming to him, and he had no idea whether he could win, no matter what he said to the contrary.

He looked down at his clenched fists. For the first time, they seemed pathetically weak. Maybe he'd been hiding for too long, passing as a human when he was anything but. He used to be one of the strongest gods to walk on Olympus: the god of the sun, the god of prophecy and the arts. But he was out of practice. Not so long ago, he would have had that little rat Hermes skewered and roasting over a pit with a snap of his fingers. He flexed his fists again. Maybe he really was growing weaker. Maybe he hadn't escaped the curse that was killing the others after all.

"You're not thinking of taking her away from here, are you?"

Aidan turned, ready to rip Hermes in half, but his anger dissipated as quickly as it came. It wouldn't have been possible anyway. Hermes peeked out from behind another pine, his legs loaded on springs. If Aidan so much as pulled his fist back Hermes would run, too fast and too far to ever be caught.

"It would be a waste of time," Hermes warned. "And she wouldn't be safe."

Aidan smiled ruefully. "Is she safe here?"

"She's not safe anywhere."

He looked at Hermes. The god of thieves had changed over the centuries, but not much. He wore his hair shorter, and he dressed like he'd fallen out of a Hilfiger catalog. And he was thin, so painfully thin. The kind of thin that eventually killed you. But the mischievous light in his eyes was familiar and so was the curve of his mouth. The stance too, edgy and tense, was so much the same that he might as well have had wings on his feet.

"You look like shit," said Aidan, and Hermes smirked.

"You're one to talk. What are you supposed to be, anyway? A seventeen-year-old Bela Lugosi?"

Aidan pulled the cape off his shoulders. It did seem ridiculous now, standing before his eternal half brother. Like playing at children's games. "I'm sorry I tried to kill you." He looked up in time to see Hermes' quick shrug. "But you can't have her."

Hermes crossed his arms. "I think Athena's going to have a different opinion."

Aidan clenched his jaw. Athena. Always proud and haughty, always Daddy's favorite. She was used to being strong and getting what she wanted. But the gods were dying. He knew that much. If Hermes was any indication, Athena would be weaker than she used to be. She'd be fading. He wondered what her death was, whether it made her angry, or crazy, or both.

"I'll fight you," Aidan said quietly. "I'll fight you with everything I can."

Hermes nodded, considering. "You know, Apollo," he said finally, "Athena would like to save you. But if you make it come down to a choice between her survival and yours, I think we both know which way it's going to go."

Aidan looked down. Resignation weighed on his shoulders. The stance felt unnatural. The god of the sun should never hang his head.

"What's it like?" Hermes asked. "Living with them? Loving one of them? It's been quite a while, for me."

Aidan smiled a small, regretful smile. "It's amazing. I never thought anything would matter as much as she does. Just one mortal girl."

"One mortal girl," Hermes repeated.

"Hermes."

"Yeah?"

"Please leave us alone. I'm asking you, if we ever really were brothers. Get her to stay away."

Hermes blinked. For a minute Aidan thought it had worked. That hearing him beg and say they were family had shocked Hermes into compliance.

Hermes sighed.

"We are brothers," he said gently. "So I hope you'll believe me when I tell you that I wish that was a choice we had."

A soft rush of air passed Aidan's cheeks. When he looked up at the tree, Hermes was gone.

12

WHAT HAPPENS ON THE ROAD

"Shouldn't we leave this thing somewhere farther off the beaten path?"

Athena looked over her shoulder at the silver Taurus. It stared back sadly, like a dog being left at the pound, parked in the rear of the lot of the travel plaza just outside of South Bend, Indiana. She shrugged.

"Well, shouldn't we take the plates off or something?"

"Don't see why." Athena shrugged again. "We're going to be long gone before anybody finds it, and the trucker probably didn't get the plate number anyway."

"You're wrong there," Odysseus said as they walked. "He was probably on the radio as soon as we started swerving over the lines."

"What are you worried for? We've already crossed a state line, and the car was probably stolen in the first place. They can't tie it to us, and even if they could, we'll have disappeared. We don't have time for this. Let's just get something to eat and catch a ride to New York."

Odysseus sighed and shut up, and Athena looked at the travel plaza. It was made up of a Shell gas station-slash-souvenir shop, a very large set of restrooms, a McDonald's, and a Dunkin' Donuts. Both of the restaurants were greasy. One was greasy and sweet. She pulled open the main door and looked in both directions. The whole place smelled like hot oil and diesel fuel.

"You go to one and I'll go to the other. Grab some food and try to find us a ride. Preferably a trucker."

"Why a trucker?"

"They'll be going farther and they usually have a sleeper in the cab. You have money, don't you?"

Odysseus nodded and pulled out his wallet. He gave her a ten and headed toward Dunkin' Donuts. Athena walked into the McDonald's side. There was a short line and a few of the people waiting were truck drivers, men with cheap ball caps, thin legs, and blue jeans pulled over cowboy boots. She glanced down at herself. She looked like total shit; if not like a criminal then at least like a runaway who'd had a rough couple of days. She buttoned her cardigan up as far as it would go to cover the bloodstains. The tears in her jeans might at least pass for a fashion statement.

When she got in line, she made sure to smile and nod at the guy in front of her. He was thirtysomething, with a goatee and mustache and a long, black mullet hanging down from his baseball cap. She checked the logo: New York Yankees. She smiled again; he turned around.

"You look like you've been on the road awhile," he said with a nod to her clothes.

"Yeah," she replied. "There was a sort of mix-up with my ride. A difference of opinion."

He nodded and gave her an understanding smile.

"I wound up losing all of my bags. It's been kind of a nightmare."

"Well," he said, and glanced up at the plastic, backlit menu. "To ease the blow, how about I buy you some lunch?"

"Oh, no, I couldn't," Athena replied. The restaurant had just switched over from serving breakfast and the smell of rubbery, overcooked eggs and cheese mingled with the grease of burgers. The smell was thick enough to coat her skin. She should have gone to Dunkin' Donuts. As she opened her mouth to ask for a ride rather than lunch, Odysseus grabbed her by the elbow.

"Hey," he said around a mouthful of chicken Parmesan flatbread. "I found us a ride." He waved to the guy she'd been talking to, then looked at her. "Do you want to get food from here? I got an extra sandwich and some donut holes. We're supposed to meet him in the lot. He drives a red Freightliner."

"That was fast," Athena said as they walked to the idling truck. Odysseus grinned. He always worked fast. Fast and clever. He opened the white paper bag. She fished out a donut hole and rolled it between her fingers, leaving a circular trail of sugar. She hadn't eaten in a day, nothing at all except those few blackberries at The Three Sisters. She popped the donut into her mouth and it enlivened her taste buds. Her stomach rumbled, and she eyed the paper sack hungrily. He'd said something about an extra sandwich.

Odysseus waved at the driver through the window of the truck. He was older than the driver Athena had talked to, by a lot. His hair was gray, and he was heavy, maybe 260 pounds and still gaining. The buttons of his shirt looked like they were under extreme pressure. He smiled as they opened the door and climbed into the cab. Odysseus introduced her and she shook the driver's hand. His name was Craig Melville, and he was doing a run from Minneapolis, with drops in Toledo and Buffalo. He could take them as far as that. After Buffalo, he'd drop his trailer and head for his home in Pennsylvania.

"Thanks again for the ride," said Odysseus, and then, to Athena, "I told him what a jumble it's been. He couldn't believe that Jimmy actually got mad enough to leave us behind. But he doesn't know Jimmy. Crazy bloke. I told you we shouldn't have ridden back up to school with him."

Athena smiled at Craig. "Well, I never thought he'd leave us either. I just hope he doesn't throw our stuff out of the car before he gets to campus."

Odysseus grinned. The lie came together naturally and nostalgia hit her in a warm wave. Side by side they were devious and slick.

"I wouldn't worry about anything." Craig checked his mirrors and situated his coffee thermos. "I've had plenty of crazy friends, and they always turn out right in the end. He'll probably be damn sorry, the next time you see him." He put the truck into gear and it jerked forward. He seemed nice enough. He told them about a few of his "crazy" friends; Athena listened and smiled while she ate the ham and cheese flatbread Odysseus had bought. While she chewed, weariness began to sink in again. The truck was nice and clean, and there was a sleeper in the back. She was about to ask Craig if she could use it when he tapped her on the knee.

"Hey," he said gently. "You both look exhausted. Why don't you sneak in the back and get some sleep? You'll have plenty of time to keep me company after we get through Toledo."

"Thank you," she said, and was surprised by how much

she meant it. It would have been nice to have something to give him in return, something more than a lie and polite conversation. She reached out for his hand. "You're a very nice man, Craig," she said. "I hope you have a lot of prosperity and good health." Craig grinned, and they shook. When they touched, she thought she felt something small pass between them, some slight bit of warmth and electricity, moving from her skin into his.

Of course she might have imagined it. The blessing of a dying goddess probably wasn't worth much. But at least she'd tried.

Odysseus held back the curtain between the cab and the sleeper. She lumbered into the back and sat down heavily on the small bed.

"Just give a shout if you want us to chip in for gas, or snacks or something," Odysseus told Craig, then closed the curtain and sat down on the bunk.

"Should we talk now?" he asked softly. Whispering wasn't necessary. Craig had turned on the strains of an oldies station, and the engine noise from the truck covered their voices well.

Athena sighed. "I'm exhausted. And what you're going to tell me . . . I have a feeling is going to keep me up." *I don't have time to be sleeping. I should make him talk now, so I can think of what to do next. I should make him talk now so I can dream battle plans, for fuck's sake.* Her mind's arguments were weak. The soft bed spoke much louder.

"It can wait. We've got a long ride ahead." Odysseus' tender voice soothed her ears. But the concern on his face edged too close to pity.

He's losing faith in my strength. I'm messing everything up. I can't protect him. I have to be stronger, faster. I will be, as soon as I get some rest.

"I'm sorry this is happening to you," Odysseus said. "You don't deserve it. Of all the gods on that damned hilltop, all of those vain, stupid prigs, you don't deserve it. You never did."

It hurt her heart that he gave her so much credit. She wasn't something to be worshipped; she was something to be contended with. Everything that had gone wrong in his old life could have been blamed on her, or on some twisted member of her family. What did it matter if she tried to fix it? Fixing it was her responsibility. It had been then, and it still was now.

She watched him as he moved down to the floor of the sleeper, as he rolled up a sweatshirt from his bag for a pillow. This was the most time they had ever spent together all at once. In the old days, there had been more to her existence, things for her to do, and she'd dropped in on him only when she was needed. But she'd always watched. She had always made sure he was safe.

Will I fail this time? Will I finally have to watch him die, not in his bed an old man but young, and soon, and painfully?

Her tongue found the slowly healing wound on the roof of her mouth and twisted into it. Bitter tears gathered in the corners of her eyes.

Without thinking, she reached down and put her hand on his arm. He jumped at the touch before letting himself be pulled up onto the bed.

It felt strangely natural, even though she had never in her long, long life slept beside a man. It went against everything her father had created her to be. And she'd never wanted it, until now.

Odysseus lay down uncertainly. He kept his eyes on her until his head hit the pillow and released his breath in a slow, nervous shudder. She felt his heartbeat, and heard it, fast and strong in his chest. Words were there, between them, but they went unspoken. It was only moments before they were both deeply asleep.

When Athena woke, the truck was stopped, and the engine turned off. Something had jolted her awake. She waited and felt a soft jerk from somewhere behind them. It was the movement of the trailer, pulling the truck back as it was unloaded. That meant they were already in Toledo.

Athena looked around in the dimness. Only two shafts of light cut through a gap in the faux leather curtain dividing the sleeper from the cab, and even that light was gray. The weather must've turned overcast while they slept.

Odysseus stirred by her side and shifted against her hip. She tensed. The bed was small. They were completely wrapped up in each other. How had that happened? She'd been so deeply under it had felt like oblivion. He was lucky she hadn't shoved him off onto the floor.

Why did I ask him here in the first place?

She couldn't remember. A deep breath brought aftershave to her nose, and she didn't know if it was his or Craig Melville's. It was probably Craig's. If it had been Odysseus, it would have smelled like cinnamon massage oil from The Three Sisters. The corner of her mouth twisted into a smile, and she pushed dark hair back off his forehead.

In the shadows, he looked softer, relaxed and innocent, the working of his brain reduced to slow clicks and whirrs. He looked almost harmless, almost gentle, nothing like the swashbuckling liar she knew he was. She leaned closer and studied the curve of his jaw, the easy pulse at his throat. His fingers rested on the small of her back; she'd turned men into stone for less. But she didn't move. Something grew inside her chest and stomach, some new, unnamed need, unfurling and trying out its wings. She let herself press closer, and shivered.

This is what men risk so much for; this shiver, this acute heat and desire. This is what they think eternity feels like.

The words moved through her mind without warning. Thoughts like that were not meant for her. She was removed from it, completely outside the jurisdiction of Aphrodite's lasso. But she had to admit it was intoxicating. It took over completely.

I should move away.

Except when she did move, it was her hand, slipping mindlessly up underneath the fabric of his shirt.

Even the touch of my ungainly hand makes him tremble. This is dangerous. It rebounds on everything. I've seen it ruin lives.

Athena held her breath, but couldn't stop. Or she wouldn't. Boundaries blurred as he woke beneath her hands. His fingers squeezed down on her hip. His eyes opened.

Odysseus pushed the veil of her hair back and drew her closer, nothing but the sound of his quickened breath and moving fabrics in her ears. He was practiced and she was new, the Don Juan of the Aegean and the Virgin Goddess, but it was all instinct, all sensation and response. The heat of his tongue, the firm strength of his body and the way he moved her, they might have done it all a hundred, a thousand times before.

This isn't real, this feeling. I'm not made for this.

He rolled her onto her back, their fingers entwined. The desperation in his movements filled her with a strange sense of power, and the way he shook and sighed. In her mind an image flashed from long ago: Odysseus in the middle of an ocean, standing on the deck of a ship. He stared out over the water, his expression determined but desolate, skin bronzed by decades of sunlight far from home. He grasped onto the ship's railing and shouted something, the same word, three times. Penelope. Penelope. Penelope. He screamed for his wife, the wife he loved and continually tried to return to. The ship's hull had been painted with a depiction of Athena's eyes.

"Athena," Odysseus whispered, and kissed her neck.

It was just an image. One brief flash. She didn't even know if she had really seen it, or if it was her own invention. Penelope was dead, she had to be, she'd used up all her devotion two thousand years ago. And besides, it didn't matter. Athena was a goddess. She took from mortal women as she liked. Odysseus was hers. He always had been.

Stop. Stop this. Those are Aphrodite's words, Aphrodite's justifications. Penelope might be gone but I'm not. He and I are separate. Divided. Just because I'm dying doesn't mean I give up what I am.

"Stop," Athena whispered. Odysseus' arms clenched tight around her, his fingers in her hair.

"Stop," she said again, and when he hesitated she shoved him, harder than she wanted to. His shoulder struck the wall over the foot of the bed.

It was embarrassing. She could see the mortified expression he wore in the shadows as she pulled herself up.

"I'm sorry," he said quickly. "I don't know what happened. We were asleep—I half thought I was dreaming!" His hands moved roughly over his face. "Look, just don't do anything drastic, all right? Don't turn my eyes to stone in my head or—" He glanced downward. "Or anything worse." He leapt up and turned toward the curtain. "I'm going to go find a soda or something. I'm sorry."

He pulled back the curtain and light cut through the sleeper.

"Odysseus," she said, and he paused. "It's all right. You didn't do anything wrong."

He wouldn't look at her. She hadn't thought he would be so ashamed. He acted like he'd been cut open.

"Don't feel so bad." She tried to smile. It had been her fault. She should say something to make it right. "This is—well—it's what you always do."

"What I always do?" he asked, and his eyes darkened. "What I always do. Like on Circe's island, you mean. Or dallying with Calypso."

Athena blinked. When he was angry, his accent got thicker. Her neck stiffened as he pointed a finger at her.

"That was a bloody lifetime ago."

"I was trying to make you feel better."

"Feel better? By making me sound like a dog? It was thousands of years ago!"

"I found you two *days* ago in a naked tangle of whores!" Her mind winced at defaming the witches of The Three Sisters, but she couldn't take it back. They were nice whores, very lovely people, but she was trying to make a point. "I suppose that was just an innocent game of Twister in between readings from *Macbeth*?" She held up her hands before he could explode. She used to be so good at de-escalating. But then she never would have allowed herself to be in this position. "I'm not saying that it's wrong. I never judged you. I was never even annoyed; I was amused, mostly—"

Odysseus shook his head. It wasn't helping.

"Don't you get it?" he asked. "This is different. You're not like them."

Athena swallowed. Not like them. No, she wasn't like them. She wasn't beguiling. Enchantments and seductions were mysteries to her. They were ridiculous wastes of time.

A heavy feeling built in her chest, just at the base of her throat. The image of Aphrodite's golden apple rippled into her mind. *To the Fairest*, it had said.

"I've always shown you respect," Odysseus finished lamely, and she looked away. He said her name and got no response. She might as well have been a statue. So he turned and left, slamming the door of the cab behind him.

Athena stepped out of the Freightliner and took a breath of Toledo. It smelled about the same as South Bend, only colder. The wind had come up too, and it whipped her hair into her eyes. She couldn't tell what time it was. The clouds blocked out the sun.

They were parked in the loading dock of a long, navy blue and white warehouse. Half a dozen other trucks were lined up beside Craig's, a few of them idling, most of them turned off. Workers passed by on forklifts, moving pallets of white boxes. She looked around. Odysseus hadn't made it far. He stood about fifty feet away, near the hot lunch truck, talking to the driver while he ate a hot dog. She walked up behind him.

"Once you start eating you just don't quit."

He turned. Uncertainty floated over his features, like he still half-expected to be turned into a toad. He cleared his throat and his brows lifted.

"I'm a bottomless pit. Can I get you anything?"

"Maybe just a Coke."

He paid the worker and handed her a cold can. Athena walked away and motioned with her head for him to follow, past the line of parked trucks and over to the end of the lot, where a lonely picnic table stood in the middle of dead brown grass.

"Well," he said and threw a leg over the bench, "this is awkward."

"Talking about why Hera and Poseidon are after you?" Athena asked lightly. "Why would that be awkward? Is it that awful?"

She looked him in the eyes. *Deal with the problem at hand. The rest we can worry about later.*

Odysseus nodded slightly and Athena took a long drink of her soda.

"You know what they're doing, don't you?" he asked.

"Looking for tools to help them eat us, you mean?"

He gave her a weird look, and she waved her hand.

"I don't think the eating part is literal. But who knows? They're just trying to save their own skins."

"For them to live, other gods have to die."

Athena nodded. "So everyone keeps saying. Though nobody seems to be able to say why."

Odysseus shrugged. "Because that's the way that it's been fated to happen. No one escapes Fate. Not a single one of us, after we're born. Not even you."

Athena rolled her eyes. He sounded like her father. "So why even bother fighting? If we're fated to lose, then we lose. If we're fated to win, then one way or another, we'll come out on top. Right?"

"Don't get philosophical on me. For the record, I don't believe in Fate. I believe that the pieces have been placed. The ending hasn't been written yet."

Athena ground her teeth. She did believe in Fate. It was almost impossible not to, after having the king of the gods drive it into her head for so long. But she'd always hated it. It made her feel powerless. Why people saw it as a comfort, she would never understand.

She twisted the tab off of her Coke and flicked it into the recycle bin. "So what are they doing, right now? Do you know?"

"They're looking for a weapon."

"I figured on that. What weapon? It can't be Cassandra. You didn't even know about her."

He hesitated, which was good. The fewer who knew the better. But she was the leader of the damned resistance. He needed to cough it up.

"There's just the one weapon that I know about," he said softly.

"Okay." She waited for him to talk. When he didn't, she nudged him with a finger. "So what is it? And why do they need you in particular to get it?"

Odysseus swallowed. "Because I'm the only one who knows how to find it."

"How to—?" she asked, and stopped. Suddenly she knew. It was just like it had been before. During the war against Troy. Greece had needed a weapon, and only Odysseus had been able to convince it to come out and fight. Only Odysseus had known where it was hiding.

"It's Achilles," she whispered. "They're looking for Achilles."

Achilles. The greatest warrior the world had ever seen. She hadn't thought of him in ages. During the time of the Trojan war, he'd been necessary, but even then she'd wished he hadn't been. He was cold, smart, and narcissistic. He knew the price of glory and he didn't care. The slaughter he left in his wake was red and spread with entrails. He knew nothing of pity, and when he was angry, even the gods were afraid.

Of course, the standard for brutality had changed over

time. In the twenty-first century, Achilles might actually be comparatively sane. But somehow she doubted it. Somehow she knew that he'd only gotten worse.

I've seen mortals do horrifying things. Impale people on pikes, stretch their limbs until the joints blew apart. I looked into the eyes of those torturers, searching for just one spark of recognition, wondering if it was really him, come back again and again.

"When the Cyclops jumped me in England, they weren't going for the kill. That's probably why I got the better end of it. They wanted to take me alive, so I could be Hera's Achilles-dowsing rod. So what do we do?" Odysseus asked. "Do we find him first? I can take you there. We could leave now."

"No. Nobody finds him." There was no point. He'd never fight for their side; there wouldn't be enough blood to sate him. He would fight for Hera, for glory, and a place amongst the gods. If they went looking, they'd lead their enemies right to his doorstep. "I don't want any part of him. He's mad, and evil. He always was."

Odysseus sighed. "No, he wasn't. He was just an angry boy, caught up in your struggle. Like we all were."

Athena nodded and bit her tongue on disagreement. He had known Achilles better than she had, after all.

"What about you? Why are you looking for your weapon? Planning to 'eat' Hera and Poseidon before they can eat you? You trying to save your own skin?"

She sighed. "It wouldn't be the worst thing to say yes. It would be nice if Hermes didn't have to die." She chuckled.

"What's so funny?"

"Just something Hermes said back in Utah. He called us 'the last of the sane gods' and said I had my cape of Justice on again. Seemed stupid. But after what Hera did in Chicago . . ." She looked down, and her voice grew somber.

"The world doesn't need that running around, I suppose. The world has enough of *that* as it is. So, yes. I'll take her out. I'll handle my own, before they wreck anything else.

"We need to get out of here." She struck her fist against the softening wood of the picnic table. How long did it take to switch loads on a truck anyway? She didn't even know where Craig was. Eyeballing the red Freightliner, she wondered just how hard it would be to steal it and how fast it would go.

"Don't," Odysseus said. "Just, don't. We're not hijacking a semi."

Athena smiled. Then she coughed. At first it was just a light tickle in her throat, but it got worse. She felt something moving, coming loose down in her right lung. It itched. She coughed harder, until she was bent over, hacking.

"Athena!" Odysseus held her by the shoulder. She took great, whooping breaths; her coughs sounded like someone ripping a bed sheet.

Finally she sputtered. She'd managed to dislodge it and work it up her throat. Her fingers fished around on her tongue, and held the feather in front of her face.

Just one, and mostly white, with a little brown speckling at the edges. Only the shallowest bit of the left side had any blood or tissue stuck to it. The rest was just wet.

"Don't get upset," she said shakily. "It's just a small one. Hardly attached to anything."

Odysseus stared at it before she crushed it in her fist and flung it off into the grass.

"How long do you think you have?" he asked.

Athena smiled, still a little breathless. "Forever."

13

THINGS YOU LOSE

The day after the Halloween party, Cassandra sat around the kitchen table with Andie and Henry. Henry crunched through M&M's with circles under his eyes so dark they looked like bruises. Andie and Cassandra split their third Kit Kat. Andie's leg bounced up and down at a jittery pace, and even though she'd showered her costume makeup off an hour ago, Cassandra knew she still looked dead.

"This is too much chocolate on too little sleep," Henry muttered. But he reached back into the bowl anyway.

"You should stop. Dad wants you to help rake the yard later."

"Ha-ha," Andie said between chews.

"You wanna help too?"

Andie dropped the candy bar. "Yeah, sure." She sighed, and stretched in the chair. "I'll tell you one thing. That is the last time I lace these bad boys up into a corset. How did women wear those, anyway?"

Nobody answered. Henry's eyes drifted over Andie's chest and he looked almost disappointed by the news. Cassandra kicked him in the shin.

She glanced out the window while Andie and Henry talked about taking naps. The day was gray, pale, and disgusting. Leaves shedded off of the trees like pieces of dead skin and frost clung to the brown grass and frozen dirt. Everything was so cold. Cold to the point of cracking.

Henry stood and turned on the TV on the kitchen counter, just a small-screen Panasonic their mother liked to listen to while she cooked. It was tuned to CNN and they were broadcasting more coverage of the attack in Chicago. This time it was footage taken from someone's camera phone. The video was shaky, shot while running backwards. The collapsed building went in and out of frame, only one half of it visible through the clouds of dust.

"Can you change that? It's pretty much the last thing I want to see." She still didn't know why Hermes and his sister had blown up the warehouse. Not for sure. But he sure as hell hadn't seemed very sorry about it when she'd seen him.

Henry turned the whole thing off and leaned over the sink to look out the window.

"Hey, it's Aidan."

Cassandra stood just in time to see his head pass by the glass, a few seconds before he knocked and came through the front door. His eyes found hers and he smiled. There wasn't a scratch on him. He was safe. She hadn't realized how scared she'd been. Her heart thumped like she'd run a mile.

"Aidan!" Cassandra's dad walked down the hall and clapped him on the shoulder. "You're just in time to rake."

He sipped his coffee and raised his brows at the rest of them in the kitchen. "With so many bright-eyed helpers it should only take a few hours."

"Sure thing, Tom." Aidan smiled. "Do you have leaf bags?"

"In the garage. I'll go get the rakes. You guys meet me out there in five minutes."

After ten pulls on her rake, Cassandra felt ready to fall over. They were spread out in the backyard, dragging damp brown and yellow leaves into sad-looking piles. Wetness made the piles heavy and flat, and far too cold to jump in.

"Here, let's get this one." Aidan handed her a leaf bag and she held it open while he used their two rakes to gather leaves and stuff them inside. Cassandra looked over her shoulder at her dad, who saw and flashed a smile.

"It feels like lying now," she said.

"What does?"

"Not telling my parents. It didn't before, because it didn't feel real. But Hermes was real last night. They're really here. So now it feels like lying."

"The less they know, the safer they'll be." He didn't look at her when he said it.

Will they really be? Or will the gods blast through them whether they know or not, if they get in the way?

"Cassandra?"

"Yeah?" She let go of the bag and took her rake back to start the next pile.

"We should think about leaving soon."

Her rake stopped. There was no pretending that she hadn't heard, and really no pretending that she hadn't known, deep down. Not in the dark space in her mind but someplace lower: in her heart, or the pit of her stomach. She looked again at her dad, and at Andie and Henry. They were throwing leaves at the dog, who barked and raced around them in circles. Her mom watched through the kitchen window while she put a casserole together for lunch.

She and Aidan would have to leave. To run. She didn't know why she felt so shocked; it wasn't like they'd be able to hide in Kincade. It wasn't like they could make a stand there. Not against what was coming.

"When can we come back?" she asked.

"I don't know."

"Will they be safe here? Will they go after them anyway, even if we're gone?"

"I don't know. But it's their best chance."

"When?" she asked, and held her breath. Whatever he said would be too soon. Too abrupt and cold.

"I thought after this, we could go to my house and figure it out."

A tear slipped down her cheek. "Why is this happening?"

Aidan lowered his eyes. "I wish I had answers, or better things to tell you. If it was anything else, I could stop it." He clenched his teeth. "But I can't. Believe me when I tell you, running away isn't my style."

The breeze whistled through Cassandra's hair. It smelled like winter. Like change and dying things. She searched the gray sky for the sun and couldn't find it.

"What am I going to say to them? They're not going to understand, Aidan."

He put his arms around her and tears slid down her cheeks.

"I hate this," he whispered. "And I hate them."

Cassandra leaned against his shoulder and stared at her family.

"I'll kill every one of them, I promise. And I'll give you your life back, as soon as I can."

———

The light in Aidan's bedroom was scant, silvery, and indirect, filtered through layers of clouds before it hit the window. Long, dark curtains blocked most of it, and they hadn't turned on the bedside lamp. Aidan paced quietly in front of his open closet, like he wasn't sure where to begin, and Cassandra didn't push. If she didn't push, maybe the moment would drag out, and everything would go away on its own.

"I think we should go south, find the coast. Athena doesn't care for the sea; she might avoid it." He stopped, swallowed.

"If you think so."

"I don't know what to think. It's a guess, and a wild one. I don't have any idea what my sister might or might not do anymore."

The muscles in Cassandra's arms and back ached from raking and from plain old fatigue. It didn't matter where they went. They were going away. She felt numb and exhausted. Aidan would have to drag her along, wherever he decided to go. She'd asked him when they could come back and he'd said he didn't know. But they were running from gods. Gods. They'd never be able to come back.

I'll never come back. This life is over.

Aidan started to move suddenly, like someone had flipped a switch. He grabbed clothes out of his closet and stuffed them into a black duffel bag; he emptied his drawers of socks and t-shirts and shoved them in too.

"I'm going to have to get money out," he said. He'd paused at his desk, his eyes moving over his things: his laptop covered in stickers, a few paperbacks, a small curved snake figurine made of pewter with gold gemstone eyes. His parents had gotten it for him at a festival they'd gone to. Cassandra watched him slide it into the duffel with his laptop.

"I should write them a note. Tell them we went to—tell

them we went somewhere together and will be back in a few days. Maybe then they won't call the police until we're too far to be caught." He flipped open a notebook and grabbed a pen. "You should write one for your parents too."

His hands shook, and he put pen to paper three times before setting it down and taking a breath.

It's hard for him. But he's had to do it before. He's had to love people and leave them before they knew what he was.

She didn't know whether that made it easier. Whether it made it better or worse.

"I'm scared," she said.

"I know. But you're brave too."

"Am I? Is that why I want to call you a liar? Why I want to run through that door, and down the stairs, and go back home like nothing ever happened?"

He turned and knelt at her feet. He would be with her. She wouldn't be alone. But she wanted Andie and Henry. She wanted her parents. Aidan's hands rubbed along the sides of her legs, like he was trying to warm her after coming in from the cold.

"We'd better get going back to your place," he said. "And we'd better hope that Henry is napping."

"Why?"

"Because my parents have both of the cars. We're sort of going to have to borrow his."

Cassandra laughed humorlessly. "He's going to kill us."

14

CONVERGENCE, OR,
WELCOME TO KINCADE,
EMERGENCY EXITS ONLY

He cut a welcome figure on the side of the highway. Athena sighed with relief. She knew he could take care of himself.

Hermes lifted an arm in greeting. Odysseus waved and tucked his poor, mortal neck in like a turtle's against the light, cold mist, too light to complain about, just cold enough to make him miserable. They'd only been walking in it for a few miles, since their ride on Route 17 had let them out, but Odysseus looked about ready to catch pneumonia.

"Took you long enough," Hermes said when they reached him. The orange polo shirt and black jacket he wore were damp and clinging, but he didn't shiver. Neither did Athena, standing tall in her wet, filthy cardigan.

"It annoys the hell out of me that I'm the only one uncomfortable." Odysseus tucked his hands under his arms while Athena greeted her brother.

"You're not the only one uncomfortable." Athena had

been coughing off and on since they'd parted ways with Craig in Buffalo. And Hermes' bones looked ready to burst through the skin. Odysseus nodded.

"How did you know where to wait?" Athena asked.

"There aren't too many ways into this city," Hermes replied. "I played the odds." He eyed Odysseus as he stood, teeth chattering. "Let's get going. I picked up some new threads for you. They're back at my room."

"Your room?" Athena asked.

"It's a Motel 6. I figured that would be an appropriate compromise between the Hilton I deserve and the dirt burrow you'd have wanted me to dig."

He stalked off with attitude to spare. Athena and Odysseus followed, smirking.

"There isn't even a Hilton here," Athena said.

"Believe me, I know."

They walked quickly up the side of the highway, the Motel 6 sign visible a quarter mile up the road. When they reached it, Hermes let them into the room and got them towels from the bathroom to sponge off with. Odysseus skinned gratefully out of his wet jacket and went in to take a shower without another word. Hermes tossed Athena a bag from Nordstrom. She looked inside and promptly threw it back.

"There are sequins," she growled.

"Not on everything! Besides, you can't walk around looking like *that*." He pushed the bag back. It tipped over and spilled its contents on the garishly colored bedspread. There were a few t-shirts and sweaters and a couple pairs of jeans. The sequins comprised only a small patch on the front of one of the shirts, winking at her in red and silver.

Athena sighed and ran the white terry towel over her hair.

"Thanks, Hermes."

"Don't mention it. How was the road?"

Through the bathroom wall she heard the shower turn on. The road. He asked about it so innocently. What would she tell him? That everything had been screwed? That she'd almost fallen to one of Aphrodite's plots? That she'd allowed herself to cross a line with Odysseus that should have been a brick wall? No. Some things could be omitted. She looked at Hermes regretfully. If he'd have been with them, none of it would have happened, and there wouldn't be this uncomfortable tension.

Athena leaned against the dresser. "Aphrodite sent someone to kill me." She shrugged. "Well. 'Kill' might be a strong word. I suppose she just sent someone to maim me."

"Aphrodite?"

"Yes. Why do you sound so surprised? You knew she was with Hera."

Hermes shifted his legs and pulled a pillow out from under the comforter. "I didn't know that. *You* thought so because of the glamour, but we didn't know."

"And you didn't think so."

He shrugged. "Are you sure it was her?"

"Yes."

"How do you know?"

She bit down hard to keep from snapping. When had she become so easy to doubt? Why didn't he just trust her? The details came forth slowly, laid out with logic from a careful tongue.

Don't argue. Please don't argue.

"She used the only weapon she ever had. Lovesickness. Obsession. And it *felt* like her. Deceptive and wild."

Hermes shrugged again. If he did it one more time, she'd reach out and throttle him.

"She was never like that to me. She was always sweet and kind."

"Of course she was. You're a boy."

"And you're not?"

Athena snorted. He was right. There was no reason for Aphrodite to dislike her. She wasn't beautiful like Aphrodite, and she didn't fall in love. There should've been no contention between them. But they'd disliked one another anyway. Even before the debacle with the damned golden apple.

"She told me once that she could make me fall in love with the Minotaur if she wanted." Athena smiled, thinking back to that day, when some slight too small to remember had brought them nose to nose yet again. "She said I'd have ugly little Minotaur babies and suckle them at my breast. Then she'd looked at my bronze breastplate and said the poor things would probably starve." And then she'd gone, in a flash of gold gauze and white skirts. She could say awful, childish things, but no one thought less of her. Certainly not any of the gods. Even Hera would go to Aphrodite when she needed something beautiful.

But I wouldn't. Her ways were never my ways.

"See, now that sounds more like her. Petty and pouty, but harmless." Hermes grinned. "I mean, you never did have little Minotaur babies, did you?" He laughed at the look on her face. "When you said Aphrodite was with them, I thought she'd only be along for the ride. That she went to Hera for shelter, because she was afraid."

"I'm sure she is afraid. Like you were afraid."

Hermes looked away, but she hadn't meant to shame him. They were all afraid in varying degrees.

"I wasn't sure I'd find you here. I thought you might hide the witches and go. Or maybe . . ." She shook her head.

"Maybe join up with Stepmommy and Uncle?" Hermes' smile faded fast. "Don't think it didn't cross my mind. But after what she did to Circe's coven . . ." His hands tightened around the pillow on his lap. "I don't have a lot of loyalty to mortals anymore. But they were our people. Or as close to it as we've got. And she killed them. I want to live forever, but not as a monster."

Athena smiled. "I'm glad you're here."

"Right, right, right. But enough about my temporary cowardice. If you're sure it was Aphrodite, then I believe you."

"I'm sure. The boy she sent was mad for her. She wanted me out of the way and Odysseus brought to them."

Hermes nodded toward the bathroom and the running shower. "What do they want with him, anyway?"

"It's just like before. He knows where their weapon is. They're looking for Achilles."

"Achilles, huh?" Hermes said with a lift of his eyebrows. He took in the information somberly, which was difficult. His entire existence had been apathetic and light. Now everything was a long struggle. Sometimes Athena could see him fight to keep his shoulders still, to keep from trying to shrug the gravity off.

"Well?" Athena asked. "You're thinking something."

Beside her, the bathroom door opened and Odysseus walked out without a shirt on. He tossed his towel underneath the sink and carried his bag to the bed, rifling through it for something to wear.

"Thinking something about what?" he asked. The gauze on his back and neck had been removed; large, puckered scabs disturbed the skin near his shoulder and down his spine. Circe's witches had healed him well, after the Cyclops attack. The scabs were a lot smaller than they could have been and there was no infection. But he would still carry the scars for the rest of his life.

Athena's eyes moved over the cuts with strange regret. They were no worse than the spear wounds he had taken in Troy. But in her mind they were a portent; she saw them widening, cracking open and bearing him down to the ground. They were a taste of what was to come, and she would survive just long enough to see him torn apart and dragged to Hades. When Odysseus looked back, she turned away.

That's my imagination. It's my fear playing tricks. Odysseus always finds ways to survive.

She put her hand to her head. It was cloudy with stupid shit and she needed to focus. The prophetess, the girl they sought, was only miles away now, and Athena couldn't even begin to remember where she'd tossed her game face.

Hermes sucked on his cheeks.

"I'm thinking the Fates have a hand in this," he said softly.

"What do you mean?"

"Well, they're looking for Achilles," Hermes reasoned. "And we just found Hector. At least I think so. Why don't you hit the showers and then I'll tell you everything."

Hector. He was Cassandra's brother, the crown prince of Troy, who would have become king had Athena and Hera not helped the Greeks to raze his city to the ground. He was Troy's greatest hero, the only one who could stand against Achilles for more than two minutes. Of course, in the end, Achilles had been greater. Hector was outlasted and ended up with a spear through his chest and his body desecrated, dragged behind the wheels of Achilles' chariot.

Athena reached up and cut through the vapor on the bathroom mirror. Her eyes stared back at her in the streak of silver.

I'm the one who lured him onto the battlefield that day. It was me who lied to him, who convinced him to face that madman. He never had a chance. I destroyed their world and now I'm going to ask them to save mine.

But that wasn't quite right either. She wasn't going to ask them. She was going to make them, whether they liked it or not.

She rolled her tongue against the roof of her mouth, which was already mostly healed. It hadn't turned into a sore after all. She felt only slight relief. More feathers would come. They would keep coming, until they filled up her lungs or twisted into her heart. They wouldn't stop until they killed her. It would be the end of a goddess. The end of a monster.

The mirror fogged up again, slowly blotting out her face. She pulled a dark gray t-shirt over her head, some designer thing with black swirling from the shoulder to the hip. Toweling her hair dry, she still saw traces of the purple she had dyed into it a year earlier. She was the commander of the apocalypse, and she had purple streaks growing out in her hair.

Her eyes blinked hard. There was no time for a bitching and moaning identity crisis, no matter how well deserved. She pulled open the bathroom door and walked out into the room, where Hermes and Odysseus were watching a re-broadcast of *Spartacus* on Starz. They were stretched out, one on each of the double beds, their hands behind their heads. When she came in, Hermes reluctantly turned the TV off.

"The witches are all right?" she asked.

"Hidden safe as houses," he replied. He flashed a winning smile. He was covering something up.

"What is it?" Athena asked.

"You're going to be pissed," Hermes said. "But trust me, you're lucky that I did it."

"Did what? You did something? I told you not to do anything until we got here." Her voice rose, and she talked more and more, aware that she was only filling space, trying to delay his delivery of yet another hiccup in their plans, another complication, another setback.

"Apollo is here."

The room went silent. Hermes and Odysseus waited, tense, for her reaction.

Apollo. Their half brother. God of the sun, god of prophecy. He'd fought against them in the Trojan War, but he was strong and smart. And unless something had changed drastically, he would never bow to Hera.

"Good," she said.

"Not exactly," said Hermes. "He's here protecting Cassandra. Apparently, from us." He let the rest of the story fall out of his mouth in a jumble, making sure to emphasize the fact that Apollo had tried to dye the cellar floor red with his innards. As he spoke Athena's eyes turned darker and darker.

"Do you know where he is?" she asked.

"Yes, but—"

Hermes and Odysseus exchanged looks and grabbed their jackets. They bolted through the door of the motel room after Athena, who was already halfway down the sidewalk.

Aidan and Cassandra took the long way back to her house, following the roads rather than cutting through yards and tree lines. She'd started walking that way, and he hadn't stopped her, even though they shouldn't waste the time. As they went he watched her from the corner of his eye even though she tried to keep her tears discreet.

Keep it together. He feels guilty enough as it is.

"I'm okay."

"You're not." He kept his hands forcibly in his pockets. "I wish there was more time. Or something else we could do."

"I know." It wasn't easy for him, either. She'd seen the deep breath he took before they left his house. One last breath of the Tide that clung to his blankets and clothes, the rose hip potpourri that Gloria put in bowls all over the upstairs.

"I should've left a different note." He'd left it under the glass of bamboo shoots in the middle of the kitchen table. Gloria would see it as soon as she came home. And her son would be gone. Cassandra slipped her hand through his arm, rested her chin on his shoulder.

"They're your parents. They'll understand." *But they won't. Because they won't really know. No more than mine will.*

"It didn't say anything I wanted to say. It didn't even say good-bye. It just said lies."

"I know." And she was sorry that she'd ever thought they weren't really his parents. "We'll come back someday and explain." She rested her head against him. "Don't we have to believe that?"

"Yeah. We do."

They walked slowly through a light mist that threatened to turn into light snow. Cassandra looked out through the trees. She'd come this way so many times. The deadfall stretched out on their left, a long, downhill path of grass where a tornado had gone through years before. It cut through the middle of the forest and no one had bothered to clear it, so the bones of downed trees lay across the ground, grown over with moss, fallen over at various angles. Cassandra always thought it looked too precise. Almost deliberate. But it was strangely beautiful. Another thing about Kincade to miss.

"Wait." Aidan stopped and put his hand over hers.

"What?" He didn't answer, but his grip tightened. Goose bumps worked their way up the back of her neck.

"Aidan, what is it?" He stared down into the deadfall and she followed his gaze. An owl sat quietly on a low branch. Another sat in the tree beside it. And another in the one after that.

Owls in the daytime. Shouldn't they be asleep?

She opened her mouth, but before she could speak, the feathers of the first owl began to seethe. Blood showed beneath the down, between the quills, and the bird started to shed feathers and skin in a grotesque waterfall.

Cassandra shut her eyes tight. When she opened them again, the owl was just an owl. Healthy, watching her with wide yellow eyes.

"Aidan?"

"She's here. And Hermes is with her. There's no point running."

The clearing flickered into view, the fallen trunks sketched across the ground like long hash marks in the mostly dead grass. Apollo and Cassandra stood on the other side, as if by magic, as if they'd been waiting. Athena put a cautious hand over Odysseus' chest.

"Don't worry," he said. "I won't run headfirst into anything."

Athena took a deep breath, trying very hard not to be

annoyed with Apollo before he even opened his mouth. It felt something like a snake trying to swallow an egg.

When she reached the tree line she walked past it without pausing, and her legs struck the cold earth confident and fast. Just fast enough to be threatening, to see whether he would twitch or give ground.

He didn't. He stood silent, his hands balled into fists at his sides, wearing jeans and a navy blue hooded sweatshirt. The hood covered most of his hair, but it was still visible across his forehead, bright gold. Steel blue eyes regarded her without blinking.

Athena almost smiled. Did they all look so handsome at first sight? She didn't think so. It was just him, beautiful even by a god's standards, forever the lord of the sun. He was apprehensive; she could see that in the way he stood, tense and ready for anything. But he was confident too. He thought he had the edge.

They were almost close enough to shake hands. In the electricity of the moment, the slight form of Cassandra was almost forgotten, behind and a few steps back.

Athena shifted her weight onto her hip.

"Apollo."

"It's Aidan now."

She snorted. "No, it isn't. And it never will be, no matter how many years you spend playing human house."

His eyes narrowed. It wasn't how she'd meant to start things. Confrontation was counterproductive, but angry words backed up in her throat. What was he doing here? Why was he, one of her favorite brothers, standing in her way?

Aidan took a deep breath. "Still the same, Athena, after all this time. Guess it was too much to hope that a few thousand years would've humanized you a little." His eyes flickered to her jeans, to her tattoos. She lifted her wrist to give him a better view.

"They're just costumes we wear. Like that sweatshirt of yours." She raised her chin. "Take off that hood. You look like a punk."

He smiled and shook his head, but he pushed it back. "Better?"

"It's a start."

"I hear you're dying," he said. "I can see what's happening to him"—he nodded toward Hermes, several feet behind her with Odysseus—"but what's your story?"

Athena glanced at the owls sitting all around them in the trees. Two more drifted in while they spoke.

"The owls. Their feathers. Choking me, worming through my guts." She shrugged. "What about you?"

He smiled. It was a smile of triumph. Her knee moved to take a step, whether forward or back she didn't know. She wanted to touch his face. She wanted to inspect him. She wanted to tear a branch off of one of the fallen trees and beat him until the blood flew.

"He's not dying." Athena felt Hermes and Odysseus move closer, crowding against her back for a better view.

It could be a bluff.

But it wasn't. Apollo was perfect, unblemished. She looked him over carefully, assessing him like a horse. How was it possible? How had he escaped? And then the darker questions: Could it be duplicated? Could it be taken from him?

"I know why you're here," he said. "And the answer is no. So I want you to go, before you bring worse trouble."

"Worse trouble?" Athena studied him. He was no natural-born liar. His eyes told her everything in the space of a second. "You've been hermit-crabbing in the mortal world for too long. You don't know anything."

Certainly not as much as he wanted her to think he did. He knew they were dying. He knew she wanted Cassandra.

But he doesn't know why. He doesn't know about Poseidon, or Hera, or Aphrodite. He probably doesn't even know about the war.

"Brother. The worse trouble will come knocking, with or without me."

"I said no, Athena."

"Don't be an idiot. You don't get to say no." She looked at Cassandra. "And neither does she."

At the mention of her, he stepped in front of Cassandra, blocking her from view, and stared at Athena, hard as nails.

"Neither one of us is going to give," he said.

Athena smiled, but didn't mean it. She knew what was going to happen.

I don't want to hurt you. She looked at his shoulders, at the strength of his arms. *And I'd rather you not hurt me.*

"I suppose compromise, for a god, is a very dirty word."

"Cassandra," he said softly. "Run home."

His attack was fast enough to impress even Hermes. He sprang without thinking, without tensing, without giving any clues, and the lunge caught her by surprise. He plowed into her rib cage and threw both of them halfway down the deadfall before Hermes and Odysseus even had time to shout.

When they struck the ground, he broke away and rolled quickly onto his feet.

Athena was up a second later. She was getting tired of acts of desperation. It felt like they were all they had left.

"What are you trying to do? Do you really think you can beat me? You never could before."

He bared his teeth. "That was before you started spitting up owl pellets." Her eyes narrowed. "But I don't want to. Just turn around and go."

"I can't. Cassandra is the key."

"The key to what? She doesn't have anything you can use. She can call a coin and tell you the weather."

"You're lying again. You really suck at it."

"She's just an ordinary girl."

"Never. She's a prophet. Thanks to you."

He lunged, but this time she was ready; her hands caught hold of his head and twisted him around. He was no human, and no Nereid; his neck was strong and close to unbreakable. But she did manage to pull him off balance and brought a knee up into his back. She felt his grimace between her palms before he jerked loose.

Up the deadfall, Hermes and Odysseus moved closer, and Cassandra moved beside them like they'd forgotten all about one another. Athena took a deep breath, careful not to wince. A swelling bruise had already bloomed up around her ribs from their trip down the trees. When Apollo circled, she backed off. There was something in his eyes she didn't like.

"How far are you willing to take this?" she asked.

"Until you go, or one of us is in pieces."

She frowned. Dying was one thing. Spending the rest of her time alive with her legs and torso in different time zones was another.

He charged again and reached into the grass for a large stone. It struck the top right side of her head with a sickening, dull crack, and hot blood flowed into her hair. She fell to the ground.

She heard Odysseus scream and Hermes yell at him to stay back, but she couldn't reply. She lay frozen with shock, watching the rock rise and fall, feeling it strike with sharp thuds against her skull.

He's killing me.

Odysseus would see her head crushed into the grass, unrecognizable. Just a wet, red mess.

He can't kill me.

Or perhaps he could. She was already dying, after all, and that wasn't supposed to be possible either. Maybe the rules had changed completely.

Apollo raised the rock again, and Athena screamed. But it wasn't a scream of fear or pain. She screamed at the sight of her blood on the stone. She wasn't dead. She wasn't anywhere near dead. Her arm came up, grabbed Apollo's, and threw him off to one side. When she lifted herself to one knee, she felt the right side of her head flop down, bleeding and torn open, but the skull was intact. She heaved herself to her feet and threw him again. Then she grasped his throat and lifted him like a fish from a stream.

"No!"

Cassandra, running down through the fallen trees.

"No! Let him go!" She stopped just short of Athena. Aidan had dropped the rock and struggled nervously as his sister's fingers squeezed, threatening to tear through the skin of his neck.

"Let him go," Cassandra demanded. "Let him go, now!"

After a moment of consideration, Athena dropped him and he fell in a heap. Cassandra darted forward and wrapped her arms around him.

"You were supposed to run the other way," he said.

"You shut up," Athena snapped. Blood dribbled liberally down her shoulder, matting down the hair on the right side of her head. She looked like the victim in a Robert Rodriguez film. Cassandra looked at her with wide eyes. Mixed expressions of awe and revulsion rippled across her face.

She thinks she knows me. She just can't remember from where. She's not like Odysseus. She's still asleep.

Even as she held Aidan, there was confusion in Cassandra's eyes. Of course she was confused. She'd just seen him bludgeon someone with a rock, and run to his defense afterward.

"Athena," he said. "Don't hurt her."

She glanced at him with irritation. "Ridiculous words, coming from you."

You were the one who cursed her in the first place. You gave her the gift of sight and then made her never be believed. And now she kneels at your side, protecting you from me, who could twist her in half.

The innocence in Cassandra's eyes made her want to scream. The blind affection in how she held him. There was something so sick about it. That she didn't know.

"Don't, sister. I love her."

"I notice the 'sister' only comes out when you want something." She crossed her arms. "She doesn't even know who you are."

"I know who he is," Cassandra said. "He's Aidan Baxter."

Athena snorted.

"But he used to be called Apollo. Who are you?"

"You used to know."

Cassandra's brow knit. "What do you mean?"

"Athena, don't." He started to rise, but Athena put him down with a finger.

Don't blame me for this. You found her, made her love you again. I'm sure it was done with the best of intentions. But you're an idiot if you thought it wouldn't all blow up in your face.

"I mean, you aren't you. But back when you *were* you, you would've known who I am." They hadn't come all this way to find half a prophetess. They needed her whole. They needed Cassandra of Troy.

Blood dripped down Athena's cheek, warm against her skin. Owls in the trees hooted absently. She gestured vaguely toward Cassandra's body.

"This. It's empty. Hollow. There's a hole inside you in the shape of a girl." And even then it didn't look special. Athena had hoped for more. Some flag or shining space to let her know what Cassandra was capable of.

"What are you talking about?"

"Don't you deserve to know who you are? Isn't that justice?" She looked at Odysseus, at his throat, at the heart in his chest. Make her remember. Isn't that what Demeter said? Make her remember, and she'll be much more than that. Wheels turned inside her head. "I mean, if there was something about me that I didn't know, I'd want to know. Wouldn't you?"

Apollo struggled to his feet and pulled Cassandra up with him. He put himself between them. Futile. Silly. Athena's wrists tingled. It felt like springs had formed in the balls of her feet. She knew what she had to do.

And I'll do it. Even though it's cruel. Even though I hate to. There's no one else.

"Let me tell her, at least," Apollo said. "Please."

"You turned me into a cherry snow cone." Athena gestured to her bleeding head. "Why should I do you any favors?" She looked at Cassandra. A pale, scared girl with long brown hair, the tips of her ears and nose starting to turn red from the cold. Odysseus reached for Athena's arm and she turned to him.

"It was better for you, wasn't it?" she asked Odysseus. "After you woke up?"

He knew what she was up to; she could see that. "I didn't wake up quite like this." He glanced at Cassandra. "Maybe it would be better, if he explained first."

Athena looked at Hermes, who hung his head. She sighed. "This isn't the Cassandra we're looking for. It's only half. If there's a less unpleasant way to make that happen, you've got thirty seconds to think of it."

No one spoke, and Athena gritted her teeth. "Look, I wish we didn't need her at all. I'm not a fucking tyrant. I don't want to turn someone's world on its ear."

She looked at Odysseus, but he said nothing. She turned to Hermes.

"Would you hold him, please?" She nodded toward Apollo. Then she smiled sadly at Cassandra.

The soft brown hair. That petite, lanky frame. I remember you now, standing with your sister on the walls of Troy. Watching your family die with a stone face. So brave. I'm ashamed that I forgot. And now I'm sorry that you'll remember.

"What are you doing?" Cassandra backed up as Athena advanced.

"Don't be afraid." Beside them, Apollo struggled in Hermes' grip, but it was feeble. He knew when he was beat. It was just more of a show for Cassandra's benefit.

"You're a goddess." Cassandra smiled shakily. She raised her brows at Athena's clothes. "With tattoos and a faded t-shirt. I saw you through Aidan's skin. The feathers."

"Cassandra, don't say anything!"

Athena smiled. So much for only predicting the weather. "We need your help."

"Help with what? What's going on?"

"Stop backing up. I don't want to feel like a wolf stalking a rabbit."

Cassandra scowled. "Then stop stalking. What are you talking about? What didn't Aidan tell me?"

"Do you really want to know?"

Aidan jerked toward her. "Cassandra. Don't."

"Don't what?" she asked. "Why not? Would someone just please tell me what's going on?"

"That would take too long." Athena moved forward. Her hands closed around Cassandra's throat and squeezed. "Don't be afraid."

15

RESURRECTION

The struggle was brief. What chance did she have, anyway, against a goddess?

Cassandra clawed at the hands around her neck. Her mouth worked frantically, trying to suck in just the tiniest bit of air. It hurt. Beneath the panic it burned and stung. Her lungs felt like they'd grown claws and were shredding her rib cage. Aidan yelled something, her name or maybe just expletives. His voice faded as her ears failed and the sky went black. It was like being filled up with ink.

Athena kept a steady grip. The impact of the girl's fists against her shoulders and arms didn't matter at all. She looked Cassandra in the eyes and tried to keep her expression soft. Not angry. Not gleeful. The whole thing would have been easier had a third of her scalp not been hanging off the side of her head. It must have been a terrifying image to die to.

Behind them, Hermes had his hands full trying to hold Apollo. His bellowing had driven all of the owls high up into the trees. But it didn't matter. The life in Cassandra's eyes flickered. The pulse beneath Athena's fingers slowed, then stopped. She waited a few more seconds, then laid the girl carefully on the damp, frozen ground.

"Odysseus," she said, and he darted forward onto his knees. He would know what to do; he'd be ready, had known what she was up to. He tilted Cassandra's head back.

"I hope you didn't do any damage to the windpipe," he muttered. Then he sealed his mouth over hers. Once. Twice. He gave her breath, but there was no sign of life.

"Chest compressions," Hermes said. "Do you know the count?"

"It's fifty to two," Aidan said. "Or is it fucking thirty? I can't remember!" He dragged his hands through his hair, pacing wildly. "Cassandra, wake up. Oh god, you bitch!" He spun on Athena and shoved her hard.

"Shut up." Odysseus pressed down on Cassandra's chest, elbows locked, counting.

Time stretched out. Athena tried to stay out of Apollo's way, her eyes on Cassandra. It seemed that she should've come back already.

Every second she stayed dead felt longer. Doubt crept into Athena's chest and caught in her throat. Cassandra's lips had turned a chill purple. Her skin seemed paler. A thin haze of mist collected on her cheeks. She was sixteen, murdered in the middle of a forest, dressed in a long, khaki jacket and a red sweater. Two thousand years ago, she'd been nineteen, murdered as a slave in a land a sea away from her home, an axe buried in her chest.

Breathe. Breathe, dammit! We need you, and three gods are willing it, so BREATHE!

"I think I heard something." Odysseus leaned in close to her mouth, his eyes wide and excited. "Yeah. Come on, girl, pick it up." He pressed down on her chest again, lightly. The color was coming back into Cassandra's skin. Her eyelids fluttered when he rubbed her hands.

"Pulse is back online." He looked up at Athena, out of breath. "Next time you're going to do that, you might give more of a heads up. For the record, I don't know the ratio for doing full CPR."

"What does it matter? You did it," Hermes said. He shook his head. "I thought you'd killed her."

Apollo rushed to Cassandra and drew her onto his lap. Tears wetted his cheeks and he stroked her hair.

Odysseus rose and put a brief hand on his shoulder. There was a surprising amount of empathy in the gesture and Athena frowned. To Odysseus, what she'd done must seem monstrous.

Apollo gently touched Cassandra's face and smoothed her hair back. Against his warmth, color began to return to her cheeks and dark bruises blossomed. They circled her throat in a broad collar; she'd be wearing scarves and turtlenecks for the next few weeks. Swallowing and talking was going to be a real bitch too, at least for a couple of days.

"Cassandra? Can you hear me?"

Cassandra's eyes stared into the distance, unfocused and just shy of blank. Then she blinked, and Athena exhaled.

The eyes that looked back at her were the eyes of Cassandra of Troy.

The world came back fast. Trees and water and sky splashed in buckets across the darkness. And not just before her eyes, which fluttered open. The world drenched her brain too, a whole other world, of yellow sand and white brick, days spent in woven dresses and sitting at looms. Images of bronze shields and sharpened spears, of her brother laughing in front of a fire. The taste of goat meat in her mouth. It all soaked in, colder than the ground beneath her head, another life immersed with her present one.

"Cassandra? Can you hear me?"

She blinked. That voice. Apollo's voice. The god who had loved her. And cursed her. He was there. And he was Aidan. Memories linked together in her skull like pressed-together LEGOs.

"I can hear you."

Aidan kissed her hair. "You almost killed her," he said to Athena.

"I did kill her," Athena corrected. "And now she's herself again. Isn't that right?"

Cassandra tugged free of Aidan and got to her feet, trying not to wobble. Athena nodded, and Cassandra knew what she must see. The difference was slight, but it was there. The way she held her shoulders. A scant bit of stiffness in her spine. The awkward ease of youth had fallen away. Memories of another person, another life, had settled onto her like layers of snow.

"No, that's not right," Cassandra said. "But I do remember. Is that what you wanted? Athena?"

Athena exhaled. "You know me. Good. It's what we needed."

"It wasn't what I needed." Cassandra cocked her head and narrowed her eyes. "I saw you, once, on the battlefield below the wall. You threw a spear through four men. One was a boy I'd made jewelry for when we were children. He wasn't much more than a child when you cut him down. And you laughed."

Athena frowned. "I suppose it isn't fair to say that's not me anymore. Not when you've just remembered."

"No. It isn't."

"Cassandra." Aidan reached for her.

"Don't, Apollo." Cassandra shrugged him off, which wasn't hard. When she used his real name he recoiled like he'd been burned. She walked up the deadfall and back to the road.

"Are we just going to let her go?" Hermes asked.

"She needs time." *We've done enough to her for now. Give her a moment to put two lives together.* "When she's ready, she'll come looking for us, and we'll see what she can do. Until then, just keep an eye out. Make sure she's safe."

Apollo turned. "Stay away from her. Nothing's changed. If you try to use her, I'll find something that really will crack your head open."

Athena clenched her jaw. "Nothing's changed? Everything's changed. She won't want you within a mile."

"I was making it up to her. I wanted to make it right."

Athena shook her head. "How could you have righted a wrong she didn't know you committed? When could she have told you it was enough? That you'd paid for it, and been forgiven?" Gods. Forever making their own rules.

"This wasn't the way."

"We needed Cassandra of Troy. No one had any other suggestions."

Apollo glared at her. "Not even a shred of guilt. Minutes after you strangled an innocent girl. Everything is a means to an end with you."

"It was justice. She had the right to know who she was. And what you did to her."

"You hide behind justice. Athena knows best." He looked at them with disgust. "I'm glad you're dying. I wish that I was. It's what we all deserve."

Having one's head sewn back together hurt. A lot. Particularly when there was no anesthetic involved. Athena sat on the counter of the sink at the Motel 6 while Odysseus dragged black surgical thread back and forth through her scalp with a sterilized needle. The awkward tugging and stinging did nothing to improve her mood. She still seethed over Apollo, walking away like a kicked puppy, trying to make her feel guilty for doing what had to be done.

But was there another way? Maybe I was in too big a hurry.

She thought of Cassandra's eyes, the way their innocence had turned to bitterness. It was hard, and cold, and more than a little cruel.

"He's just like the girl," Hermes said from the bed on the other side of the room, where he lay lazily flipping through channels. "Apollo just needs time. Time to see the bigger picture."

We don't have the time that everyone seems to think we have.

She inhaled and felt the tickle of feathers.

I don't have the time.

"And shouldn't we be investigating why he's not dying?"

"Apollo can get bent," Athena snapped, and winced when Odysseus poked harder with the needle than he had to. "What?"

"Oh, come on," Odysseus groaned. "Are you two really so thick that you don't understand why he's doing this? Your war doesn't matter to him. The only thing that matters is Cassandra."

The needle slid through her skin again, tugged as he

made a knot. It would heal quickly; the makeshift stitches could come out in a day. Odysseus clipped the thread off and started to clean up. Red dots and wads of gauze and tissue moistened pink with blood and water decorated the sink. Athena turned and looked in the mirror. He'd done a good job. The stitches weren't even visible through her hair. She sighed.

"Apollo will fall in line once he realizes that Hera is coming for her. And for him. He's smart. And we've always been close, by godly standards. And," she said, arching her eyebrow at Odysseus, "I wouldn't put too much stock in his 'love.' The last time he loved her, he drove her completely bughouse. Remember that."

"I remember." He tossed reddened tissues into the trash. "But haven't you ever heard of atonement?"

"Great movie," Hermes supplied. "Better book."

Odysseus ignored him. "The way you grabbed her throat today—I've never seen anything like that from you. Maybe you should start thinking a little *less* about the big picture."

He refused to look at her while he finished cleaning, throwing away pieces of thread and wiping down the counter. The rejection stung like a tightly squeezing ball in her chest.

"How can you say that?" More words rose and died in her throat. The way he ignored her, the aversion in his eyes; it pierced like needles. She expected loyalty from him, if from no one else.

I need it. That's more the truth. I can't let him turn his back on me. It would hurt more than these stupid feathers.

Athena stalked across the room and slammed out the door. The air had turned colder since they'd come back and the mist had turned to snow; small, dense flakes hit her cheeks like tiny razors. Her feet struck the pavement as she paced, almost hard enough to crack it. She didn't know how long she was out there, turning ice into steam, before she heard the door open and Odysseus walked through it.

"Do you think any of this is easy? Dying? This stupid Twilight? You, Hermes, Cassandra—Hera and Poseidon will send all our worlds sliding off the edge and I'm the one holding on to the rope, so don't tell me not to think about the bigger picture! Thinking of the bigger picture is the only thing I can do these days."

"Don't give me that," Odysseus said. "This is exactly your element."

"What are you talking about?"

"I'm talking about what you did back in the woods. It was cruel, and that's just the way you wanted it. You got to be a god again. You're so bloody scared of being the tiniest bit human—"

"Bullshit. Hard choices have to be made. How can you accuse me of wanting to do that? Do you think I liked it?"

Odysseus took a breath. How must she look, her head full of sutures, still wearing the t-shirt soaked in blood? If she wanted to, she could tear his limbs off, one by one. He should be afraid of her. He always should have been. But he never was.

"That's not what I'm saying." His brows knit and his palms lay flat, trying to explain. "I know it needed to be done, believe me. But you used to be patient. Compassionate."

Athena exhaled. "Back then I had the luxury." She pressed her hands to the side of her head and wanted to squeeze, to reopen the stitches and scream. "But I know, I know. I came here to save her, to protect her, and instead I killed her in the first five minutes." Her arms fell to her sides. His words hung around her neck like lead. "I had to, you know. 'Make her remember, and she'll be more.' That's what Demeter said. Unless I misinterpreted the riddle." And maybe she had. The immediate battle was over, the adrenaline rush subsided, and she was so incredibly tired.

"At night I imagine feathers cutting through my insides," she said softly. "I see them, making their way to the surface, tearing me up before they tear me open. When they come through it's slow. They twist up and rise, like plants from soil." She laughed a humorless laugh. "I'm going to die, Odysseus. And when I do I'm going to look like a monster. I suppose you think that's fitting."

He stepped closer and took her by the elbows. Heat flowed into her from him in a powerful, strange wave. *This is what it feels like to want someone.*

"Look at me," he said, and pushed her hair back over her shoulder. "You're not going to die. If there's a way to survive, you'll find it. You always do."

"I thought the same thing about you not a day ago. But it might not be true anymore. So many things are different now." *Like us, standing here. With your hands on me. Like the feelings for you that I shouldn't feel.*

"You're right. Things are different."

"We're still goddess and hero."

"What if we're not? Just that." He smiled at her, his eyes soft.

"That's what we are, always." Her heart sped with curious hope. The urge to fall was utterly new and made her dizzy. He could catch her and hold her up. She knew he could.

If this is how Aphrodite feels every day, it's no wonder she's such an idiot.

"Always," he said, and let go of her arms.

———

Cassandra's head itched from the odd sensation of having one too many brains inside it, brushing against each other. Everything she remembered ordered and reordered, stacked and shuffled. It felt like her mind had grown longer and larger, that it stretched out behind her several thousand years.

The cloud of her breath puffed like steam from a train. The cold mist that had been falling for the last hour was slowly turning to sleet. It left icy trails in her hair. The only parts of her that felt warm were her neck and throat, which throbbed and ached underneath Athena's handprint bruises. She swallowed.

It hurts worse than strep. Worse than when I had it for a week in third grade.

Third grade. In third grade, she'd already been thousands of years old. She just hadn't remembered.

"Athena," she croaked. Blaming her was easy. It was her handprints wrapped around her neck. She was the one who had asked her if she wanted to know, without giving warning about what that might mean. And she was the one who'd lured her brother Hector to his death.

Hector.

Hector.

Henry.

The knowledge forced its way through her ears, and she stopped short; the sounds of her shoes slapping the slushy sidewalk cut off sharply. Hector, Troy's hero, was her brother, Henry. She could see him on the city wall, smiling as he pointed down into the market. She could see him throwing Lux's Frisbee.

And Andie too. With long hair, twisted through with hand-dyed ribbon. She'd taught Cassandra to use a bow. Her name had been—

"Andromache." Hector's wife. Henry's wife. Gross.

"Cassandra." Aidan. Apollo. She remembered him too.

"Are you—?" he asked.

"Don't ask if I'm all right. And don't tell me you're sorry." *Even if you are.*

He stuffed his hands in his pockets. "I wouldn't do that. It's stupid. I just—never knew what to do. How do you make up for driving someone out of their mind?"

"Do I look the same as I did before? Didn't it ever bother you?"

"You look more like her now," he said. "And it did bother me. It bothered me every day."

"Could've fooled me. Did fool me."

The wet sweatshirt on his shoulders looked like it weighed a million pounds. Of course it wouldn't, to a god. It wouldn't even be uncomfortable. They didn't feel the cold, or the heat. They didn't feel. Cassandra looked up into the gray sky, let the sleet hit her cheeks and melt onto her lips. It didn't taste of tears, just of cold, and she swallowed it down. The bruises made her wince but she didn't care. The cold water felt good. It eased the nausea of having an extra lifetime crowd in behind her eyes.

"I've always loved you. I looked for you for so long. After what I did. After you died."

"Was killed," she corrected. "I didn't just die. I was killed. They took me hostage and put an axe in me when I hit the Greek shore. Like a sacrifice." The memory made her shiver. It was real, but far away, and so strange to remember her own death. "You cursed me. It was your fault Troy fell. More than the Greeks'. Even more than your stupid sister's. You gave me prophecy and then made people think I was crazy." She glared at him. He didn't even look the same. Images of Apollo and Aidan danced over each other. The boy she loved and the god she hated. "And now you lied. You lied when you said you had no more secrets. You knew who I was the whole time! And never said anything. It's sick." Her throat tore every time she raised her voice, but she didn't care. Her head felt like it might explode.

He grabbed her shoulders. "Please. What was I supposed to say?"

"It might've been hard in the beginning, but not now. After I knew what you were, then you could've told me the truth." She hated him. Hated him for being what he was, for standing in front of her wearing the face she loved.

But I do love him. I love him even when I hate him. Even back then when he could do that to me. That's the worst part. Worse than dying. Worse even than our walls crumbling.

"I know," he said. "I know."

"You don't know anything. And I don't want to be with you anymore." She thought she wanted to see his face when she said it, that she wanted to see pain, but it only made her own hurt worse.

He turned away and put his hand on his head. For a second she thought he'd turn and leave.

"I can't—leave you alone yet. I'm sorry. But Athena and Hermes are still here."

That's right. I need you. I need a god, to keep other gods from ruining our lives again. But even then a sliver inside her was glad. He'd been so much a part of her. For so many thousand years. Cutting him out so fast felt like it would tear half her chest away.

"We aren't going to run from them anymore, are we?" she asked.

"I don't think we'd make it if we tried."

"So what do we do then? How do we keep my family safe? How do we keep them away from Andie and Henry?"

Aidan glanced up and she nodded. *Yes. I know them too.*

"Let me talk to Athena," he said. "Find out exactly what she's after. They want to make an ally of you. But I don't know why, or against what."

"We won't have much time to choose sides," she said, and suddenly knew it was true.

Aidan reached out hesitantly and touched her cheek. His hand was so warm and her heart thumped like it always had. She let it linger there for a moment, then brushed it away.

"Don't. It's not like that anymore."

"I love you," he said. "I made a mistake, a long time ago. It was a god's mistake, so it was big. But I'm sorry. I've been sorry for thousands of years."

He was sorry. But what did he know about time or consequences? How long could you hold a grudge when someone broke your life like an unwanted toy? Was a thousand years enough? Two?

"So you'll talk to them?" she asked. "And come back?"

"As soon as I can."

She reached out and pulled his wet hood over his head.

"You're still you," he said softly. "And I'm still me."

"I know," she said. *We are, and we aren't.* Her fingers trailed down the front of his sweatshirt. "Be careful."

He nodded. "I'm going to swing by my house first and tear up that note I left. I'll call you soon."

16

YOU CAN RUN

Leaves had already found their way back into the yard, blown in from the neighbors' or fallen down from the last clinging bunches high up in the maple branches. It was only a scattering. Their dad wouldn't make them rake again, but he'd be in the yard on his own next weekend, clearing out the last of them.

As Cassandra walked up the driveway, she tried to be unsurprised that the house was still her house. That she still remembered growing up in it, sliding down the banister and almost breaking her leg, and decorating sugar cookie reindeer with her mom, candy sprinkles spread out across the tabletop. It still felt like it was hers.

It's mine, like Troy is mine. And I'm me, and I'm not me.

She walked through the door and the heat inside immediately made her nose run. By the time she got a tissue from the bathroom across from the den, her fingers tingled and the sting of thaw bit the tops of her ears. Across the hall, machine-gun fire issued from the TV. The backs of Andie and Henry's heads sat above the brown suede of the couch while they watched a movie.

I saw you die. I was there on the wall when you fought Achilles.

The memory was completely clear. He'd fought so well, so bold and fast, that for an instant she'd thought her vision could be wrong and Hector would win. She'd hoped so, right until the moment he stumbled. Right until the moment Achilles' spear thrust into his chest. Andromache had screamed then, and Cassandra had wanted to cover her eyes. No one should have to remember the sight of their husband trying frantically to get a spear out of his chest while someone else drove it farther in.

She shivered hard, and wet, brittle clothes rattled on her body. Andie turned on the couch and her mouth dropped open.

"Kill the TV."

"What? What for?"

"Just do it." Andie spun off the couch. "My god, Cassandra, what happened? Henry, call the police and your parents." She pulled an afghan off of the hope chest and pulled Cassandra's jacket off of her shoulders before wrapping her in it.

"Cassandra? Jesus, what happened?" Henry lifted her chin. The bruises, black as an inner tube, circled all around her throat. The fact that they were finger marks was unmistakable.

"Don't call the police," Cassandra whispered. "And don't call Mom and Dad."

"What do you mean, 'don't call'? Look at you! What the hell happened?"

"I got in a fight."

"That's not a fight, Cassandra; that's someone trying to kill you. You have to report it. Do you know who it was?"

Someone did kill me. And someone brought me back.

"Where's Aidan?" Andie asked. Concern and fear etched her features in equal parts.

Can they know, somehow? Can they sense it?

But no. They were just afraid and thinking the worst.

Cassandra closed her eyes.

"Could you please just make me some tea? With honey?"

"You should take some Tylenol or something too," said Henry, and went to get it from the bathroom.

Cassandra followed Andie to the kitchen and pulled out a chair to sit. She listened to drawers and cabinets open and shut. The kitchen smelled like melted cheese and butter from the casserole they'd had for lunch.

"Where are Mom and Dad?"

"Grocery store and errands in town," Henry replied. He ducked under Andie's arm on his way to the sink to fill the teapot and Andie turned the wrong way and got honey on his shirt. It was ridiculous just how effectively they could get in each other's way, how one innocent arm movement from Andie could manage to entangle her in Henry practically up to the shoulder.

It's how they always were. The prince and the Amazon fell in love while wrestling and never really stopped.

At least until the gods had run their lives into the dirt and killed them. And now here they were: Henry her brother again, and Andie her friend. It felt unfair. They'd paid for it once already. It should have been enough for a hundred happy lives.

But that's not how it works. Fate has its way. Fair or unfair doesn't matter. Hector told me that once.

"Here. It's pomegranate antioxidant something or other."
Andie set down a steaming mug of purplish tea. It smelled
of bitter citrus and dark bits of leaves swirled near the bottom. The heat of the ceramic mug sank into Cassandra's
sluggish fingers.

Henry stared as she sipped. Andie briefly looked into the
teapot like she might pour herself a cup, but then set it
back on the stove to cool. Neither one of them seemed to
know what to do. They waited quietly, watching but not
really watching, in that way people have when they know
you have something unpleasant to tell them.

*I don't have to tell them at all. Whatever happens next, I
could leave them here. Leave them out of it.*

Only she didn't think she could. There were things at
work, threads being pulled that wound around and around
them. It was almost visible, thin as gossamer, draped over
their heads when the light hit just right.

"What would you say if I told you we aren't who we
think we are?"

"What?" Henry asked. "Cassie, what happened to your
neck? Who did that?"

Cassandra swallowed her tea and felt honey coat the
bruises.

"Athena did that," she said. "A goddess did that."

"Like Aidan." Andie pulled out the chair beside her and
sat. "A god, like Aidan. Which one?"

"His sister." Cassandra nodded. "You'd know that, though,
if you were really you." She winced. It was almost exactly
what Athena had said.

"His sister? The one from the jungle?"

"No. It was Athena. And Hermes was there too."

Andie looked at Henry; Cassandra waited until he'd sat
down in the chair opposite and had Lux's head on his knee.

"I'm not just Cassandra Weaver. You're not just Andie Legendre. That's why I've been seeing the things I have. They've been looking for us. Me mostly, but she'll use you too."

Andie tried not to look skeptical and failed. But Cassandra was patient.

"Listen. Your name used to be Andromache. His used to be Hector. Past lives, get it?" She stopped abruptly when her voice got too loud. Talking loud still felt like coughing up a crumpled ball of aluminum foil. They didn't believe her, and why should they? The only way to make it real would be to strangle them and bring them back from the dead. And she wasn't about to try that.

But Athena will. I have to get them away from here. Away from her.

"Andromache," said Andie softly, trying it out in her mouth. "And Hector. From Troy." She paused. "Wait. I totally saw that movie. And this guy is no Eric Bana." She shoved Henry in the shoulder.

"This isn't a joke. Look at my neck. They did this to wake me up. So I'd remember being the other Cassandra. So they could use me for something. They'll do the same thing to you."

They stared at the blackening fingerprints around her windpipe. "You remember being . . . the other Cassandra?" Henry asked.

She nodded. "And I remember you. When you were Hector. It's true. I'm not crazy."

"What—what are they going to use you for?" Andie asked.

"I don't know. Aidan's trying to find out." She didn't tell them what he'd done to her back in Troy. There was so much to tell.

And it doesn't matter. Not in the middle of everything else. Not even when it feels like my heart's stopped beating.

She took another sip of tea. It had cooled, or maybe her throat had gotten warmer. The purplish liquid swirled in the bottom of the mug; leaves and bits of flower floated and swayed in suspended patterns, like drifting seaweed. Cassandra watched as the pattern became less random, as the leaves strung together into shapes. An open, screaming mouth and long, drenched hair. She blinked and tried to unsee it, but couldn't. It was like seeing the hidden shape in a Magic Eye puzzle, or catching the shape of Elvis in a grilled cheese sandwich. Once you saw it, it was all you could see.

"Is it cold?" Andie asked. "Do you want me to nuke it? Or make you more?"

Cassandra glanced up. When she looked into the mug again, the face was gone, blown apart.

"No, I—"

Water coated her eyes. Bubbles churned against her cheeks and her own hair found its way into her mouth and choked her. Someone was holding her under. Her lungs felt ready to bleed.

It's not me. It's someone else.

She took a deep breath and her lungs filled with air. She was safe, in the kitchen, her back firmly planted against the wood of the chair.

It's just a vision. No different than any other.

But this was monstrous, seen through a blurry surface, like a windshield sheeted with rain. The air smelled of moss and wet rocks, of freezing saltwater. The only light seemed to be light reflected off of water; it danced over every surface and made her dizzy. They were in some kind of cave. Or a cove, in the cliffs.

She felt Andie and Henry's hands on her arm and shoulder. They asked questions, but she didn't understand them. Their voices were muffled and echoed. They might have been shouting through a cement wall.

In the center of the cave a hole of dark, greenish water rippled. Then the surface exploded and a girl was tossed out with a wave, thrown onto the stones. The sound of her slapping against the rock hurt Cassandra's bones. The arms that threw her were just visible inside the retreating water: slimy and scaled and cut through with stiff seaweed. Wet rot blackened the tips of the fingers.

The girl hacking and vomiting water on the stones wore jeans and a sweater, clothes that didn't belong to her. They were cheap and the sweater was too large. She pulled in deep breaths and kept her eyes on the rock. She seemed afraid, but not panicked. Water ran out of her thick mass of red hair as she tossed it back over her shoulder.

A foot clad in a slingback heel stepped before her and the vision opened up. Two women stood in the back of the cave, both dry and hideously beautiful. The one nearest had dark blond hair, cropped short. The second lingered behind and swayed on bare feet. Long yellow hair hung down her back. Dirt streaked across her fragile blue dress. She was young, and unbelievably beautiful, except for the bruises that marked her arms and legs.

Those aren't from fighting. It's sickness. And she isn't young. She just appears that way.

Her big blue eyes blinked, vacant and wild. Insane.

Aphrodite. And the other . . .

She saw a stone fist, heaviness in her limbs. A peacock feather.

Hera.

Hate streaked through Cassandra's blood, hate that she hadn't known she had. The vision jerked; it sped up and skipped ahead in a montage of torture. Something dark erupted from the greenish water and dragged the red-haired girl back down. Red clouds bloomed in the water and churned up flashes of pale bits, pieces of loose skin. Screams mingled sound with bubbles and spit.

Poseidon. And not Poseidon. At least, not the sea god I knew.

When he slammed the girl back onto the rocks, he rose out of the water to his waist. Sea plants shot through his skin, cracking it. Long, red cuts crossed his torso from kelp leaves working their way inside. His once handsome beard was infested with shells and creeping claws, and in the place of his right eye was a piece of bone-white coral, jutting from the socket. Where his blood oozed, it was oily and reddish black. The sea was polluted, and so was he.

Cassandra remembered the god he'd been, golden like the sand and strong. The waves on the rocks used to ring with his laughter. At least two Trojan girls a year came back from swimming giggling, with Poseidon's babies growing in their bellies.

They'd run from him now. They'd run screaming.

Across the slippery sound of water, Hera's voice rolled like thunder off every wall.

"We can bring the others. Is that what you want?"

The girl shivered and twitched on the stone.

"Talk, you stupid witch!" Aphrodite shrieked and threw a stone. It bounced off the girl's shoulder and drew blood.

"Don't, daughter. We don't have to be cruel." She held out her arm and Aphrodite ran to her and held her tight.

"She says nothing. She lets us die. Lets us burn and bleed and crack!"

Hera shushed her and stroked her hair. Aphrodite keened softly for a few moments, then quieted. "She'll talk. She'll talk because she knows we are their gods. The witches of Circe do not belong to Athena alone."

The girl shivered. "You killed us."

"I had to, little one. You took things from me and my family. Things we have looked a long time for." She kissed Aphrodite's brow and sent her away, back to hug herself in a corner. Hera stepped forward and knelt before the girl. She reached up and tucked wet strands behind the girl's ear, almost tenderly. "Look. You see Aphrodite. Goddess of love and beauty. She's dying, and dying cruelly. Losing her cheeks to clotted blood and her mind to madness. Because love is madness." She wove her fingers into the girl's hair and twisted, yanking it tight. "Love is madness. We kill for it like you do. I'll kill you and every remaining witch to save Aphrodite and my blighted brother. Or I can spare you and kill somebody else."

The girl breathed hard. She looked at Aphrodite and glanced back toward the green water. But she said nothing. Hera sighed and nodded to Poseidon.

Cassandra wanted to look away as he threw himself onto the rocks. He wrenched his jaw open and sank his teeth into the girl's leg, his expression horrible and vacant, close to mindless as he tore her skin away and chewed. He would have bitten again had Hera not held up her hand.

The girl fell back, clutching the wet red hole above her knee. She trembled, her breath shallow and ragged. She'd go into shock soon, and then it would all be over.

"Go back for the others."

"No."

The girl spoke, her voice deep and sweet, softly accented with French. "No. Leave them alone!"

"I will and gladly. If you strike the bargain."

The girl wept. She took several deep breaths before she spoke again. When she did, it was only a few words.

"Kincade. New York."

Hera smiled. And snapped her neck.

The vision threw Cassandra back hard. The legs of her chair skidded across the hardwood of the kitchen.

"Cassie?" Henry jumped forward and held her steady. But that was no comfort. Hera, Aphrodite, and Poseidon had killed that girl. Even after she told them what they wanted.

They know where we are. They're coming.

She swallowed and looked at Henry.

"We've got to get out of here."

Athena was at the mirror when he came in, leaning close to the glass, using her fingernail to coax a small, blood-tinged feather out of her eye. It had been floating just below the lid for the last hour, making her eye water and sting. When Apollo came through the door, he didn't bother to knock, and her reflection shot him a sour look. Then she went back to scraping her nail along her eye.

Hermes sat up quickly, but with more curiosity than alarm. Apollo couldn't stand against them when they were all together.

Odysseus clicked the TV off and cleared his throat in the awkward silence. He bounced up off of the bed and extended his hand.

"Ody," he said.

"Aidan. I remember you. You used to be trouble."

He smiled. "Still am."

Behind them, Athena let something drop loudly against

the countertop. The feather had come out; she rolled it between her fingers, staining them red before rinsing the lot of it
down the drain. Odysseus raised a brow in her direction. She
arched hers back, but her expression softened. Apollo looked
like walking shit. His clothes hung on him in a wet bundle.

"I've come to find out what the fuck's going on," he said.

"Might've been a better question to ask before you attacked me." Athena turned from the mirror and rested her
hip on the counter. She'd changed into a different t-shirt and
sort of wished she hadn't. She should have worn the blood
like a badge.

"Don't waste your time," said Hermes. "He's gone Rambo
on us. Break bottles first and ask questions later."

"I was only trying to protect her."

"And look how well that turned out." Hermes lay back
on his propped-up pillows.

It was enough. Anyone could see that Apollo was beat.
Athena pushed away from the counter and walked toward
him.

"We're trying to protect her too," she said gently.

"You killed her."

"She was dead already. She still is. She's been dying for
as long as we have. Her fate is tied to ours." She clenched
her teeth. No matter how she tried, she couldn't seem to be
anything but harsh with him.

Apollo straightened. When he did, he almost looked like
a god again, instead of a post–garage band sack of rags. "Why
is this happening? What's killing you?" Athena shrugged.
Those were stupid questions to ask. "I heard about Artemis," he said. "Cassandra had a vision of her, hunted down
in her jungle. Something was running her to the ground.
Was it true? Is she dead?"

"Maybe not yet. But that's the end result. The means are

different for all of us. Have Hermes tell you about Demeter." Apollo's eyes fell, and she restrained the urge to place
a hand on his shoulder. Denial was strong, and so was
panic. His actions weren't so unforgivable. Hearing about
Artemis couldn't have been easy. Athena thought of her,
just for an instant. Skin as pale as the moon, hair that always looked silver no matter what color it really was. She'd
hunted everything in the forest. Now she was the prey.

Why does it have to be so cruel? So humiliating?

In her mind she saw a flash of a green leaf, dripping with
dark blood. She smelled carrion breath.

Is that my vision, or Cassandra's?

"So what do you want?" Apollo looked from Athena to
Hermes and back again. "Do you want to save yourselves
somehow? Do you think Cassandra can stop whatever is
happening to you?"

"To us," Hermes said. "And why isn't it happening to
you, exactly?"

"I don't know."

"I hate to burst your bubble," Odysseus interjected, "but
it probably is. There's no good reason for you to have escaped. You probably are dying in some way that hasn't
shown symptoms yet. I mean, face it, mate, aside from your
questionable decision to reenter high school, you're no different than any of them. You're not separate."

Apollo shrugged. "I don't care. Dying or not dying. I just
want to know what you want from Cassandra. She can't be
harmed."

"But she can't be left out," Athena warned. "Demeter
said that she could be the key to everything. That she'll
become more than just a prophetess."

"How the hell would Demeter know?"

"Let's just say she kept her ear to the ground," said

Hermes, and looked at Athena meaningfully before dissolving into giggles. The little asshole was always being inappropriate. But she had to cough harshly to stop from laughing herself.

Keeping her voice even, Athena told Apollo everything they knew. She told him how they'd found Demeter, stretched across the desert. She told him about the Nereid, and what it had shown her. She told them what they'd learned at The Three Sisters, and what Hera had done. As an afterthought, she told him about Aphrodite's asylum escapee. When she finished, he walked around the room thoughtfully and sat down on top of the cheap plastic-wood table next to the TV.

"Hera, Poseidon, and Aphrodite. That's who we're fighting?"

Athena exhaled. "I like it when you say 'we.' I don't want us on opposite sides, brother."

Apollo narrowed his eyes.

"I haven't made any promises yet."

Athena clenched her jaw. She'd shown her olive branch too early. "Well, you'd better make some. Because if Hera gets her hands on Cassandra, you can bet she won't survive it. I might have killed her to bring her back, but Hera will use her, then kill her, and let her stay dead."

"You don't know that."

"Take her word for it," Hermes said, his voice low. "She's gone insane. She was cold as ice when she murdered Circe's coven."

Apollo hung his head and stuffed his hands into his pockets. "Well, that's a shame. Since no one's ever been able to hold Hera back when she gets a hair across her ass. No one except maybe Zeus."

"Yes," said Hermes. "Where is good old Dad when you need him?"

"Wait," said Odysseus. "That's a bloody good question. Where is Zeus? You've said that Hera is dealing in some serious strength, right? What if he's giving her some extra juice?"

The three gods looked at one another. They were Zeus' children. One of them, Athena, was his favorite child. But not even that made her really special. Certainly not indispensible. Zeus had fathered almost too many children to count. He had made her; he could make another one of her just as easily. Their minds circled the idea warily before turning their backs on it.

"No. Zeus is gone."

"Maybe Hera—"

"No," Athena barked, and winced. When she spoke again, her eyes were soft. "Even if he is still alive, he's chosen not to interfere. I'm sure he sees all this as Fated, and if there was ever anything he was afraid to fuck around with, it was that. He was always concerned with keeping the balance between us and them. Besides, he never took sides between me and Hera."

Apollo ran his hand roughly across his face. "I don't think we should fight. I think we should run."

"Interesting idea," said Hermes. "And I'm totally open to it. But with the world ending, I don't know where you suggest we run to."

Athena crossed her hands over her chest. They couldn't run. And even if they could, they still had a stake in this. They still had some responsibility. Hera had killed dozens. She'd kill more while hunting them if they ran, Athena was sure. Apollo was willing to forget everything he was for

Cassandra. He had shed his godhood, tossed it away like it was nothing, to live like a mortal with her. He'd have to be watched. If they didn't keep him close, he'd break all the rules.

Odysseus caught her eye, and she looked away. Once upon a time, she'd broken plenty of rules for him, and she was in no mood to feel like a hypocrite.

A knock at the door made all four of them snap to attention. An uneasy expression rippled through the room. They weren't expecting anyone. The knock came again, louder and more insistent. None of them made a move, and Athena watched curiously as the handle turned and the door swung open.

"You don't lock the door?" Cassandra asked.

"There isn't much point," Hermes explained, relaxing. "Anything strong enough to hurt us could just take the door off its hinges."

"I guess." She stood framed in the open doorway. Silvery sleet fell onto the sidewalk, turning more and more to ice as the sun sank lower. Behind her, Henry's black Mustang idled in the parking lot with Andie and Henry inside.

Cassandra swallowed. When she spoke her voice came out a dry crackle, and the handprints on her neck stood out like a neon sign.

I hope they do. She stared at Athena. *I hope the handprints look like yours. That if you turn your palms over they'll be stained the same black as my bruises.*

"Come in," Odysseus said. "Close the door. You're not the only one who feels the cold, you know."

Cassandra stepped through and shook moisture from her

hands and jacket. Odysseus helped her brush off. In the chaos of the deadfall, she hadn't really looked at him.

"You're human," she said, and another piece of the puzzle clicked into place. "You're the boy I saw in my dream. Being attacked by the Cyclops." The dream came back for an instant, the smell of cold and caves and blood, the wry curl of his lip, and the Cyclops falling on him. Looking closer, she saw fading red punctures down the back of his neck.

"Here." He twisted to give her a better view, and she felt her cheeks flush. He was good-looking in the daylight. In a rough-around-the-edges, shaggy-haired sort of way. "It goes most of the way down in the back."

"I thought you were dead."

He chuckled. "That makes two of us."

"What are you doing here?" Athena stepped forward, and Cassandra regarded her coldly. She seemed less crazy than Aphrodite and less powerful than Hera. Her left eye was red and watery and someone had sewn the flap of her scalp back in place. She could just barely see the stitching of black thread behind her hairline.

Aidan stood apart, saying nothing. He didn't greet her or try to protect her. Beside the others, the similarities in their faces were more apparent.

He looks so inhuman. I can't believe I didn't notice before.

She thought of Aphrodite's shrieks, of Poseidon tearing the girl apart. She thought of Hera, snapping her neck. Three gods. Three monsters.

Athena can't stand against that. And Hermes looks about ready to fall over, he's so skinny.

This is the losing team.

"I had a vision," she said. Aidan's arm twitched, to comfort her maybe, or just to touch her shoulder, but in the end he stayed still.

"What did you see?" Athena asked. Eagerness lit her eyes. It was like watching all the hackles rise on a hunting dog. The possibility of an advantage had crept into the room. They looked so hopeful, Cassandra almost wanted to lie and give better news.

"I saw a red-haired girl. Hera and Poseidon were torturing her. And before they killed her, she told them exactly where to find us."

17

HEROES

The announcement was met with silence. Cassandra watched it sink in, watched each of them process it individually. Their eyes lost focus and then snapped back. Aidan shifted his weight. Odysseus' eyes narrowed and stared through Cassandra's head. Hermes' mouth dropped slightly open, and his brows knit.

"We have to get out of here," said Aidan. "We have to get out of here now."

"And go where?" Athena asked. Her expression hadn't wavered for more than a second. "Was there anything else? Could you see where they were?"

"A cave, maybe. Someplace near water. Nothing definite. Who was that girl? Why did they kill her? How did she know where we were?"

"Her name was Celine," Hermes whispered. "She led the coven in Chicago. She knew where you were because we asked her to find you. And they killed her for it."

Cassandra blinked slowly. "The building in Chicago. You didn't blow it up."

The stricken look on Hermes' face confirmed it, but Athena shoved past him and snapped, "Of course we didn't blow it up." She paced near the foot of one of the beds. "Hera blew it up as punishment. And to stop us from getting to you. So if you can remember anything else from your vision, pipe up. I'd like to know where she's at."

Aidan stepped toward his sister. "It doesn't matter where she is if we know where she's going. We should be gone before she gets here."

"Hang on," said Odysseus. "How much time do we have? I mean, how does it work exactly? Are these visions, or premonitions? Has it happened already, or is it just going to happen?"

Cassandra shook her head. "I'm not sure. The building blew in Chicago about two days after I saw it. When did you get attacked by the Cyclops?"

"I don't know." Odysseus ran his hand across his face. "Days on the road tend to blend together. Not to mention the days I spent tangled up with the girls at The Three Sisters." He glanced at Athena and cleared his throat. "That's not much help."

Hermes grasped her arm. "Were there other witches there?"

"No. That's how they got her to talk. They said they'd spare the others."

His face crumpled. "Spare the others? Hera doesn't spare the others." He looked at Athena miserably. "I didn't run fast enough. I didn't hide them well enough. Celine. Mareden. Estelle. Bethe and Jenna and Harper." He said their names like a lament. "That coven spanned thousands of years and that bitch wiped them off the planet."

Odysseus put a hand on Hermes' shoulder. "You did what you could. And so did you, Athena."

"Did I? I could have stayed. I could've fought her in the rubble. I might have lost, been beaten to paste, but I could've taken part of her with me." Cassandra watched as Odysseus touched Athena's arm. The way his fingers lingered, and the concern in his eyes. He loved her. Athena didn't touch him back, didn't put her hand over his. She didn't even look in his direction.

She's a virgin goddess. Men aren't supposed to fall in love with her. She'll break him, and she won't care.

Hermes pressed to the front. "It doesn't have to be enough. It doesn't have to be all. She might not have gotten to the others yet!" He looked to Athena for permission. He seemed ready to force wings through his back, as long as there was a chance. "I could still get there. I could save them."

"If they listened to us, they won't be where you left them," said Athena. "They'll have moved on. And we don't know how much time Cassandra's vision gives us. It might not give us any."

"If I get there too late, then I'm too late. I'll come back."

It was a lie, there for everyone to see. He cared about those witches. If he arrived too late, he'd do something stupid and heroic. He'd take on Hera alone, and she would forcibly remove his spine. Cassandra wanted to ease his conscience. He seemed so guilty, and so earnest. She'd thought she'd hate them all, but she couldn't hate him. Not with so much desperation in his eyes to save someone he cared for.

Athena shook her head, once.

"We can't risk it. I'm sorry."

"Athena—"

"We have to stick together now, brother."

Cassandra watched Hermes slowly sink back into himself, into his prominent bones and hollow cheeks. The light that had briefly flickered went out. *Athena should have let him go*. But no. The way Athena looked at him, and the sad fury in her face told the whole story. *She wants to let him go, but he's too weak. He'd never win.*

"This wasn't your failure," Athena said. "It wasn't the way you hid them, or how fast you ran."

"Right," Hermes muttered.

The TV beside them was still on, and Athena struck the button with the side of her hand, hard enough to knock it back against the wall. In her frustration, she seemed to swell three sizes, and the space in the motel room grew small.

Hermes glanced at Cassandra.

"What use is she? If she doesn't even give us time? What use are visions that you can't change?"

Athena peered at her. "Do you feel any different now? Now that you remember your old life?"

"No." Cassandra thought a moment. "The vision was a little strange, but they've been evolving since . . . I guess since you started looking for me. But I don't feel any different."

"Useless," Hermes muttered.

"Hey," said Aidan. "She'd be more than happy to be useless. Why don't you face Hera and tell her so? Then you can leave us alone."

Voices broke out, the voices of gods, and they forgot themselves. The sound of their argument rose over everything else. It thundered through walls and rang out across the nearly empty parking lot. Odysseus couldn't do anything to shut them up, but he did try, with an elbow in each of their chests.

Cassandra and Athena looked at each other. The time for bargaining had come and gone. So had the time for laying blame.

"Quiet," said Athena, and the room fell silent. Cassandra stared into the flowered wallpaper. Outside, the city of Kincade went about its business in cars and shops. Meals were made and eaten. TVs played too loud. Lights turned on and off. Just like every other Kincade evening.

This was her life. Her city. And they meant it to be their battleground, just like it was before.

"What good will running do?" Athena asked. "How far can we go before Hera burns up all the land behind us? We'd never be safe." She looked at Cassandra. "They'd never be safe. We'd run until Hermes' body eats itself from the inside out and I'm too stuffed with feathers to breathe. Our fall would be pathetic. Unworthy of an epithet."

"So what?" Hermes shrugged. "Let it be. After we're dead, it won't matter anyway."

"You don't mean that," Athena said softly. "And besides, what about them?" She nodded toward Cassandra and looked at the door. Cassandra edged into her view, like she could shield Andie and Henry from her thoughts, but Athena had already looked back at her brothers. "Will you let them try to stop Hera on their own?" No one had an answer. They stared at their feet.

"If you want to know the truth, giving up would be easy. As easy and comfortable as falling into a bed. Stopping these feathers . . . Saving my life doesn't seem any more possible than it is important."

"If it's not important," Cassandra said, "if you don't care, then why are you here? What are you doing?"

Athena looked at her, and for the first time Cassandra

saw less a goddess and more a girl. A girl who had fought a hard battle and still come up cornered. Athena smiled, a small smile, through closed lips.

"There isn't much to me anymore that isn't push me and I push back. There hasn't been for a long time. Maybe it doesn't make sense, but there it is. And besides, I can't do nothing, when they stand here looking, waiting for me to say what to do."

"So what are you going to do?"

"We have to make a stand," she said.

"What? Here?" Hermes sounded horrified.

"Kincade is as good a place as any for the world to end."

Hermes shook his head. "It most certainly is not. Kincade is a place of unclean motel rooms and a mall that's several dozen stores too small. I vote with Apollo. Running. Running I'm good at. We could run halfway around the world, to places worth seeing once more before dying: London, Paris, Florence. Maybe all the way to fricking Delphi."

"More than that," Aidan said. "Kincade isn't the best place to face an enemy. It's settled into a valley in foothills. Not exactly the high ground. You should know that. You should seek advantage."

Cassandra swallowed. He talked so casually of war and strategy.

"Putting it off will only make us weaker." Athena looked at Cassandra. "And I think she's the only advantage we're going to get."

"What is it that you think I am?" Cassandra asked.

"You're a weapon."

Hermes crossed his arms.

"But what sort of weapon? An amped-up prophetess? What use is someone who tells you the boat is sinking when you're already bailing it out?"

"I don't know, Hermes. But Hera is afraid we'll use her. If she wasn't, she wouldn't go to so much trouble. I thought, maybe, after I made you remember . . ." She shook her head. "All I know for sure is she's a link to the Moirae."

"The Moirae? You mean the Fates?" Cassandra looked at Aidan. "Is that what my visions are? A link to Fate?"

Aidan shrugged. "It's what we've always thought. But the Fates don't talk to us."

"Except through me."

No one responded. They'd already moved past it to the matter at hand, thinking of strategies and contingencies, and not one of them looked like they expected to win.

"I suppose I should watch the waterways," said Hermes. "Maybe check the river. That's where Poseidon would come from. Or Nereids, if he sends them on ahead."

Athena nodded like she was relieved. "I half expected you to refuse, or to go spend one last season in Paris or Rome."

"Nah. I'll stay." When he breathed, the skin over his ribs stretched and the bone of his sternum was visible. "I wouldn't have been able to run for that much longer anyway."

Athena put a hand on Hermes' shoulder. Cassandra watched the bones and tendons shift underneath his shirt. Most of the muscle had been eaten away.

Athena squeezed. "Not everything's hopeless. If we throw Hera down, you might heal and grow strong again. I might escape this cage of feathers." She looked at Aidan.

"I don't think so." He moved nearer to Cassandra. "If we stay here, and fight her . . . You saw what she did to those witches in Chicago. Do you even know what she wants? Is she trying to kill her or trying to use her?"

"Does it matter?" Athena asked, and glanced at Cassandra. Cassandra didn't reply, but had to admit that one didn't seem more desirable than the other.

"If we stay here, she could level this place."

"If you leave, she might level it anyway, looking for you."

Level it. Cassandra held her breath. Her hometown. The house she grew up in, and her family inside it. Everything up until then she'd managed to swallow, even the idea that she was once again just a tool, a toy for immortals to play with. The longer she looked at Athena, the more she disliked her. That reasonable face. That voice, so steady and unruffled. For her, leading battles was a matter of course. Never mind that innocent people would die. Never mind that a whole town might get caught in their stupid cross fire.

She thought of the freshman with the mop of brown hair who had watched her call the coin. She thought of Sam, unsinkable in his stocking cap, and sweet, sort of slutty Megan in her Bo Peep costume. Every one of them had lives, and plans, going on that very minute. And none of them had any idea it was days away from being ruined. That the gods' mess was going to ruin it all.

"We can't do this. Not here." She looked at Aidan. "Our friends are here."

"It'll come to this eventually," Athena said. "You know I'm right. We live or they do."

"We live or they do," Cassandra said. "Us or them. But it isn't us that you mean. It's you. Just you, and yours. We die so you can live, just like always."

"That's not true, Cassandra," said Odysseus.

"You're blind," she growled. "And you." She turned on Athena. "I'm not helping you. Not here. Maybe not anywhere. I'm getting out of here. And you'd better find a way to tell Hera I'm gone." The bruises on her throat cut inside like broken glass when she spoke. She had to turn away quickly to hide the tears prickling the corners of her eyes.

"Wait." Athena reached for Cassandra's arm. The goddess's touch sickened her, ignited a heat deep inside her head and in her chest. Her arm trembled. She wanted them out, all of them; she wanted to break them down with her bare hands. The goddess's grip was iron. Athena had forgotten everything about being soft, or compassionate, or human, if she'd ever known in the first place. Without thinking, Cassandra drew back her free hand and slapped Athena hard across the face. In the half second it took for Athena to recover from the surprise, Aidan got between them.

"I'm not going to hurt her." Athena stood still, her hand against her face.

"Of course you're not. You need me."

Odysseus narrowed his eyes from where he stood at Athena's shoulder. "Don't be so sure. Might be just as smart to get rid of you. At least then Hera couldn't use you either. Level the field a bit."

Cassandra felt the muscles in Aidan's arm tighten. Odysseus was lucky Athena stood in his way.

A half-hearted, hurried knock broke the tension just before the door swung open and Andie and Henry burst halfway through, blinking in the sudden change of light from the dark parking lot. Cassandra looked from them to Athena and back again. They'd sworn they would stay in the car.

"You were taking so long." Andie fidgeted. The way she looked at Athena and Hermes, Cassandra knew her friend could sense something was off. Even if she hadn't known there were gods in town, she would've sensed it—that something was unnatural about these strangers.

Andie stared wide-eyed at Athena's slightly shocked face. Her gaze dragged slowly down and then back up without blinking, like she could discover some secret behind the human costume.

"She looks less human than Aidan. Even with those tattoos. Why is she looking at us like that?"

"Leave them alone," Cassandra warned.

"But you told them already," Athena said. "Hector and Andromache. They look so much the same. Untamed. And he's still so tall and broad-shouldered. He could help, if we woke them up."

"Don't touch them. Aidan, don't let her touch them."

Odysseus gestured to Henry. "They'll kill him too, if they find him. They're after Achilles. That means they'll kill anyone who could possibly stand against him, and that means Hector."

"What are you talking about? Who are you?" Henry asked. Andie backed into him to get him to shut up.

"I know what you're thinking." Aidan stepped just to the center. "That you should just get it over with. Wrap your hands around their throats and let Odysseus bring them back. Then you'd have two soldiers instead of a pile of questions. But it should be up to them. Let them decide. That's justice."

"Since when are you the authority on justice?"

Athena shifted her weight, her eyes on the lines of Henry's muscles. Cassandra nudged Aidan's side, and he stepped farther forward.

"Aren't you tired of using them? Aren't you tired of moving them around and spending their lives like pocket change? You're a monster, but you're also a god. Don't you have any grace?"

Athena's eyes snapped to his. "It's not like we have the luxury of time. It's a hard choice, but this is why I lead. No one else has the stomach to do the unpleasant things that sometimes need doing."

Odysseus cleared his throat. "Do they really need doing?

Look at him." He nodded toward Henry. "You already killed him once."

Cassandra's eyes snapped to Athena. Odysseus had caught her off guard. She didn't know what to say.

"Take them," Athena said finally.

"Come on." Cassandra shoved them out the door like children. Aidan followed behind, but she still glanced once over her shoulder, half convinced that she'd see Athena coming after them with hooked fingers.

Athena listened to the car peel out of the parking lot. She thought of the boy behind the wheel. Hector. Who was now called Henry. When she'd stared at him, he'd stared back with strong brown eyes. Shell-shocked for sure, but he didn't run. He never ran. That's why it had been so easy to trick him onto the battlefield to face Achilles.

I lied to him. I put on the disguise of an ally and said he was blessed. That he wouldn't fight alone. So he came and stood face-to-face with a madman.

She still remembered the look on his face when he realized he'd been tricked. And later, the look in his eyes when Achilles drove the spear into his chest.

Odysseus was right. She'd killed him as surely as if she'd thrust the spear in herself. Back then, Andromache's screaming could barely compete with her own laughter.

"Well, now what?" Hermes threw up his hands and collapsed on the bed with a bounce.

"Athena." Odysseus moved in front of her.

"What?"

"Your face." He stared at her cheek, which still tingled where Cassandra had slapped her.

Tingling. Almost burning. But she's just a human.

She twisted to look into the mirror. There was a red handprint painted across her cheek.

"Why are you smiling?" Odysseus asked.

Athena studied the impossible wound. As she watched, it tingled and burned deeper.

"Because even though Cassandra doesn't feel any different"—she pressed a cool palm to her face—"she *is* different. More than a prophet. A weapon."

18

FATE'S A BITCH

The scent of granite hung on the air. Whether it was real or just in her imagination, Athena didn't know. The sleet had stopped, leaving the world wet and black in the absence of the sun. She inhaled; the scent faded. It probably hadn't been there in the first place. The air was completely still, no breeze to carry news, or to dry the slushy puddles in the street.

It didn't matter. She stood at the tree line along the highway where she and Odysseus had walked into Kincade. This was the way that Hera would come. She would follow them in, rising up behind them like some gruesome specter. The move had bravado. It had menace. Doing it any other way wouldn't even cross her mind.

The city of Kincade was cut through by one large river and five tributaries. There was also a lake, Lake Reilly, medium-sized but quite deep, and fed into by the river.

Athena's eyes scanned the horizon. The tributaries were no problem; they were too small for any water-dwelling bastard to move through that quickly. But the river and the lake were perfect hiding places for Poseidon. As for Aphrodite, well, they'd probably leave the sniveling brat back home. Or they would, if they were smart.

She heard footsteps coming cautiously up from behind. Odysseus. She'd only been gone from the motel for twenty minutes.

"What are you doing?"

"Getting my bearings," she replied without turning. "Preparing for battle. Doing what I do."

He came up to her shoulder and tried to rubberneck around the front of her to see her cheek.

"Quit it." She jerked away. "It's gone."

"But what was it?"

"An injury put on me by a mortal. And if she can do it to me, she can do it to the others."

"But it was just a handprint. I don't even think she knew what she was doing. It could be nothing."

But it wasn't nothing. It was something. Only she had no idea what, and it seemed Cassandra wouldn't have much time to figure it out.

Oh, Aunt Demeter. I wish I hadn't respected your wishes. I wish I'd pulled you out of the sand and rolled you up. I could use you. I could really use you.

Odysseus' hands thrust into his jeans pockets against the chill and his neck turtled slightly. She didn't want to look at him, so she kept on studying the terrain.

"Kincade's not exactly the high ground, I suppose," Odysseus mumbled.

"Nowhere is the high ground where Hera is concerned."

He leaned against her and heat moved into her from his shoulder. Why did he have to be so damned comforting? What was it about him that could make her so soft? Maybe it had always been this way. Thinking back, she remembered the fondness she felt every time she looked at him. When she watched him charge the battlefield at Troy, his eyes terrified but determined, he'd been so alive; it had made her want to laugh and scream. But it hadn't been like this. Back then she was a goddess and he a mortal. Back then the lines between them were clearly drawn.

Ahead, the world seemed to stretch on to forever, but she knew it didn't. Not really. Somewhere, Hera was coming for them. And no matter how she planned, or what strategy she used, it wouldn't be enough.

"Not getting down on us already?" Odysseus nudged. "Are you still angry that Aidan didn't let you kill Hector?"

"His name's not Aidan. And we could have used Hector. We could have used them both." She shrugged him off. Odysseus made a disgusted sound. He would chastise her now, call her inhuman, which was a stupid argument anyway. He would call her selfish. And if he went much further, she'd knock his ass in the wet dirt.

"You're not alone in this. No matter what you might think." He crossed his arms over his chest, staring out in the same direction she had. "I know you think you've got to make all the hard choices. Someone has to lead us, right, and you're the one. So you come out with mud on your face. You get to be the villain, the one that everybody blames."

"It doesn't matter," she said. "Someone's got to do it."

"Someone does," he agreed. "But don't think it means you're the only one with blood on their hands. That bitch is out to kill us all. It's our fight as much as yours."

The words set off a sting someplace deep inside her. She moved against him again so they stood side by side, looking down the highway.

"Cassandra thinks I'm doing it to save myself. And I am.

I mean, I was. When Demeter told us we'd need to use humans to fight, I barely shrugged. I just wanted these feathers out of my throat. I just wanted Hermes to grow strong again. If humans could help that happen, then great." She took a breath. "I've gotten really bad at looking after people."

"It'll all come back," said Odysseus. "You took care of me well enough, back then."

Athena snorted, remembering his epic ten-year quest for home. "You were almost drowned. I don't know how many things tried to eat you."

Odysseus shrugged. "Eh. It all turned out well. Besides, you made me a legend."

"Stop this. You're not yourself without your ego."

They smiled at each other. Let the rest of them hate her. Let the whole world blame her for its end. It didn't matter, as long as he knew who she really was.

Lux whined. The big German shepherd walked restlessly from Henry to Cassandra and back again, trying to fix whatever was making the room so tense and quiet. Henry finally grabbed his collar and told him to sit. Andie rubbed his fur absently.

"So I was in the Trojan War."

"Well, not exactly." Aidan leaned against Cassandra's closed closet door. "You were Hector's wife, and he was in the Trojan War. You mostly just watched from the wall."

"Lame," she whispered.

"Lame that you just watched, or lame that we were married?" Henry asked.

"Both." They smirked at each other.

"Hey," said Cassandra. "This isn't a joke. There isn't really time for the denial phase you've both got coming."

"Nobody's denying anything." Andie squared her shoulders uncomfortably and brushed dog fur off her hands.

"But you are. You've got this look on your faces, telling your jokes, like there's going to be an explanation soon. Like everything's still normal and this has been the most elaborate April Fools' joke ever."

"It's nowhere near April."

"Screw you, Andie."

Andie's mouth dropped open. Henry pushed off the wall.

"Come on, Cassie. Give us a break. It's a lot, you know? If you walked into the woods and saw a rabbit hiding colored eggs would you just buy it? Just like that?"

Cassandra ground her teeth. Unless that rabbit was about to turn and snap them like twigs, it wasn't the same thing. She ran her hands over the stitching of her quilt. If there had been a loose thread, she would have grabbed it and torn the whole thing apart. The need to run grew in her belly; it grew stronger every minute.

"Look, I think we just need to take a step back." Andie stood up and stretched. "Get a good night's sleep. Everything will look better in the morning."

"We don't have until the morning. We've got to leave. Now."

"What are you talking about?"

Cassandra wanted to hit her. "I'm talking about my vision. About gods knowing where we are, coming to Kincade to kill us."

"You don't know when she's coming. Or if she really will come. You just saw someone tell her. 'Kincade,' you said. Just one word."

"If we don't leave now, we won't get away. And they'll burn this place down looking for us. If we go, they won't waste time on Kincade. They'll chase us instead, and by then we'll be far enough ahead."

Andie raised her chin. "Do you really *know* that? Or is this just a hunch? I'm not giving up my life over a hunch."

Cassandra stared at her, eyes wide. She looked at Henry, but he didn't know what to do either. They would stand there, paralyzed by indecision, until Hera and Poseidon were at their door.

"Athena said we stand and fight, or we run. And she was right about that at least. Hera will be here. Soon. We have got to get out."

Andie tapped her foot and shook her head. It wasn't getting through.

"Andie." Aidan stepped close and took her by the shoulders. "Do you want to remember?" He looked into her eyes, and the heat in the room jumped, driving the thermostat up ten degrees. His hands moved from her shoulders and wrapped around her throat.

"Aidan, don't." Cassandra started to get off the bed. Lux whimpered and nosed his way behind Henry's knees.

"It's her choice," he said evenly. "Hers and Henry's. It's not Athena's or mine. And not yours either." His fingers closed around Andie's neck and squeezed. He lifted her until she was on her toes, so easily his arms barely flexed. Cassandra remembered the ease with which he lifted her the night of the party. She remembered Athena's iron fingers around her throat. But Andie could still breathe, even though her hands rose to try to pry him loose.

"Do you want to remember?"

Andie's eyes were ringed with white. Cassandra had never seen her so scared.

"No!"

He let go. Andie held her throat with her hand and fell back on the bed with Cassandra, but she was all right. The skin wasn't red. There wouldn't even be bruises.

"No, I don't want to remember." She looked at Cassandra and started to cry. Cassandra hugged her. Andie never cried. Not when her hamster died in second grade. Not even when her dad left to start a new family.

Henry stood up, hands balled into fists. "You shouldn't have done that."

"I'll do it to you too, if you want."

Cassandra shook her head, not quite sure who she was shaking it at. The heat in the room lingered, but wasn't radiating off Aidan like it had when he'd grabbed Andie. Still, he seemed taller and more beautiful. More of a god.

I shouldn't regret that. We're going to need him to be before all this is over.

"Don't jump to my defense." Andie sat up and wiped her eyes. She gently pulled free from Cassandra. "I'm not your wife. I'm not Andromache. It's gross."

"That's not why I did it." Henry's legs twitched, like he couldn't decide whether to pace or storm out. He ended up doing nothing.

"What are we going to do?" Andie wiped her eyes again and sucked in a hitching breath. "Go home, pack our bags, leave notes saying we're headed to California? What about my mom?"

Henry sat down heavily. "I can't believe this. Cassie, she's right, we can't both go. What about Mom and Dad?"

"There's nothing we could tell them that they'd understand. But we'll come back." *We'll come back. Whenever we can. After all the gods are dead, and who knows how long that will take?*

"Maybe they don't want us. Maybe they just want you."
She said the words, but Andie's voice held no hope. Cassandra couldn't let them stay. She couldn't leave them behind to have their necks snapped.

"We'll come back."

"We should probably tell Athena." Aidan stood apart from them, near the door, arms crossed.

"No. It'll slow us down. And besides, I don't trust them."

He nodded, staring at the carpet. "I've got to go back to my house. Get my bag again. Rewrite the note."

"We'll meet back here in an hour, okay, Andie?"

An hour. Not much time. Certainly not enough to say good-byes, or to do anything that they'd have liked to do one more time in the city they grew up in. Andie got up and walked out the door. Henry and Lux followed behind. After they'd gone, Cassandra reached under her bed for her duffel bag and started to fill it with clothes from her dresser.

"Do you think Andie'll come back?" Aidan asked. "She was pretty upset. Maybe I shouldn't have done what I did."

"No, you were right about that," Cassandra said. She pushed past him to get into her closet and yanked shirts and jeans off plastic hangers. "Even if you were wrong about everything else." In the corner of her eye she saw his shoulders slump. He hadn't touched her since she'd brushed him away near the deadfall. But he wanted to. And angry as she was, part of her wanted to let him.

"Cassandra, I'm sorry."

"About what exactly? About the fact that we're all probably going to die because gods can't stand the thought of going quietly? They've been around forever. Isn't that long enough?"

"It's not easy for them. You don't really understand . . .

anything about forever. About what that word really means."

She rolled a sweater up and stuffed it into her bag. "I guess I don't. I'm just a human. I just live. And die. Nothing I do is eternal." She threw makeup and moisturizer into the bag. She wanted to throw them against the wall. Makeup and moisturizer. Ridiculous.

"Why did you come here? Why did you find me?"

"Because I never stopped loving you."

"That's a selfish reason." She went to her dresser, opened drawers, and slammed them shut. "You made me feel things I shouldn't feel. And I can't make them go away just like that. Yesterday I loved you. Now it's all over. Except it's not. It's still in here." She struck her chest with her fist. Her heart burned. It needed to be torn out.

"A thousand times I opened my mouth to tell you."

"To tell me what?"

"Everything. Who you were. Who I was. What I'd done. But then I'd look at you. And I knew no matter what I did, I would lose you anyway. To death, or disease, or a fucking car accident. I've felt your heartbeat, and it's so delicate it makes me ache. It paralyzed me, how different we are, and in the end I was a coward. But I've loved you a thousand years, and another thousand."

"You asshole." She stopped angrily packing and threw her bag on the bed. A thousand years and another thousand. That's how long he'd spent loving the girl he'd gotten murdered. "You made me love you more than I did before. Knowing what you did. It's a violation."

"What do you want me to do?"

"There's nothing you can do. You can't make it like it was before. Neither of us can. No matter how much I want you to." Everything was hard now, and cold, but it was a million times harder without him. "You should go. Get your stuff. Get out money for us."

He nodded and turned, then stopped with his hand on the doorknob. "I came here to make sure you had the life you should have had if not for me. But I couldn't. I wish I could take it all back. Or make this go away."

Downstairs, the door opened and Lux barked and ran down to the entryway. Cassandra froze, listening to her parents talk to the dog and stomp their feet on the rug. Grocery bags crinkled and clinked down on the countertop, filled with aluminum cans and cardboard and bundles of vegetables.

"Cassandra!" her mother called. "Henry! Come help with the groceries!"

Cassandra threw her duffel into the closet like they might see it from downstairs. They were home. Her mom and dad.

"I thought we'd be gone before they got back. That there wouldn't be any choice. We just wouldn't have been able to say good-bye."

Her knees felt like water. Aidan grasped her arms and held her up.

"It's okay," he said. "I'll go. I'll help them. You stay here."

"No," she said. "I want to." She couldn't decide if she felt like crying or throwing up. "Aidan. I don't know if I can do this."

He pulled her close and held her.

19

THE THINGS YOU CAN'T
SEE COMING

Nobody looked back until the lights of Kincade were far behind, an orange glow thrown up into the black sky as the Mustang flew down the highway. It was close to four in the morning. The road was empty except for a few scattered semitrucks. They'd waited until Cassandra's parents were asleep to leave. Then they'd waited longer, dragging their feet until Aidan finally grabbed their bags and took them silently to the car. Henry was the last to come. He'd knelt on the front steps with his dog, scratching his ears and whispering. Then he'd locked Lux up inside and helped Aidan push the Mustang down the driveway and along the road until they were far enough away to start the engine.

"Is anybody hungry?" Aidan asked from behind the wheel. He'd suggested he drive, since he wouldn't get tired, but any of them could have done it. Cassandra had never felt more awake in her life. "We could stop at the travel plaza and get something from the gas station. Some chips or soda or something."

"We've got a full tank. Let's wait." Cassandra glanced over her shoulder. "Andie, I'm sorry I snapped at you earlier."

"It's okay. I'm sorry for—you know—being myself." She shrugged, her face pale and washed out. She was okay for the moment. They all were. But sooner or later it would get bad. Sooner or later they'd realize what they'd left behind, that their lives had been severed and they couldn't go back.

Let it feel unreal. For as long as it can.

"Aidan, do you even need to eat?" Andie asked. "I mean, you eat all the time, but do you need to? You don't get tired, so do you need to sleep?"

He swallowed. "Yes. No. I don't necessarily need to eat. But I want it. And a god needs to do what he wants." He and Cassandra glanced at each other, waiting for Andie's smart-ass comment, but it never came.

Trees flashed by in the Mustang's headlights. The road was still damp, but the sleet had stopped. If Cassandra strained her eyes against the interstate floodlights, she could see stars in the sky.

"Where are we going exactly?" Henry asked.

"I don't know," Aidan replied. "Away. Just away." His foot pressed down on the accelerator, taking them south.

Hera had never been known for her subtlety. When she made announcements, she liked them to be loud and shiny, taking up all the air in the room. This time was no different. She leveled two buildings in Philadelphia: one an office building on Market Street and another along the western edge of Logan Square. Both were skyscrapers, stretched buildings of steel and windows that shone like crystal as the sun moved over the city. She seemed to choose them completely at random, though both did have a relatively high composition of glass. Athena supposed she wanted to watch it fly, glittering prettily in the light before it embedded itself into other buildings and the soft flesh of people passing by.

The news, of course, leapt all over it. Death tolls were estimated to be in the thousands. Various terrorist groups cropped up to claim responsibility, and they were already linking it to the Chicago attack. But Athena knew a diversion when she saw one. Resources from the surrounding states would be drained, called in to deal with the carnage. The stables would be left empty and the drawbridge unguarded. Hera could slink into Kincade casually, wreak her havoc, and leave their stinking carcasses far behind long before any human authorities came around to gawk.

In the room at the Kincade Motel 6, two gods and a reincarnated mortal watched the TV, barely breathing. Images of smoke and flashing emergency lights played across their irises. None of them needed to say anything. They sat on the garish bedspreads and Athena clicked through channels, searching for new information, looking for the whole story. The humans weren't getting it.

Buried within the emergency news broadcasts, almost as a footnote, were reports of a storm rapidly approaching the East Coast. They were calling it a nor'easter, covering it only because of the problems it could cause regarding the search and rescue efforts in Philadelphia. Meteorologists were optimistic. They expected the storm to swing farther north, making land closer to Connecticut before swinging back out to sea. Idiots. The storm had come out of nowhere, the ocean a fury of waves and wind. It wasn't a fucking nor'easter. It was Poseidon, come to drag the lot of them down into the deep until they churned in the sandy bottom. Hidden inside the waves would be creatures they hadn't known existed: dark, scaled things with fins and claws, piranha's teeth and lidless eyes. It was happening. Their time was up.

"We need Apollo," Athena said without taking her eyes from the screen. "We need all of them here, quickly."

Hermes stood shakily. Sweat stood out on his forehead. He'd been running a low fever on and off for the last few hours. "I can't believe she's really coming. That we're really going to face her." But he took a breath and headed for the door. His courage wouldn't fail. She wouldn't doubt him.

"Hermes," Athena said, and he turned back with a jump, as though she'd shouted. "Don't bother trying to blend in."

He nodded and left. Odysseus touched Athena's arm, and when she turned she was surprised by the fear bleached across his face.

"She's showing us what she can do. Showing us she's on her way. And she's not one bit frightened."

Comforting words rose up in her mouth, but she swallowed them down. They were lies. He would've seen right through them, anyway. The images on the screen were screams in Hera's voice. She had nothing to fear. She could run at them brazenly, without armor or subterfuge. She was stronger. She would win.

"I don't want to split up." Athena looked down at the bedspread, mauve splashed through with green and gold. "I don't think you'd be any safer if we did. But I'll do everything I can to keep them off you."

"Who's going to keep them off you?" His hand slid across the blanket and covered hers. "I didn't want to say anything. I guess I've had a case of, what you call it, denial. But there's no time for that anymore. Athena—" She felt the mattress shift as he moved closer. "You're strong. Stronger than Hermes and stronger than Apollo, but—"

"But not stronger than her." She kept her eyes low. It wounded her pride that he had said it, and that it was true.

"When Apollo bashed your head in, I thought—" He shook his head. "But this is Hera, pissed off beyond reason and desperate. She's not playing around. That stone fist—"

"Will go through my face and come out the back. I know. But what else am I supposed to do?" She looked up, into his eyes, watching him search for an answer to that question, frantically scrambling through his clever brain for any possible alternatives. It made her smile.

"I can't let you. I can't let you go without knowing."

"Odysseus." *Please don't. Don't make it any harder. We were never meant to have this, anyway.*

"Athena!"

The door burst open and clattered against the wall before it wobbled and fell onto the carpet. Hermes had taken it clear off of its hinges.

"What? What is it?" Athena asked, rising.

"They're gone. All of them."

"Gone? What do you mean 'gone'?" Odysseus asked, but Athena wasn't listening.

Apollo, you softhearted idiot, what have you done? Where have you taken them?

In the background, the news from Philadelphia blared from the TV. All of that movement to their south. It felt almost like a wall. Like they were being herded. Again it crossed Athena's mind that the blasts in Philadelphia had been a diversion. Now she wondered just how many purposes it served.

"So, do you think they're freaking out yet?" Henry asked from the backseat.

"Who? Our parents?" Andie shifted against the leather seat next to him.

"Yeah. Do you think they're looking for us?"

"Why would they look for us when we left a note telling them where we were going? I think they're on the phone with each other. Plotting our punishment." She smiled. "It won't be until after we should've been home that they'll really start to worry." Her smile faded.

Aidan slid his hand across the seat and took Cassandra's. She laced her fingers through his, and he pulled her palm up and kissed it. He was grateful for the touch; it was written all over his face. *I should tell him that it's all right. That I forgive him. That the past feels less and less important.*

Only it wasn't true. Not yet. The past felt less important, but it was still there.

"We're going to have to stop for gas soon." Aidan glanced at the fuel gauge. "Maybe get something to eat."

"Gas already?" Andie nudged Henry in the shoulder. "You might think of investing in a car with better fuel economy."

"When I bought it, I didn't think it'd have to go on a cross-country chase." He shoved her back.

After a few disagreements and slight changes in direction, they had decided on southwest, toward Pennsylvania. Aidan had suggested catching a flight somewhere, but no one seemed to know where they should go, and no one was certain that Hera and Poseidon couldn't just rip the plane out of the air anyway.

Cassandra yawned. Her eyelids felt thick and weighted.

"It'll be a little while yet," Aidan said. "You've got time for a nap." She let go of his hand, and her head fell against the headrest.

When she woke, they were stopped and she was alone in the car. Turning, she saw Andie and Henry, leaned up against the door, watching the gas pump as the gallons tried desperately to keep up with the dollars.

Andie reached into her pocket and pulled out her phone. "It's my mom." The first call. "I'm shutting it off. I can't— I don't want to listen to her messages. I'd want to call her back too bad." She stuffed it back into her pocket. After a second, Henry pulled his out and shut it off too. He sighed.

"Are you sure you don't want to let Aidan choke you out?"

Andie laughed. "What for? You want me to be in love with you?"

"No." Henry snorted and shuffled his feet. "It just might be nice to feel like we knew what we were doing. Like maybe we'd know how to fight or something. Besides, it can't be all that weird. Cassandra's still Cassandra."

Andie shrugged. "I guess so. But I don't see what good it'd do. So you'd know how to use a sword. And I might know how to shoot an arrow or something. Big deal. The flipping Mustang's a more useful weapon. Besides, you'd also remember what it was like to die with a spear in your chest. Doesn't sound like fun."

"It might give us a better chance." The fuel nozzle clicked off, and Henry pulled it out and put the gas cap back on.

"I'm just not doing it. I—" She exhaled. "I'd rather die as me."

"You're not going to die, Andie."

"Look at us, Henry. Look at what we're doing. None of us knows what's going to happen. Not even Cassandra, and she's frickin' psychic."

Cassandra opened the car door and stepped out. The day was bright and cold. The parking lot of the travel plaza they'd stopped at was already busy, filled with the sounds of idling engines and the scents of oil and gasoline. She stretched her back and legs and cracked her neck.

"Look who's up. Want to go in and grab something to eat? Aidan's in there already, but he never knows what to get you." Andie gestured behind them, toward the Sunoco convenience store.

"Sure." Cassandra smiled. "You coming, Henry?"

"I'll stay with the car. Can you grab me a Chuckwagon sandwich?"

They walked through the aisles of motor oil and cold medicine, toward the cold cases in the back. Andie craned her neck toward the hot chocolate and cappuccino machines. It felt too early for soda, but they stocked up anyway, grabbing bottles of Mountain Dew and Diet Coke. Aidan walked up holding both a Grape and an Orange Crush. Cassandra could never decide which she wanted.

"I've got a couple of breakfast burritos in the microwave. We should really eat on the road."

Cassandra nodded, even though the thought of getting back into the car so soon made her want to scream and kick her feet. She'd better get used to it. They had days and days of car ahead of them. Who knew how far they'd have to run before they felt safe enough to get a motel room? Who knew how far they'd have to go before Aidan felt safe enough to sleep?

There was a short line for the cash register, and it took extra time as the guy in front of them wanted to cash in scratch-off lottery tickets and buy several more of each different type. Cassandra took the opportunity to stretch and flex her legs as much as she could. She wouldn't even have noticed the footage playing on the TV mounted in the corner had the clerk not taken it off mute and turned up the volume.

At first she thought it was a rebroadcast of the Chicago explosion. The piles of debris and clouds of dust looked so similar. But this structure was more twisted; there was more iron to it, and the destruction hadn't been as complete. The frame of half of one of the buildings was still visible, charred and jagged. And the "live" tag blinked in the corner of the screen.

"My god," she heard someone say. The camera panned over fire trucks and ambulances, flashing red and yellow lights everywhere. People were panicked and crying. On the periphery of every camera angle there was blood: someone walking with gauze pressed to their head, paramedics running past with stretchers.

"Where is that?" asked Aidan, and the guy with the lottery tickets said, "Somewhere in Philadelphia."

Philadelphia. The same way they'd been heading.

Aidan threw two twenties down on the counter and nudged Cassandra and Andie toward the door. "It's more than enough for what we got," he said when Andie looked worried. She needn't have bothered. No one even looked their way when the bell dinged to announce their exit.

Andie jogged ahead with Henry's Mountain Dew and Chuckwagon.

"It was them, wasn't it," Cassandra said.

"I think so."

"Of course it was. It was just like Chicago." She clenched her fists, felt heat behind her eyes. "How many people do you think died this time? Were they people who knew, like the witches, or were they just regular people?"

"It doesn't matter if they knew or not. She killed them." Aidan's face was a mix of blank and terror. "She's insane."

Cold fear clamped around Cassandra's heart. If Hera found them, they wouldn't have a chance.

Walking back to the Mustang, her feet felt like lead. She couldn't hear anything. The images of smoke and blood took over her senses. She didn't see the figure shuffling toward her until he was close enough to touch. Close enough to smell.

He stank of urine and something faintly medicinal. He wore the clothes of a vagabond, stained and torn, just a green sweatshirt and gray sweatpants. The sides of his Velcro tennis shoes had burst. He giggled and pointed at her. Stringy brown hair trailed along his hollow cheekbones, and underneath the shock she felt sadness. He couldn't have been more than twenty-five.

"She'll have you." His grin stretched, showing every black-stained tooth in his mouth. "She'll have you now."

"What?" Cassandra asked. "Are you all right?"

The man's eyes widened, stretching impossibly until it seemed that his lids had retracted into his skull. His hazel green eyes trembled and skittered wildly back and forth— until all at once, they were blue.

Aidan grabbed Cassandra and pulled her behind him.

"What?"

"I know those eyes. Even half mad and sick with disease, I would know them anywhere. Aphrodite."

Cassandra looked toward the car. Andie and Henry stood behind the wide open door, their faces scared and confused. She tried to drag Aidan away, but he wouldn't budge. He grabbed the man by the collar and dragged him around the side of the Sunoco station. Cassandra hesitated, then followed. She rounded the corner just in time to see the man's body buckle at Aidan's feet.

"No," she breathed. He took her by the arm.

"Walk, don't run."

"Where are we going to go now?" Cassandra asked, just before the vision struck.

It sent her to her knees. Pressure squeezed down hard on

her arms, hard enough to crack the bones. The world went by in flashes, whipping from right to left. She saw trees, a flash of blue sky. Ice-blue eyes beneath a crown of dark gold hair. Hera laughed as she wrenched her back and forth and lifted her up high. The sky whipped past, like leaning her head back on a playground swing. Panic took hold and her fists connected, digging into Hera's strange surface, soft and hard, warm flesh dotted through with granite. And then the ground rushed back. She felt her head strike pavement and heard something crack. After that, everything went dark.

"Cassandra." Aidan shook her gently. They had to move; people had seen her fall from inside the gas station and were starting to come out to help. The clerk was on the phone.

She gripped his arms and let him pull her up. Her head felt heavy. It seemed like she could feel the blood sloshing around inside it.

"We're okay," he called to the people coming toward them. "She's okay. She just slipped."

"Aidan. I saw."

"What? What did you see?" He watched in horror as blood began to drip from her nose.

"I saw Hera. I saw her kill me."

He scooped her up and ran to the Mustang. "No. Everything's going to be fine. She's not going to touch you." He shouted at Andie and Henry to get in the car, and put Cassandra gently into the passenger seat. The tires squealed as he pulled out onto the on-ramp.

"What? What's happening?" Andie gripped the back of Cassandra's seat.

"They found us. So easily. They're stronger than I am. Stronger than Athena is." Aidan mumbled. He drove too fast; the Mustang surged forward. "I don't understand it."

"You're babbling. Cassandra, he's babbling." That seemed to scare Andie worse than anything, but Cassandra couldn't reply. She was numb. Shocked and outside of herself. When Andie put a tissue to her nose and held it there to catch the bleeding, she barely noticed. She'd seen herself die. She'd felt it.

"I should've been faster. Smarter. You won't die. I swear that you won't." He reached over and touched her, twisted his fingers into hers. "I won't let her touch you. Don't be scared. Please, believe me."

I want to. But my visions are never wrong. And now I've seen it. So now it will be.

Everyone in the car was silent and bleach white with fear. Aidan watched the passing road signs and gritted his teeth, then took the next exit ramp hard and turned around, back to Kincade.

"Athena . . . it was a mistake to leave you."

They were going to need a car. That was certain. Hermes would have to steal them one. But a car didn't solve the problem of deciding which direction to drive in. The world had become so busy and vast. Even a god could get lost in it.

"Maybe they headed for the Canadian border," Odysseus suggested.

"That's no better than a guess," said Hermes. "He's evading Hera, not the Feds." They were starting to snipe at each other, pacing in their cages. Only Athena stood quietly, leaning up against the wall.

As hard as she tried, she couldn't zero in on Apollo. He wasn't even a blip on her radar. Of course, eventually her radar would light up like a circuit board. As soon as Hera and Poseidon found them, their combined presence would be a flashbulb behind her eyes. And then it would be too late. Hera would render Apollo into pieces. She'd kill Andromache and Hector, and take Cassandra, while the bits of Apollo screamed impotently in her wake, dragging themselves along the ground.

And if I face her, she'll really kill me.

Athena snorted bitterly. How she'd loved to watch her heroes fly into battle to meet the end of a spear or a sword. The glory and valor was breathtaking. She'd never figured on doing it herself.

She looked at Odysseus, his eyes bright and alive, and let her gaze wander over his features, down his shoulders and chest. These were the last few moments of quiet. Soon, they would make a decision and begin moving forward toward their end.

I'll die protecting him. There are plenty of worse ways to go than that.

Then she heard it, a whisper in her ear. It carried with it the scent of dust and a blast of dry, dry heat.

"You must go, and soon, child. He's coming back to you and bringing all of them along besides."

"Demeter."

Odysseus and Hermes stopped talking. They couldn't hear Demeter's voice. To them, the room was empty. Hermes started to ask what Athena meant, but she held up her hand.

Miles of highway passed by behind her vacant eyes. It was a road she knew would lead them straight to Apollo, with Hera still just following after, if they were lucky.

"He's on the freeway. He's forsaken stealth for speed. But he won't stay there. He's going to turn off and—" Athena stopped, and swallowed. "Thank you, Aunt."

"We are more monsters than gods now," Demeter whispered. "But some are worse than others."

For a second, Athena thought she felt a soft, dry brushing against her shoulder, like leathery fingertips. And then Demeter was gone. Athena's eyes flashed back to the present.

"I know where they are. He's on the road, and he's making a wrong turn."

"Not that I doubt a god's ability to drive," Henry said from the backseat, "but shouldn't you look ahead of you, at least once every few miles?"

Aidan cleared his throat and mumbled an apology, then went back to staring into the rearview mirror. Cassandra knew why. He was waiting for the sky to go black behind them, waiting for a ball of fire, or a flash of lightning, or whatever-the-hell entrance Hera would decide to make when she burned up their trail.

Aidan glanced at the fuel gauge and struck the steering wheel with his palm.

"This thing gets shit for gas mileage, Henry."

"So everyone keeps telling me. Why didn't you take another car, then? And why don't you have one of your own? Super rich, undying god guy?"

Andie heaved herself toward the front seat. "Stop bickering!" She put her hand on Cassandra's shoulder.

"He could've bought us twelve Priuses if he was worried about fuel economy, is all I'm saying."

"Shut up, Henry!" She gestured toward an exit sign. "Just get off the freeway. The back roads are secluded. We can slow down and save gas and still have cover. We can't stay on the interstate much longer anyway without risking a high-speed police chase."

Cassandra sat quietly in the passenger seat, holding an

open bottle of Orange Crush. Andie had finally gotten her to drink a little of it, though she'd refused anything to eat. She glanced up through the windshield. The sky was so incredibly blue and Aidan was driving so fast. But it wouldn't matter. Her death waited for her beneath blue skies and pines. On a day just like today.

"Aidan."

"Yeah?"

"If this doesn't work, will you promise to protect them?" She touched Andie's hand, still on her shoulder. "I mean it. Will you get them somewhere safe, even if I'm dead?"

"Don't talk like that," Andie snapped. "We're not going anywhere without you."

Cassandra ignored her and watched Aidan. He was a god, and gods were single-minded. She'd always thought Andie and Henry were his friends. But maybe they didn't matter if she wasn't around. Maybe he'd just leave them, out of grief, or out of indifference.

"Nothing's going to happen to any of you." Aidan looked at Cassandra. "They're my friends too."

"Promise."

"I promise."

You promised me too, once. That you had no more secrets.

The word of a god. Was it worth anything? He'd only known them for a few years, barely a blink in his long life. She would be gone before the sun began to set, and he'd go on forever. She closed her eyes.

"It's not going to hurt. It's just going to be scary, and then everything will be dark. Do you think that's how it is? My head will crack open, and I won't know anything anymore. I won't *be* anymore."

"It's not going to happen." Aidan ground his teeth and signaled for the exit toward Seneca Lake. "We'll cut through the Finger Lakes back to Kincade. But we're not staying. I'll just . . . tell Athena to be ready, and then we're going north."

"What if she tries to stop us?"

"She won't. Not this time."

Cassandra slid her fingers against his. "This isn't your fault. Not really."

He squeezed her hand and held it to his lips. "Don't give up. I'll stand against anything that tries to hurt you. Even my crazy-ass stepmother."

They drove, fast and silent, along the curving highway that bordered the lake. Aidan kept one hand twined around Cassandra's. He muttered to himself, curses and plans and possibilities. She watched him check the fuel gauge for the hundredth time since they left the freeway.

"Aidan!" Henry shouted.

Aidan looked up just in time to see the person in the road. He jerked the wheel hard, and the tire caught the edge of the shoulder. For an instant, the Mustang tilted precariously, and the screaming of rubber against asphalt and gravel rose in Cassandra's ears. But then the car slowed and straightened out. Aidan hit the brakes hard and the jolt of the stop threw Cassandra mostly onto the dashboard. The Mustang sat half on and half off of the road, the front end pointed toward a slender but imposing-looking pine tree.

"What the hell was that about?" Andie asked breathlessly. The person in the road had been an old woman, and she'd walked right out of the trees into the path of the car. "Some old lady, just walking across the road? Where did she come from? Did you see a house?"

The stretch of highway was secluded, bordered on both sides by pines and orange-and-brown autumn trees. Farther out, Cassandra saw the slate gray edge of Seneca Lake peeking through the trunks. She thought back over the way they'd come.

"There was no house. No driveway, not even another car for the last five miles. What was she doing, popping out of the trees?"

"Thank god we didn't hit her."

"It would have been better if we had." Aidan stared into the side mirror, looking back with dread. Cassandra craned her neck to look out the window.

The old woman stood in the middle of the road as though dazed. Her arms hung slack at her sides, and she swayed on her feet, which were planted wide apart. Something was off. Something wrong. The vacant way she stared at the car made Cassandra want to crawl under the seat.

"What's the matter with her face?" Henry asked. As they watched, the old woman's cheeks began to sag. The lines became deeper, and the corners pulled down until her mouth was a leering scowl. Then it dripped off, leaving behind a wet, black spot.

"Get it in gear, Aidan," Andie said shrilly as more of the old woman's face detached and hit the pavement. All of her skin liquefied; her hair slid down her head to reveal the skull beneath: obsidian black and covered in slime and scales.

"What is that thing?" Henry asked, but Aidan didn't answer. He threw the car into reverse.

"Buckle up."

We have to go faster. Much, much faster.

Athena sat in the passenger seat; her knee bounced and twitched nervously. Odysseus was driving as fast as he could, but it was nowhere near fast enough. They were headed south, toward the Finger Lakes, on Route 89. Seneca Lake was close enough to smell, but they were still at least twenty minutes from finding Apollo and Cassandra. She glanced toward Hermes with annoyance. She refused to believe that there hadn't been anything faster in the car lot than a '91 Dodge Spirit. She looked back to Odysseus. He was scared. Much of that fear was concern for her. Was he really driving as fast as he could?

She pushed her neck back slightly and checked the gauges. Eighty miles an hour. Any faster and the engine in the piece of crap would fall out onto the highway.

Apollo, you fool. What would make you run anywhere near these deep, dead lakes when you know that Poseidon is on your tail?

The tires squealed; the smell of burnt rubber bloomed instantly in the air. The Mustang growled into reverse, aiming straight for the old woman.

Cassandra would have winced, even if she had been the most evil old woman on the face of the planet. Even if she had been granny-Hitler, she would have winced at the idea of running her down. But the thing standing in the road looked nothing like an old woman anymore. It was hulking and webbed, with teeth like an anglerfish from the depths of the ocean. The last of the old woman sat in a puddle around its feet.

The Mustang hit it with a heavy thud, and Cassandra bounced as the body passed beneath first the back and then the front set of tires. Aidan braked hard, and the car slid to a stop.

"What the hell is that thing?" Henry asked again.

"It's a Nereid," Aidan growled. "It's disgusting and warped, but that's what it is. They serve Poseidon."

"Poseidon?"

"Poseidon." Aidan ground the gears in the Mustang. "You know, god of the sea, brother of Zeus. My uncle, and a real prick." He dropped the car into first and revved the engine.

As they spoke, two more Nereids emerged from between the trees and sprang onto the highway. Above the burning rubber, the scent of wet rot and fish permeated the air.

"Hang on." Aidan popped the clutch and the car squealed forward, aiming straight for them. Cassandra squinted her eyes and turned her face away from the impact. Their huge, muscular bodies were likely to come right through the windshield. Her mind flashed on the image of one of them covered in shattered glass and bleeding on her lap, the rotten, fishy reek smeared across her clothes.

It seemed that neither Nereid was going to move. But at the last second, one of them dodged around the car, slamming its fists into the passenger side, crushing Cassandra's door and cracking the window. The other Nereid went the same way as the first, under one set of tires and then the other.

"Are you all right?" Aidan asked, and she nodded, her eyes wide. He turned toward her, his eyes moving across her arms, making sure she hadn't been hurt. He didn't see the goddess step in front of them until everyone else in the car screamed.

Aidan hit the brakes instinctively as Aphrodite raised her arms. When they slammed down onto the hood, it was like being struck by pillars of marble. The Mustang's engine was driven six inches into the asphalt, and the rear end of the frame jerked upward, lifting off the ground two feet before bouncing back down again.

Aphrodite stood amidst the steam rising from the wrecked hood, a broad smile stretched across her flawless face. Her eyes locked with Aidan's, hot with madness. She leaned against the boiling black paint, laughing a maniac's laughter as golden hair lifted in waves around her shoulders. The whimsical, gauzy dress she wore was beautiful and ruined, shades of differing blue and green, stained and torn in a hundred places. Cassandra remembered her from the vision, the shadows and water reflections swirling over her features. She was worse in the daylight, with no shadows to hide under.

"Get out of that car, baby brother. Get out of that car and come home with Mother."

"Cassandra," said Aidan softly. His hand went to the door handle. "When I take her on, you have to run, do you understand?"

Cassandra looked at the mad thing in front of the Mustang, and the bent steel of the hood. In the mirror, wrecked black bodies of Nereids littered the road, but there would be others. Aidan would be outnumbered. They'd run over the top of him and come for her anyway.

"No. We stick together. I'm not leaving you."

He grasped her hand and kissed it. "You're the one they're after. Remember your vision." He let her go and opened the car door.

Cassandra watched as Aphrodite backed off to give Aidan space. He kept his body between her and the Mustang, and she seemed happy to let him do it. She circled and crouched and made mock charges, laughing when he jerked to block her way.

"It doesn't make me happy to see you this way, sister."

Aphrodite clucked her tongue. "Apollo, Apollo, still so pretty. Give up the girl and come home. Mother will not be angry."

"Hera isn't your mother."

Cassandra tensed, watching the exchange. In the corner of her eye something dark moved, just a shadow in the trees. Another Nereid. If she and the others ran now, they'd be caught, whether Aidan had a hold on Aphrodite or not. She could feel them, and smell them, moving in closer, tightening around them like a knot.

"You shouldn't have run," Aphrodite scolded. "You shouldn't have shielded her. You made us chase, made me sad, made Mother tear witches in half." She looked at him petulantly, her full lips pouting. Then she smiled and half turned away, before hooking her fingers into claws and aiming for his eyes.

"Aidan!" Cassandra shouted, and opened her door. Before she could get out, Henry lunged from the backseat and pulled her back in, just as the Nereids attacked the car. Three of them beat into the side panels and rocked the frame back and forth. One smashed in the rear window and reached for Henry; Andie punched it in the face over and over, oblivious to the cuts left on her knuckles by fins and scales.

Aidan twisted out of Aphrodite's grip and tried to help, grabbing the nearest Nereid and shoving his fingers deep into the creature's eye sockets, then ripping back hard enough to dislodge the skull. Aphrodite shrieked and clawed at his back, drawing deep furrows of blood, but Aidan kept moving, using the head of the first Nereid to bludgeon the one who attacked the back of the car.

Henry scrambled to the front seat and covered Cassandra with his body, protecting her from glass and clawed fingers.

"Henry, door prize!" Andie shouted, and Henry savagely kicked his door into a Nereid on the passenger side. The impact sent it rolling back toward the ditch. He looked at Cassandra, shocked only for a moment before his eyes darkened.

"Stay here. Both of you." He got out and slammed the car door, going after the Nereid he'd struck.

"Not a chance." The door opened again and Andie followed. She scooped up a thick branch as she went.

Cassandra sat frozen in the car. It felt suddenly quiet and alone. The Nereids had gone off after Andie and Henry; she saw Henry duck a black, scaled arm and punch the creature in the face. In front of the Mustang, Aidan struggled with Aphrodite on his back. Cassandra looked around the interior, at seats covered with spilled soda and snack wrappers. Nothing she could use for a weapon.

What am I supposed to do? How do I help them?

Aphrodite's hands searched for Aidan's neck.

"I'll snap your spine and tear your head off," she shrieked. "Then I'll keep it as a pet."

"So you can bitch at me at your leisure? I don't think so." He reached back to flip her over the front of him, but she was hooked in. Her teeth sank into the meaty part of his shoulder, and he screamed.

"Aidan!" Cassandra's hand went to the car door and she stepped out, ready to do she didn't know what. "Get off him!"

Out of nowhere, Hermes blew in like a breeze and collided with Aphrodite. The hit knocked her off of Aidan's back and dumped her rolling onto the side of the road.

"You make a fairly nasty turtle shell, bitch." Hermes' sides rose and fell rapidly, but his eyes were bright.

"Where did you come from?" Aidan asked.

"About ten miles back, Athena opened my door and told me to hit the ground running." He gave Aidan a small smile. "You shouldn't be so hard on big sister. She always comes through in the end."

At the edge of the ditch, Aphrodite got to her feet, crying at the fresh dirt streaks on her already stained dress.

"Bastards," she hissed, and Hermes and Aidan made ready to fight, but she turned and fled through the trees, down to the water. The Nereids too had pulled back. Andie and Henry backed up toward the car.

"What are they doing?" Andie went to Cassandra and held her shoulder. Henry came too, his forearm bleeding from cuts made by sharp gills and razor teeth.

"Cassie, get back in the car."

"Don't bother." Hermes watched the Nereids. They stood on the edge of the highway, their posture attentive, like they were listening for something. They had all turned to face the lake.

Something's coming.

The dark water rippled along the shore. Cassandra could almost feel it against her arms, the depth and the cold. It raised goose bumps across her shoulders. She thought she saw something skimming along under the surface, some ragged, shadowy shape, hulking and enormous, the Loch Ness Monster in the flesh.

When Poseidon reared his head out of the water, his jaw jerking open to reveal shark's rows of jagged teeth, Cassandra gasped. Next to her, Aidan stared at the monster his uncle had become.

"Big sister better not be far behind."

The road twisted north and curved; Odysseus had to slow down, sometimes to as low as fifty miles an hour. Athena struck the dashboard, eyes bright with fear and frustration.

"I'm sorry," Odysseus said. "It won't help anyone if we

flip the car." He glanced at her, a question in his eyes. She shook her head.

"Don't ask me to turn back. And don't try it. I'll just throttle you and drag you bleeding back into the fray."

He smiled. "I know. Is Hera there yet? Can you sense her?"

Athena shook her head. She'd sensed Aphrodite and Poseidon clearly enough. Their arrival, so malevolent and sudden, had practically blown a circuit out the back of her head. But Hera had not yet made the scene. It was the only thing that gave her hope.

"They won't last long," Athena said.

"Don't sell them short. Apollo got the drop on you for a minute, when he bashed your head in. He can do the same to Poseidon."

Athena looked at him doubtfully.

"Just drive faster."

A Nereid sprang out of nowhere and dove for Cassandra. They'd all been so busy staring at Poseidon that they hadn't noticed it coming close. It knocked Andie and Henry aside like toys. Cassandra tried to dodge, but it grabbed her by the wrist.

"Aidan!"

It was so strong. No matter how she dug her feet in or clawed at its grip, the ground only seemed to go by faster. Her ankles caught on the dirt and rolled painfully.

Fall. Let me fall. Slow down.

But it didn't. It held her up and kept on, speeding her mindlessly toward the lake, while Aidan screamed her name. She glanced back. Nereids had swarmed the Mustang like black beetles. Hermes had his hands full with three, and two dragged Aidan down toward the ground. Andie and Henry fought back–to-back, but there were too many. Cassandra shouted as she saw one rake its claws across Andie's stomach.

Ahead of her, Poseidon yawned like a nightmare, barnacle shells eating away the surface of his arms, blood like black oil draining from cuts made by coral that twisted up his body and sliced tunnels into his face. She remembered his teeth in the witch's leg, and her own legs turned to rubber.

"Cassandra, I'm coming!"

She looked back; Aidan had gotten free and dashed down through the trees. Black Nereid bodies littered the ground around the car. Hermes tore another head loose and dashed down after him, so fast. But in the next instant, cold struck her belly and closed over her head as the Nereid dragged her into the water.

She held her breath as they went under, all her limbs twisting toward panic. Panic at the teeth with her in the lake; panic that her lungs already burned from lack of air. She kicked against the Nereid's side and it let her break the surface.

"Aidan!"

Her teeth chattered in the frigid water. The shock of it made all her muscles seize. If the Nereid let her go, she wasn't sure she'd be able to swim to shore. Through weak splashes of protest, she could still see Poseidon, standing suspended, his torso covered in seaweed and slime, a god purified and corrupted all at once. His death transformed him, made him elemental, enormous. More a Titan's offspring than he had ever been.

He'll kill him. If Aidan faces him, Poseidon will drag him down like a shark.

She turned toward the shore.

"No! Go back!"

But he wouldn't. He wouldn't even hesitate.

Hermes stood at the edge of the lake watching her. He caught Aidan by the arm.

"Wait, brother."

"There's no time!" He tried to jerk loose, but Hermes held him fast.

"He'll kill you and take her anyway."

Aidan looked at Cassandra. She could barely see for blinking back water. *Hold him there. Make him wait.*

Aidan turned to Hermes.

"Not if you help me." He twisted out of his brother's grip and ran into the water, diving in fast.

Hermes shook his head. "Shouldn't we say something heroic first?" he shouted, but he plunged in, plunged in afraid, and swam after them both, toward a god diseased by shells and the claws of crustaceans.

Fresh adrenaline reached Cassandra's blood and she struggled, kicking and splashing. Her fingernails dug into the Nereid's scaled hand. She twisted them and drew blood, but it didn't matter. Poseidon watched them come, his one remaining eye coated with film. Except for the hungry gape of his jaw, he almost looked disinterested.

The Nereid let go and darted away, and for an instant Cassandra felt mad hope. But it had left her for *him*. Left her and swam away fast to keep from falling to the god's teeth. She felt a massive hand grip her leg and drag her down. Cold drenched her to the bone. It flooded into her ears, blotted the world out in heavy, murky darkness.

I don't want to drown. I can't, I don't. I die on a road, my head cracked into pieces.

She opened her eyes as something passed by: Hermes. He drove his fist into Poseidon's cracked flesh, but it was resilient as the rubber of a tire. It didn't matter how he wrenched and fought. Poseidon didn't release his grip. Through the silt-churned water Cassandra saw another massive hand cut through and close on Hermes' arm.

It'll snap. There'll be a snap, and his arm will break, the muscle will tear away and turn the water red.

But no. It would take more than a Titan's fingers to break Hermes' bones. All around them, black bodies of Nereids slid past like curious sharks, but none of them struck. She didn't know why. Perhaps they'd been ordered not to. Or perhaps they were afraid of Poseidon too.

Her lungs tightened. Hermes twisted toward the arm that held her and bit down on tendon; the grip loosened just enough for him to push her toward the surface.

"Get to the shore!" he screamed, but she had just enough time for a breath before Poseidon dragged her back down.

Her head spun, growing dizzy from lack of oxygen and fear. She finally caught sight of Aidan through the bubbles and moving currents. He'd gotten around Poseidon's back and hit him repeatedly. The reverberations of his fists passed through the water again and again, but weren't doing much.

We have to get out of the lake; we have to get to shore.

The pressure of the water against Cassandra's skin and the sensation of being swallowed by the lake was too much. Poseidon would drown her and drag her corpse to the ocean with Aidan swimming behind.

Cold fear and despair took over, and she tore again at Poseidon's hand. Her fingers found a piece of coral embedded near his palm and latched on, jerking at it, trying to tear it free. Hermes saw her and joined in, his hands brushing hers aside. It pulled loose like a long root from the ground and left a deep, twisting gash up Poseidon's wrist, all the way into his elbow. Blood like black ink drifted around them in a cloud, but it worked. Poseidon let go, and Hermes shoved Cassandra toward the surface.

She coughed and sputtered. Hermes yelled for Aidan, who was there in an instant.

"Get her to the shore." He looked at his golden brother. "And then come back. Don't leave me here." He dove back under, and Aidan put his arm around Cassandra's waist and swam while she sucked in air. She tried to help when her heels hit soft sand, but her legs were weak and rubbery. He set her on the bank, away from the water's edge, and smoothed back her hair.

"Are you all right?" He inspected her arms and legs for cuts; there weren't any.

"I'm fine." Her lip trembled. She didn't want to cry, but it was there, in her throat. Terror and despair, big enough to make it hard to swallow.

"Go back to Andie and Henry. Wait for Athena. Don't worry. You've shown us how. Now we'll take him apart." He was back in the water before she could tell him not to go.

He wouldn't have listened if I had. His brother is there. Fighting for us.

She struggled to her knees and to her feet, backed away from the water another few yards. The lake churned around Poseidon, churned and splashed like the site of a feeding frenzy. Mad as it was, she wanted to be back in the water, back under the dark. On the shore, she couldn't see what was happening, whether they were all right.

A form broke the surface and someone screamed: Hermes. Poseidon had sunk his teeth into Hermes' ankle. His massive head twisted and Hermes twisted with it, but even as he did, he reached out for a pearlescent shell embedded in the other god's chest and ripped it loose.

Poseidon let go and roared, but Hermes didn't swim

away. He stayed in close and went to work, fingers like whirlwinds, tearing out shells and pieces of sea trash, carapaces of crabs and lobsters half submerged. Even strands of thick-bladed sea grass with roots twisted into Poseidon's veins. Discarded pieces of the sea god floated around them before they slowly sank.

Poseidon continued to rage; he plunged his hand beneath the surface and dragged Aidan up by the arm. His head twisted to bite and Cassandra screamed as he wrenched his head back and forth, ripping at Aidan like a crocodile, his lidless eyes expressionless. Red bloomed in the water and Cassandra saw a Nereid flit closer, smelling the blood. They had to get out of the lake. The Nereids would rush in to help sooner or later, whether they were ordered to or not.

"I'm not going to die underwater, you prick!" Hermes reached for the coral in Poseidon's empty eye socket and twisted savagely. It broke with a sickening crack and Poseidon howled, pain driving him out of the water to the waist.

"It's working!" Aidan shouted. "Keep going!"

Skin and muscle hung in loose shards across Poseidon's chest and shoulders. They were dismantling him. Piece by piece. But it wasn't fast. Poseidon drew his arm back and struck Hermes, sending him splashing back. He turned on Aidan, a horror with razor teeth and an eye socket leaking black down a cheek webbed with seaweed.

No. Don't touch him. Don't hurt him.

Far up the hill, she heard Andie and Henry shout as Poseidon lunged. Her heart hesitated in her chest as the teeth descended and took Aidan underwater.

"Aidan!" She scanned the ripples, the splashes. Long seconds ticked by with her stomach in her throat. "Hermes! Where are you?"

"I'm here."

He limped out of the water, dragging his mangled foot in the sand.

"No. What are you doing here? You can't leave him!"

Hermes looked back toward the lake. His eyes were distant and exhausted. "I didn't. He won."

"What?"

"Poseidon's dead." He thumped his chest. "I know it. It's leached into my bones, passed into my blood like an electric shock. The sea no longer has a master."

"But where's Aidan?" Cassandra stared out at the calming surface, but Hermes paid no attention.

"There were pieces of him everywhere. As I was coming out, I think I saw a Nereid glide by and eat a chunk." He chuckled sadly. "Poetic justice."

Cassandra gave a small cry as Aidan's head popped out of the water, bleeding from the nose and mouth. He swam slowly, awkwardly, and as he came into the shallows she saw why: Poseidon's bloated, ragged head hung from his right hand. The god of the sea was dead.

"Guess that answers that question," Hermes muttered, and turned up the hill toward the sound of screeching tires. A champagne-tan Dodge Spirit pulled up in front of the Mustang. The door opened and Athena rose out. She stared down at them in amazement. Odysseus got out of the driver's side and his mouth spread in a wide grin.

Cassandra closed her eyes. Time had stood still since Aidan went back into the lake. But he was all right. He was there, drenched, holding an enormous severed head. Black blood drained from the ragged neck hole, staining his jeans and shoes. The Nereids were gone, slipped away toward the ocean once Poseidon was dead, or perhaps carrying his body along with them.

"Aidan." She went to him as fast as she could on shaky legs. "Are you okay?"

"Well, he bit me." His shirt was red from shoulder to elbow, and the water that dripped from his fingers was tinged pink. But he would heal. He looked at Poseidon's head, which lost its color as it drained. The one remaining eye stared back at them. "Zeus' brother. Earth-shaker. Dead at my hands."

"He hasn't really been Poseidon in a long time." Hermes swallowed as Aidan moved to lean on Cassandra and kiss her head.

"Want to carry it?" Aidan asked and held out the head. "My shoulder—"

"You carry it." Hermes recoiled. "You're the one with two working legs."

Aidan smiled. He tossed the head down into the sand. Cassandra kissed his cheek, shivering. He held her closer. "You need a blanket."

"You need a doctor."

"No. We have to go." He looked up the hill, where Athena waited, smiling down at them and shaking her head. "We'll take that POS until we find something better. Big sister can cover our tail." He took a breath. "We might make it. Athena's here and Poseidon's dead. We will make it, Cassandra."

She looked into his eyes. "I was so scared, when I couldn't see you."

He smiled. "I'm sorry."

"Then why are you smiling?"

"Because of what it means. Because of the chance."

Hermes huffed. "Make kissy faces later. Let's just hobble up this damned hill." He jump-limped ahead, bitching under his breath.

Cassandra hid her grin. "He's a good brother."

"So's yours." Aidan nodded toward the destroyed Mustang, where Henry and Andie waited, side by side. "Killed a few Nereids and never once yelled at me about the car. You're shivering." He pulled her closer. The warmth of his arms and the nearness of him made her heart jump. He'd saved her life, and they might make it. They might make it and get past everything.

"The lake was cold. Could you do that sun-god thing you do?" He smiled, and heat radiated into her, soaking into her skin, drying her clothes and hair.

"Apollo!" Athena screamed. Cassandra looked up toward her, confused. The confusion lasted only an instant before Aphrodite raced out from between the trees and plunged a cracked branch through Aidan's chest.

20

ARISTEIA

Aphrodite wrenched the improvised spear out of his chest, her sneer like a spoiled child. Aidan dropped to his knees.

"No!" Athena raced down the slope, not caring as Aphrodite turned tail and ran, only pausing to scoop up Poseidon's severed head before fleeing up through the trees toward the road, her stained dress mocking them like a flag, blue and green.

"Get him to the car. Hermes, help me." She grabbed Aidan under his arms and dragged him back up the hill. Cassandra scrambled along with them, crying and pressing her hands down on the wound. Leaves crunched and rustled beneath them in a thick, shifting carpet. Hermes tried to take hold of Aidan's legs, but his ankle was ruined, and he kept slipping against the soggy ground. There was so much blood. Aidan coughed and Athena saw it on his teeth.

He's all right. He's a god, he's fine. It won't kill him. He's fine.

They got him up to the road and leaned him against the side of the Dodge.

"I need water and a towel, something to stop the bleeding," Athena barked. Odysseus nudged Henry and they ran to get what they could from the Mustang. "It's okay, brother. It hurts, but you'll recover."

"He'll recover," Cassandra repeated, and Athena nodded. The way Cassandra stared at her, eyes coated over with tears, jaw clenched down tight to keep from screaming, what else could she say? She needed to believe her. They both did.

"Cassandra." Aidan held out his hand and Cassandra took it, wincing at the blood. She wiped tears quickly from her cheeks.

"I'm not crying. Your sister's right; you'll be fine."

"I'm sorry I scared you. I'm sorry for lots of things."

"Don't try to talk." His hair clung to his forehead, still wet. She pushed it back and rubbed blood off his chin with her thumb. "Athena's going to stop the bleeding. It'll be okay." She looked at Athena. "Aren't you? You're going to stop it?"

Athena glanced at the wound, at all the red pulsing out of it. Cassandra's eyes were desperate, but she kept her voice even and measured, like she didn't want Aidan to be afraid.

"Here." Odysseus handed Athena a rolled-up shirt and a bottle of water.

She knelt and gently moved Aidan and Cassandra's hands away from the wound. The bleeding was bad, spurting slowly through their fingers. *It should have slowed. It should be slowing.*

"We'll have to wash this out when we get back to Kincade." She pressed the shirt against his chest as hard as she could. "And you'll need to be stitched up. Don't worry. Odysseus is pretty good at it."

Aidan barked a short laugh and grimaced. "We can't go back there. They'll find Cassandra."

"Don't argue with me right now." Blood soaked through to her fingers. His eyes were glassy. Cassandra held his hand to her chest.

"Don't argue. And don't worry about me." She looked at the blood and again at Athena. "Why isn't it stopping?"

Athena shook her head helplessly and pressed down harder. She didn't know what to do. "Take a sip of water," she said. Aidan tried, but coughed most of it back up.

"I was just yanked under a lake. I've had plenty of water today." Sweat stood out on his forehead in fine dots. *His skin is cold. He's never cold. He's god of the sun.*

"But this isn't enough," Hermes whispered. "It shouldn't be bad enough to—it shouldn't be able to. I don't understand."

"Somebody do something," Cassandra began to shake. She looked at Athena. "Do something!"

Athena held Aidan's shoulder.

We all go in our own way. This is Apollo's way. He's dying a mortal's death. Aphrodite killed him and she probably didn't even know what she was doing.

"It's not her fault, Cassandra." Aidan put his hand over Athena's, over the wound in his chest. "You can't let anything happen to her, sister. Promise me."

You're her protector, not me. Stay. Stay, brother. Don't go somewhere I can't find you.

"I promise." The blood beneath her fingers slowed to a crawl. There simply wasn't any left to bleed. He looked at Cassandra with such love and such regret, it almost stopped Athena's heart.

"I'm so sorry."

"Don't apologize to me." Cassandra kissed his hand. "You're not going anywhere. You're immortal. I've got my whole life to—"

Athena's shoulders slumped. She'd felt it pass through her as Cassandra spoke. He was gone. Her fingers clenched into his shirt, tight enough to wring it out.

"No," Cassandra moaned. Andie took her by the shoulders, but Cassandra looked like she was choking. Like her screams would explode inside her chest.

He can't be gone. All this life, leaked out onto the pavement.

He was a god. There had to be some way to put it back. Athena wanted to scream, to cry, to crack the earth. Odysseus slid his hand onto the back of her neck. Behind Andie, Henry stared, looking like he was about to be sick.

"Why did this happen, sister?" Hermes asked. But she didn't know. There were no answers, and the leathery flap of Demeter didn't come to whisper wisdom into her ear. Apollo was dead. Poseidon was dead. It all felt pointless.

"Poor, idiotic Apollo." Hera's voice rolled across the asphalt, deep and mocking. She had come up from behind them, as Athena had known she would. The weight of her strides made the earth tremble.

Hermes stood quickly, his posture like a prey animal. Athena twisted and watched Hera approach. She stopped thirty yards away, arms crossed over her chest.

"I'm not going to say that it didn't have to end like this," she said.

Athena stood and gestured toward her fallen brother.

"Like this? Are you mad? He's dead. You'll save yourself by killing your family?"

Hera looked at him, and for a moment it seemed that sadness flickered across her hardening face.

"He was a stepson, only. Another bastard put upon me by my husband. Yet I would've welcomed him, had he not forgotten what you've forgotten. That he was a god. That gods are not meant to die."

Aphrodite scurried to her, Poseidon's decapitated head clutched to her breast.

"They killed him! They killed him!"

"And she killed Aidan!" Athena shouted, and Aphrodite edged toward Hera's protecting arms.

Hera cocked her head.

"Who?" Then she studied Aidan's jeans, his hooded sweatshirt. She shook her head, disgusted, and stroked Aphrodite's hair. "I know, pet. I felt the sea god's light go out. I'm sorry I wasn't here. I would've ground them to paste before they ever touched him."

Athena took quick stock. What did they have? A slow Dodge and a fleet-footed god with a broken ankle. Their getaway would be sad and short.

"Why are you doing this?"

Hera snorted. "Don't ask stupid questions."

"Do you really think you can kill us all? All of us and these mortals besides?"

"I know I can."

Hera whispered to Aphrodite and she slipped quietly to the side of the road, Poseidon's blood mingling with the dirt streaks on her green and blue dress as she hugged it. "I lived with mortals too, you know. I loved them. Raised them." She shrugged. "I even married a few. But I never forgot what I really was. The choice between them and us isn't a choice. It's just us."

"Us. But not Hermes and me."

Hera cocked her head. "Perhaps Hermes. But not you."

Athena turned an ear back to Hermes, half wondering if the next sound she heard would be his feet, dragging and hopping to the other side of the battle line. Instead she felt the press of his shoulder against her.

"And why not Athena?" Hermes asked. "What's she

done? She's not a bastard, not a betrayal of you by your husband. He made her out of himself. No paramour required."

Athena watched Hera's jaw set bitterly.

That's why. All this time. All these years. That's why she's never been a mother to me, when she was the only mother I knew. I was evidence that she wasn't necessary.

"Athena." Cassandra spoke quietly from where she knelt, holding Aidan's cold hand. Athena turned toward her. "This is what I saw. Why Aidan turned us back. The blue sky and evergreens. The silver-black of asphalt on the highway. Hera's face, vicious and full of glory, even as chunks of granite form on her arms and shoulders. I remember the exact sensation of striking her skin." She looked at Aidan's empty face. "I remember the light going out." She stroked his pale cheek, then turned to Athena with steel in her eyes. "This is it. This is the end."

"The end?" Athena looked down at her. "But it can't be."

"I don't have all day, stepdaughter," Hera called. Her kitten heels tapped against the road. "Come closer so I can kill you and your half brother."

Athena couldn't form a thought. As she looked at Aidan's body, Hera's words landed sour, like a wrong strike against a tuning fork. They made her spine twitch and sent sharp bursts of rage ringing across her surface.

"Apollo lost his life to save a mortal girl. So now I will too."

"No," Cassandra said, and grasped her wrist. "You can't stop it."

"It's not a choice. He wanted you safe. And we need you safe, so—"

"No." She clenched her fist around Athena's arm. Athena's mouth dropped open. Where the girl touched her, it

[320]

burned. Like the tingling on her face, after she'd slapped her. She looked up, her chest full suddenly with absurd hope and the words of Demeter urgent in her ears. *She could be the key to everything. . . .*

Cassandra trembled, then grew still.

"I feel it too, whatever it is. And I've seen this. I've seen this day and this fight. I'm in it with you."

Athena looked at her, deep into her brown eyes. *What is this thing? Like looking at a frozen surface through a pane of glass.* She didn't know what it was exactly. But she knew it was power.

She grasped Cassandra's hand. "How does it end?"

Cassandra shook her head.

Athena nodded. "Okay."

They took a deep breath. Conviction laced the air between them, white hot.

"I don't know how much strength is left in me," said Athena.

"Enough," Cassandra said softly. She looked one last time at Aidan's face.

Together, they rose to their feet and looked down the road. Hera stood with Aphrodite hiding behind. The stone fist hung heavily at her side. More patches of stone were visible too, spattering her neck and cheeks with flecks of gray granite. She wore a finely woven black coat and dark blue jeans. She looked cold, almost indifferent. Someone who didn't know her would never guess at her violent temperament. She kept it carefully hidden. Swallowing so much vindictiveness and rage must have been like swallowing shards of metal.

"I don't know how much use you'll be with a crushed foot," Athena said to Hermes. "But keep the others safe, if you can." She glanced over her shoulder at Odysseus. When she turned away, he caught her by the arm and pulled her back.

"Athena." They looked at each other for a long second. Fear shone plain in his eyes, and for a moment she thought he might actually say it, that he might actually grab her and kiss her and throw her completely off her game. Instead he smiled his cockeyed smile and pushed the tire iron from the Dodge into her hand.

"Don't get hit," he said quietly. She wrapped her fingers around the weapon.

Good advice.

"Give up the girl," Hera commanded.

"And you'll let us live?" Athena asked sarcastically.

Hera smirked. "Of course not."

Athena looked over at Cassandra, who stared straight ahead. She didn't know what she was doing, leading a mortal against the Titans' queen. It felt crazy. It felt against everything she'd ever known about war and battle and strategy. It felt completely right.

When she walked, the girl walked with her. The tire iron settled into her palm. As they came closer, Aphrodite scurried away, a rat going to hide in the sewers and wait until it was all over. Hera bared her teeth. The stone fist twitched. There would be no bombs this time, no tricks. *She wants the satisfaction of murdering me with her bare hands.*

"How noble. Standing against me together? All for one and one for all?"

Athena clenched her jaw. "Me first." The tire iron spun, slicing through the air as she ran and sprang, using it to strike and slash. Hera ducked and dodged, her face a twisted grimace. When the iron finally connected, it caught her in the back of the shoulder and barely knocked her forward.

In the corner of her eye, Athena saw a flash of granite and pulled out of the way.

Don't get hit.

Cassandra watched Athena and Hera, fists and iron, moving sharply through the air. Fear laced through her insides, but it wasn't alone. An odd certainty ran in her blood, infusing it with heat. She knew what she had seen in her vision. She remembered what the world had looked like, flying by. Her death was here. And it wasn't. The images shimmered, becoming transparent. She should have been terrified. She should have been mad with grief, collapsed over Aidan's body. Instead she waited. Waited for Athena to give her an opening.

Athena was struggling. Speed was the key, both to landing blows and to keeping her skull in one piece. But it was also tiring. Hitting Hera was like hitting twelve tons of rock. It sent painful shock waves all the way up to her shoulder. And Hera's fist came dangerously closer.

She swung once more and leapt away, breathing hard; the feathers lining the lower part of her lungs held her back. The tire iron sat heavier and heavier in her hand. Hera's arm swung and Athena leapt out of the way, half a second too late. The ribs on her left side cracked and disconnected. The world turned colors as she flew through the air and her lower back thumped into the base of a tree. In comparison to Hera's arm, it felt soft.

"You're supposed to be so smart," Hera said. "What do you think you're doing? I'm going to smash you to pieces.

I'm going to grind you into the road until you're nothing but a stain." Kitten-heeled footsteps jarred the pavement as Athena pushed up onto her elbow, and then her knee. "You killed your uncle, my brother!"

"You killed mine!" Athena shouted, and suppressed a cough. Her left lung had mostly collapsed, and breathing through the feathers made it feel like a flapping curtain. Hera advanced, glittering eyes and stone.

"And now I'll kill you."

"Maybe. But not before I put a few decent chips in your ass." Hera threw her fist and Athena dodged to the side. She heard a wet crack as Hera's arm cut through a tree trunk. Quickly, she swung the tire iron in an arc and caught Hera on the cheek. It gave a sharp crack, followed by the sound of a pebble rolling across asphalt. Athena looked toward the road and saw a sparkle of skittering granite. Hera's cheek bled from the new hole, leaking down over her jaw. Athena smiled. "See?"

Hera screamed and advanced, moving faster. The weight of the stone slowed her down and Athena used the trees, dodging and scrambling, listening to wood splinter all around. She gritted her teeth. Ducking and running. Scrambling around in the dirt for a hold. She'd never fought this way. The wound to her side sapped her, and the certainty and resolve of the moments before battle seemed a thousand years in the past. She staggered toward the road and glanced over her shoulder, saw Hera bearing down. The tire iron swung once and missed.

"The goddess of battle runs like a rabbit," Hera shouted. "Olympus would be ashamed of you."

"Olympus doesn't exist," Athena growled. She feinted behind a tree.

I was wrong to try this. Running isn't a plan.

Hera wouldn't tire, but Athena would. She had. Her breath dragged through her throat, and she stumbled.

It was an unlucky accident. There were no trees between them, no seconds of advantage. Hera surged forward. She caught Athena by the hair and dragged her onto the road, presenting her like a trophy while Aphrodite chattered and clapped. Through half-closed eyes, Athena saw her ragged band; saw their faces suspended over terror, believing she would win, willing the tire iron in her hand to rise up. When Hera threw the stone fist into Athena's side, the ribs that were broken crumbled like chalk.

She went down on one knee, trying to hold her lung inside her body. From somewhere, she heard Odysseus shout. He couldn't come anywhere near. Hera would kill him instantly, or take him to use to find Achilles. Either way, she wouldn't be able to stop it. She couldn't breathe. She knelt at Hera's feet and waited for the blow she knew would come, for the searing pain through the back of her head, and then the darkness.

Do it quick. And then let them run. Let Hermes take them far away from here.

"Honestly, Athena. I expected more out of you."

She looked down at the toes of Hera's well-kept heels. The Titan was so close. Her breath moved through Athena's hair.

"I'm going to kill them all, you know. Hermes, and Hector, and Andromache. Even Cassandra and your precious Odysseus, after I'm done with them. I'll peel the skin right off of their bodies. And they'll curse you."

Athena clenched her teeth. It was true. If they died, they would curse her. It would be her fault.

"Get up, child. The goddess of battle does not die on her knees."

Am I to die then, Aunt Demeter?

"There is glory on that stretch of road. Glory, and cracked stone, and blood . . . "

"She never answers the damned question," Athena muttered.

"Last words?" Hera leaned down close, smiling.

Athena clenched her fists. Demeter might be just a flap of skin, but she was right. If she died, she'd die in pieces and rage, not kneeling with a bowed head. She took a great, tearing breath and erupted off of the ground, bringing the tire iron up against Hera's chin and knocking her back. Silver slices passed across Hera's chest and face in a flurry. Chipped granite and blood rained down on the pavement.

"Athena!" When she heard Cassandra shout, she dropped the iron and snapped her hand through the air, locking it around Hera's stone fist. She held it wide while her other hand clawed for Hera's throat.

"Cassandra," she shouted, but hadn't needed to. Her footsteps ran closer and she dove onto Hera, driving Athena's weight forward, knocking all of them to the ground. Athena's fingers struggled to hold on. With fury and adrenaline she held, but each breath was like swallowing fire.

Cassandra grimaced and put her hands on Hera's cold skin. A strange electricity passed through her. Beneath her touch, Hera became colder and harder. Her skin solidified, turning more and more to stone.

Hera screamed and thrashed; Athena tried to absorb the blows. Cassandra was human; if she was struck, whatever bones were hit would be more than shattered, they'd be powder. But Cassandra moved wisely, dodging and pulling back at the right moments. She was cool and focused, her movements precise as she used her hands to infect Hera further with her own curse, to spread her death across her body. Stark patches of rock ran like fissures through her shoulder and up her neck. Her head whipped back and forth and her jaw shuddered as it hardened.

Aunt Demeter, who is this girl? What did you send me to find?

Hera's left arm slipped free and Athena heard it hit the ground, crumbling the asphalt. It had been close. Cassandra rolled away before locking her fingers in again. The look on her face carried thousands of years of resolve, thousands of years of vengeance. Hera screamed.

Will she turn that power on me next? Will I explode in a mass of feathers, just a pile of white and speckled brown, cut through with ribbons of skin and sinew?

In the midst of the thought, Hera's arm swung again. It caught Cassandra in the chest and threw her back. Athena twisted just in time to see the girl bounce onto the pavement, and to hear her head strike the road with a sharp, final crack.

"No!" When Hera shoved her away, she barely felt it, too busy scrambling across the road to Cassandra's limp body.

She wasn't moving. Was she breathing? Fresh prickles rose on the back of Athena's neck. She was afraid to touch her. Behind them, Aphrodite keened, and a scraping sound told of Hera's rock-infested flesh being dragged from the road. It didn't matter. What mattered was Cassandra. Apollo's Cassandra. And the death she'd faced even though she'd known it was coming. Athena knelt. The others called Cassandra's name as they ran closer.

"Get up," Athena said. "Get up and breathe. I won't have failed my brother so soon."

Cassandra's head swiveled, and she locked upon the goddess with empty eyes. Athena backed off a step. It was like looking into an abyss, power she didn't understand. And then Cassandra blinked, and the window slammed shut.

Cassandra pushed herself up onto her shoulders. The strange electricity was gone.

"It's over."

Athena nodded. It was over. Hera would be dead soon if she wasn't already. Poseidon drifted in pieces at the bottom of the lake to be swallowed by his own servants. Aphrodite, even though she lived, was mad and unable to make much mischief on her own.

Athena looked down at her wounds. Adrenaline still sparked through her exhausted frame, and blood saturated her left side. The impact of Hera's fist had turned her rib cage into a mess of pick-up sticks and paste. She took a hesitant breath and felt the itch of feathers. They were still there.

Just because they don't disappear instantly doesn't mean anything. Maybe it doesn't happen all at once.

She swallowed. It sounded like bullshit even in her head. Hermes was going to be so disappointed.

Odysseus jogged up to her, his eyes bright. She walked back and picked up the tire iron.

"Not a bad plan, was it?" He grinned, and she shoved it into his hands.

"Then don't look so surprised that it worked." She took his shoulder to lean on.

Andie and Henry stood on either side of Cassandra, holding her arms for support even though she didn't seem to need it. The darkness that had swum up and around her in waves when her skull struck the pavement was gone. Hermes limped around behind her on his crushed foot.

"What do we do now?" he asked, and looked at Athena.

"We take them back to their homes." Her eyes rested on the unmoving form of a god propped against the tire of the car, dressed in a boy's clothes. "All of them."

EPILOGUE

The coffin was overlaid with flowers. A huge spray of calla lilies, creamy white, draped over an obsidian black box, arranged in such a way that they strained toward the ground. They were good flowers for funerals. Their stems dipped, hanging their heads mournfully. If a plant could weep, it would be a calla lily.

The service was crowded, full of students from the high school and many members of the community. They had all come out for the funeral of the boy they only thought they knew.

Cassandra sat to the side, with Aidan's parents. Throughout, she said nothing, but she kept her back straight, even as tears coursed down her cheeks. Andie and Henry sat behind her, their faces constricted. Both of Andie's hands were bandaged, and under her shirt were stitches forming the lines of claws. Henry had a broad cut on his forehead from the window glass, and another stitched together on his hand from sharp gills.

Such a shame, people said, to lose a promising young man to a car accident. It was a miracle, they said, that all four of them hadn't been killed. The Mustang was completely mangled. State police would never be able to figure out just what happened, how fast they had to be going to lose control of the car so badly.

The service ended, and people began to stand, began to come to her, to Aidan's parents, and tell them how much he'd be missed. How much he was loved. Cassandra did her best to not hear a word. A hot, seething ball hung suspended in her chest, and she wasn't sure what it was made of. Screams? Tears? Love, or hate, or all rolled up together. But Aidan's funeral wasn't the place to find out.

"I'm so glad he had you, Cassandra." Aidan's mom squeezed her hands.

"I'm glad he had you." She looked at both of his parents. "You gave him a family."

But then, he'd always had a family. Athena, Odysseus, and Hermes stood on the outskirts of the cemetery, underneath the bare branches of an elm tree. Cassandra waited until everyone but Andie and Henry had filed out, even Aidan's parents, before nodding for them to come closer. Hermes and Athena leaned on each other. The damage done to her rib cage and his ankle still needed to heal, but Cassandra supposed that wasn't the only reason.

They stood around the coffin, lost and drained.

Athena's eyes wandered over the black box. He was in there, her brother, or what was left of him.

"This doesn't want to sink in. He was eternal. Now he's in that box."

"Jesus," Andie hissed. "Don't say things like that. Not today."

Athena looked up and blinked at them like she was bewildered. Cassandra supposed she was. She didn't have any experience burying family.

"I'm sorry," she said, and nodded. "But it feels wrong. And I can't do anything about any of it."

Cassandra drew a shaky breath.

"I don't have the energy to say anything to you. He's dead." Tears slipped out of her eyes and fell softly on the chest of her black dress. "I think it was a mistake. I want you to take it back." They would lower the coffin into the ground soon. They would cover him over with dirt. "I was supposed to spend my life with him," Cassandra said. "And then you showed up."

"Hey," Odysseus said gently. "It wasn't her fault."

Cassandra clenched her fists. "But whose fault is it, then? Are you still dying?"

Athena glanced at Hermes, then at Odysseus. She nodded, but Cassandra didn't really need an answer. Athena had coughed twice on the walk across the cemetery, and Hermes shook with fever as much as mourning. It hadn't stopped. Aidan was dead, and they still hadn't saved themselves.

"Maybe this was never about saving our lives." Athena looked at Aidan's coffin. "Maybe it was about redemption."

"Or maybe it isn't over." Cassandra wiped her eyes. "Do you know what happened? What went through me?"

Athena shook her head. "You kill gods. It must be what Demeter meant. That you could change everything. That you'd be more."

"Why? And how?" Beneath her gloves, her hands burned. It was still inside her. "It's not over."

"It's over," said Hermes. "It has to be."

Cassandra stared at Aidan's coffin. There were other gods out there. Gods who would fight, just like Hera did, to stay alive. They'd be coming. And the one who had killed Aidan. She was still alive. "This isn't over. Not for me."

"Cassie." Henry shrugged helplessly. "Maybe everything can go back to normal now. Maybe we're safe."

"They're not safe." She turned to Athena. "You can't just leave. You promised Aidan you'd protect us."

"Maybe with Hera and Poseidon gone, you don't need protecting. Maybe Henry is right."

"I'll need protecting when I go after her. I'll need your help."

Andie grabbed her arm. "Go after who?"

"Aphrodite." Cassandra shrugged her off. Athena and Hermes exchanged a glance, and Cassandra's fists tightened. *If they say one word about revenge not being what Aidan wanted, I'll scream.*

But Athena only sighed.

"I wasn't going to go far. People with destinies like yours are rarely safe."

"So you'll help."

Athena lowered her head, and Odysseus edged forward. "Hey. We shouldn't be talking about this today."

"There's a lot that shouldn't be today." Hermes spoke loudly, his eyes on the overcast sky. "He shouldn't be put beneath the dirt. He was the god of the sun. He should be burned on a pyre of oak, hot and bright. It should be glorious." He looked at his sister and took her hand. "So let's make it so." He nodded toward the gray clouds.

Athena exhaled. "It won't work."

Cassandra studied the sky, felt the chill of the wind against her cheeks. Hermes was right. It was all too cold.

"Try," she said softly.

Athena and Hermes closed their eyes, using the will of gods to move mountains, to wield the power they once had.

Not even Cassandra expected anything to happen, until she felt the warmth of sunlight on her face and hands.

Athena opened her eyes and watched the clouds roll back.

"I should have told my brother I loved him."

Cassandra swallowed hard. "I should have too. I guess I thought he'd be around to hear it later."

Athena stepped to the coffin and ran her fingers along the shining edge of black. "He was proud to die like this. Like a human. Like one of you. He died a hero."

Cassandra's breath hitched. She felt Andie and Henry's hands on each of her shoulders. Odysseus and Hermes put theirs on Athena's.

"Good-bye, Aidan," Athena whispered.

Cassandra stared with wide eyes into the clearing sky, as the clouds dissolved and drew back like a curtain. It took a long time, but finally, a small smile started to curl at the corners of her mouth.

They left the cemetery together. Behind them, the black of Aidan's coffin blazed like fire beneath the bright light.

And thus was their burial of Apollo, god of the sun.

ACKNOWLEDGMENTS

I have to start off by thanking my publicist, Alexis Saarela. Not only because she is a publicity wiz, which she is, but also because for two whole books I've forgotten to thank her. So thank you, Alexis, and I apologize for being such a huge butt.

Thank you to my agent, Adriann Ranta, for being the best advocate a writer could ask for. She also made sure this book got a much better title than the one I had originally planned.

Melissa Frain . . . what can I say? If there's any downside to having her as an editor, it might be that I'm becoming completely dependent on her expertise. Something weird? And it don't look good? Who'm I gonna call? Mel. Duh. She'll see it in an instant. (I apologize for the *Ghostbusters* reference. I miss writing those.) So thank you, Mel!

Thank you to the lovely and talented novelists Sara Bennett Wealer and Daisy Whitney. Without Sara this book would be firmly lodged in 1985, technology-wise. Daisy, thank you for your focus and fixing the ending!

Art director Seth Lerner, thanks for another striking cover. The entire team at Tor is incredible, and deserves undying gratitude.

I feel like I should thank Homer, but he might not have even existed. Still, *The Iliad* and *The Odyssey* were badass. So thanks for those, Homer, or the multiple people who actually wrote them.

As usual, thanks to Ryan VanderVenter, Missy Goldsmith, and Susan Murray, who continue to read everything I write even though they're very busy and are probably pretty annoyed at this point. Thanks to Dan and Kristin, for support and excellent catson-watching. And of course, Dylan Zoerb, for luck.